Zeus Is Undead:
This One Has Zombies

BY

MICHAEL G. MUNZ

Red Muse Press
Seattle, WA 2019

Written by Michael G. Munz
Edited by Bethany Root
Cover Design by Greg Simanson

This is a work of fiction. Names, characters, places, brands, media, and incidents are either the product of the author's imagination or are used fictitiously. Any resemblance to similarly named places or to persons living or deceased is unintentional.

Print ISBN: 978-0-9977622-5-9

Library of Congress Control Number: 2019901495

For everyone who made Zeus Is Dead a success, with special mention of Crystal, the Ciderbacon Folk, and all the Muses who let me put words in their mouths.

. . . Also Uncle Frank, who didn't take offense to my last dedication and gave me a really nifty pen.

OTHER FANTASY AND SCIENCE FICTION NOVELS BY MICHAEL G. MUNZ:

Zeus Is Dead: A Monstrously Inconvenient Adventure

Mythed Connections: A Short Story Collection of Classical Myth in the Modern World

Four Fantastical Ways to Lose Your Fingers

The New Aeneid Cycle
A Shadow in the Flames
A Memory in the Black
A Dragon at the Gate

TABLE OF CONTENTS

CHAPTER ZERO

"He's actually a decent enough chap. A tad strict, perhaps, but it's his job to keep the dead out of the world of the living. You don't want someone like me in charge of that. One good distraction and wham! Zombie apocalypse!"

— Hermes speaking of Hades, press conference, June 18, 2009

"The world would simply have to do without Aphrodite, Ares, Hades, and Hermes. The fountain flung them into the void between the stars, never to return without Zeus's explicit permission — or at the very least some other contrivance of plot should it become necessary."

— Zeus Is Dead: A Monstrously Inconvenient Adventure,
Epilogue

LEIF RACED INTO THE café, his phone clutched against one ear. "First lines are hard," he grumbled into it. Empty round tables and wooden chairs crowded his path. As he scrambled around them, his hip clocked a chair. It overturned with a clatter and he winced from the impact, but he didn't stop.

Tracy's voice came through the earpiece, annoyed yet calm, oblivious to Leif's predicament. *"Stop making excuses,"* she insisted. *"You've written most of the script. Suck it up, and finish the beginning, right?"*

"Like it's that easy," Leif grumbled back.

A snarling figure burst through the wall to his left. The café had been flimsily constructed on a movie set. Behind Leif, Wilhelm shouted in alarm, and they both spun away. Wilhelm rushed ahead. Leif followed.

"Leif, come on. It's a movie! There'll be twelve production company logos

and whatever sweeping landscapes Wilhelm puts in before the first line of dialogue is even spoken. First impression's already made by then."

A gurgling growl erupted behind Leif as a hand grabbed for his shoulder. Leif batted it away, increasingly irritated. "Not the point!" Ahead of him, Wilhelm smashed his own hole through the wall to make a shortcut, heading for the stage door beyond. "The first line of dialogue has to be fantastic! It needs to grab the viewer and make them feel—"

A spotlight crashed from the rafters to his right, bringing a wailing lighting technician down with it. Two more snarling figures flailed their way after her. With a roll of his eyes, Leif kept running.

"Leif, the only reason I could get the studio to even let you write this movie is because you experienced the real thing with me. You've got zero script writing experience—"

"But I've *seen* plenty of movies—"

"I told you before, just start it with some action and no one's going to care about the dialogue."

Leif balked. "*In media res?*" He dashed through the stage door after Wilhelm into a narrow hallway between sound stages. The fluorescent lighting flickered wildly. "God, that's so over-used!"

"Leif! The second unit starts filming tomorrow. No more delays, right? We're already over budget since you talked Wilhelm into motion-capture razorwings."

Leif and Wilhelm reached a T-intersection and turned left. They joined a rush of stage-hands stumbling over themselves to get away from what chased them.

"The puppets looked fake!" said Leif. It was the one time Wilhelm, the movie's obstinate director, had enough sense to listen to him about anything.

"The puppets were already paid for."

"Well nobody asked me!"

"This is what I am saying!"

Behind him, some klutz screamed and fell. Exuberant, near-inhuman snarls followed after. Leif and Wilhelm shoved their way through a fire door to Stage 14.

"Hey, what's going on over there anyway? Are you running?"

Leif glanced over his shoulder. "Just zombies," he answered.

"*What?*"

"Chased by zombies."

"*You wrote* zombies *into* Zeus Was Dead?"

He grimaced. That lousy title! *Zeus Was Dead?* Talk about spoilers. When he and Tracy had pitched their idea for a film about the previous year's events—the real return and departure of the Olympian gods—while identifying themselves as the two mortals at the heart of those events, he'd wanted to call it *Murdering Zeus for Fun and Prophet.* Nobody had listened.

"No, I didn't write them in! It's not part of the movie!"

The "zombies" had actually burst into the *Zeus Was Dead* sets just as the crew had taken a break for lunch: about thirty grasping figures, in fake-looking undead makeup, swarmed through the doors in a shambling rush. They'd bypassed the craft services table and made straight for the crew. Obviously, they had come from *Zombies vs. Landsharks 2: Brains A-Poppin',* the much lower budget horror flick filming on the stages across the street. He hadn't known if it was a publicity stunt or if *ZvL2* just meant to mooch their catering. After the "zombies" slammed into the *ZWD* crew, knocked people over, ripped off a few arms, and broke someone's smartphone, Leif figured it was the former.

And so he ran. He had a smartphone *and* a new gaming laptop; no way he would risk those for some dumb publicity stunt!

The stunt was, he'd begrudged, well-coordinated. Even the *ZWD* actor playing Thad Winslow was in on it. It had looked so real when two of the "zombies" ripped his arm off and bit into his skull!

The producers would throw a fit if this caused any delays, of course. So would Tracy. Now Leif had even less time today to write the opening scene.

"It's pretty nuts," Leif said. "Did the studio tell you about this? Were they in on it?"

"*Never heard a thing.*"

A crewmember running beside him with a "Redshirts!" T-shirt screamed and went down, tackled by one "zombie" and then swarmed by more in a wild gurgle.

Leif cradled his laptop closer.

"They're fast zombies, if you can believe that." Leif grumbled.

"Fast zombies belong in video games, not movies!"

"What the hell are you talking about?"

Wilhelm burst through another door with Leif at his heels. Suddenly they were racing across a sound stage facsimile of the rocky Greek mountainside where, last year, a resurrected Zeus had exiled from Earth the gods who had conspired to murder him. And also where Tracy, Zeus's daughter by a mortal mother, had forced Zeus to once again withdraw the gods and monsters from the public world . . . and maybe where, just prior to that, Leif had made a massive miscalculation, failed to usurp Zeus, and gotten his ass kicked.

He'd opted to leave that final part out of the script. Purely for brevity's sake, of course.

On the set, the fake rock outcroppings and bushy ferns in front of them were already festooned with "zombies" making a disturbingly realistic feast of assorted crew members.

Ahead of him, a plump zombie in a turtleneck sweater suddenly sprang from behind a fake rock and grappled Wilhelm.

"Uh-oh!" Leif cried with mock terror. "They got Wilhelm!" He couldn't help but grin. Despite the danger to his electronics, the adrenaline of the chase was giving him a thrill, and he decided to embrace the stunt and role-play. "Fear not, greasy director-man! I shall save—"

As evidenced by the preceding em-dash, the turtlenecked zombie bit into the aforementioned greasy director man's throat before Leif could finish. Wilhelm screamed. Fake blood splashed across Leif's face.

Wilhelm's head rolled to the set floor.

Leif licked his lips. The fake blood tasted incredibly authentic.

. . . *Wait.*

A realization lurched into Leif's forebrain. Distantly, he wondered why this particular Greek mountainside had such a talent for making him look foolish.

"Um, Tracy?" He backpedaled away from the turtlenecked zombie's horrid feast, trying and failing to work out a non-lethal explanation for Wilhelm's sudden lack of an attached head. "Are there any other directors available?"

The rasp of the zombie that Leif suddenly backed into drowned out any response. Leif shrieked and spun away before it could get hold of him.

He escaped; his smartphone did not. The grasping zombie's flailing hands knocked it from Leif's grip.

Lamenting the loss of its 4G LTE, 16-megapixel, 64GB-of-storagey goodness, Leif bolted for his life (and his laptop) through the sea of rocks and bushes to the other side of the enormous stage. Ahead of him loomed the mock-up of the temple where Tracy and Apollo had resurrected Zeus, and—more importantly—a ladder within that might get him to the building's rooftop and—most importantly— safety.

In the way swarmed at least a dozen dead-eyed figures in various states of decay who presumably had other plans.

Wait, did zombies make plans?

After hearing another snarl behind him, Leif decided to leave that topic for the Internet to debate. A ladder lay against a tall boulder to his right. He scurried up and then kicked the ladder away as the zombies tried to follow. Their hands and feet scraped the boulder's sides, unable to find handholds on the smooth, fake stone. More zombies clustered in behind them. Taking a deep breath, Leif made a running leap over grasping fingers to another rock. His feet hit, slipped, and scrambled, but finally found purchase. Looking around for his next jump, he spotted a few ZWD crew members atop other boulders.

"Get to the temple!" he yelled to them. "We can get to the roof!"

Without waiting to see if they understood—it was a simple statement, and if they didn't comprehend it, maybe they deserved to be zombies—Leif sprang to another rock. He jumped to still another, grateful for his long legs and their continued attachment to the rest of him. Within moments, he leaped off the last available rock and dashed up the fabricated stone steps into the temple set itself.

The temple, mercifully, featured no zombies. More mercifully, he hadn't imagined the ladder! It hung from a hole in the ceiling fifty feet above, dangling on the far side of the temple's altar.

Leif dashed for it. None of the other ZWD crew had followed. He seized the metal rung of the chain link ladder, stepped one foot up on a lower rung, and realized that his other hand still clutched the laptop.

Leif sucked in his gut. He shoved the laptop halfway down the front of his pants and resumed climbing just as half a dozen zombified catering staff shamble-rushed into the temple after him.

Leif climbed faster, hand over hand, making for the hole at the top where the ladder met the stage ceiling. Above lay scaffolding and a roof hatch. The dangling ladder shook with his spastic movements. Could zombies climb ladders? If so, they would surely try to follow. He didn't look down.

Okay, so he looked down once and wished he hadn't. Because they were following. And the lead zombie wore a Justin Bieber T-shirt. Leif screamed and climbed faster.

So, okay, now zombies existed. *Real* zombies. After finding out the Greek gods existed and meeting several of them a year or so ago, reconciling a real zombie attack wasn't so hard. But where were they coming from?

If he didn't get his ass in gear, he might not survive long enough to find out.

Zombies! he thought to motivate himself. *Zombies zombies zombies!*

Leif reached the top of the ladder and scrambled over the edge of the hole. Rather than the open-sky clifftop expanse present at the real temple, numerous wooden panels laid across scaffolding and five feet of headroom surrounded him. Also, there was a bearded zombie wearing a sheriff's hat. The zombie gnawed at the brains of a surprised looking stagehand just below the roof hatch. But hey, at least the roof hatch existed, right?

The sheriff-zombie looked up from its meal and began crawling toward him. "Brains!" it snarled in greeting.

"Oh, come on!" Leif yelled. "Finish the brains you have!"

"Brains!" it countered.

"That's just wasteful!" Leif screamed, eyeing the hatch.

"*Brains!!*" came agreeing shouts from the ladder below.

It was like arguing on Facebook.

The sheriff-zombie lunged, its bloodied fingers grasping. Leif jumped to one side. Unstable plywood rattled beneath his feet. He wobbled, nearly losing his balance before righting himself and backpedaling for the hatch.

Sheriff-zombie whirled, advancing again. Leif scrambled away, but his heels crashed into the zombie's previous meal. He fell to his butt across the stagehand's chest. The zombie bore down on him. Leif seized the first thing he could find for a weapon and bashed the sheriff across the face with . . . his laptop.

The crack of its screen against the zombie's skull tore a yell of anguish from Leif's lips. A renewed energy surged in him. The zombie reeled, and Leif kicked out with both feet. It flew backward, arms flailing, and toppled through the hole into the temple below.

"Damn it!" Leif shouted, examining the damaged laptop.

"*Damn it!*" Leif yelled as a new zombie crested the top of the ladder.

"***Damn it!***" Leif screamed before hurling the laptop at the zombie's face. It cracked her nose and sent her—and the laptop—back through the hole. Over the snarls of the other zombies below, he heard the distant shatter of expensive-laptop-on-fake-stone that broke his heart.

Taking little solace in knowing his writing was at least backed up on a flash drive, Leif scrambled off of the stagehand and reached up to open the hatch to his freedom.

It wouldn't budge.

Leif tugged. He pushed. He heaved and banged and even tried joggling it a few times (he'd never joggled anything before). But it held fast. Another zombie clawed its way up through the hole. One eye hung from its socket like a soggy teabag. The sight kept Leif too busy retching to do anything else.

Suddenly: a clank from above. Daylight streamed down onto Leif as the hatch opened. A man jumped down in front of Leif, feet slapping on the plywood in a moderately-quiet fashion. Metal glinted—a sword drawn!

"Flee!" ordered the man. His blade slashed through teabag-zombie's neck. Its head toppled away. The zombie's body crumpled.

Leif, perhaps like a buffoon, just stood there.

"To the safety of the roof, I tell you!" the newcomer cried. "Defy not my suggestions yet another time, Leif Karlson!"

Leif groaned as he recognized his rescuer: Ryan Seth Sloude. Just under six feet tall. Pale skin. Black, finger-length hair only slightly more unkempt than Leif had seen it previously. Not *this* guy again.

On the other hand, three more zombies had just climbed out of the hole, and safety was safety. Leif hoisted himself through the hatch and into the sunlight.

He just wished his rescuer hadn't been that—what was it he'd called himself again? A former member of the "Ninjas Templar," was it? Twice the guy had barged into the studio offices—and once into Leif's own apartment—demanding that his stupid little ninja group be written into the movie.

"They are humanity's true deliverers from the false gods!" the guy had exclaimed. Like, constantly. (He was really big on exclaiming.) "I demand they be given their due!"

When Leif *and* Tracy had told him that they'd never even heard of Ninjas Templar, he'd been undeterred. When they'd explained that it was Tracy herself—and not any Ninjas Templar—who had gotten Zeus to make the gods depart from public life again, he'd declared that "the Almighty works in mysterious ways!"

And when Leif had said they'd never seen a single ninja amid the whole Olympian mess, the guy had merely exclaimed that of course not, they were *ninjas*. Leif thought it interesting that not only could he see this particular ninja just fine, but that studio security had no trouble whatsoever tasering the guy and hauling him out the front gate.

Repeatedly.

While he kept exclaiming.

Except now, Leif owed the guy a favor. It didn't take a genius to figure out how he'd want it repaid, and that meant something even worse than zombies.

It meant rewrites.

Squinting against the California sunshine, Leif surveyed the area as his rescuer scrambled up onto the roof after him. Sirens rang from multiple directions. Smoke rose down the block. Atop adjacent rooftops, other survivors milled around, two of whom were tossing a Frisbee for some reason.

The ninja slammed closed the roof hatch and secured its latch. The drawstrings on the ninja's bright orange hoodie fluttered in the wind. Leif's stomach twisted, realizing what he needed to do. He steeled himself.

"Thank you," Leif managed at last. He shuddered.

"Your gratitude is appreciated. Some most-heinous devilry is afoot."

"I was thinking more 'zombie apocalypse,' myself," said Leif, "but sure, let's go with that."

~   ~   ~

For a reference index of the so-called "mythological" characters in this novel, as well as Edward Bulwer-Lytton for some reason, please refer to the Who's Who at the back of the book. Or don't. Up to you. Think of it as a spare tire in the event of a recognition blowout; you probably won't need it, but it's there if you do.

Part One:

Return of the Return of the Gods

CHAPTER ONE

"Does the so-called 'danger' posed to the populace by not acting to reduce what some may call 'the dead rising to eat the living' outweigh the economic costs to the country?"
—Michelle Theremin, United States Speaker of the House (Z-plus 10 days)

"Brain-eating zombies are portrayed as harmful, but there isn't even one study that can be produced that shows that zombies are a harmful menace. They are a harmless menace."
—Flip Larriman, Straight Truth Talk That's True *satellite radio show (Z-plus 14 days)*

"The science for this so-called 'zombie apocalypse' just isn't there. In fact, there are just as many corpses staying dead as there are coming back to life and eating people."
—Jeb Sherman, U.S. Senate Majority Leader (Z-plus 25 days)

"The concept of the zombie apocalypse was created by and for the Canadians in order to make U.S. moviemaking non-competitive."
—*popular Twitter blowhard (Z-plus 30 days)*

ONE MONTH AFTER THE MORTALS reported the initial zombie outbreaks across six of the seven continents (Australia was strangely lacking undead of any fashion), Athena reached her limit. No longer could she stand by while the mortals fought the undead scourge unaided. No longer could she leave unused all the tactical plans she had devised in the shower to battle said creatures. And especially no longer could she stay silent while an opportunity lay before her to prove her worth to Zeus—and so regain the divine power of which he had stripped her as punishment for failing to bring his murderer to justice.

Yes, Zeus had delivered such punishment to nearly all the Olympian Council gods—save for Aphrodite, Ares, Hades, and Hermes, whom he'd banished from the planet entirely for murdering him in the first place. But to Athena, it especially stung. As Zeus's bodyguard, she had borne a special responsibility. That he had been murdered at all was a mark upon her honor. That she, well, maybe kind of let the crime go unanswered and got caught up in reveling after the gods returned to the public eye . . .

Very well, so *maybe* she had felt a tiny bit of guilt about that.

But what good would dwelling on his murder have done, really? Zeus was already dead. The fact that someone had somehow killed an immortal god, to say nothing of the most powerful of them—it had spooked everyone! Wiser to forget the whole thing. After all, she recalled telling herself, it wasn't like anything could've been done to bring him back.

In hindsight, it had been her worst tactical error since getting drunk during the U.S. Civil War and assuming Major General George Pickett would get her sarcasm when she whispered in his ear that languid charges into artillery emplacements were sexy.

Now, dressed in heavy black jeans, her lucky green leather jacket over a black T-shirt, and a jeweled garland of olive leaves, Athena climbed the cerulean marble staircase toward the largest outdoor balcony in Zeus's wing of Olympus. Apollo walked beside her, clad in a dark suit and orange dress shirt without a tie. He carried a lyre, at which he plucked absently.

"*Must* you do that?" she asked, with a nod to the lyre.

Apollo cast her a sidelong frown. "Yes."

They continued, each step punctuated by random plinks of the strings.

"You have no cause to be nervous, you know," she said. "Zeus likes *you*. I'm the one without my divinity."

"I am not nervous."

"Then quit it with the lyre, Half-Brother."

"Or," Apollo said sourly, "I could go right back down this stairwell and let you speak to him without my support."

She heaved a sigh, reminding herself to pick her battles. "Fine. Plink on." Fates-alive, how long was this wretched staircase?

Apollo, thankfully, put the lyre away. "Feeling irritable?"

"No."

"Uh-huh."

The aroma of flame-sizzled meat filled the staircase's final turn. At the top stood an archway, which led outside to a dazzling marble balcony. A pair of oak trees grew out of either end of the balcony itself, providing partial shade from the sun shining in the brilliant blue sky. In the balcony's exact center, on a low dais up against the railing, stood a giant barbeque grill. Smoke rose from the grill. Tending it was Zeus, king of the gods, ruler of Olympus, and proud wearer of an apron that read "Just try to beat my meat!"

Also, he wore an old San Diego Chargers hat festooned with lightning bolts, which Athena thought might be laying the motif on a little thick.

"Apollo!" Zeus cried upon seeing them. "Welcome! You are early!" His gaze flicked to Athena only long enough for an acknowledging, "Daughter."

"Forgive us, Father," Apollo said. "We wanted to speak with you."

"And now you are speaking to me!" he laughed. Zeus jabbed a thick cut of steak with a fork. He lightning-seared it with a flick of his fingers, and then tossed it on the grill with a grin. The king of the gods loved a barbeque, which was one reason why Athena had chosen to broach the topic now. He was guaranteed to be in a good mood.

Apollo opened his mouth to speak again, but Athena silenced him with a hand on his arm. She stepped forward. "Father, have you been watching the mortals?"

"All the time."

What about when they're not in the shower? Athena stifled the comment. As the goddess of wisdom, she had learned to stifle a lot of comments, especially around Zeus. "Then you know they do not fare well against the zombies."

Zeus picked up a dish full of sauce marked "Hestia's BBQ sauce formula #2,187" and dipped a basting brush into it. (The goddess of home and hearth had been plying her brother with condiments, hoping to regain her divinity by feeding his barbeque habit.) Zeus slathered the sauce across a lamb shank and said, "They'll get the hang of it. The mortals can be quite adaptive when they must."

"Individually, yes, but as a group?" Athena asked. "Less so. They lack the collective will to organize quickly, and the longer the crisis goes on, the greater the threat becomes. I have prepared a brief presentation. With your permission?"

Zeus grimaced as if he'd just swallowed the BBQ fork, but motioned his consent nonetheless.

Athena nodded to Apollo. He made a motion of his own, fashioning the available sunlight to project in mid-air the presentation she'd prepared. (That she'd needed to prepare it using productivity software instead of pure divine power still galled her to no end.)

"First of all, the rate of dead-to-undead conversion is increasing," she began, pointing to a lovely graph that hovered in the air between her and Zeus. "While no corpses dead for longer than a year have re-animated—yet—and the dead are not all rising at once, more are doing so each day."

Zeus smirked. "So, the number of dead that are rising each day is itself rising."

"Correct."

"And does the rising rate rise after sunrise?"

"I haven't noticed a specific correlation between the sun's rise and the rise of—" Athena stifled a scowl. "You are mocking me, aren't you?"

Zeus shrugged with a smile. "But I am listening."

"Understand, Father: the longer the mortals take to get organized, the greater the danger the crisis will get away from them." She motioned to Apollo again, and the graph changed. "Especially when we factor in the near total conversion rate for those who die from zombie bites, scratches, or other sources of infection."

"Other sources?" Zeus asked.

She grimaced. "Some mortals have eaten zombie meat."

"That is disgusting, Athena."

"Agreed. Some chefs will do anything to be avant-garde."

"And then there are the necrophiliacs," Apollo added with a shudder.

Zeus arched an eyebrow. "You're telling me that some mortals find zombies . . . sexually attractive?"

"Apparently."

"Well." Zeus appeared to give the idea genuine consideration. "That's a Saturday night approach I hadn't thought of. A swan, yes, but . . . "

"Please forget I mentioned it, Father." Apollo shuddered anew. "I implore you."

Athena stabbed for her argument's heart: "Bottom line, we need to help them."

Zeus arched an eyebrow. "The zombies?"

"*No*, Father, the mort—" She grimaced. "Mocking?"

Zeus winked. Athena merely crossed her arms and stared him down. Zeus's grin grew wider before it broke on a sigh. "We are withdrawn from the mortal world, Athena. We cannot intervene."

"So, we return! We cannot abandon the mortals to defeat! Who would fill the world with life? Who would create art, culture, and conflicts for us to appreciate?"

"Who would you watch in the shower?" Apollo added. Athena shot him a scowl, despite the likely persuasiveness of the argument.

Zeus sighed again, almost wistfully. "Much as I would like to agree with both of you, I cannot. I swore to Tracy Wallace, *by the Styx*, no less, that the gods would leave the mortal world alone, just as we did in those millennia before my murder. My word is my bond. I am the god of law! I cannot simply cast that aside when it becomes inconvenient. We must trust the mortals to take care of themselves."

Athena boggled. "Trust the mortals . . . to take care of *themselves*?"

"Have faith, Daughter. They do have the capacity to be responsible."

"Like they are responsible for driving over eight hundred species to extinction in the last century?"

"While they may stumble . . . "

"Let's not forget the scourge of terrorism and seasonal pumpkin spice overdoses. The mortals have cleaned that right up, haven't they?"

"They're working on it."

"How about New Coke?"

"Enough! I command it!" Zeus boomed. "Do you think I do not see the problems down there?"

"You see all, Lord Zeus."

It was a lie that Zeus would allow for the sake of his ego. None of the Olympian gods were omniscient, not even Zeus, but flattery had its place. Athena steeled herself and continued. "In places, the mortals are indeed fighting the good fight. Countries with a highly-armed populace, and a high exposure to zombie movies, television, and video games, are managing alright. They know to shoot for the head, they are informed about the dangers of infection, and they are familiar with many ways the foolish may die. But even that is not enough; their governments are paralyzed by zombie deniers and petty deadlocks.

"Just yesterday, during a U.S. government debate on the use of military force to protect the populace, one senator claimed more research on the cause of the zombies was needed. Another senator called him a pinhead, the first in turn called him a 'pompous dick koozie,' and a brawl erupted."

Apollo switched the presentation to C-SPAN footage of the altercation. Chairs flew through the air amid podium-shattering fist fights.

"The conflict was short-lived," Athena said, "but it ended with everyone agreeing to shut down the government for a week until cooler heads prevailed."

Zeus sighed.

"Consider, Father," Athena said, "you swore to Tracy only that we would withdraw again. You never specified the *length* of that withdrawal."

Athena watched her father. Surely Zeus had thought of that loophole already. Yet with the suggestion came from another, he could save face—and he would owe Athena a debt of gratitude for the excuse. If Zeus had not yet thought of it, then he would further owe her for the idea itself. And with Apollo there to both witness her and back up her argument—

She glanced to Apollo, suddenly worried that he might back out. He only stood there, the look on his face as pensive as when he'd plinked at the lyre.

"Athena makes a good point, Father," Apollo finally added.

Zeus turned back to his barbeque and tended to some swollen hot links. "Apollo, why are *you* supporting this?"

"Because I believe it is the right thing to do."

"Yet you were among the least happy with the Return. The overwhelming mortal attention? The unending hassles of dealing with prayers? Now you lobby for that to happen again? Fates only know how much more you would have to deal with."

"It is a burden I am willing to bear." Apollo straightened with a reluctant pride. "It is also my hope that we would return with some caveats—some limits on how often we should respond to mortal requests, perhaps. I am working on learning how to say no."

Zeus lay down his meat fork and rubbed his knuckles across the thick brown stubble along his jaw, considering.

Athena waited. Apollo waited. The reader waited.

"IS IT NOT A GLORIOUS DAY FOR THE CELEBRATION OF FATHER ZEUS AND HIS MAGNIFICENTLY SEASONED MEAT!" The voice boomed from the balcony entrance. Athena stiffened and battled to keep a scowl from her face. It would not do to show displeasure at her father's new favorite.

"Baskin!" Zeus beamed. "Welcome!"

Baskin, the seven-foot-tall divine ice cream sundae upon whom Zeus had recently bestowed godhood (because reasons), swept up beside Apollo in a flurry of milky forcefulness.

"Apollo, my comrade in arms!" he bellowed in greeting. "Glory of Zeus to you!" Baskin's eyes, shot through with red and yellow sprinkles, flicked to Athena. The two shared a glare, but the usurper had no words for her. She considered it an improvement. It was only a month ago that Baskin, Zeus's new shield-bearer and bodyguard after Athena's disgrace, had ceased insisting she pledge her loyalty to Zeus at the start of their every encounter.

"Apollo, Athena," Zeus said as other Olympian denizens began to arrive. "I will consider your words. For now, enjoy the sunshine and the feast."

"But Zeus—"

"Enjoy, Athena!" Zeus said again, thrusting a forked hot link at her. "I command it!"

Baskin surged between her and Zeus. "You will enjoy the barbeque as Father Zeus ordains, or else taste the fury of my frigid fists!"

Athena stared up at the ridiculous god, silently daring him to try, and stepped around him to pluck the link from the end of Zeus's fork. She bit off a hunk and chewed, directing a predatory grin at Baskin.

"Delicious."

Four hours later, Zeus gazed down over the balcony as the last of the guests filed out. Invisible servants cleared away the dishes and uneaten food. (Most of the leftovers were gelatin desserts; Apollo always brought too many). The barbeque grill, of course, cleaned itself. It was just one of the many marvels Hephaestus had crafted for Zeus in the three months since Zeus had restored his divinity.

In return, Hephaestus, god of the forge, had promised to work unendingly for a year to craft new inventions for Zeus. The self-cleaning propane grill, which would never overcook meat or allow any charcoal within 500 meters, was Hephaestus's first gift. Soon after followed such treasures as a lightning bolt supercharger, a new divine chariot (which, through illusion, matched each observer's ideal of the sexiest vehicle), and, most recently, a remote-controlled ice cream scoop with a compass in the stock and this thing that tells time.

All in all, the barbeque had gone well, even with Eris's presence. (Ares's sister, the minor goddess of discord who was now picking up some of the slack for her exiled brother, had brought a potato salad that concealed not only a virulent strain of Olympian E.coli but also—and here Zeus shuddered—*pineapple*.) Hestia's sauce had been a hit. He would have to return her divinity sometime soon. Maybe when summer ended.

For now, Zeus pondered the zombies. They swarmed the mortal world below, an ever-growing menace spawned from—well, no one yet knew their source, did they? Did Athena know how much Zeus himself wished to return and put a stop to it? Or how much he wished to simply return, even before the zombies had arrived? For three thousand years he had forced the gods to stay hidden from the mortal world, interacting with humans only in disguise—and even then, in the most mundane ways possible. He had cut himself off from glory, from worship, and from merchandising, all because of that blasted prophecy, which came to pass regardless! He'd misinterpreted it and fallen from power anyway! They'd actually *killed* him! *Him!* And he only managed to come back because of his foresight into—

(It is at this point that we will cut away from Zeus's internal monologue about the events of the previous book, as his indignation and temper can get pretty long-winded. This is not to say that Zeus is not within his rights to harbor lingering resentment over such familial betrayal, murder, and insult. Nonetheless, we should not have to listen to it. But he should be done by now . . .)

Zeus sighed, collecting himself. And to think now that the only thing preventing him from enjoying the fruits of another return was his promise to Tracy—under duress!—that the gods would withdraw again!

(Nope, he's still going. Let's just jump forward again until after he summons Baskin, shall we?)

"I am here, Lord Zeus! My congratulations on a mouth-wateringly successful barbecue! Do you wish me to smite she who brought the most corrupted potato salad?" Baskin hefted his Mighty Pink Battle-Spoon™, which audibly vibrated with the god's own eager righteousness.

"Ignore Eris, Baskin. Do not feed the trolls, as the mortals say."

"Trolls?" Baskin raised up to his full height. "Trolls have breached *Olympus? But HOW? The palace walls should rise higher, force shields should activate the moment a threat is detected!*"

"No, it's—forget it," Zeus said. "And I can handle my own smiting. But report: what more have you learned of the zombies?"

Baskin grumbled, positively radiating preoccupation with the troll issue. "Not enough. Persephone claims no knowledge of their origin."

"She has checked the underworld for leaks? Breaches?"

"She has! No leaks! No breaches!"

"Did you *bellow* a demand for an answer, Baskin, or did you ask nicely, as I instructed?"

Baskin's chest puffed with pride. "I bellowed *nicely*, Lord Zeus!"

"That's—" Zeus faltered. That was about as subtle as he could really expect. "Alright. And do you believe her answer?"

"I detected annoyance, but no falsehood, Lord Zeus!"

Zeus folded his arms, pondering. "And yet, she is new to ruling the underworld without Hades."

"There is always a learning curve, Lord Zeus!"

"My thoughts exactly."

"Despite her best intentions, a zombie impetus may have slipped by her, Lord Zeus!"

"That's what I was implying."

"Just as the trolls invading Olympus have somehow slipped by me, Lord Zeus!"

Zeus sighed. "There are no trolls invading Olympus, Baskin."

"So suddenly? Then they are now defeated?" The shame melted from Baskin's face and he hollered a victory cry. "On swift wings does victory come to you always! By my honor, the surreptitious trolls shall not return!"

"Athena and Apollo now lobby me to allow our return to the mortal world. To deal with the zombies."

"Aha!" Baskin seemed to forget the troll issue immediately. "Just as you had hoped! Then there is to be a new Return?"

Zeus weighed the question. It was indeed true that he had hoped for the other gods to suggest returning, so that the idea would not appear to come from him. It was doubly true that his arguments against the matter were merely feigned so he could appear as beholden to his vow as possible. Yet the idea of actually declaring a new Return brought a sensation to his gut akin to a nest of nervous rattlesnakes. Was he so concerned about his reputation? Or was it simply against his nature to so swiftly cast aside such a vow?

On the other hand, he had bent rules before. Philandered behind Hera's back while in the grips of their marriage vows. He had even drank beer before liquor when it served his own needs. So, probably, the rattlers were just indigestion. Confound Eris and her potato salad . . .

"I am considering it," Zeus said at last. "But there is the matter of my promise to Tracy."

"Tracy betrayed you, Lord Zeus! Despite her taste for ice cream, she deserves no more consideration than you have already given." Baskin edged closer. "And I hear the whisperings of the others when they do not see me. They long to return as well. They will not fault you. Not in this time of need. Not when others have entreated you to do so."

"Mm," ruminated Zeus. "There is also the difficulty, once the zombies are dealt with, of staffing certain godly responsibilities. So many of your fellows are still without their divinity."

"Surely you can defeat any staffing issues, Lord! Are you not the king of us all? Command, and we shall follow!"

Zeus turned to Baskin, grinning his approval. The young god beamed broadly back, basking in the blessing.

"Then we shall return!" Zeus announced. "Go now. Descend upon the Earth and locate the most dramatic battlefield for our first strike against the undead! Tomorrow I shall lead that strike!"

Baskin quaked with excitement. Sprinkles and fudge sparked from his shoulders until he finally burst, "*As you command, Lord Zeus!*" In a flurry of fealty and whipped cream, he sprang to his assignment. "*To GLORY!*"

Zeus watched him go, his own excitement rising. "To glory!" He stripped off his apron, summoned his greatest lightning bolt, and rushed to inform the pantheon. Tomorrow they would descend from Olympus! They would make themselves manifest among the mortals once again! Then, with the might of a million headshots, they would rid the world of the zombie hordes, once and for all!

Or so was Zeus's plan.

Spoiler warning: it didn't exactly work out that way.

CHAPTER TWO

"You've seen tons of zombie movies, comics, and TV shows, so you know all you need to survive in our new zombie-infested reality, right? WRONG! You've studied FICTION! The walking dead in our cities, forests, and dentist offices are real! Do you want to pin the safety of your children, your pets, and yourself on inaccurate knowledge gleaned from fake tales made up by hack writers and charlatans? Of course you don't! Are you afraid to pay only $39.99 a month for your subscription to the only zombie survival e-resource to be endorsed by the University of Western Indiana? Of course you're not! Subscribe to The Sweeten's Guide to Real Zombies *now!"*
—*advertisement,* The Sweeten's Guide to Real Zombies

"Don't get eatens! Read your Sweeten's!"
—*James "Jimmy Joe" Sweeten, author,* The Sweeten's Guide to Real Zombies

THE OLYMPIAN GODS, fresh off the bench from their year and a half of rest, gushed onto the modern scene like a pack of sugared-up nine-year-olds at a water park. Zeus, a host of minor gods at his back and Baskin by his side, first plunged into the defense of Manhattan. They saved the entire NYPD 7th Precinct and the "ZombieBusters" volunteer militia in two minutes flat via sword-delivered decapitations of the undead hordes that had cornered the mortals on the Williamsburg Bridge.

Apollo and his twin sister Artemis—whose divinity Zeus had restored first due to some first-rate cajoling from Apollo—waged roving skirmishes across Europe, Asia, and Africa. Every arrow they lanced twixt a zombie's eyes spawned a new argument between them about who was the better shot. Demeter took it upon herself as goddess of the harvest to cleanse the farmlands of Asia from any ounce of brain-eating menace (and also locusts, for good measure, because eww). Even Eros, god of love and Aphrodite's son, devoted his skills. He set the zombies' hearts aflame for each other until they were too busy making out to eat brains or defend themselves.

Yet all that stuff was mostly just for show.

Such battles, though glorious, were as efficient as stopping a termite infestation by drawing-and-quartering each drone with horseflies. Not being fools—at least not in this paragraph—the gods also combined their divine power in wide-banded blasts to put down the majority of the zombies from a distance before engaging in closer combat. It's just that the publicity from playing hero in person was too tempting to pass up. Also, come on; who hasn't fantasized about fighting real zombies while in god-mode?

Not everyone was fighting, of course. The gods had returned anew, and despite their visibility on the front lines, it was important to properly announce their renewed presence in the world. The messenger goddess Iris, taking a cue from the now-banished Hermes, called a press conference to ensure the Second Return received its due coverage.

The conference garnered little attention. Perhaps it was that Iris was one of only a handful of gods at the press conference, and few mortals had heard of her. Perhaps it was that Eris also attended and accused every member of the media in attendance of being dirty liars out to get her. Or perhaps it was the fact that the world—still save for Australia, for some reason—was crawling with undead, and a few gods calling a press conference at 3 p.m. on a Tuesday just didn't rate anymore.

Nonetheless, the Second Return beat the zombies back, and within three months, helped humanity crawl back from the precipice of undead annihilation. But the thing was . . .

"Why do the zombies keep coming *back*?" Athena puzzled aloud.

"Do you expect an answer, or are you being rhetorical for mystery's sake?" asked Melpomene. "Because I approve of either."

Athena glanced at Melpomene, the Muse of tragedy, horror, and (since 1960) children's books. "Thinking aloud," Athena said. "Though if you know the answer, this would be an ideal time to voice it."

You had to ask these sorts of things of Muses lately. With Aphrodite, Ares, Hades, and Hermes banished, Hecate dead, Diomedes presumably trapped in Tartarus, and assorted others still stripped of divinity, the nine Muses—like other minor Olympians— had been called upon in the four months since the second Return to provide logistical support to the gods who remained. Yet there was a side-effect of relying on entities for whom drama and presentation is a primary concern: life itself began to unfold somewhat more dramatically than it used to. Bomb squads defused explosives within no more than five seconds of detonation. Instances of "meet-cutes" between budding couples in laundromats skyrocketed. Ninety percent of all football games ended in double overtime. As a result, Athena had begun to operate on the assumption that the Muses themselves, while generally helpful, might not always volunteer information unless dramatically prompted.

Melpomene, clad in thick-heeled, black leather boots, white leather pants, and a black *Hamlet* T-shirt, posed formidably with her hands clasped behind her back. Straight white hair fell down past her shoulders. "Any claim I could make to know of such things would be, I fear, dreadfully false." She offered a wan smile.

"Shh!" urged Clio (Muse of history, historical fiction and travel writing). "It's ready."

Athena turned her gaze back to the viewing pool around which they stood and watched the recording unfold:

A maelstrom of red and black energy whipped around a broad, white obelisk that Athena knew to be the Balefire of Hades. Hades had forged the device early in his rule. Not only did the Balefire track the deaths of every single mortal on Earth so as to draw their spirits inexorably to the Underworld—while giving off a lovely scent of citrus to freshen the area—it marked one of the Underworld's primary metaphysical focal points. As such, around it gathered Zeus, Persephone, Demeter, and Death, all manipulating the aforementioned maelstrom—a historic moment recorded dutifully by

Clio just two months prior.

Athena had heard what had happened, but now she would witness it herself. There had to be a clue somewhere.

The four stood at compass points around the Balefire: Zeus, his hands raised high with power. Persephone, Queen of the Underworld, eyes blazing with beams of UV light. Death, a.k.a. Thanatos—or Doug, as most on Olympus knew him lately—his scythe extended into the maelstrom. Demeter, goddess of the harvest, glowing gold. She was the only one of Zeus's generation so far to have her divinity returned, so her power was needed for the ritual.

"The undead force diminishes!" wailed Persephone. Her usually deep voice came shrill, as if distorted by the maelstrom or a bad recording. "Yet it will not relent! I cannot isolate it!"

"~Ever shifting~" called Death. "~In the storm. It shatters not. Fluid in form~"

"I just adore when he rhymes!" Demeter shouted above it all. "I know it's because he's stressed, but it's still a delight!"

"Demeter!" Zeus growled through clenched teeth. "Stay focused!"

Demeter *tsk*ed. "I am most assuredly focused, Brother, enough to see that this is not working! I did not wish to be negative before, but as you mentioned it, we are running out of time!"

Perhaps taking his own advice, Zeus did not answer, but seemed to redouble his efforts. Even without her old divine senses, Athena could tell the power flowing between Zeus and the maelstrom then grew stronger. For a few moments, the others followed his lead. Lightning crackled around Zeus. Demeter's eyes flared with golden light. Persephone quaked with the effort, and Death actually seemed to phase in and out of existence.

"Persephone?" Zeus shouted above it all.

Athena caught a glance shared between Persephone and Demeter. "If we cannot isolate the source of the undead, Lord Zeus, we cannot extinguish it!" Persephone cried. "We must try my mother's idea!"

Zeus gave a bellow of frustration that, for all Athena's scrutiny, did seem genuine. He wasn't faking this defeat. "Demeter!" he called. "Proceed! Now!"

Demeter clapped with glee and stepped back from the maelstrom.

"Plan G!" She seemed to withdraw into herself, as if culminating strength, and then blazed forth with an amber light, like a sunrise over a wheat field. Or like a blazing ball of wheat over a sunflower patch. Maybe both; Athena couldn't decide. But there was a definite bloom of agrarian power that poured forth from Demeter to plow into the maelstrom, sowing the seeds of change within the rich soil of swirling energy before her, until it finally culminated in a harvest of—

Athena shuddered and pulled herself away from the pool, nearly overwhelmed with farming metaphor. She rubbed her eyes in an effort to clear her head from the aftereffects of Demeter's power. Wheat. Grains. Cornucopias. Tractors. Cornucopias driving tractors?

Fates-alive! She wouldn't be having this problem if she'd kept her divinity! When Athena found the strength to view the pool once more, the ritual had ended. The Balefire stood quiet, the swirling maelstrom now gone as the four gods around it relaxed their efforts.

"Well?" Zeus asked of Demeter.

"I am *mostly* well, thank you," said Demeter, "though a mite shaken from the effort. So nice of you to ask!"

"He was asking if it worked, Mother."

"Hush, dear. Mommy is talking to your uncle-father."

With a huff, Zeus touched a hand to the Balefire's white stone surface. "Something does feel different."

Death nodded. "~There is a change, of a sort~"

"Oh, most definitely!" Demeter declared. "*Something* was most certainly successful. I cannot wait to see what it is!"

In the recording, Zeus nodded, his brow knit in the way Athena had learned to recognize during her millennia of guarding him: his concern was indeed genuine. Some had suggested to Athena, in conspiratorial whispers, that perhaps Zeus had orchestrated the zombie crisis to provide the gods an excuse to return once again. Athena's instincts—and the recording—told her otherwise. If Zeus could have ended things at the Balefire ritual, he would have. Besides, why would he have given Athena permission to investigate the zombie issue further if he were responsible?

"Come," Zeus said to the others around the Balefire. "Let us see what changes we have wrought."

The recording ended. The pool cleared.

"Ooh, 'wrought'," said Melpomene. "One of my favorite words. Just behind 'sinew' and 'viscera'."

Athena turned to Clio. "I had hoped to find more here, but really was just as they described. Whatever force that's causing the zombies wasn't something they could just shut off."

Clio shook her head. "But as we've seen since, Demeter's plans to redirect it were not totally in vain."

Indeed. Though it took time to become apparent, the gods' efforts had blunted the zombie menace on a number of levels. The chances of the newly dead rising as zombies plunged to a rate of only thirteen percent, and instances of buried corpses rising had dropped to nearly zero. A majority of zombies could no longer run. There were even signs that zombie infection vectors had diminished. No longer were humans at any appreciable risk from zombie bites, scratches, and fluid contact. Now the only real infection threat was zombies sneezing, which made battling them much easier in areas with a low pollen count. (Athena found it odd that creatures who did not need to breathe to survive still got hay fever, but as they also did not need to eat to survive and still got hungry, she chose not to dwell on it.)

The greatest change, however, was the difference in zombie behavior. No longer did the hordes of undead roam the world's cities and countryside with gurgling cries of "Brains!" to herald their insatiable cravings. Now, in what surely was owed to Demeter's direct intervention, these cries—and those cravings—had changed.

Guy scrambled up from the wet grass where he'd fallen. The car was just ahead at the bottom of hill. Snarls from the pursuing trio of zombies chased him toward it. He wiped his hands on his red shirt and mocked, "Let's have a picnic! What could happen?!"

His girlfriend, Showna, was still running. "You're the one who brought the gods damned baguettes!" she yelled back.

Guy caught up with Showna as they both reached the car. "I hate gluten-free bread! It's all chewy and weird!"

"Are you *kidding* me? If we get out of this alive, you and I are through!"

Guy thrust his hands into his pockets. His fingers found only loose change and pocket lint. *Where were the car keys?* "Just because I forgot zombies like—"

"GRRAAAAAAIIINNSSSS!!!!"

The zombies had chosen that precise dramatic moment to crest the hill and snarl their endless demand. The lead zombie still had the remains of Guy's turkey-on-wheat clutched in its decaying hands, but its eyes were fixated on Guy himself, craving more. Its two fellows had eaten nothing, and their hunger drove them down toward Guy and Showna.

He'd only eaten a quarter of the sandwich! Could they still smell the wheat on him? Would they tear out his stomach to get at it? *Where were the freaking keys?!*

The answer to Guy's questions, in order, were as follows: Yes, they could. Yes, they would. And locked inside the trunk, because Guy is a nimrod.

We now return you to the primary narrative, already in progress.

Athena blinked. "Did something just happen?"

"Narrative cutaway," Melpomene explained. "Just ignore it."

Clio nudged Athena. "I believe you were busy thinking aloud?"

"Er, yes," remarked Athena. She shook off the odd feeling of being elsewhere and went on. "That Zeus and the others could only redirect this undead force rather than simply terminate it . . . it's almost as if they were dealing with a force of Nature itself."

Clio shrugged. "Such things are beyond my expertise. Unless you would like to see a history of all the tornados recorded in the last two hundred years?"

Athena shook her head, trying to concentrate.

"How about hurricanes? They all have wonderful names. Mortals have started to give them men's names lately, also . . . "

Athena shook her head again. "No, thank you. But what I am wondering—"

"I've drawn up some strikingly accurate charts and graphs . . . " Clio loved charts and graphs. So did Athena, but there was a time and place for everything. "Are you sure?" Clio fished.

"That's—"

"Each uses multiple colors!"

"No, I really—"

"The fonts are amazing!" Clio cried.

Melpomene threw up her arms. "Sister, *please!*"

Clio calmed, blushing. Melpomene motioned to Athena. "You were saying?"

Athena stifled a grumble. "If I'm right, and the undead are somehow now a legitimate force of Nature rather than an aberration, then it stands to reason the Erinyes know something about that. They have to authorize any changes in the natural order, after all."

"Again," said Clio, "that's outside my area, but—"

"No, that's correct," said Melpomene. "Apollo's still trying to push through the paperwork for a slight solar course change. Something involving Hera and pomegranates. I don't think his heart is truly in it, though."

That was it, then, Athena thought. She would talk to the Erinyes. Except . . . "Zeus surely would've thought to ask the Erinyes about it himself by now."

"No," said Clio. "That angle may have been overlooked."

"How could it possibly have been overlooked?"

Melpomene smirked. It was one of her trademark chilling smirks that a cat gives a cornered mouse. "Because it's more dramatic that way. You didn't think of it yourself until just now, did you?"

CHAPTER THREE

"The Erinyes pretty much do not get along with anyone. Initially, one could hardly blame them. If you were born out of blood spilled from the castration of Zeus's grandfather, you might be a little bit cranky about it too. Yet even such traumatic beginnings can be overcome, and after so many thousands of years, it has become apparent to even the most forgiving individuals that the Erinyes are, put simply, spectacular jerks."
—Zeus Is Dead: A Monstrously Inconvenient Adventure,
Chapter 14

"Few mortals ever witness the Erinyes and live to tell the tale. These beings of vengeance excel at four things: punishing those who offend the gods, punishing those who violate the natural order, punishing those who commit murder without proper authorization, and burpees. Some scholars suspect the Erinyes may serve as fitness instructors in their off hours, but this has yet to be proven."
—A Mortal's Guidebook to the Olympians' Return, 2nd
Edition

IN A HOLE IN THE SKY there lived the Erinyes. Not a wormhole, with swirling lights and protruding dimensions carrying people off through space-time to who knows where-when, nor yet a comfortable hole with carpeted floors and paneled walls with lots and lots of pegs for hats and coats. This was an Erinyes hole, and that means discomfort.

The hole being in the sky, it also meant that Athena needed a rope and grappling hook to reach it, and thirty-six tries to get the hook in place. Though the hole was only twenty-five feet over a rose quartz gazebo on the extreme southern edge of the Olympus grounds, it was also invisible to Athena in her current state, and so she had to aim based entirely on memory and occasionally vanishing birds.

Millennia ago, when the Erinyes had constructed their base of operations—which was of course where the hole led—they had made it as visually repellant as possible. Hera had taken one look at the place—with its unflattering angles, entrails-spewing fountains, and billboard advertising—and covered the hovering monstrosity with an invisibility field to preserve the beauty of the grounds. So, really, it wasn't so much a hole that Athena climbed into, but an open doorway into a floating invisible eyesore.

Once Athena entered, the interior was very much visible. Blood dripped from patches on the ceiling. Spikes in the walls skewered the occasional mortal head, many of which—though not all—were severed from their bodies. The spaces lacking head spikes displayed either motivational posters with pithy sayings or bar charts of vengeance efficiency across the decades.

It was as if Vlad the Impaler had opened up a consulting firm.

"Subtle" was rarely in the Erinyes' vocabulary. As Athena made her way through the Erinyes' foyer toward the grand staircase that led to their audience chamber, she noted that "air freshener" wasn't likely in their vocabulary either.

When she reached the foot of the staircase, a scraping from above heralded the arrival of a six-foot long fire ant. It scuttled down the steps, reared up on its hind legs five steps above her, and adjusted its spectacles.

"Do you have an appointment?" it asked.

"I'm here to speak to Megaera." Really, any of the three Erinyes would do, but Megaera was the most organized.

The fire ant's pincers twitched in annoyance. "Do you have an *appointment*?" it repeated.

Athena set her jaw and climbed to the step beneath the ant. "I am she who is called Athena, patron of the Parthenon temple, protector of civilized life, master of handicrafts, creator of the North Atlantic Treaty Organization, inventor of the gyro sandwich, and she who sprang fully armored from the head of Almighty Zeus!" (She would have used "flashing-eyed" too, an epithet from Homer she'd always enjoyed, but she could not currently make her eyes flash, so it felt wrong.) "I have as much need for an appointment to visit the Erinyes as my sword needs an appointment to visit your vital bits."

The fire ant rasped a put-upon sigh from between its pincers and stepped aside. "Very well. Piss off my Mistresses, then, if you like." It scuttled over the edge of the staircase and out of sight.

That was easier than Athena had expected, but she wasn't about to complain. She climbed the rest of the staircase unimpeded and, taking a deep breath, passed through a set of heavy iron doors into a pitch-black corridor. An unsettled, wretched feeling wrapped Athena even more closely than the darkness; nonetheless, she persisted. Though the effect weighed upon her more heavily than it had during her visits as a full goddess, she knew it was only an illusion, designed to impress upon visitors that this place was the Erinyes' domain.

She could have done without the out-of-tune bagpipe music, though.

Fortunately, within another twenty paces the darkness lifted, the feeling lightened, and Athena stood within the Erinyes' command center. It always reminded her of a NASA control room: View screens plastered the walls. Smaller workstations sat in rows of three along either side of the wide space, at which sat five-foot-long monitor lizards, all busy monitoring. Pallid, red lighting bathed the area, broken only by two sources of pale daylight—a triangular window at the center of the front of the room, and a ten-foot-wide hole in the floor. Devoid of any safety railings whatsoever, it was an open-air drop of miles and miles (and miles) down to Earth from the edge of Olympus. The hole served as the Erinyes' launch tube for their vengeance sorties. (While they could simply teleport to their targets, they preferred the rush of first diving out the hole and teleporting after.)

"Athena," came a shrill voice. "The ex-goddess of failed protection! You dare to come before us, Cousin?" The Erinys Tisiphone sneered from behind one of the three command podiums near the window. She was in her more presentable form: her blond hair lacked any vipers; her back concealed her white bat wings; and her eyes failed to gush blood, as they were apt to do when she was actively dishing out vengeance or chopping onions.

"I would speak with you about the zombies."

"You would, would you?" Megaera stepped from the shadows to Athena's right, holding a tablet computer. The room's lighting gave her already red hair an even bloodier sheen. "And you simply expect—without an appointment!—that we will fit you into our busy schedule of punishments?"

"Pun-ish-mennnnts . . . " Something crawled along the ceiling to Athena's right, a winged form concealed in darkness. Judging by the voice—and process of elimination—it was the third Erinys, Alecto. Yet something seemed off with her. "*Pun-ish-mennnts!*"

Athena ignored Alecto. (It was usually a good policy.) "I am here to request—"

"No!" Tisiphone shrieked. Wings sprang from her back. Snakes burst through her hair. Tisiphone pounced at Athena. "Our time is valuable!"

Talons seized Athena's neck and jerked her off her feet. Megaera followed suit to grab Athena's ankles, and faster than you can say "clichéd expression," the two had Athena dangling upside down above the hole in the floor. Suddenly, the only thing between Athena and a miles-long drop was the Erinyes' grips.

Athena swallowed. There was enough wisdom in her to know that getting dropped, even if it wouldn't kill her, would hurt like a colonoscopy-by-cactus. She had no fear of heights, but faking it for the Erinyes' benefit was easy enough—easier than it had been to stifle her instinct to dodge their attack in the first place. It kicked her pride in the crotch, but if she didn't allow the Erinyes a bit of torturing fun, there would be no dealing with them at all.

"Oh gods, no," Athena tried. "Please, set me down. I beg you." Styx, it was humiliating.

Her feigned protests only got her lowered through the hole until she dangled outside in the winds of Olympus. With the Erinyes' base now invisible above her, it was as if she floated in open air, save of course for the two cackling, bat-winged hags clutching her ankles.

"Impudent failure!" Megaera shouted. "This is our domain! We should drop you like a hot stone!"

Tisiphone shook the ankle she'd captured. "Your winged sandals won't help you now!"

Athena rolled her eyes before she could stop herself. "That's *Hermes*. Hermes has winged sandals."

"Well—" Tisiphone stopped shaking her. "Well, they're *still* not going to help you, are they?!"

"Please!" Athena tried again. "I'm here at the behest of Lord Zeus! Or do you deny his authority as well?"

"Zeus sends *you*, wee Athena?" Megaera scoffed. "Does he think so little of us?"

"A lie if I ever heard one!" Tisiphone added. "We have nothing to tell the likes of you!"

As one, the two Erinyes dashed left and then right, jerking the still upside-down Athena through the air like a rag doll. Immortal blood rushed to her head, which packs even more of a kick than mortal blood if you're no longer divine enough to handle it. Athena thought of positive things like bulletproof vests and spectacular looms in an effort to clear her mind.

"Not even about the undead disruptions of the natural order?" she managed finally.

The Erinyes came to an abrupt stop. "The natural order is *our* business!" Tisiphone snapped. "*We* enforce it!"

"Which is why I wish to inquire about it."

"Inquire about it at your peril!" Tisiphone cried.

"Perrrilll . . . *Perrilll!*" Alecto added from somewhere up inside the building.

Megaera handed the ankle she held to Tisiphone and floated down to stare Athena straight in the face. Was that suspicion in Megaera's eyes, or something more?

"We give you leave to inquire," Megaera said.

Tisiphone hissed at Megaera. "*What?* Pus-cockles! No, we do *not!*"

Megaera swiped at Tisiphone. "We will not have this debate here! I said she may inquire! I did not say we would answer!"

"But—"

Megaera teleported straight up into Tisiphone's personal space and screamed, "Silence!"

". . . not the boss of me . . . " Tisiphone muttered.

". . . smarter than you . . . " Megaera muttered back.

". . . Megaera . . . braiinnsss . . . " Alecto purred from inside.

Megaera pointed a finger down at Athena. "Speak!"

"Understand, I have reason to believe the cause of the zombies may be a legitimate force of Nature rather than an aberration," said Athena. "I come to ask if your superior senses have noticed this as well, and if so, what is behind it."

Tisiphone and Megaera shared a look. The snakes in Tisiphone's hair writhed a little faster.

"We have noticed nothing!" Tisiphone burst, shaking Athena's leg. "Everyone knows there is nothing to notice! Fake notice!"

Megaera gave no notice of her sister's lack of notice. "Why do you believe this?"

"The ritual that Zeus and the others tried at the Balefire of Hades," Athena answered. "If the zombies were just a glitch of some kind, it should have worked."

The two Erinyes shared another look. "We should drop her right now, Sister." said Tisiphone.

Megaera took hold of both of Athena's ankles. "No."

"She knows too much!"

"The fall would not kill her!"

"But it would cause her pain!" Tisiphone shouted. "A lot of pain! And then maybe she'd keep her trap shut until we can decide what to do!"

Athena strained to sit up. Though she was dangling upside-down, she still had godly abs, so she got pretty far. "I am no longer goddess of wisdom, for now, but I still have wisdom to share! I see you are torn by something. Tell me what is going on, and I will give you good counsel!"

"No!" Tisiphone spat.

"She will not be disgraced forever," Megaera observed. "Zeus returns divinity eventually, despite his anger. And when Athena has hers again, she will owe us *favors*, sister. She will send to us more sinners and hubris to punish!" Megaera looked down at Athena, her lips wide in a toothy grin like a shark at the dentist. "Won't she?"

"Of course!" Athena punctuated it with a rapid nod. Transgressions did require punishment, after all. For one thing, a plague of adventurer-archeologists were desecrating her temples for treasures for the past eighteen months, insisting such things belonged in a museum. They were galling her beyond belief.

"See?" Megaera said to Tisiphone. "We will tell her!" She began to pull Athena up into the building.

Tisiphone didn't budge. "No! Shut up, Meg!"

"We'll let Alecto break the tie!" said Megaera. "Alecto! Should we tell her?"

"Telll herrr . . . Telllll herrrr!" came the reply.

Tisiphone thrust a finger at Megaera. "That is *not* fair! You knew she would repeat—"

Megaera cackled and hauled Athena back into the command center. The monitor lizards had remained at their stations, although Athena spied one switching his screen back from a game of *Frogger*.

Tisiphone smacked her hands together. "Out! All of you!"

The response was instant: throughout the control room, all monitor lizards crawled down from their monitors and trotted to the exit for parts elsewhere. Megaera plopped Athena into the nearest vacated seat. Unhappy with the seat's saurian reek and lousy lumbar support, Athena took to her feet again as Megaera and Tisiphone landed in front of her. Megaera resumed her less-objectionable form. Tisiphone had folded away her wings, but Athena still saw serpents swimming just beneath the surface of her hair.

Alecto remained out of sight in the shadows above. Athena was really beginning to get suspicious about that.

"Your guess was correct," Megaera said. "The zombies are part of the natural order." Athena waited for elaboration, but Megaera's green eyes merely watched her.

"Yet how can that be?" Athena finally asked. "There were never zombies before. Or were there?"

"There were not," Megaera said. "Except for those raised for specific tasks, and in those cases the animating magic burns right through them. Before too long they fall apart like a frog on a firecracker."

"Delightfully horrifying when timed right," Tisiphone added with a grin. "Spectacular shock value."

"But that's not what we're seeing now," Athena said.

"No."

"So, then, hasn't the natural order changed?"

"Yes," Megaera whispered.

"But the Erinyes safeguard that order! How could that change occur without your being consulted?"

Megaera grimaced. "It is . . . complicated."

"How?"

"Hah!" Tisiphone crossed her arms. "You wouldn't understand!"

Athena sighed. "Okay, then who did it?"

"Did what?" Tisiphone snapped before Megaera could answer.

"Who changed the natural order?"

"Changed it to do what?" Tisiphone snapped again.

"Hey!" Athena shot. "Do you want my counsel or not?"

"Do you want the hole again, fail-goddess?" Tisiphone spat.

"We do not know!" Megaera cried. "The paperwork was filed! The change authorization forms were signed! But we do not know who did so!"

Athena blinked. "Well—if you got the forms signed, how do you not know. . . ?"

"Alecto got them signed!" Megaera said, casting a glare up at the shadows. "She followed a lead, went to confront whoever it was, and took the usual paperwork *without* telling the rest of us!"

"She's always doing that!" Tisiphone grumbled. "Too much impulse, not enough brain . . . using!"

Megaera went on. "Alecto, *presumably*, discerned who was behind the zombies. But now, she cannot tell us!"

"Can't, or won't?"

Megaera sighed. "Alecto, come down here."

Alecto let go of the ceiling and, with a robe-muffled bang, slammed to the floor behind a bank of monitor screens. "Downn . . . herrrre . . . "

Megaera rolled her eyes. "Alecto, you braindead scab-stain, stand *up* and come here!"

"Yes, let the ex-goddess have a look at your pretty face," Tisiphone added.

Alecto stood. In the dim, ruddy light, Athena could only make out the top of a brunette head at first. When Alecto emerged from behind the monitors, her mouth was hanging open, framed by the dark tangles of hair that fell over the shoulders of her blue robes. Pale skin stretched tight over her bones, yet paler still were Alecto's eyes: completely glazed over and thick with cataracts. Or rot. Or maybe— though Athena counted this unlikely—air-puffed marshmallows.

"She has become a zombie?" Athena asked.

"Somewhat," Megaera answered. "Some abominable form of undead immortal."

"At first we didn't notice at all," said Tisiphone. "You know how Alecto is. There's really not much difference, except now she smells a little funny."

Megaera fished out her tablet. "She found out who had altered the natural order"—"Or what," Tisiphone injected—"and went to them without telling us, and returned to us in this state, with the signed forms. And you can see how helpful *they* are."

Megaera handed the tablet to Athena. On it, at the bottom of page two of the Clearance Agreement to Alter the Natural Order Form (version 287), to the left of the notice "This form complies with the Olympus Paperwork Reduction Act of 1598," just above Alecto's initials of authorization, in the box marked "Initiator," someone had made their signature.

They had signed with an X.

CHAPTER FOUR

"This ridiculous idea that zombies have switched to craving grains instead of brains is nothing but propaganda from the gluten-allergic deep state. Or the Celiac-industrial complex. Or at the very least, a typo. Look, we all know how zombies act. They've eaten the brains of our families. Our friends. Our neighborhood bakers. Their brains! *Do not let this wild grains rumor endanger your lives or alter your eating habits. Protect your brains, but keep eating grains!"*

> —Ondrea Noble, president, Bread Makers Guild of North America
> (Z-plus 68 days)

"Despite clear messages to the mortals about avoiding grains— television announcements, social media, Surgeon General warnings on packages of flour—some still don't get it. I can only guess some of them fear that the very act of using their brains might attract zombies."

"Also, wheat is delicious!"

"You are not helping, Demeter. Can you people edit that out?"

> —Apollo and Demeter, Good Gods, Y'All—What Are They
> Good For? *podcast interview (Z-plus 87 days)*

"Their (sic) gonna eat all the Twinkies, aren't they?"

> —alley graffiti in Tallahassee, Florida (artist unknown)

LEIF TUGGED, HIS EYES and teeth clenched. The final lug nut didn't budge. "Are they coming?" he gasped before giving it another try. The tire iron ground into his palm. Still nothing. Muffled groans and lip-smacking mastication drifted from across the road.

"Not yet," Tracy whispered.

Leif spared a moment to reassure himself that she wasn't

wandering off. Tracy stood, her back to Leif and their disabled pick-up truck. She aimed her shotgun toward the ten zombies swarming the overturned bakery van that lay across half of the two-lane mountain highway. Leif's heart pounded. It didn't matter that he hadn't eaten any bread in days. Zombies were like sharks; with enough grains to feast on, they could go into a feeding frenzy and lash out at anything within their reach, food or not. The ones gorging across the street hadn't reached that state yet, but it was only a matter of time.

Just a few minutes ago, Leif and Tracy had rounded a bend in the road and spotted the overturned van. There had been ample time for Leif to react. Really, there had been no need *to* react. Wedged into a roadside waterfall on the far shoulder, the van blocked only part of its own lane. Leif didn't need to swerve the pick-up in order to pass safely. Maybe it was the shock of seeing the van's contents spilled across the road; English muffins, pretzels, and bread—both sliced and un-sliced—lay everywhere, gorged upon by zombies. Maybe it was sunlight gleaming off the water that spilled across the pavement from the redirected waterfall—a minor water hazard. Or, just perhaps, it was that bonehead Ryan reaching in the window from the pickup's cargo bed, yanking Leif's arm and exclaiming "STOP!"

Whatever the cause, Leif had steered the pickup toward the guardrail on their right, overcompensated enough (while screaming) to fishtail them across to the left shoulder, and then driven directly over something that blew out the front left tire. When the pick-up had finally skidded to a stop, they were in a slow-vehicle turn-off back on the right side of the road, about thirty yards from the bakery van and its undead buffet line.

Now, Leif planted one foot and heaved on the tire iron anew. *What kind of hydraulic maniac fastened this thing?* The lug nut might've moved a fraction of a nanometer. He heaved again. The sixteenth time was the charm: it turned! He unscrewed the nut the rest of the way like a toddler after three shots of espresso. "Finally! We might actually get out of here if Ryan doesn't do anything else stupid!"

"Trying to rescue that van driver is not a stupid thing!" Ryan answered.

"It is when you nearly get us killed," Leif grumbled, pulling the punctured tire off the lug bolts.

Ryan stood beside Tracy at Leif's back, katana unsheathed. It was the same sword with which he'd saved Leif's life on the first day of the zombie outbreak. Soon after, Leif had learned the man was an ex-Ninja Templar—not that Leif entirely believed there was ever such a group as the Ninjas Templar in the first place. Yet Ryan was insistent about this. Ryan was insistent about a lot of things, really.

Ryan Seth Sloude. Sheesh. What a dumb name. What was that, Welsh? Sure, it was nice having a guy who could use a sword tagging along on a journey across zombie-speckled country. Sure, Leif did owe the guy his life, so he couldn't really send him away. But did he have to be so . . . asinine?

"We have a responsibility to battle—"

"The driver was dead already!" Leif shot.

"Which we did not know when—"

"When we saw the van already overturned and swarming with zombies?"

"There was still hope!"

Leif shoved the spare tire into place with a grunt. "That doesn't mean you can just—"

"Quiet, the both of you!" Tracy hissed, turning around. "Maybe Leif can agree that it's important to try to help people sometimes, and maybe Mr. Sloude can agree that sometimes the risk is too great!"

"And that you shouldn't yank the wheel away from the driver of a moving truck on a mountain highway!" Leif added.

Tracy turned back to watch the bakery truck, stopping only to glare at Ryan. "Oh, he'd better agree about that."

With a crunch of gravel, a tall, thin, zombie-shaped shadow loomed to Leif's right. Something had crawled up behind them—possibly a zombie.

"Tracy!" Leif shouted.

"Shit!" Tracy shouted.

"GRAINNNS!" the now-highly-probable zombie shouted.

Leif ducked back against the side of the truck. Tracy fired. The zombie fell back, obliterated. A green ball cap that read "Fishermen do it with a pole!" dropped at Leif's feet.

"It came up from the river," said Tracy. "I'll check for more.

Sloude, guard Leif. Leif, get that tire on!" She darted behind the truck.

Leif fastened the lug nuts as swiftly as he could. In his rush to thread the last one, it slipped from his fingers. The nut bounced under the truck, out of reach. Crap. Well, lug nuts were like fingers; four out of five was still pretty good, right? He cranked the jack down until the spare tire was back on the ground.

"Um, done!" Leif shot to his feet. Most zombies at the bakery truck were still distracted with their meal, but two had begun to stagger toward the pick-up. Bits of soft pretzels dangled from their mangled jaws, like half-eaten intestines. (The simile perhaps leapt to Leif's mind because other things dangled from their jaws that were half-eaten intestines.) Tracy stood by the guard rail between the shoulder and the slope to the river. Something down there had caught her attention.

Leif slapped the top of the cab. "Tracy! Everybody back in the truck!" Pausing only to toss the jack and tire iron into the back of the pick-up, he jumped into the driver's seat. Thankfully, Tracy jumped into the passenger's seat a moment later.

"Three dead down there," she said with a jerk of her thumb. "Fishing. Drinking beer. Must've been attacked a few days ago and the one got turned. Dumbasses!"

"People like beer," Leif said.

"It's made with grain!" Somehow Tracy managed to say this as if it weren't an obvious fact that Leif and probably most readers of this book already knew.

"Since when do people stop doing things they like just because it's dangerous?"

Leif gunned the engine and shot the truck back onto the road. The bakery van disappeared in the rearview mirror. Ryan had climbed into the back of the pick-up before they'd driven off.

That was probably good, Leif supposed.

They passed a sign: *Leavenworth, 7 miles.*

Leif checked the fuel gauge. "We should stop in Leavenworth. Get some gas and a new tire before we go on."

Tracy gave an affirmative grunt as she watched out the rear window. They passed another sign: *Leavenworth Oktoberfest, September 29–October 8.*

Leif swallowed. "This is September thirtieth, isn't it?"

"All day."

"Well, poop."

It was a lovely night in this part of the Olympian gardens, but that was not unusual. Non-lovely parts of the Olympian gardens were not permitted to exist, and it was always night in this particular one; Hecate had set it up that way so that she might always have a starlit pool in which to watch her favorite mortals

Melpomene, a fan of darkness herself, had taken a liking to the spot long ago. It was here that Athena met with her tonight. After Hecate's accidental death the previous year in Titan War 2 (Olympic Boogaloo), Melpomene had appointed herself the area's caretaker. Thanks to her efforts, blue roses continued to bloom in the shadows. The chutes around the starlit pool still wafted bewitchingly in the evening breeze. The ambiance remained the perfect combination of inviting and mysterious, even if Melpomene had planted more deadly nightshade than Athena thought necessary. Now, the two sat around an intimate, black lacquer table, glasses of ambrosia between them.

"So the Erinyes don't even know where Alecto went to get the form signed?" Melpomene asked.

"Nope," said Athena. "None of the other information written on it was helpful either; some was just gibberish. They won't follow up on it for fear of turning out like Alecto, and they're afraid to tell anyone that they haven't followed it up for fear of being blamed for the whole zombie thing in the first place."

"And they told you . . . why?"

"Because I'm clever," said Athena. "And they're conflicted. They're hoping I'll do the follow up for them. So far, they're right, since getting to the bottom of this was my original goal regardless." Athena actually suspected Tisiphone would rather she get to the bottom of a dark, spikey pit, but Tisiphone couldn't always get what she wanted. "Also, I promised I wouldn't tell any of the gods about this yet."

"But they're okay with you telling me?"

"They only specified 'gods,' so, technically . . . "

Melpomene sniggered. "Erinyes, not very smart."

"Yes, but I'd still rather not argue the point with them, so don't spread it around either," Athena said, and then added, "Please."

Melpomene smiled the smile of a vampire who's just been invited into someone's home.

"You're showing more teeth than most would consider comforting," Athena observed.

"Muse of horror." Melpomene licked the tip of a canine tooth. "Can't stop practicing."

"Which leads to why I'm confiding in you in the first place."

"Mmhmm, I'm good at dialogue segues, too. You're welcome."

"You just ruined it by interrupting."

"I'm a Muse, not an editor."

Athena plunged onward. "Megaera said that around the time the forms were signed, the location tracking on Alecto's tablet showed a few trips to the Underworld."

"Trips to the Underworld aren't exactly outside of the Erinyes' job description," Melpomene pointed out.

"I am aware. It might only be coincidence. But I had already planned to interview Persephone next, so this is hitting two birds with one stone. First, however, I need to *get* to the Underworld —"

"I can't take you to the Underworld, Athena. You know Zeus's rules: no helping the Punished with travel arrangements."

"That's not what I mean," Athena said. "I'll make the journey myself, but that means going down to Earth first."

"Ah. Where the zombies are." Melpomene grinned.

"Please stop helping with segues."

"Is it *scary* how helpful I am?" Melpomene grinned wider.

"Bottom line: what tips can you give me on moving through zombie-infested areas?"

"Ooh!" Melpomene grinned so wide the corners of her lips met at the nape of her neck, and her head popped off for a moment before she returned to normal. "Now there you've definitely come to the right person! Let's see. Number one: never trust anyone who seems sketchy enough to hide it if they become infected. They're bound to get infected eventually, and it's always trouble."

"Sounds wise enough."

"Number two: never, *ever*, back up."

"Not even when—"

"I said *never!*" Melpomene shouted. "See, that's when zombies get sneaky. No matter how much they normally snarl, groan, or rasp, they'll all turn silent on you if you don't watch where you're going. One moment you're backing around a tree, and the next you're food for a whole pack of the bastards tucked behind it who got quieter than ninjas in a library."

Athena frowned. "How is that even possible?"

"Don't ask silly questions. Number three, and the most important: if you stumble upon an isolated community of survivors securely holed up behind excellent defenses, what do you do?"

"That sounds like an excellent place to rest and re-supply."

"Wrong!" Melpomene slammed a hand on the tabletop. "You do not dare trust them! I cannot emphasize that enough. Really, you're better off just bloody running, because nine times out of ten there's something severely deranged transpiring in places like that."

Athena grumbled wordlessly. Her hand slipped into her jacket pocket and toyed with the tiny silver ball Megaera had given her before she'd left Erinyes HQ. With one squeeze, and enough angry thoughts, Athena could teleport, Erinyes-fashion, to anywhere she wished. Tempting. Yet the ball was only good for one use. Though it would be difficult to reach the Underworld on her own power, it was wiser to save the ball for an emergency. Also, the Erinyes' teleportation methods caused blood to gush from their eye sockets, and, frankly, screw *that*.

"There you are!" cried Thalia from the edge of the clearing. "You're just sitting around, sipping ambrosia, shooting the breeze or breezing the chutes, or whatever, while I'm off busting my shapely butt picking up your slack? I've got so little business covering for you I can't even tell you, but now you're just going to have to deal with it because gods forbid Nyx gets even more cross-grained than she already is just because you can't be bothered to keep an appointment! Oh, felicitations, Athena, how're you?"

Athena waved two fingers in greeting. "I've been—"

"Do you know what she did?" Thalia thrust both arms at Melpomene, who rolled her eyes.

"I—"

"She was *supposed* to meet with Nyx tonight to help her make sure the midnight fog wafting about the Scottish moors is sufficiently creepy, but she stood her up!" Thalia, seemingly on the verge of tears, huffed at Melpomene. "You don't stand up the goddess of night, Melpomene! Not when you're musing horror! Or, wait, were you trying to tweedle her off because you think that'd be scary? She called me up asking where you were, then demanded I help her instead! Why did Nyx call the Muse of freaking comedy? It's like the set-up to a joke, except it isn't funny!"

Melpomene sighed. "Nyx is just a divine personification playing at being a goddess. She fiddles too much. There are zombies roaming those moors; they're creepy enough. I'm busy helping Athena."

"Oh, hi, Athena," Thalia said again.

"You already said that," Athena answered.

"Yes, that's what makes it funny," Thalia said.

"Does it, though?"

"You try being funny after dealing with Nyx!" Thalia shrieked. "It's like trying to talk after someone takes away all the *e*'s in the room! Like this!" She snapped her fingers in a display of Muse-power.

"I'm sorry," Ath_na tri_d. "I r_ally didn't m_an to mak_ you f__l put upon."

M_lpom_n_ glar_d. "Fix that this instant, Thalia, or I'll tak_ away th_ *a*'s."

"Hrmph!" said Thalia. "As if you could maintain it."

"B_tt_r than you!" M_lpom_n_ snapp_d h_r fing_rs. "Scr_w you!"

Th_ two Mus_s glow_r_d _t __ch oth_r until th_ir f_c_s turn_d blu_. Th_y st_r_d _nd gl_r_d.

"Stop! Pl__s_!" _th_n_ d_m_nd_d.

Tog_th_r, both Mus_s snapped their fingers again. "Drama queen," Melpomene muttered.

"Goth hag!" Thalia spat.

"I really wish you wouldn't do that sort of thing when I am in the room," Athena said.

"Hey, you started it!" Thalia crossed her arms. "Never tell the Muse of comedy that she's not being funny. Even if that's an accurate assessment." Sulking, Thalia sank into an easy chair made of moss-covered stone — and then beamed so cheerfully that Athena wondered how she didn't get whiplash. Her eyes bright, her smile joyous, Thalia asked, "So anyway, what do you need help with, Athena?"

Athena waited to see if Thalia's mood would turn on another dime, and when it didn't, answered finally, "I'm going down to Earth, so I'm getting zombie advice."

"Why ever are you going down to Earth?" Thalia demanded. "You'll have to walk!"

"Because that's the only way I can get to the Underworld."

Thalia gasped, horrified. "Why ever are you going to the *Underworld*? You'll *really* have to walk!"

Athena hesitated. She probably shouldn't tell the Erinyes' secret to everyone just yet. The best way to distract Thalia was usually with a joke. "Um, because I may as well once I'm down on Earth?" *Ba-dum-bum.*

Okay, so it was barely a joke. Thalia gave a courtesy chuckle. "This is something to do with your quest to stop the zombie thing, isn't it? Melpomene, you *have* given her the Talk, yes?"

The Talk?

Melpomene sighed. "She's a grown immortal, Thalia. She can make her own choices. She doesn't need the Talk."

Athena cleared her throat. "You two do know I dropped the chastity thing a century ago? I hardly need —"

Thalia talked over her to Melpomene. "You just want her to have a harder time of it, don't you? Haven't mused enough tragedies lately?"

Melpomene stiffened. "I simply didn't think it necessary to influence —"

"Story before genre, Melpomene!" Thalia cried. "She has to behave as if this might be a sequel!"

Melpomene glared. "She has to make her own choices!"

"We still have a responsibility —"

"Stop!" Athena shouted. "What are you both talking about?"

The two Muses turned toward her like children caught plundering a cookie jar.

Melpomene sighed. "If you're going to Earth, you should get mortal help."

"*Familiar* mortal help," Thalia added. "Leif Karlson. Tracy Wallace. Even if they're just ancillary, supporting . . . help, if you know what I mean."

"Familiar?" Athena said. "I've never worked with either before, save for fighting on opposite sides."

"No, not familiar to *you*," Thalia said. "Familiar to the—okay, look, it's a Muse thing. Just trust us."

"You mean trust *you*," Melpomene said.

Thalia stuck out her tongue at Melpomene. "I mean trust *us*."

"Hrmph," Melpomene said.

"Shush, or I'll take away letters again, and then there will be no vowels for *anybody*."

CHAPTER FIVE

"Leavenworth Oktoberfest: The next best thing to being in Munich before zombies tore it to shreds!"
— Things to See While You Flee the Z! *(Pacific Northwest travel blog)*

"Keeping the undead alleviated so you can get inebriated!"
— *motto, Leavenworth Volunteer Traditional Bavarian Anti-Zombie Brigade*

THE TOURIST TOWN OF LEAVENWORTH, situated 35 miles east of Steven's Pass on Highway 2, is a charming little community with traditional Bavarian architecture, traditional Bavarian mountain views, and traditional Bavarian gift shops, eateries, type fonts, and two-and-a-half grocery stores made over to look (traditionally) Bavarian.

The fact that Leavenworth was originally a logging town called Icicle Flats—and only shifted to Bavarian-themed tourism after a change in the railway lines—made no difference to most visitors. It especially made no difference to the thousands of tourists who descended upon the town each autumn for a traditional, beer-fueled Bavarian Oktoberfest. As for the sparse clusters of undead outside the town's hastily constructed anti-zombie fences, their opinion on the matter could not be ascertained. Questions were answered only with "Grainns!" or "Nno commennnt!"

Some might say that in light of recent events, Oktoberfest should have been canceled that year. Indeed, some made this very argument to the Leavenworth Oktoberfest Council. Yet by then the beer had already been purchased. The hotels had already filled their reservation books. As the Mayor put it, "Leavenworth is an Oktoberfest town. We need Oktoberfest dollars. Now, if the people can't drink here, they'll be glad to drink at the festivals of Chelan, Hanford, Long Island . . . "

And so, Leavenworth Oktoberfest had continued. The first day had gone well. Sounds of defenders' rifles pulverizing the zombies encroaching on the fences and entry gates could barely be heard above the shouting of drunken tourists and polka bands. It was not until mid-afternoon of the second day that anything even resembling ultimate horrific disaster occurred.

It was mid-afternoon by the time the pick-up truck carrying Leif, Tracy, and ex-Ninja Templar Ryan Seth Sloude finally rolled through Oktoberfest Zombie Screening Checkpoint West. Following a half-hour wait in a one-mile line of vehicles stretching back along Highway 2—the final section of which was bordered by ten-foot chain link fencing festooned by the occasional zombie—they had passed through a gate staffed by men and women wearing red "VOLUNTEER" sashes. Beyond lay a fence-bound holding area consisting of the main road and the parking lot of a burned-out drive-in restaurant. There, a plump woman with long, graying red hair and a clipboard quizzed each of them. Had they come into physical contact with a zombie in the past 48 hours? Were they transporting any wheat, sorghum, or other major grains in amounts greater than two pounds? Were they carrying bags packed by anyone other than the living?

Each of them had each given three *no* answers. Leif breathed a silent thanks to no one in particular that Ryan had skipped his usual self-righteous exclamations of detail. After all, none of them did have any *physical* contact with the zombies on the road. Technically.

As a few stray zombies repeatedly bumped the fence just thirty yards away, the clipboard woman adjusted her sash and then stamped the backs of their hands.

"Welcome to Leavenworth!"

Leif glanced at the stamp, which read "NOT a zombie." It was the nicest thing anyone had said about him all week.

They soon drove out of the holding area and into the town proper. Parked cars crowded the sunbaked street shoulders. Clumps of walking tourists became denser and Bavarian buildings inched taller as they drove toward the town center. Bass drums and tuba-borping beckoned all forward, and the intoxicating aroma of beer crept heavy through the air.

Traffic crawled. Leif perused a pack of pickled pedestrians—two of whom wore Pope hats for some reason—shuffling along a crosswalk toward a beer garden that filled a side street. He sighed. Leif hadn't risked a beer in a long while. Lucky fools.

"Much farther?" He asked.

Tracy checked the map. "About a thousand yards up, past the town center, across from a Queequeg's Frozen Yogurt."

A gas station sign loomed on their left. $12.99 per gallon? That was nearly two dollars more than where they'd filled up last! Maybe the mechanic's garage they were heading toward would have a more reasonable price.

Stupid zombie-addled economy.

"That's outrageous!" Tracy scoffed. "For a single tire and a fill-up?"

The man named Rod grinned. "That's the price."

The garage price had not been more reasonable. Now, the three of them stood at the counter in its tiny office. Shadows cast from barred windows fell on a service counter covered in toothpick sculptures and flyers for local restaurants. On one wall was an ad for the *Sweeten's Guide* ("Subscribe for a year and get a free Sweeten's 'Zombie-Survivor Superstar' tote bag!"). Behind the counter stood Rod, the garage's owner.

At least, that's what the nametag emblazoned on his coveralls said. Given the coveralls' heinous rips and suspicious dark stains, not to mention the shady look in the guy's eyes, Leif considered it possible that this man had simply pried them from an unfortunate Rod's corpse.

Leif had such a bad feeling that he stifled his urge to complain in order to avoid having to defend his own clothing from "Rod." After all, survivor-on-survivor theft was just the kind of thing that happened out in the wild of small towns in a zombie semi-apocalypse.

Tracy, apparently, did not have such concerns. "That's not even a discount on the gas!" she said.

Leif cleared his throat in warning. "Tracy, now, let's not be bad customers . . . "

"Hinder us not with your highway robbery!" Ryan added. "We toil on an errand for the glory of Almighty God!"

"Ryan—" Leif tried.

"Oh yeah?" said Rod with sudden interest. "Which one?"

Ryan blinked. "Which *one*?"

"Is it Hermes?" tried Rod. "I love that guy."

"Hermes is no more a god than I am!" exclaimed Ryan. A globule of spittle arced through the air to land on Rod's sleeve, and a dangerous color rose in Rod's cheeks.

Leif turned and put a hand on Ryan's shoulder. "Let's talk outside, huh?"

To Leif's relief, Ryan allowed himself to be guided outside. Soon they were alone in the shadows beside the gas tanks.

"Don't antagonize him!" Leif whispered.

"I am educating him!"

"We don't need him educated, we need him to fix our tires and give us gas, so we can get out of this place as soon as possible. The longer we stay here, the greater the chance something'll go wrong. Either the zombies get in somehow and we have a fight on our hands—or worse, this guy decides to pull the 'humans are scarier than zombies' trope and kills us to sell the truck for parts or something!"

"Ahh," said Ryan. "Like that bowling alley in Vancouver."

Leif winced at the memory. "No, that was . . . a misunderstanding." The incident had been a week after the zombies had risen. Leif later admitted he might have jumped to conclusions there, and he really did hope the doctors managed to reattach that guy's hand.

Inside, Tracy continued to haggle with Rod. Leif took a deep breath. "Look, just wait out here and watch our backs while Tracy and I make a deal, okay?"

"I'm a deal maker too," Ryan whispered. "I make the best deals.

Everybody says so."

"You're also the one with the sword. Guard our backs, okay?"

Ryan nodded. "I have the best sword."

Leif gave him a thumbs-up and ducked back inside. Tracy was leaning over the counter with both hands pressed against its top. "Rod" stood rod-straight, his arms folded across his ragged coveralls. He had a smile on his face like a turtle who's been asked to get out of the way.

"You do know that Hermes isn't around anymore, right?" Tracy was saying. "Zeus exiled him. There's no point in gouging us in his name."

Rod laughed. "Oh, sure. The sneakiest god disappears, and we're all supposed to believe it's exile?"

"Trust us," said Leif. "We were there."

"Sure you were, guy. See that?" Rod angled a thumb to an upturned hubcap on a shelf behind him. On display in the hubcap's center was a $100 gift card to Queequeg's Frozen Yogurt. Surrounded by tea light candles and coins of both U.S. and Canadian origin, it looked like a shrine. Next to it, and possibly unrelated, sat a half-drank pint of beer—or a half-un-drank pint, depending on your philosophical leanings.

"That's proof," Rod continued. "Last March I was working on a fuel pump replacement. It was a bastard of a job, and I was already running up against the maximum time I'd promised to bill for labor. So I said a prayer to Hermes to help me get it done fast. Well, he does me better than that. I get it done, fast as you please, and as I'm backing the car out of the garage for pick up, thanking Hermes aloud as I do it, that card just falls out of the sun visor, right into my lap!"

"And you kept it?" Tracy asked.

"Hermes bestowed it upon me! It's practically a holy relic! So don't tell me he's not out there. He's just testing your faith. Or hiding from Zeus. And even if he weren't, it's still in my interest to gouge you." Rod grinned and fixed his gaze on Leif as he said "gouge."

Leif shivered. "Is your name really Rod?"

"Rod" raised an eyebrow.

The door burst open a moment later. Leif turned, expecting Ryan, and found instead an out-of-breath, pudgy-faced man in his mid-forties. An orange hat emblazoned with the logo of the Leavenworth Volunteer Traditional Bavarian Anti-Zombie Brigade sat askew on his head.

"Afternoon! Just a heads-up, folks! Nothing to be alarmed about, but there's just the smallest hole in the town fence down the way near Gerry's Bait Shoppe. Nothing to be worried about—we're already fixing it back up, but be on the lookout just in case one of those grainers wandered through. And if you see one, call the hotline! But nothing to worry about! Just a minor penetration, if any!"

With that, the brigadier checked something on a clipboard, nodded to Rod, and dashed out the door before anyone could say anything. Leif watched the brigadier's eager egress through the window and suddenly noticed Ryan was nowhere to be seen.

Meanwhile, Tracy pulled back from the counter. "Right. Minor zombie penetration. One more reason to just take our business elsewhere, then. Let's go, Leif."

"You're not leaving," said Rod. "You need my gas. And my tire. You'll pay my prices. Where else you gonna go?"

From the door behind Rod came a violent clatter of wood, metal, and a few other items Leif couldn't identify, but sounded like either paint cans or watermelons. What followed, though, Leif immediately identified:

"Die, undead hordes!" came Ryan's scream. Another clatter came on its heels.

Rod looked back with an alarmed, "Son of a Bavarian bitch!" Rod grabbed a double-barreled shotgun from beneath the counter and beat feet through the rear door so quickly that Hermes would've been proud. In the blink of time before the door swung closed, Leif spotted the glint of Ryan's sword and several pale, bloodied figures in the middle of the mechanic's garage.

Leif and Tracy exchanged glances. Leif was about to run after Rod to assess the situation, but Tracy grabbed his arm.

"Get out to the pump," she urged in a whisper. "Fill up the tank!" She rushed around the counter, punching keys on the electronic register before Leif could move.

In the garage, Rod launched a volley of profanity too rapid to understand. Leif stood rooted, torn between obeying Tracy and investigating.

Tracy pointed toward their truck. "Zombies bad! Gasoline good! Hurry!" After a couple slaps on the counter to spur Leif on, she grabbed a nearby tire iron and dashed into the garage.

Leif scrambled out to the gas pump like a pug chasing a slice of bacon. He yanked the nozzle from the pump holster, unscrewed the truck's gas cap, and jammed the nozzle inside.

Rod, meanwhile, hollered loud enough to be heard through the walls. "What have you done, you—! *Those aren't zombies!*"

"They look exactly like them in the shadows!" came Ryan's answering yell.

As the pump's dial spun all too slowly, Tracy asked a muffled question somewhere inside.

"*Yes,* I'm building a zombie parade float!" Rod hollered. "It's for Zombvemberfest next month! And this sword-wielding jackass just hacked all my mannequins to pieces! You can forget about the tires and the gas until you help me fix all of this!"

2 gallons. 2.4 gallons. 2.8 gallons . . .

"We did nothing wrong!" Ryan exclaimed. "We will not fix graven zombie images that I rightfully destroyed!"

Tracy's muffled voice sounded once more.

"It doesn't matter if you haven't heard of Zombvemberfest!" Rod shouted. "It's a new Leavenworth tradition! Attracting more visitor dollars in the lull between Oktoberfest and the Christmas tree lighting! It's a Hermes-inspired idea!"

4.4 gallons. 4.8 gallons . . . Tracy said something else.

"That doesn't matter!" Rod yelled. "Now you two stay right here and start fixing this! I'm going to—!"

Rod's shout aborted with a wordless yell, a torrent of cursing, and finally a gurgled scream.

"Die, undead hordes!" came Ryan again. At least three growls of "Grrrains!" issued above the clatter of items knocked over and the squelching cracks of sword-through-neck. Leif left the nozzle to its work, grabbed his crowbar from the back of the truck, and looked around the pumps for zombies. Some must have gotten through the fence and surprised Rod while he was yelling—unless his parade float was just that realistic in simulating them.

Leif forced himself to stay put. If he left to help Tracy, logic dictated that more zombies would surely find the truck and ambush them when they came out—possibly even leaking gas everywhere and then blowing the place up in the process.

7.6 gallons . . .

Or would that happen if he did stay by the pumps, alone? They'd swarm him, attacking—a missed crowbar swing would dislodge the nozzle, send gas everywhere, and probably spark something with him standing right there . . .

8 gallons . . .

From inside, a rifle shot rang out, followed by multiple heavy things crashing into each other. Then all was silent.

"Tracy?" Leif shouted.

There came a tinkle of glass, followed by a *ffwwhoom!* that was either something igniting or someone unfurling a really big flag.

"Tracy?" Leif tried again.

8.8 gallons . . .

Suddenly, a tire rolled around the far side of the garage, guided by Ryan. His sword was sheathed. His face was energized. His foot struck a crack in the pavement. He fell forward, lost control of the tire, regained his balance, and then ran to catch up to the tire, which rolled straight to Leif's feet.

"Where's Tracy?" Leif barked.

"Coming!" Ryan scooped up the tire. He shoved it into the truck's cargo bed, and then climbed in after it.

The gas pump clicked off at 10.00 gallons exactly, which Leif thought was pretty neat. He yanked out the nozzle, thrust it back on the pump, and fastened the gas cap.

A plume of flame erupted from behind the garage.

"Um," said Leif.

Tracy burst out the front door. Zombie blood stained the right leg of her jeans—or Leif assumed it was zombie blood. She carried two twelve-packs of bottled water and a fistful of beef jerky.

"Get in the truck!" she yelled. "Start the engine!"

Leif did so. In moments, Tracy had dumped the water in the back and slid into the passenger seat. Hardly waiting for her door to close, Leif threw the truck in reverse and drove them away from the burning station and back to the main road.

"What happened?" Leif asked. "I mean, I heard about the parade float, but . . . "

Tracy pulled some granola bars from her pockets and stuffed them into the glove compartment. "Rod backed out of an open door," she said. "Into the lot behind the garage. I don't know why. Four actual zombies were standing right there, dead silent, waiting."

Tracy pulled Rod's $100 gift card to Queequeg's Frozen Yogurt out of her pocket, examined it, and thrust it back inside.

"Zombie-ninjas?" said Leif. "Bummer."

Tracy nodded and took a huge bite of beef jerky. "Rod didn't have a chance," she said between chews. "Then fighting. Fire. A whole mess."

Leif caught the faint sound of fire engine sirens in the distance. He sighed. Rod surely didn't deserve all that. Unless the guy really did kill the real Rod and take his coveralls. Leif realized he had no proof that wasn't what had happened. That made him feel a little better.

"What the hell kind of stupid idea is 'Zombvemberfest,' anyway?" he asked.

"I know, right?" Tracy thrust a handful of dried meat his way. "Beef jerky?"

Chapter Six

Let it be known: Those gods and goddesses stripped of their divinity for Crimes Against Zeus (the details of which I shall not dignify by listing here), henceforth known as "the Punished," in addition to their godly demotions, may only travel off Olympus by their own reduced means. They may climb, they may walk, they may construct an ill-advised hang-glider out of wax and toilet paper, but they must do so without divine aid. No other Olympians shall provide the Punished with transport assistance outside of Olympus, nor may the Punished access or borrow any divine vehicles without my express written permission. Providing teleportation assistance to the Punished is right out. Of these things I command, I shall tolerate no violation.

P.S. None of the Punished should even think about asking to borrow the keys to my new Harrier AwesomeJet. In fact, none of the rest of you should, either.

—Decree of Zeus, one week after the Second Withdrawal

THE STARTLING THING FOR TRACY wasn't so much that the woman was standing in the middle of the road, but that she had chosen to do so almost immediately around a blind corner. The next startling thing was the sound of Leif's shriek mingling with the squeal of the tires as he swerved. And then it was the feel of the beef jerky trying to escape up Tracy's esophagus as the abrupt stop hurled her into the seatbelt.

And then, finally, it was recognizing just who the foolish woman in the middle of the road *was*.

Her clothing was different than when Tracy had last seen her. From the heavy gray jeans tucked into boots even heavier and grayer, to the black leather bomber jacket (set off with blue and, yes, gray stripes), to the dark hair and gray-framed sunglasses, there was little to distinguish her from any other muscular woman who had a thing for gray. But the handgun at her hip made an impression, holstered as it was next to the shining hilt of a sheathed short sword. As for the shirt she wore beneath the jacket—gleaming like gold chain yet moving like fabric and, Tracy knew from experience, hard as steel—that was pretty much a dead Olympian giveaway.

The woman wore a charcoal T-shirt under the gold shirt, but that was neither here nor there.

"You can't just stand in the middle of the damn road like that!" Leif shouted at her. "We just *fixed* this truck!" Recognition finally seemed to hit him as the woman walked to the passenger side. "Oh. It's her."

"This truck bed is not restful," came a pained moan from Ryan. "And needs seatbelts . . . "

The woman rapped smooth knuckles on Tracy's window. Tracy rolled it down with some reluctance.

"Tracy Daphne Wallace? I require a few moments of your time."

"Hello, Athena," said Tracy. "What were you doing in the middle of the road like that? Weren't you the goddess of wisdom?"

"Key word being *were*," said Leif.

Athena frowned, mostly at Leif. "I am still immortal," she said. "This was the best way to ensure you would stop."

"Right, well, this isn't the best place in the world to have a conversation right now."

"Then I shall travel with you. Slide over."

"Why should I?" asked Tracy. "The last time we met, you were trying to kill me."

"I was trying to *defeat* you, which is not the same thing. Now let me in before you get rear-ended."

Leif sniggered. "That's what she said."

"That is indeed what I said, Leif Karlson, but I'm certain Ms. Wallace heard me the first time." Athena turned back to Tracy. "If it helps, Thalia says hello, and bade me tell you she can always lighten you up again if you need it."

Tracy rolled her eyes at the memory. A concentrated look from the Muse of comedy once had her running through the desert giggling about ping-pong and clowns.

An orange Porsche Boxster rounded the corner behind them and swerved, tires squealing like a mob snitch. It narrowly missed their back bumper, and then sped on as the driver flipped them off through the sunroof. The Boxster's license plate read *PANDORA*.

Tracy grit her teeth and opened the passenger door. "What's this about?"

Athena climbed in, sandwiched Tracy between her and Leif, and closed the door. "Solving the zombie problem," she said.

"Hey, who's she?" came Ryan's voice from the back. No one answered.

"Did you guys do that?" Tracy asked. "Create the zombies so you'd have an excuse to come back?"

"I do not know their source." Athena fastened her seatbelt. "But—"

"How would she know?" said Leif as he stepped on the gas. "She's not a god anymore. You're not, right?"

"Neither are you, Leif Karlson. Be quiet while I'm speaking." Tracy couldn't help but smirk as Athena went on. "I am striving to learn the source so that I may stop it, and I require your assistance. I am going to the Underworld."

"Why do you need our—"

"Because I no longer have the power to travel there as a goddess would, and you, Ms. Wallace, previously traveled there by foot. And because, *apparently*, I cannot do so without bringing you along."

"Says who?" asked Leif. "We've got our own urgent business right now."

"Says a pair of Muses," Athena said.

"It wasn't Terpsichore, was it?" Leif asked. "She's given me really bad advice before."

"She has," Tracy agreed.

"Melpomene and Thalia. They claim it is a 'sequel thing'."

"Oh," Leif said, somehow mollified by that. "Say no more."

Tracy cleared her throat. "Well, say a *little* more, right? Because if I'm going back into the Underworld during a zombie crisis, I want to know why. Plus, Leif's right. We're in the middle of our own business."

Tracy told Athena about the *Zeus Was Dead* movie, how in the wake of the zombie apocalypse the studio collapsed and the movie subsequently folded, and of her and Leif's determination to salvage their already invested time (and potential profit) by getting the movie made through another company.

"Except I don't have rights to the script *I* wrote because for some stupid legal reason it still belongs to the dead studio!" Leif moaned. "Now if I rewrite it, I can't mention the gods' names, which is freaking ridiculous."

"Though we could use their Roman names," Tracy added.

"Apollo is the same in both Greek and Roman!" Leif said. "I looked it up! What am I supposed to do, call him Paulie?"

Athena fished a metal buckler out from between her back and the truck seat and lay it on the dashboard. Greek engravings circled a painted olive tree on its front. She set a holstered handgun beside it. "Leif Karlson, you are not rapidly approaching your point," she said. "Fix that now."

Tracy eyed the handgun. Was that a Glock 21?

"Er, sure," said Leif. "So, since Apollo apparently has some controlling interest in the entertainment industry—"

"Now that Zeus broke his word," Tracy injected, "and let you all come back again . . . "

"Zeus did not break his word," Athena warned.

"Whatever," Tracy said.

"—we're going to one of Apollo's temples to pray for his help," Leif continued. "And since he doesn't seem to have temples in convenient places where normal people go, we're stuck coming out to eastern-frakking-Washington to do it. Is it really true that the gods don't have to listen to any prayers not made from their own temples anymore? If we're driving all this way for nothing . . . "

Athena nodded. "Zeus decreed it as a favor to Apollo to help keep his workload manageable. And also to increase mortal efforts at temple construction so as to provide more jobs and help the economy."

Leif snorted. "Are you the Olympian Press Secretary now?"

"You did inquire."

"It's just that it's awfully inconvenient going all this way just to ask a favor from a 'god' who, frankly, really owes us big."

"That is not my problem, Leif Karlson."

"Do you even know how expensive air travel is now after that zombie near-apocalypse?" Leif burst. "How much of a pain in the ass this trip has been so far?"

Tracy considered telling him to shut up, but frankly, his rant mirrored her own feelings. Also, she still wasn't over the whole gods-trying-to-kill-her thing. Not to mention the gods-unleashing-monsters-for-sport thing. Or the gods-possibly-being-responsible-for-the-zombies-in-the-first-place thing, which had been on her mind for the past few months.

"I sympathize with your predicament," Athena said. "But even you, Leif Karlson, must agree that stopping the undead infestation of your world, blunted though it may be now, surely takes priority over any copyright issues you may have."

"What do you mean 'even you'?" Leif demanded.

"You are the least-wise person in this cab."

Tracy turned to Leif. "Sloude *is* in the cargo bed."

Leif grumbled something inaudible but cranky.

"My point stands," said Athena. "There is an Underworld entrance near the Grand Coulee Dam. That should take you out of your way only marginally."

"Right. Only a marginal distance, plus a jaunt into *Hades*," Tracy corrected.

"Hades was exiled," Athena countered. "We don't call the Underworld that anymore."

"So you just call it the Underworld?"

"Yes. Or 'Jerry'."

Leif perked up. "Oh, hey! How *is* Jerry?"

More importantly, thought Tracy: "Zeus put *Jerry* in charge of the Underworld?" That was liable to explain the zombies right there. Tracy liked Jerry—as the sentient, temple-guarding tree given divinity by Zeus had taken to calling himself. But the last time Tracy had seen him, Jerry had still been getting the hang of his new divine power—not to mention the novel and complex concept of *walking*.

"Jerry did have the guarding thing down pretty well," Leif offered.

"He was only in charge for a few weeks after Hades's exile, in the interim before Persephone was entrusted with full control," said Athena. "That was long before the zombie troubles. However, in that time, he managed to put through the name change, and Persephone hasn't yet cared to bother Zeus about it. Unfortunately, 'I damn you to Jerry' doesn't have quite the same kick to it. So we mostly call it the Underworld."

"Whatever you call it, we don't want to go there." Tracy fixed her gaze on Athena to better portray her resolve. The ex-goddess's eyes were a crystalline gray, like cloudy diamonds, and just as hard. Athena stared her down, and Tracy was struck by the impression that Athena could, if she chose, fold Tracy up and stuff her in the glove compartment. This would be a feat even more incredible than it sounds: the glove compartment had been jammed ever since they'd bought the truck in Oregon from an old woman in a roadside tent.

"You used to be a heroine," Athena said.

Tracy swallowed. "And I used to be Zeus's mortal daughter before I renounced that, too. I got tired of being used."

Athena folded her arms. Those biceps were impressive. "You were being used for the gods' purposes back then. Now you would be helping your world."

"That's exactly what someone trying to use me would say."

Athena scowled. "I am not a trickster, Ms. Wallace. But if you wish further incentive, after your aid is given, I will put in a good word for you with Apollo regarding your film troubles."

"Did you hear Leif's 'Apollo owes us big' bullet point earlier?"

"You are not the only one in this truck that he owes. Keep in mind that your cause can be sabotaged as easily as it can be aided."

Something pounded on the cab's back window. Tracy jumped before realizing it was Ryan. "Speak to me of the newcomer!" he shouted. "Why have we taken this woman into our fold?"

Tracy ignored him, though it did give her an idea. She unfolded their map. "How about this: We give you a ride to where Highway 174 branches off of Route 2 toward the dam. From there you can make your own way the remaining"—she peered at the map, trying to gauge distance and missing the luxury of battery-draining smartphone navigation—"call it twenty miles to the dam."

"That is not—"

Tracy pointed a thumb back at their tagalong ninja-cargo behind them. "You can even take Mr. Sloude in our place as our representative!" Tracy offered. "Doesn't that satisfy your need to get our help?"

"Helloooo?!" Ryan shouted through the glass, as if sensing his involvement. Athena glanced back, and Ryan waved. "Has anyone informed you that you look very much like one of the old false gods?" he yelled. "They're all very bad! Everyone knows it!"

Tracy cleared her throat. "He is handy in a fight. Comes with a sword. You can haul him into Hades."

"Into Jerry," Leif corrected.

"That, too."

"Ms. Wallace," said Athena, her tone dipped in frost, "are you truly so unconcerned with eradicating the zombies that you will not take a chance on the goddess of wisdom?"

"Technically, *ex*-godde—"

Athena silenced Leif with a glare. As Tracy considered further, however, Leif's silence didn't last.

"What if our truck gets damaged?" Leif argued. "Or if we stop the zombies but it turns out that the gods really did cause the zombies, and so you make them withdraw again, and we never get the chance to talk to Apollo! Then we might never get the rights to the movie back!"

"That would be kind of a recycled plot," said no one in particular.

Tracy's conscience tugged at her. Or maybe that was her seat belt. "Okay," she sighed. "We'll take you all the way to the damn dam."

Leif groaned. "All the way?"

"Did I stutter?" Tracy shot.

"Er, a little, actually."

"All the way to the dam," Athena repeated. "And then?"

"And then," Tracy answered, "we'll see."

Ryan banged on the window again. "Helloooo?"

"And until then, we'll continue to ignore the guy in the back," said Leif.

The truck drove on.

CHAPTER SEVEN

"Hear me now, my worshippers! For those who are not otherwise enlightened, the so called 'dark' side of the moon — as the indelicate refer to the far side — is not truly dark. It simply is not visible *from Earth. It always faces away. While this makes it an excellent place to hide things, the far side is no darker than the side mortals see. 'Dark' in this context originally meant hidden, but this has caused much confusion. We must therefore eradicate this slanderous term, lest further misunderstanding of my wondrous celestial sphere be spread!*

"I, Artemis, goddess of the moon, compel you: spread my word to the mortal populace. Anyone referring to it as the 'dark side of the moon' is a buffoon to be publicly ridiculed and barred from use of my temples, forests, and my planned chain of archery ranges."

— *"It Ain't Made of Green Cheese, Either!"* Artemis's Official Temple Newsletter, *Issue 12*

ON THE DARK SIDE of the moon, along the edge of the largest crater he could find, surrounded by piles of bent iron swords, shields, spears, and poorly-constructed assault rifles that looked like a half-blind monkey had tried to manufacture an AK-47, lay Ares: god of war and conflict, inventor of the Internet comment section, and mastermind of the only successful plot to murder Zeus.

Certain fools, were any on the moon to give their opinion, would claim that he was only the *ex*-god of war and conflict due to his exile from Earth. Yet, as Ares had endlessly repeated to himself, those fools were assholes, and hypothetical to boot! (At least, he would have repeated that to himself if "hypothetical" weren't two syllables longer than his personal lexicon generally allowed.) *He* was the only god on the moon at *all*, so he could be god of anything he damn well pleased! Ares, god of craters! Ares, god of power! Ares, god of kicking shit to pieces!

It should be mentioned that the whole "mastermind of the plot to murder Zeus" thing is also false. Ares was involved, but he neither came up with it nor commanded anyone in its execution. Any of his co-conspirators would point this out, were they around to argue the point. Yet they were not: Aphrodite had dumped Ares after their exile and ran off to parts unknown with Hermes. Dionysus remained trapped in Tartarus with most of the Titans. Hades seemed to have vanished.

Hidden away on the ass-end of the moon, Ares spent most of his time building little moon-men out of moon dirt, giving them life and weaponry, and then telling one group of moon-men that another group said they were jackasses, telling the second group of moon-men that the first group not only said they were jackasses but that they were made from inferior moon dirt, and watching the ensuing battles.

They weren't the best made moon-men. While Ares retained his divinity in his exiled state (though one step anywhere near Earth would strip his power entirely), creation had never been his strength. What life he could give the moon-men only lasted a few hours before they reverted to moon dirt.

The weapons he'd made for the moon-men—and this is what really galled him—weren't much better. No, they didn't fall apart, and yes, there was plenty of iron to be found on the moon to make them. Yet while weapons design was something Ares truly excelled at, weapons *forging* was something he'd previously left to that lame cuckold Hephaestus. Forced to do it on his own, the resulting implements made him glad no one else was around to see them.

And so it was that Ares lay along the crater, staring into the sun and brainstorming ideas of how best to start a three-way moon-men free-for-all battle that would end before half the combatants crumbled to pieces. No ideas were forthcoming. Ares punched his own brain, demanding it work better. It did not.

And then: a twinkle! Not from an idea, but from a particular star floating just above the lunar horizon. It twinkled purple. It twinkled red. It twinkled perzoid, which is a peculiar shade of boz, both of which were extra-dimensional colors only visible to supernatural beings and a few hyper-competent interior decorators.

Also, the star was bobbing slightly and growing closer.

Ares grinned, leapt to his feet, and rubbed his hands together. A visitor! Someone to break the monotony of a year and a half of moon-men and mock battles! Ares donned his new wolf's head helmet (which wasn't nearly as nice as the one he'd left behind on Earth, but he wasn't some pansy artist), drew his solid iron, double-headed Lunar Axe of Glory-Slicing, and fired out a beacon of godly energy. It was a damned fine beacon of godly energy, designed to both attract the newcomer's attention and imply the enormous size of his swinging celestial gonads.

Almost instantly, the newcomer changed course to widen the distance between them. It changed again a moment later, now heading directly toward him, and then zig-zagging back and forth in a fashion so wobbly that Ares started to get dizzy following it.

"Hey!" Ares yelled across the vastness of space. "Get yer ass over here!" There being no sound in space, it had no effect save to remind Ares how much the vastness of space pissed him off.

The newcomer continued its nauseating approach. It grew larger in the sky as it drew near. Ares shifted the grip on his axe into a more offensive posture and yelled—telepathically this time—"*It ain't smart to mess with the god of war, whatever ya are! Stop wiggling yer butt and get over here or yer gonna get cleaved where the sun don't shine!*" He imbued the axe with a blast of crackling power to better make his point.

The newcomer stopped, maybe a mile off? Ares squinted. Whatever the damn thing was, he had a hard time getting a fix on the distance. It quaked, flaring again in colors across the extra-dimensional spectrum, and then it flattened itself in a way that reminded Ares of a particularly ungrateful Macedonic king that he'd once dropped an altar on, but with less blood and screaming. It hung there in the sky, ugly and arrogant.

Ares sneered. *Enough of this crap.* He leapt into the sky on an intercept course. It was a *direct* intercept course, with none of that spinning, spirally crap! Now *this* was how you moved across the sky, damn it!

When Ares got within a hundred yards, the newcomer exploded.

Alas, it was not a fun explosion, with lots of glorious flame and force and flying viscera. It was an explosion of sensation and . . . *parts*. Where once bobbed a ball of light, there now burst forth grasping tentacles, which encircled it in a sea of writhing flesh. Mouths of all shapes and sizes boiled out of them, teeth gnashing. Amid those, bothersome shapes surfaced and submerged: trapezohedrons, hyperhedrons, hippopotamohedrons, and—what really turned Ares's stomach—ovals.

The ovals were the worst. Aside from Ares' general hatred of ovals, with their smug roundness and bastardized curves, these particular ovals were so perfectly two-dimensional that each time one burst out of the writhing mass, they slashed a hole in three-dimensional space before sliding back whence they came. Disquieting things spilled out of those dimensional slashes: nauseating floral scents, uncomfortably adorable baby penguins, and hundreds upon hundreds of kazoos.

Ares, his axe raised for a counterstrike, nonetheless backed off as the whatever-it-was swelled in size. Two thoughts gave him comfort in the face of the monstrosity: The first was its chaos reminded him of his sister Eris. (He missed her greatly. Eris could destroy Facebook friendships with a single comment, or pick the precise fruit that need be thrown to start a major war at any given moment.) The second thought was he did not have to suffer the penguins' cuteness for long before, fuzzy wings flapping helplessly, they tumbled into the vacuum of space and asphyxiated.

"What in Medusa's butt crack are you?" Ares telepathy-growled at it.

Forty-two eyes ruptured into existence across the thing's surface. Some were green, some were perzoid, some were atop stalks or even other eyes. All peered at him. Thirteen blinked. Being eyes, of course, none spoke.

That was all Ares could take. He bellowed silently into the vacuum, sent a blast of energy into the largest of the eyes, and, axe raised, surged forward to strike.

His axe never found its mark. Tentacles and kazoos gushed into his chest. The impact hurled him backwards. His ass slammed into the moon before he knew what hit him. A cone of energy burned a shaft into the lunar surface, down which Ares plunged. The entire shaft flooded with blackish pink ichor that filled Ares's nose, ears, and other assorted orifices. Ares was trapped under its festering weight. His knuckles began to itch.

Above, the newcomer closed the maw in its middle that had spewed the ichor. It folded back in upon itself until it was once more a bobbing ball of light. Then, after spending a few moments hovering over the newly filled shaft in what was either suspicion or arousal, it continued toward Earth.

Speaking of Eris, she had been enjoying a productive day of Internet trolling when someone had tried to shoot her out of a cannon—or, rather, to shoot an effigy of her out of a cannon. The culprits, a group of mortal anarchists seeking to curse a Canadian election rally, had snagged her attention with a sacrifice in her name of a dozen bottles of vodka. These bottles were delivered in Molotov cocktail form at the aforementioned rally. Eris had perked up when she sensed the sacrifice and turned her gaze upon them from afar. That was when she spotted the hideous, half-likeness of her, cobbled together from coffee cans. The anarchists shoved this into a makeshift cannon and blasted it rudely into the sky such that it parachuted down over the twice-aforementioned rally. The effigy's left arm dangled broken. Parachute lines tied around its neck threatened to tear its head off completely.

Eris could not fault the anarchists overly much; it was an excellent idea in principle. An effigy of literally anyone else would have tittered her fabulously, but to show such disrespect to the goddess they purported to worship? Baaaad mortals.

She had launched herself from Olympus at once, descended upon the anarchists, and repaid the favor with cannons of her own. She had not the time to bother with creating effigies, so the anarchists themselves had served just fine for ammunition. *They* disrupted the rally even more spectacularly, and wasn't that what they'd really wanted in the first place?

The incident had whet her appetite for more. Taking the form of a vulture to honor one of her exiled brother's favorite animals, she drifted on the winds, letting them carry her where they might as she kept her eyes peeled for new and interesting opportunities.

Eventually, they had taken her into the eastern half of Washington State, where she spotted the truck and, within its cab, the unmistakable form of Athena. Eris had kept her ear to the Olympian ground enough to know that Athena had a bug up her butt about the zombie issue. But why was she in a truck with two mortals and an ex-Ninja Templar? Eris dove on an intercept course to find out.

Moments later, Eris latched her talons onto the truck's passenger side mirror. She poked her bald head through the open window at Athena and stopped time in that handy way that gods can when they wish to have a few moments to speak outside of the bothersome space-time continuum. Months ago, Eris had discovered that the Punished still possessed enough celestial kick to allow her to form a time-stop, but—and this was the truly delicious part—not enough to break it. She therefore abused this quirk as much as possible, often while invisible, banishing the Punished to a private, powerless timeout just before they tried to eat something, drink something, or flush something. Eris did have to stay in the time-stop as well to maintain it, but it was a small price to pay for the high of spreading frustration.

This time, however, she remained visible, tapped her beak on the mirror, and said, "Hey!" She punctuated it with another mirror tap, just to be irritating.

Athena had the nerve to roll her eyes. "*What*, Eris?"

"I am not Eris!" said Eris.

"You speak with her voice, vulture. You have her bearing. Ergo, you are Eris."

"Or am I another, seeking to fool you into thinking I am Eris?" Eris tapped her beak on the mirror a third time, yet again to be irritating.

Athena sized her up from head to tail. "No," she said, "you are Eris."

Hrmph. "Fine. Just what do you think you're doing, *Athena*?"

"I *think* I am on a road trip and trapped in a time-stop so you can cause some strife, *Eris*. What do you think *you're* doing?"

"A road trip to where?"

"Why do you care?"

"A goddess's curiosity knows no bounds, Athena. Or did you forget that after you lost Zeus's favor?"

Near imperceptible as it was, Athena winced. She recovered quickly. "Curiosity killed the cat, you know."

Eris grinned—quite a painful feat for a creature without lips, but she was a goddess. She could take it. "But satisfaction brought it back," she said. Hearing the lesser-known half of the proverb made Athena roll her eyes in irritation, which only made Eris grin wider. Except, wait, that hurt even more. She dialed it down a notch. Damned vulture mouths.

Ares just *had* to make them lipless.

"Listen, Athena," she continued, "I know you're trying to fix the zombie problem, and I know you. You wouldn't come down here in your current state unless you had a plan. So you've got two choices: tell me what it is, or stay trapped in this time-stop and go insane while I tap out the baseline from 'Welcome to the Jungle' on your forehead for the next two days."

Athena scoffed. "Truly, Eris? You know the moment you strike me the time-stop bursts."

Eris did know that, but had been hoping Athena no longer did. Oh well. "So I'll tap other things. And though your Punished memory is more intact than I'd hoped, you would be a fool to compare our capacities for patience." She scraped her beak along the window frame, and then: *Tap-tap tap-tap-tap-tap! Tap tap tap-tap tap!*

Athena merely stared at her.

Tap tap tap-tap-tap tap-tap, tap tap tap-tap!

"Do you do such things because nobody likes you, Eris," asked Athena, "or does nobody like you because you do such things?"

"Plenty of people like me. Still mad about the golden apple thing? It's not my fault Paris didn't name you most beautiful." She went on to tap out the second verse of the Guns & Roses masterpiece.

"I am going to Jerry," Athena said. "To see what Persephone knows."

Eris sniggered. "You gave in faster than I expected. It's almost a shame."

"Or I decided you would follow me anyway, so there's no point in tolerating you longer than I must."

"You should be wise enough not to antagonize me, Athena," Eris warned.

Athena laughed. "Or am I wise enough to know the goddess of discord only respects those who don't shrink from conflict?"

"You fear me," Eris pressed. "You know what I can do to you if I choose. How outmatched you are. You're afraid I'll learn what else you're planning, aren't you?"

Athena leaned closer. "Am I, Eris?" Her eyes narrowed. Her jaw set. She lay one hand on the passenger door's window sill. "Am I really?"

Eris poked her head closer in turn until her beak was a hair's breadth from Athena's nose. "I know false bravado when I see it, ex-goddess."

"Oh? Would false bravado do this?"

Athena punched Eris's neck. The force simultaneously knocked Eris from her perch and broke the time-stop with its physical contact.

The truck drove on as Eris regained her bearings. She landed on her feet along the road's shoulder, in human form, torn between pride and anger. She adored causing discord, and few things were more discordant than physical violence, so mission accomplished there. Yet physical violence directed at her? That just pissed her off. Wavering between emotions, Eris stood virtually paralyzed by indecision for a full ten seconds.

If you want Eris to fly around in circles, bludgeoning her head with a frozen turnip in an effort to beat herself into a decision, turn to the next page.

If you want Eris to shake it off immediately and get on with her business, turn to the next page anyway, because this isn't one of those choose-your-own-misadventure books.

CHAPTER EIGHT

"Ninjas who succeed at the highest level are not lucky; they're doing something differently than anyone else, and they have really cool katanas."
—*Grandt Sledgeman, motivational ninja life coach*

"Setting goals is the first step in turning the visible into the invisible. The next is buying a lot of dark clothing."
—*Grandt Sledgeman, author, from* Awaken the Ninja Within!

"Grandt Sledgeman is, bar none, THE authority on how anyone can become a ninja in business, a ninja in love, and a ninja in life! There's nothing more important than his one-week 'ninja-vational' online boot camp: a $25,000 value, now yours for only $3,499!"
—*Grandt Sledgeman*

THE ONE CALLED Ryan Seth Sloude crept across the hillside a quarter mile downstream from the Grand Coulee Dam. Crouching low, he wore a black hooded sweatshirt that helped him blend into the tan granite geology in broad daylight just like a fifty-year-old man blends into a college rave. He skittered around boulders. He ducked behind bushes. He tip-toed across dirt paths with the stealth of a flatulent hippo. Nonetheless, Eris noted, he had almost caught up with the three figures he followed. Nearly upon them, he paused to tug his hood closer about his face before making his final approach.

All three figures turned his way. He crouched lower, undaunted.

"Must you insist upon that?" Athena asked him.

"He must," said Leif.

"We've tried to stop him," sighed Tracy.

"A.B.S.!" Ryan exclaimed as he reached Athena and stood up.

"Always Be Sneaking. Wisdom from the spectacular ninja-coach Grandt Sledgeman!"

"Mortal," said Athena, "We walk ahead of you. Your 'stealth' serves no purpose and impedes our pace."

Ryan huffed. "I have an instinct for stealth! I consented to lend you my instinct for the greater good, but I won't have its use dictated to me by one once counted among the false gods!"

Quick as thinking, Athena snatched Ryan's sword from his belt, scabbard and all. "You should count yourself fortunate I am one of the more patient members of that group, Mr. Sloude."

"Hey!" The mortal grabbed for his sword. Athena merely held it high out of reach. Ryan jumped, arms flailing. Athena shoved him back in mid-air, and he landed, surprisingly deftly, on his feet a meter back from where he'd started.

"Sneak more appropriately!" Athena scolded.

Ryan bristled. "You dare contradict the wisdom of Grandt Sledgeman!"

"Most assuredly I do."

"Mister Sloude," Tracy added, "if you want to honor our deal—"

"And make sure I write the Ninjas Templar into my movie," injected Leif.

"—just cooperate."

Eris watched as Ryan closed his eyes for a deep, meditative breath. She considered spitting on his face from Athena's direction but discarded the idea as too crude. Also, the eastern Washington air had given her dry mouth.

"Fine." Ryan opened his eyes. "But this is not a defeat, for my prize is grand, my game is long, and my drive goes deep. I go on until I win, and win I shall. Win big!"

"More Sledgeman?"

"Grandt Sledgeman's Ninja Motivation Rule Number Three! Win big!"

Leif sighed. "Can we go now, please?"

"She must return my sword! Grandt Sledgeman's Ninja Motivation Rule Number Five: A ninja is only as good as his sword! Or his headband. I do not wear headbands; they give me a rash. So return my sword!"

Athena lowered it, and Ryan snatched it back. "I have the *best* sword."

"It is a fair katana," Athena admitted.

"It is American made! It is a *freedom-tana!*"

"It seems to have been made in China, actually."

"And purchased with American dollars!"

"Come," ordered Athena, turning. "We are nearly there."

Eris rubbed her hands together in anticipation as the four trekked along the gravel path. Ryan brought up the rear, crouching again, but at an increased pace. Eris did not follow. She remained high above, invisible, and drew out a tablet computer. Hephaestus's most recent model, the tablet featured dilithium-polymer batteries, a touchscreen resolution higher than reality itself, and seventeen individual headphone jacks. Eris brought its screen to life, tapped the Olympian Skypeep app—and then cursed as the wretched thing forced her to wait while it downloaded an update.

Eris drummed her fingers on the side of the tablet. The dry wind fluttered through her hair while the app's progress bar ticked ever so slowly upward. Just before she would have hurled it into space, the app sprang into motion. The screen displayed a closer view of Athena's group, unhindered by the hillside and scrub between them.

A dark fissure split the hillside. Athena was already walking into it. Tracy followed, holding a flashlight, and behind her came Leif, outshining Tracy's flashlight beam with an LED camping lantern held out before him. Ryan continued to bring up the rear, pressed tight against the fissure wall.

"Swiftly the Ninja Templar creeps into the darkness," Ryan whispered. "He blends silently, an unseen companion of the shadows, his senses as sharply honed as the sword which he—"

Ryan went silent as Leif turned, his lantern now bright in Ryan's face. Leif turned back forward. The group continued, passing through the fissure into a roughly hewn passage large enough for them to walk two abreast if they wished. They did not, apparently, wish, and continued in single file.

"We go as far as the Ferryman's shack," Tracy told Athena. "Then you're on your own. Do you know how you're paying the fare across? The last time I was here I needed to bring some batteries."

"I came prepared," Athena whispered.

"Is the shack going to be a very long walk?"

"Stop complaining, Leif," Tracy answered. "You could've stayed behind to guard the truck."

Leif scoffed. "Oh, yeah, right. Be the guy staying behind alone? Why not just roll myself in bread crumbs and run around screaming 'zombie buffet'?"

"It should be no more than a quarter mile," Athena said.

Eris chuckled to herself as the first modification she had made to the tunnel came within Athena's view. The ex-goddess stopped short. "Except . . . this should not be." Athena's right hand dropped to her side and unfastened her Glock's holster.

Tracy moved up along her left side. "What is it?"

Athena took hold of Tracy's flashlight and directed it down the passage where it just barely illuminated . . .

"A door."

"A green door, even."

"The Ninja Templar drew his blade, steeling himself for battle with the fearsome viridian door, reading—"

"Beep beep, Ryan," said Leif.

"What?"

"I said shut the hell up."

Eris summoned up a vodka martini and sipped as the group drew nearer to her door. She had crafted the chamber behind it quicker than she would have liked, but it ought to serve its purpose. Her only regret was not being able to furnish it with a unique monster or seven.

It was three months after the Second Return, and Zeus still forbade the gods to bring monsters back into the world. Eris did not know whether he hesitated due to the ongoing zombie issue, or because he still felt beholden to his promise to Tracy to remove the monsters for good. If it were the former, Eris might be less inclined to hinder Athena's efforts to rid the world of them. A world full of zombies vs. a world full of other monsters? Either would strike Eris's discord chords just fine. A world with—Fates forbid—*neither* of them? That was just too drab to comprehend.

"There cannot be a door here," Athena told the others. "Passages to the Underworld must be open so the dead may pass unhindered to the Acheron."

Leif stepped up. "If there *can't* be a door, then this is an illusion! All we have to do is refuse to believe it!" He broke into a run and, before anyone could stop him, slammed into the door and fell back on his ass.

The mortal had run with his hands out in front of him and thus avoided any major head injuries, but it delighted Eris regardless. She grinned and whispered to herself, "Nope!"

"Hypothesis tested," Athena said, "and found incorrect. Thank you, Mister Karlson."

"Don't mention it," Leif grumbled as Tracy helped him up.

With an almost snickering creak, the door, which was still green, swung open into the chamber beyond.

"I'm taking credit for that," said Leif.

One after another, the group passed through the doorway and then paused to take stock of the marble-covered, rectangular room. Eris had fashioned the floor in a checkerboard pattern, with each square about three feet wide and alternating between teal and orange marble. A chandelier hovered below the center of a high-vaulted ceiling. Its dozens of candles burned with a roseate light, which bathed the room in an aura resembling intestinal medication.

Directly across the room from where they entered, Eris had placed another door—wooden, closed, and bound in iron. A single lever, cast in silver, protruded from the wall beside it.

Tracy nodded at the iron-bound door. "Care to take a run at that door too, Leif?"

"Gonna take a pass on that, thanks. But I am curious about that lever. I bet this is some sort of puzzle room we have to get through." He put one foot forward, but before he could take a second step, Athena grabbed his shoulder and held him back.

"Rats," Eris whispered.

"Let me," she said. "I do not trust this place, and I am less vulnerable than you."

"I wasn't going to just walk up and *pull* it, you know," said Leif. "I *have* played Dungeons and Dragons before."

"This is not a tabletop roleplaying game," said Athena.

"Not yet."

"What?"

"Eh?"

To Eris's delight, Athena moved into the room. The teal panel onto which she stepped depressed half an inch under her weight with an audible *snick!* Immediately, she ducked and rolled backwards to the mortals.

Nothing else happened.

"That was fun," Tracy whispered.

"Definitely stay where you are," Athena ordered. With a single leap, she sprang ten yards across the chamber. There, she landed on an orange panel in front of the iron-bound door, just to the left of the lever.

Snick! went the panel. Athena crouched warily.

As before, nothing else happened—albeit more maliciously this time. A sidestep brought Athena onto a teal panel directly in front of the lever. The panel gave neither a *snick!* nor any other onomatopoeia.

There, Athena examined the lever. She peered at it. She traced it gingerly with her fingertips. She squinted into the fulcrum. She even pressed her ear to the wall and rapped her nails on its shaft. What the ex-goddess hoped to accomplish by that, Eris had no idea. Eris was about to just go down and pull the wretched lever herself when Athena finally gave warning to the others, raised her left arm with the buckler strapped to it, and knocked the lever from the up- to the down-position using only the buckler's face.

Three things happened at once: A lever unfolded from each of the two side walls (one lever cast in gold, the other bronze). The earnestly green door through which they'd entered clanged shut, now locked into place. And the hovering chandelier started spinning.

There was no real significance to the chandelier spinning; Eris just hoped it might make someone dizzy.

"Well," said Leif. "That's a *kind* of progress."

"Whatever malevolence created this room now taunts us with more levers!" Ryan exclaimed.

Leif eyed the chandelier. "No, malevolence would be if that thing started playing disco."

"Oh, good idea," Eris whispered to herself, and made it so with a tune about Ra-Ra-Rasputin, Russia's greatest love machine.

"Oh damn it to Jerry," Leif groaned.

Tracy had spotted something behind them. "What's that writing?"

They all turned around to look where she pointed. Wide lettering glowed in a path around the edges of the most sincerely green door. Eris took another sip of her martini.

"It's Olympian. 'Welcome to the jungle' is what it reads." Athena said, and then scowled. "Eris."

Leif blinked. "Someone's welcoming Eris to the jungle?"

"I mean Eris wrote it."

"Eris was *not* a member of Guns and Roses!" Ryan burst. "More fake claims from the false gods that—"

Tracy elbowed the ninja, to Eris's further delight. "Eris says this a lot, I take it?" she asked Athena.

"In the truck on the way here."

"Excuse me?" Tracy glared. "The truck? You were going to tell us this when?"

"When it became relevant. It just did. Now, be doubly careful." Athena leaped across the room again, this time landing in front of the gold lever protruding from the left wall. There was no *snick!* there either. Athena paused, listening to make sure.

Tracy raised a hand. "I'm not getting Eris and Eros mixed up again, am I? Eris is female? Something of a bitch, right?"

"Goddess of discord, and sister of Ares," Athena said while giving the gold lever a once-over. "And I would counsel you against calling any goddess a bitch, were it not that Eris takes it as a compliment."

"So then I'm fully justified being annoyed that you kept this from us?" Tracy shot. "She's trying to stop you?"

"You are justified," said Athena, and, as she'd done with the silver, knocked the gold lever with her buckler. It only moved an inch before meeting resistance. Athena frowned. "And yes, she is. I do not know why." She knocked the lever again, with the same result.

"Ah, do you really think you should keep pulling levers like that?" Leif asked.

Athena sprang across to the bronze lever on the right wall. Again, her landing was *snick!*-less. "Do you have a better idea? I am being as cautious as possible, but understand: we must push forward."

Tracy put a hand on Leif's shoulder to hold him back, though he did not appear to be going anywhere yet. "No, *you* must push forward. Since you're withholding things from us, I'm thinking *we* should go back."

Leif cleared his throat. "You mean back through the door that just sealed itself?"

Athena tapped the bronze lever down with her buckler. As with the gold, it only budged an inch. "Do not be so petty, Ms. Wallace."

"Petty? I said I'm done being manipulated, and the first thing you did was lie about Eris!"

"I did nothing of the sort! You inquired, and I answered!"

Tracy scoffed. "Now who's being petty?"

"Still you."

"A theory!" Leif declared and held up a finger. "The silver lever unlocked the far door, and the rest is all just a distraction." He stepped forward onto the first teal panel that had previously gone *snick!* under Athena's foot. Under Leif's foot, it simply gave way and plummeted into an open shaft beneath it. Leif would have plummeted right after it, were it not for Tracy and Ryan grabbing him from behind. The two dragged Leif to safety—a fortunate thing for Leif, as no one survives a plummet. (A drop, yes. A fall, of course. A plunge, sometimes. But a plummet? Never.)

"Rats again," whispered Eris.

"New theory," Leif offered. "The silver lever turned all the panels that previously just went *snick* into armed pit traps, and now we're kind of slightly hosed a little."

Athena leapt back to where Tracy, Leif, and Ryan stood. "Alternate theory: you have gained us vital information and we are, in point of fact, less inconvenienced than previously. As the tiles beneath the new levers have been, for lack of a better term, *snick*-free, I believe we must now pull them all simultaneously."

"Based on what?" Tracy asked.

"Divine wisdom," said Athena, "and, at this point, narrative expedience."

"Excuse me?"

"The Muses have grown more powerful." The mortals merely

stared, uncomprehending. Athena sighed. "It would take too long to explain. Just trust me."

With that, Athena gripped Tracy's arms and leapt with her to the panel in front of the gold lever, and then, depositing Tracy there, sprang back to Leif and Ryan.

"And you say you're not manipulating me?" Tracy yelled. "*Ask* me before you do that!"

"I am not manipulating you! I am merely picking you up and placing you where you should be!"

"Oh, yes, totally different!"

"Boiiiiing!" Leif exclaimed as Athena took him to the other lever. "Hey, why do I get the bronze one?"

"As with most aspects of life," said Athena, "make up whatever reason satisfies you most." A final leap took her back to the silver lever by the wooden door. "Now on the count of three, everyone pull! One!"

"I shall take no orders from the false god!" Ryan exclaimed.

"That's probably why you don't have a lever, Ryan," said Leif. "Two!"

"Now hold on, right?" said Tracy. "How do we know this—"

"Three!" Athena shouted the integer with the practiced authority of over three millennia spent "counseling" people about what to do. Whether issued from a godly source or not, that's not something you can resist without at least half a day of psyching yourself up. As Leif and Tracy had spent the last half day very much dealing with other things, each pulled their levers.

Three things happened at once (again): The iron-bound wooden door beside Athena swung open. A nozzle on the chandelier doused Ryan in a blast of hearty whole grains. And the panel beneath Ryan's feet dropped away. Ryan himself dropped into the pit not even a moment later. (He did it with a manly, ninja-like scream, however, so at least Grandt Sledgeman would've been proud.)

Eris grumbled under her breath and then, realizing she still floated alone in the sky watching these events unfold, grumbled over her breath as well; she'd hoped it would be Tracy who would fall into that pit. *That* pit had zombies.

Yes, Zeus had indeed promised Tracy that no one would take revenge on her for forcing the Second Withdrawal, and yes, like it or not, that promise bound Eris. At least, it did if she didn't want to find herself chained to a rock while vultures gnawed at her liver or told her all about their unpublished novel for eternity. But hey, this wasn't revenge. This was just chaos! After all, Eris had only put the zombies *nearby*, with a clear warning label! It read *"Warning: Zombies"* in 1-inch high, lowercase letters on the tunnel ceiling just outside! It wasn't Eris's fault that Tracy hadn't noticed it in the dark, or couldn't read the Latvian in which it was written, or didn't have the visual acuity to make out yellow-on-white lettering. If anyone was to blame for anything that befell Tracy or her companions there, it was those pesky, unexplained zombies!

Those same pesky, unexplained zombies—a full dozen of them— now circled Ryan Seth Sloude where he lay at the bottom of the pit. Eris fiddled with her screen for a better view of the pit, hoping that Tracy or Leif might see fit to fall down there after Ryan while the zombies gnawed off his skin. Except . . .

The zombies weren't attacking.

"What the zorch?" Eris asked aloud.

Clutching at his left shoulder, which appeared to be dislocated, Ryan remained on the ground, but none of the dozen undead around him approached closer than arms' length. "I shall beard the lions in their den!" he exclaimed. "I—"

He sneezed violently, having inhaled a cloud of grain dust, and then screamed in pain as the sneeze shook his shoulder. The sneeze necessitated another deep inhale, which in turn resulted in further sneezing, which of course resulted in further pained screaming, until Ryan was trapped in an endless cycle of sneeze-screams.

All in all, thought Eris, it was exhilarating to watch—except for the aforementioned fact that *the zombies were not attacking!*

Granted, they *were* snarling, and growling for grains, and then sneezing themselves all over the place because of it. Yet they refused to attack! Why? Had she gathered defective zombies?

At that moment, one of the zombie's heads exploded in a shower of gore and bone. Athena had jumped to the edge of the pit and begun firing into it with her Glock.

"Hold on!" Athena ordered between shots. The zombies were dropping like flies—or rather, faster than flies, because flies aren't so easy to shoot—sneezing, snarling, and crumpling. Ryan had managed to recover from his own sneezing fits. Meanwhile, Tracy and Leif stood trapped next to their levers, demanding to know what was going on.

It occurred to Eris that there was no reason she couldn't expend a little power to launch the zombies from the pit up into the room above, possibly some of them directly toward Tracy. Yet the thought had barely sprung to mind when Zeus's voice rang out along divine frequencies throughout the planet:

"All divine entities are commanded to report to Olympus immediately!"

There was a pause, during which time Eris cursed, and after which Zeus's voice rang out again:

"No, do *not* stop for donuts!"

Another pause.

"I said *no*, Demeter!"

Could it be that Zeus had spied what Eris was doing? He would hardly send a group summons just to confront her, would he? No, never! Probably never. Maybe.

Athena had shot all the zombies by now anyway. Even if Zeus wasn't watching her, there'd be little point in launching the zombies' remains out of the pit before she left. Eris shrugged and did it anyway. It would make a delightful mess, and—

Whoops.

Eris's initial design for the chamber had included more levers. Some of them were to be concealed behind ceiling panels, and most of them—in a partial tribute to the late dungeon designer Gary Gygax— would trigger jets of fire, unpleasant smells, and/or ceiling collapse. Eris had completed some of those trap mechanisms before discarding the idea during her always-chaotic creative process. So, when the zombie remains struck those ceiling panels, the impact set off about half the vestigial mechanisms behind them.

Moments after the geysered remains landed on the floor, plumes of flame erupted in the chamber's corners, and the entire ceiling began to crumble amid the odor of microwaved fish. Tragically, Eris didn't have time to fully enjoy the mayhem. She allowed herself a moment to relish the horror on everyone's faces, and then departed to respond to Zeus's summons.

It was only then that Eris noticed the moon had turned purple. That was odd, she thought. It didn't usually do that on a Wednesday.

CHAPTER NINE

"Though she had her critics among the pantheon who thought her either too strange, too introverted, too peculiar, too morose, too some-other-thing, or—given her adoption—just too not-blood-related-to-them, all mourned Hecate's death. That her demise occurred at the stinger of the mis-aimed Unmaking Nexus during the Second Titan War made her passing doubly tragic.

Not even Zeus was as mourned as Hecate, in fact. (Though as Zeus's death was intentional, perpetrated by five members of the pantheon, and allowed the first Olympian Return, that is to be expected.) Said my colleague Melpomene of Hecate, 'She possessed an undeniable, almost indescribable quality about her: coy yet powerful. It lurked in the dark of her eyes, the dark of her magic, and the dark of her chocolate preferences. She shall be missed.'"

—After the Sun Sets: A Retrospective Blog by Apollo

"I am not entirely certain why Apollo started these historical retrospective blogs, though I suspect he's compensating for losing his prophetic powers to the Fates last year. While I certainly sympathize, I do wish he would stop asking me if he sounds enough like Ken Burns. I'm running out of respectful ways to say no."

—*personal journal of Clio, Muse of history*

CLAD IN HIS BEST ARMOR, his lightning bolts on his back, his lucky lightning boxer shorts hidden beneath it all, Zeus stood awaiting the arrival of the distant perzoid light source. The fact that he did so while floating in high Earth orbit did not affect his standing posture. Gods, after all, could plant their feet whenever they wished, even if the place they wished was in the vacuum of space where they had nothing whatsoever to stand upon.

It was not unlike a human arguing that vaccines cause autism.

Floating to his right was Baskin, clad in near-matching armor and carrying Zeus's Aegis shield. (As for Baskin's boxer shorts situation, Zeus neither knew nor intended to ask.) Flanking each of them were Apollo and Artemis, in gold and silver armor respectively. Their bows were slung. Their arrows gleamed. Their hands held burning braziers of blue flame that Hestia had insisted would look pretty and appear welcoming. Why blue, Zeus did not know, but Hestia knew her stuff, and Zeus saw no need to question her judgment.

Restored to her full divinity after the less-than-successful ritual at the Balefire of Hades, Hestia had resumed her duties as goddess of home and hearth. On Olympus, at Zeus's back, she now relayed his orders to the other gods as they arrived to respond to his summons. (When he had left for orbit, she had been arguing with Eris about, oh, something. It hardly mattered. Argument was Eris's resting state.) Hestia would tell Eris and the others where Zeus wished them to go in order to best strengthen the Earth's defense, should the approaching perzoid light turn out to be hostile.

When Artemis had reported the light passing her beloved moon, on course for Earth, Zeus had suspected its source. When the moon turned purple shortly thereafter, Zeus was all but certain: Cosmics. He had multiple suspicions about their intent. Yet trying to guess the mind of such . . . *entities*—he refused to consider *them* gods—was fraught with peril. Their thoughts moved along right angles to reality, rationality, and reason, not to mention some other things that didn't even start with *R*.

His lucky lightning boxers began to chafe.

"My compliments on resetting the moon's color so quickly, Sister," Zeus heard Apollo tell Artemis.

"Thank you, Brother," she answered. "The change was merely cosmetic, so it was a quick fix."

"Turned it off, and then back on again?"

"Of course."

Zeus cleared his throat and silenced them both. As god of the sky, Zeus had the power to let all nearby voices carry in a vacuum; it was easier than bothering with telepathy all the time, and also let him hear if anyone was muttering about him under their breath. But with Apollo and Artemis, sometimes the kibitzing was a bit much.

"Be on guard!" Zeus commanded. "What approaches is surely of Cosmic origin, and none of you have dealt with their kind before. Neither say nor do anything without my leave, and do not maintain eye contact for more than a moment, assuming there are eyes to make contact with."

The glowing perzoid blob grew nearer, pitching and bobbing, like an inebriated goose struggling to land. Zeus frowned and held out a hand—an instruction to stop that might neither be heeded nor even understood. The light-blob bobbed to a distance of possibly one hundred meters, though the perception eddies flickering across it made it difficult for Zeus to be sure. Zeus tensed and sent a nudge of power as a gentle warning to halt. The blob flashed the second-purest green Zeus had ever seen, and then obeyed.

"Greetings," he said. "I am almighty Zeus, King of the Olympians and supreme authority on the world of Earth."

The blob of light grew larger, now shifting in color from perzoid to sort of an eulbish-orange. (Eulb is, of course, a color midway between that of day-old bananas and apoplectic dysphoria; "eulb" being "blue" spelled backwards is entirely inconsequential.) A void opened within the blob's center, out of which floated two entities half its size, which settled on either side of it. The entity on the right jolted Zeus with a recognition that he hoped he hid from the others.

Cyot'hgha.

From the waist up, Cyot'hgha was nearly nude. Light gleamed off of her literally pearlescent skin. Breaking her skin's otherwise perfect expanse were black and red barnacle-like encrustations. These ran up the outside of her arms to her neck and across her forehead, which extended back into a bony, hairless crown extruding directly from her skull. A metallic halter of iridescent gold, red, and boz covered the bit of her torso not laid bare, yet below the waist she wore a black skirt that seemed to hold the entirety of deep space within it. Though stars twinkled there, Zeus knew from experience that gazing into the skirt's depths for more than a few moments could result in vertigo, nausea, and the unnamable urge to holler quadratic equations.

He also knew it wasn't really a skirt.

Did she remember him after so many millennia? Was their shared secret why she was here? That would be problematic, to say the least. Zeus searched her eyes for recognition, but given her eyes were nothing more than empty black voids, it was difficult to tell.

The second new entity, which floated to the now eulbish-orange blob's left, possessed no visible humanoid features whatsoever. Yet with Cyot'hgha there, it must be none other than C'oggn-yon, her . . . unknowable, genderless sibling. C'oggn-yon was formless—a cloud of violet, shifting, swarthy mist. Around the mist's borders came the occasional arc of electricity, which didn't so much flare or strike as simply insinuate itself upon reality in almost nonchalant fashion. More chalant was the way the mist tantalized the eye with half-glimpses of *something* at its center—perhaps something with many, many tenebrous elbows.

So tenebrous.

The blob that had brought them flashed again and shrank to its original size before bursting into a mass of writhing, fleshy tentacles. Yet even as an assortment of mouths, teeth, and bombastohedrons boiled out from it, the mass shrank further, and then reformed itself into something so horrid that even the mighty Zeus counted himself lucky to withstand the sight: the resulting eldritch creature possessed the body of a cuttlefish and, horrifyingly, the head of a *slightly larger cuttlefish!*

It was a disproportion subtle enough to drive a lesser mind mad with vexation.

This noisome entity was also the brother of Cyot'hgha and C'oggn-yon, a being whose name Zeus had never gotten the hang of pronouncing because it was just nine apostrophes followed by a Q.

"Cyot'hgha," Zeus acknowledged. "C'oggn-yon. And . . . '''''''''Q. It has been eons."

"Aeons," corrected '''''''''Q.

"*ZOGG!*" boomed C'oggn-yon.

Cyot'hgha said nothing.

Zeus stood taller. "On Olympus, and Earth below, *we* say 'eons.' But being barred from journeying there, I would not expect you to know that. And so, many *aeons*, if you like." He smiled, doing his best to project strength, and avoid Cyot'hgha's gaze. "Why have you come?"

"ZOGG!" C'oggn-yon boomed again.

The others simply stared at him. Zeus couldn't decide if they expected a response to that or were just trying to cultivate an unsettling atmosphere. Zeus folded his arms and stared back into C'oggn-yon's mists, waiting for more. Two could play that game.

The seconds ticked by. Four Olympians. Three Cosmic entities. Two sides. One space. Zeus waited. He anticipated. He waited some more. The moments unfolded like a TV show revival with an overly artistic director left unchecked by editing.

"Missing," ''''''''Q intoned at last.

Uh-oh. Zeus frowned. "What is missing?" He had a pretty good guess. He could have more accurately asked *who* was missing, but playing dumb was smarter.

"Needed," ''''''''Q said. "Needed in the depths. Where the leviathans jibber, and the vyriim dance, and the wild, gluttonous ones devour the non-dairy confections."

Zeus gritted his teeth. "I realize it is not in your nature, but you must be more coherent if you want this conversation to progress."

Now Cyot'hgha drifted toward Zeus, her skirt-that-was-not-a-skirt in motion as if she were carried on two long, sinuous legs. Baskin tensed; his hand moved to the scabbard of his Mighty Pink Battle-Spoon™. Zeus stilled him with a gesture and stood strong as Cyot'hgha reached his side. She lay one hand on Zeus's shoulder, inclined her head, and whispered into his ear:

"Hecate."

Styx! Suspicions confirmed.

Cyot'hgha, Hecate's true mother, remained a hair's breadth away; the twin voids of her eyes awaited his. To meet them he would need to either step back, or turn his head until his mouth met hers. Yet he could give not even a step of ground here. Nor would he, despite past indulgences, allow a kiss—especially in view of the others.

Word might get back to Hera, after all.

And so Zeus forced himself to remain unmoved. He fixated on ''''''''Q and tried to hide from everyone his consternation. The Cosmics must have sensed Hecate's death. Were they here to castigate him for failing to protect her as his adopted child? If so, the icing on top: the other Olympians would quite possibly learn the deeper secret behind that adoption.

Zeus cleared his throat, hoping he was wrong about all of it. "Hecate is . . . missing, you say?"

"ZOGG!" boomed C'oggn-yon.

"Yes." Zeus swallowed. "*ZOGG* indeed."

Part Two:

Athena's Aggravating Adventure

CHAPTER TEN

"In hindsight, I should have seen what Mr. Sloude was much earlier than I did. I can only blame myself—by which, of course, I mean my being forced to operate without my usual divine essence. And that was hardly my fault. That was all Zeus's doing. Let's face it, Eris wasn't exactly helpful at that point either. And why do I keep writing things like this in a public blog?"
—*blog entry by Athena (unpublished)*

MELPOMENE'S ADVICE echoed in Athena's ears, italicized and everything:

"Never trust anyone who seems sketchy enough to hide it if they become infected. They're bound to get infected eventually, and it's always trouble."

"How are you feeling?" Athena asked.

Trudging "stealthily" ahead of her through the dry tunnel, Ryan Seth Sloude did not face her when he answered, "Spectacular. I am trapped in a tunnel with a false goddess, separated from my companions—and with them, my primary calling—and my shoulder throbs with a huge pain. This tunnel maintains a particularly foul odor. But I shall persevere."

"This 'false' goddess also saved your life," she warned.

"And wrenched my arm delivering me from that pit!"

"Would you rather I had left you in it?"

Ryan's silence answered for him.

Once the ceiling had begun to collapse, Leif and Tracy had the wherewithal to hopscotch across the stable panels to the entry door. Trapped in the pit, however, Ryan could not have climbed out in time without divine intervention. (Okay, fine, she corrected—*ex*-divine intervention.) Athena had leapt into the pit, thrown Ryan over her shoulder, and scrambled up and out of the chamber through a shower of rubble across a re-dead zombie-carpet. That she had only wrenched his arm in doing so was something he should consider a blessing. Instead, he had complained, without even a thank you.

His complaints hadn't exactly answered her question, either.

"Do you feel any elevated body temperature?" she pressed. "Dizziness? Increased craving for, oh, say, soft pretzels?"

"Did you not witness?" grumbled Ryan. "The zombies in the pit were kept at bay! They dared not confront my righteousness!"

"I witnessed a great deal of sneezing in your general direction—"

"Righteousness!"

"—which is cause enough for vigilance."

Ryan stopped and turned. He pulled his scabbard free of his belt and held it aloft, sword and all. "*Riche! Ous! Ness!*" Each syllable he punctuated with a shake of the scabbard. "I am fine!"

Athena scrutinized him until he finally turned back around and continued walking. He returned the scabbard and sword to his belt after dropping it only twice.

"I know of the Ninjas Templar," Athena said, "as your group calls itself. Please enlighten me as to how righteousness goes hand in hand with releasing the Titans to make war upon the world. You were to blame for that, if you recall."

"False-god propaganda! I believe it not!"

"To ignore facts solely because they contradict your beliefs is a path away from wisdom. Your group set into motion events that annihilated my glorious patron city of Athens! So much destruction there! So many innocents dead!"

She swallowed the sting of knowing she was still powerless to help the Athenians rebuild. Their ancestors had revered her. After the Return, they had taken up that reverence again. Those who had survived Athens' destruction suffered its loss almost as much as Athena did. She would heal their pain the moment she earned her divinity again. Or reasonably soon after, anyway. She would need time to properly rub her restoration in Baskin's face, after all. But then, Athens!

"So," Athena finished, "you will forgive me if I question this righteousness you claim."

Ryan's step faltered, for just a moment. "Well, anyway, I wasn't a part of the group then. You know, technically."

"You deemed them worthy of joining *after* they caused my city's ruin? This is not an improvement."

"No, I left before that. Mine was a mighty sacrifice! I was already the best; I needed no more training. To help better the group, I struck out alone, so they would not waste their limited funding supporting me."

"Ah," said Athena. "They expelled you."

"*Righteously discharged* is the official term."

"Voluntarily?"

"It was a group decision."

"And did that group include yourself?"

"Er—I refuse to disclose the secret dealings of—" A sneeze exploded through the rest of his sentence. Two more followed on its heels. Athena halted immediately.

If Ryan were infected, was she in any danger herself? She retained her immortality, lost divinity notwithstanding. On the other hand, so did Alecto, who had additional power to boot, and something had happened to her. Was Alecto's condition the result of a standard zombie infection, or a special strain she had encountered in the document signing?

Athena mentally upgraded her personal defense condition level before the echoes of Ryan's sneeze could fade. It was one of her tactical secrets: at any given time, she maintained her own internal DEFCON status. It was roughly the same five-level defense condition system used by the United States North American Aerospace Defense Command, the idea for which Athena had planted anonymously in the mind of the Joint Chiefs of Staff Chairman via a particularly phallic dream about launching missiles. Athena's personal system, however, had six levels. Like NORAD, hers also began at DEFCON 5 (her lowest state of readiness), but rather than stopping at the well-meaning but possibly inadequate DEFCON 1 (imminent nuclear war, or in Athena's case, divine-on-divine combat), hers could go beyond that. Granted, Athena had yet to set herself to a state of DEFCON Zero (actual Armageddon), but there was no sense in being unprepared.

The other levels included DEFCON 4 (above normal readiness), DEFCON 3 (weapons armed, drawn, brandished, or otherwise waving about), and DEFCON 2 (below divine level combat—i.e., combat with anyone she could wipe the floor with under normal circumstances).

She did once downgrade to an unofficial state of DEFCON 6 for an entire week during the first century A.D. That week had been something of a blur, and resulted in so much retroactive embarrassment that she vowed to neither use the DEFCON 6 designation again, nor try any more of Dionysus's "special weed."

Now at DEFCON 4, Athena pulled from her pocket a NATO bandana and fashioned it into a makeshift facemask before Ryan could sneeze again. Satisfied, she then trotted to catch up with him.

"Those were the sneezes of the righteous," he grumbled, noticing the facemask.

"Indeed."

"I am destined for greatness," he mumbled.

"Many are."

"The greatest greatness."

"Surely."

"Do you have any bagels?"

Athena checked the chamber on her Glock. "Sometimes the new ferryman has donuts. It is not far now."

Athena approached the rickety shack on the shore of the Acheron River. The structure looked ready to collapse with a strong breeze, yet the door made the shack look robust by comparison. She knocked, but carefully. Somehow the rap of her knuckles did not send it bursting apart, and so Athena waited for a response.

A few yards away, Ryan squatted at the foot of a modest dock that stretched out over the river. He peered into the water below, looking either puzzled or constipated.

"Do not touch the water," Athena called. Ryan only shrugged.

With no answer at the door, Athena knocked again. The ferryboat was moored at the other end of the dock, so the ferryman who lived inside had to be around somewhere. Casting glances along the shoreline revealed nothing, save for a few warning signs bathed in the eerie, rust-and-lavender colored light that illuminated the borders of the Underworld.

The lavender was new, she observed. Likely one of Persephone's touches.

"Let him touch the water if he wants to," came a man's voice from the shack's roof. The speaker had the air of someone for whom melancholy was an aspiration. "He won't want to a second time. Experience is a better teacher."

Athena cleared her throat. "Marcus? Come down here, please."

Anyone with half a moment's knowledge of Greek so-called mythology—and at this point, that should probably include any readers of this book, but how the heck can one be sure?—would know that the traditional ferryman to the land of the dead bore the name of Charon. Even Marcus Shanks, a previously self-avowed atheist, had known that before he had stumbled upon a path to the Underworld in his basement and met Charon in person. The trouble was Marcus didn't believe a word of it. As it had happened a couple of years before the Olympians' public Return, one could hardly blame him. Then again, one might also expect that finding a vast, mysteriously lit underground cavern with an even more mysterious river and a semi-mysterious shack housing a creepy old man might bend one's beliefs just a tad. At the very least, Marcus should not have leapt to the conclusion that it was all part of a con scheme to hypnotize people into coming there and giving money to the guy "playing" Charon.

But Marcus had.

Perhaps, had he done otherwise, Charon might not have tricked Marcus into agreeing to do Charon's job for six months out of each year for the rest of his life. (The precise details of how that came to be is a long story. Or, at least, a 4,365-word story. "Long" is subjective. At any rate, we won't cover it here.) As a result, Charon now got to spend half his time—and all his accumulated fortune—taking luxury ocean cruises and lobbying the astronomy community to designate Pluto as a planet again. Marcus just got to be cranky.

"You're not the boss of me," said Marcus, still out of sight, somehow supported by whatever constituted the roof of the dilapidated structure. "And you're not dead either. I can tell. So wander off, whoever you are; you don't belong here."

"Come down here *now*," she ordered, "... and I may make it

worth your while." Athena silently thanked the inventor of the ellipsis—it was either Apollo or some Welsh soldier, she couldn't recall—as they had given her time to stifle a threat to sack Marcus's shack. This would go more smoothly if she avoided antagonizing him. She did regret losing the opportunity to actually *say* "sack your shack," though.

"Worth my while? Um, I have a girlfriend," Marcus answered.

"That is not what I—!"Athena slammed the butt of her fist against the shack. "Marcus Shanks! Do you wish to get Wi-Fi down here or not?"

"Now what the Jerry are you—" Marcus stuck his head over the edge of the roof, spotted Athena, and frowned. "Oh, it's one of *you*." He vanished again. After the squeak of a hinge, the creak of wood, and a sudden crash that she couldn't identify, the shack's door opened. Marcus looked her over as if she were covered in fish heads. "So, Wi-Fi, eh?"

"I need passage across the Acheron," Athena told him. "Once my business there is concluded, I'll ask Persephone to set something up here for you. I know it drives you crazy to be off the grid."

"Yeah." Marcus scratched his elbow. "But this is a trick, right? Goddess gets bored, decides to come down here and make fun of the Fool of the Acheron? Why's Aphrodite need *my* help to cross?"

Athena stiffened. "I am Athena, not Aphrodite. You would be wise to—"

"Whatever. I can't keep you people straight. My point's the same."

"Aphrodite is gone. Exiled. You will never see her again."

"I didn't really see her before. See, you can kind of tell that because I got you two mixed up."

"Mister Shanks!" Athena resisted the urge to turn him into a horseshoe crab. Then she had to stifle the urge to complain that she no longer had the power *to* turn him into a horseshoe crab. But she could still sack his shack if she wished!

"Mister Shanks," she said again, calming. "I am temporarily un-divine. I no longer have the power to cross. Had you kept up with Olympian events like you ought, you would know this already."

Marcus shrugged. "Let's say I believe you. Why do you want to cross? Just asking in the name of keeping up with Olympian events and all that."

"I seek to end the zombie problem, and would speak to Persephone on the topic."

Marcus blinked. "The what problem?"

"Zombie."

"The undead scourge unleashed upon the world by the false gods' arrogance!" Ryan exclaimed from near the water.

Marcus glanced at Ryan. "Who's he?"

"Ignore him."

"I dunno," said Marcus. "False gods? I think I kinda like him. But okay, let's get back to my original question: what the crap are you talking about?"

"The dead rising from the grave?" Athena asked. "Attacking the living? Nearly overrunning mortal civilization until Zeus let the gods return to the world to get things under control?"

"What?" Marcus's alarm seemed genuine.

"How have you not heard?"

"I've been down here five months! No one tells me anything!"

"You're the ferryman to the land of the dead," Athena said. "I had expected you would have noticed something."

"Well, the passengers had more bites for a while there, but—" He stared off toward the tunnel to the surface, his face dark with worry.

"Miranda is safe," Athena assured him, referring to his girlfriend. "I checked before coming here."

Marcus let out a breath. "I guess I'd have seen her waiting for the ferry here otherwise, huh?" He swallowed. "Now I know why Charon came by asking if I'd seen anything strange lately. Said he was asking for Persephone. She never talks to me herself, of course."

Athena could imagine why not. "What did you tell him?"

Marcus scoffed. "What do you think I told him? Anything strange? On the shores of the Acheron? That's a relative term, isn't it? What the heck is 'strange' down here? I said no! And the old bastard didn't even tell me why he was asking or what he meant. Freaking gods . . . "

"Watch your language, mortal," Athena warned.

"*False* gods!" Ryan exclaimed.

Marcus leaned a bit closer. "Seriously, who is that guy?"

"His name is Ryan. You've heard of the Ninjas Templar?"

"Those right-wing fanatics who released the Titans that wrecked up the planet? Yeah, *them* Charon mentioned a while back."

"He was one of them."

Marcus raised an eyebrow. "Why is he peeing in the Acheron?"

"I suppose because he drank a lot of water on the way here."

"Fair enough."

Ryan zipped up and then ambled over to the two of them. He sized up Marcus. "You're human?"

"Last I checked. Nice job wrecking up the planet," Marcus said, not without sarcasm.

"Says one who colludes with false gods!" Ryan cried.

Marcus laughed. "Do you want to be the pot or the kettle here? You're traveling with one."

"I work for the glory of the Ninjas Templar and the Almighty!"

"Well." Marcus patted Ryan's shoulder and smiled at him in the way he might a child who had proudly eaten a mud pie full of dog hair. "Isn't that nice for you. And for the record, I was tricked into this."

"For the record," Ryan replied, "only a fool allows himself to be tricked."

Athena cleared her throat. "Putting this repartee aside, Marcus, I ask you, in the name of helping your fellow mortals and getting free Wi-Fi, will you ferry me across the Acheron to speak with Persephone?"

Ryan inhaled abruptly. At once Athena grabbed him by the shoulders and aimed him away from both herself and Marcus just in time for him to burst out with a trio of sneezes. "Cover your mouth next time," she said, letting go.

Ryan sniffed, and Marcus looked him over again.

"Something peculiar about him, isn't there?" Marcus whispered. "He's going across with you, right?"

"Certainly not!" said Ryan with a glance at Athena. "My agreement was only to go this far."

Marcus looked Ryan over a third time. "Oh, I think he really ought to cross," he told Athena.

Could he sense Ryan's infection? Was Ryan technically already dead?

"Very well." Athena turned to Ryan. "You will cross with me. You cannot return to the surface without my help anyway."

"No!"

"Trust me," said Marcus, "as someone who knows: you do *not* want to be hanging around here on your own. Tell you what: I'll take you both across immediately, since saving the world from zombies and getting me Wi-Fi is a good and urgent cause. After that, I'll tell you how you can get back to the surface without her. Deal?"

Ryan gritted his teeth and twitched. Athena readied herself to deflect another sneeze and considered this time simply using her buckler. Yet no sneeze came.

Instead, he merely spat, "Fine. But I was promised donuts."

CHAPTER ELEVEN

"Foxhole Donuts: Zombies or not, we deliver anywhere!"
—advertisement, Foxhole's Armored Truck Donut Delivery

THE RIDE ACROSS THE ACHERON was quieter than Athena had expected. Marcus spoke little, save to warn them that, while their seat cushions could be used as flotation devices, actually falling into the water would so swiftly paralyze them with pain that the cushions would be of little help. He also thanked them for flying United. Ryan, meanwhile, was steadily masticating a pair of maple bars that Marcus had produced from within his shack. He stared across the water, chewing like a cow on some cud. Since they had boarded the ferry, his skin had taken on a pale cast, and his breath seemed shallower.

Athena, sitting behind Ryan, kept close watch. She had chosen to not inquire about the source of the maple bars, especially since she had made up the whole "Marcus has donuts" thing in the first place. Now freed of any burden of conversation with two mortals lacking the wisdom to worship her, Athena pondered her upcoming meeting with Persephone.

Athena respected Persephone, and that respect seemed to go both ways—save for their irreconcilable disagreement about wearing socks with sandals. (Athena thought it perfectly acceptable in chilly weather. Persephone considered it a damnable offence. She had created a thousand-acre area of the Asphodel Meadows entirely for those who died wearing socks with sandals. It was just as bland as the rest of the Meadows, but all socks there were perpetually wet.) Athena would avoid bringing footwear into their conversation. Instead, she hoped to rely on the trust she'd cultivated during the first year of

Persephone's marriage to Hades.

The *official* tale of that match-up was the following: With help from Zeus and some spectacularly eye-catching flowers, Hades had lured Persephone away from her friends, kidnapped her to the Underworld, and forced her to be his queen. By the time Demeter—Persephone's mother, frantic at the loss of her daughter—had persuaded Hades to let Persephone go, the young goddess had already eaten a number of Underworld pomegranate seeds, requiring her to live in Hades's kingdom for at least half the year. Demeter never forgave Hades for that.

Demeter also never learned what Athena, in her wisdom, had figured out soon after the nuptials: the "kidnapping" was a fake. Persephone had run off with Hades willingly. The two secret lovers had mutually hatched the kidnapping cover story—Persephone thought her mother would never accept the relationship otherwise—and had carried it out with Zeus's aid.

The whole pomegranate seed thing was utter bunk, too. Eating pomegranate seeds grown in the Underworld would no more keep someone from leaving than eating sand would keep someone at the beach. The trouble: Persephone never dreamed Demeter would take it so hard. She could not bear to tell her mother the truth and had begged Athena to keep the secret. To this day, Athena had done so.

Athena hoped her previous loyalty would provide enough interpersonal capital for Persephone to disclose any secrets she might hold about the zombie issue. If not, well, there was always blackmail, wasn't there?

That assumed Persephone had any zombie secrets at all, of course. But then, Alecto had gotten *someone* to sign that form. Persephone was as likely a candidate as anyone else.

At long last, the ferry slid aground on the dark gravel of the far shore. Athena clambered out first. She also clambered out last, because Ryan just sat there chewing.

"Come," she ordered.

Ryan gave an eloquent, "Mmrgh," and added, "Going back now."

"That's, ah, not how it works," said Marcus, leaning on the 10-foot pole he used to guide the ferry and also not touch people with. "You have to get out first so the ferry registers the trip. You don't get out, and the accounting is off. Death won't stand for that."

"Not dead," said Ryan after a moment's consideration. "Ninja."

"Doesn't matter. You have to get out before you can go back. This ride's over."

Ryan swallowed his last bite of maple bar. A moist trail of drool painted one side of his mouth. He looked back at the annoyed ferryman.

"Marcus give two rides," Ryan said.

Marcus frowned and caught Athena's eyes. "First, you really need to get out."

"Two rides."

Athena strode back to the boat, seized Ryan by the shoulders, and hauled him onto the beach before he could stop her. His skin was burning up. Marcus immediately pushed the ferry back from the shore a few feet while Ryan stared after him.

"Thanks," said Marcus.

Athena let go of Ryan's shoulders. Ryan crouched into his standard "sneaking" pose, wobbled, and fell over onto the gravel with a crunch.

"Always be sneaking," Ryan muttered without his previous exuberance. "So quiet."

Athena turned back to Marcus. "How long do you think he has?"

Marcus blinked. "Er, how long for what?"

"Until he is officially a zombie."

"Oh, is that what's wrong with him?"

Athena glared. "I thought you had sensed that already! Isn't that why you said he should cross?"

Marcus laughed. "I just didn't like how he talked to me, so I figured he could use a good stranding. Thought I might trick him into taking my job like Charon tricked me. Geez, he's going to be a zombie?"

"At this point, I believe so." At least she could observe the stages of infection as they happened. Perhaps that would provide her with key insight into its cause.

"Crap," said Marcus. "Zombies can't pilot the ferry. I think it's a union gig."

Ryan clambered to his feet, and then "snuck" straight toward the ferry. "Two rides." His feet splashed into the Acheron before Athena seized the back of his belt and hauled him back.

"Ow," said Ryan.

"Case in point," said Athena.

Marcus rolled his eyes. "Just my damned luck. The last live person who came down here was too smart for me to trick, and now this guy's about to croak."

"Yes, how unfortunate for you," Athena said. "That last person: Tracy Wallace?"

"Maybe. Why do you ask?"

"Curiosity. She was accompanying me until we were separated. I am . . . mildly concerned about her welfare."

"You think Athena and Ryan are okay?" Leif asked.

"Who knows?" Tracy answered. "Good riddance."

Leif squinted in the sudden sunlight as they cleared the cave entrance back into the open air. "That's a bit harsh."

"Sorry. I'm just hungry and cranky about being deceived and nearly dying, right? Pretty sure they got through the other doorway before things collapsed completely."

"Good point," said Leif. "I guess that's usually how these things work anyway. Back to the truck, then."

Athena and Ryan reached Cerberus's lair not long after they had bid farewell to Marcus at the Acheron's shores (well, Athena had bid farewell; Ryan had only muttered about two rides, sneaking, and "the great Grains Sledgeman").

She smelled Cerberus before she saw him. When a dog is the size of a bear and has three heads, a lizard's tail, and a strong aversion to bathing, you don't need an immortal nose to sense him in a closed space. Athena paused before the creature came into view, and halted Ryan with a tug at the back of his shirt.

"Still with me, Mister Sloude?"

Ryan's head bobbed like a cork in calm water. "Still with.

Righteous. Sneaking. Chocolate cheesecake."

Athena chose not to ponder that last one. "We're about to see Cerberus, who guards the entrance to the Underworld. He's fearsome and he's got three heads, but he won't hurt you if you keep away from him. You will, therefore, remain calm. Is that understood?"

"Cerberus. Three heads. Two rides."

"Understood?"

"Understood."

She knew he was likely just parroting her, but she wanted the acknowledgement anyway, if only for legal reasons. Of course, whether or not Cerberus would harm Ryan depended on how long he remained human. Cerberus was trained to attack zombies, so the moment Ryan succumbed completely to zombiehood, Cerberus would tear him to shreds. But then Ryan would be a zombie, so no great loss, and his spirit would have only a few feet to journey to the Underworld.

It was, therefore, win-win—not that she felt a need to explain that to him.

Athena prodded Ryan out of the dark tunnel from the shore and into the tangerine light bathing the official Gates to the Underworld: conduit to all possible afterlives and portal to the realm now known as *Jerry*. Those gates of 96% pure diamond, open and waiting like an eager maw, sat atop a broad, low set of stone steps. Atop the steps patrolled the grizzly-sized, wolf-bodied, lizard-tailed, three-headed pupper named Cerberus. His claws scraped stone at the sight of them. His body shifted to block their passage further. His three heads each growled, though the middle head also shimmied to some tune played by state-of-the-art Beats by Apollo™ headphones.

Ryan halted. His right hand seemed to reach for his sword, but froze mid-motion, either due to Athena's warning or his own deteriorating brain. He slowly sank down into yet another sneaking crouch and whispered, "Monster doggie."

"*Good* monster doggie," Athena corrected. She ignored Cerberus's posturing and, taking care not to look too challengingly into any of his sets of glowing red eyes, walked, smiling, up to his side. Once there, she scratched the left head behind the ears. That the head did not immediately bite her arm off confirmed for Athena that her immortality still held some privileges. He would let her pass.

All three heads still growled, of course; Cerberus had appearances to keep up. When Ryan took a few crouched steps forward, the growling doubled.

"Mister Sloude, stop."

"Monster doggie." Ryan's right hand was twitching. It inched closer to his sword hilt. "False dogs." He stepped closer. Immediately the left and middle heads erupted in a fury of barking while the right head—

That was odd.

The right head had stopped growling entirely and instead regarded Ryan with a quizzical look. Cerberus padded closer to Ryan, two of his three heads still barking as the right head sniffed the ninja up and down. Ryan had frozen again. The nostrils on Cerberus's right head flared. It jammed its snout into Ryan's armpit, and then less polite areas. If Athena didn't know better—and if the other two heads weren't barking louder than a terrier at a squirrel party—she'd say Cerberus recognized him somehow.

When the third head coated Ryan's entire face with a slobberous lick, Athena started to wonder just what made her think she did know better.

Wait a minute—she was Athena! She was millennia old, spending nearly all those years as the goddess of wisdom, defense, weaving, and owls! *Of course* she knew better! What the Styx was going on?

Ryan reached an arm up to pet the right head. The other two heads lunged forward, taking the rest of Cerberus's body with it. The middle head snapped at the right one, and the left clobbered Ryan so hard that he flew backward and crashed into the wall beside the tunnel exit. He slid to the ground, legs splayed outward. Athena winced in sympathy.

"Doggie punched."

"Darn right he did," said Athena, feeling vindicated. "Now, stay there. Rest. I will speak to Persephone and return for you, provided you are, oh, still here, let's call it."

"False dogs," Ryan mumbled. "Marcus give two rides."

"Uh-huh."

Cerberus returned to his spot atop the steps in front of the gate, leaving just enough space for Athena to pass by. She did just that, scratching behind the left head's ears again as she passed.

"BOOF!" said Cerberus.

Not far to go now, Athena told herself. Traveling by car and by foot was a pain in the butt. Once she regained her divinity she'd be flying everywhere. Maybe Hephaestus would build her a jet pack.

CHAPTER TWELVE

"Death is . . . oh, how to put this? Death is weird. He's not really a god, but he is. He's not really a force of Nature, but he is. He's not really a skydiving fan, but he is. He's one of the most adaptable of the pantheon, I think, which is kind of a fecking oxymoron because he's also big on keeping order, keeping to his schedules, yadda yadda yadda. I suppose when it's your job to constantly bring drastic upheaval to people's lives, you get a teeny bit used to change."

—Persephone, BBC interview, First Olympian Return

"When I first met Death—countless centuries ago next month—he preferred to go by Thanatos. He had more spring in his step and did not have a scythe. Did not give interviews. Could not care less about mortals. Yet after a while, he became interested in how the living world viewed him. I would catch him asking the dead if he was 'what they expected.' Sometimes he would change his name according to what mortals called him, if it pleased him: Mot. Arawn. Kosač. Yama. During the Middle Ages, he took to dressing in robes and carrying the scythe. Said it made him looked fearsome. Lately, he's trying out the name Doug, and likes Chicago-style pizza for some reason. He still hangs onto that bloody scythe, though. And he is always Death."

—Charon, Acheron ferryman, from Death's Little Brother: A
Memoir

IN THE BALCONY overlooking the vast royal audience chamber of the Underworld Palace, Persephone gripped the arms of her throne so tightly the tendons in the back of her hands were visible. It lasted only a moment before she relaxed, though irritation remained in her dark brown eyes. Her back straightened, which accentuated both her regality and the multicolored layers of the wine and turquoise dress that covered her from head to toe. "I am so *tired* of everyone asking this!" She glared down at Athena, who stood before her dais. "Zeus asked me. My own mother asked me! For shades' sake, I was grilled on the subject by a gods-damned dish of fecking ice cream! I am sick to *death* of it!"

"~Sick to Death? How profane~" spoke Death from a darkened alcove. "~As if I am to blame~"

Persephone rolled her eyes. "Not *you*, Doug. Holy Styx, you should be used to that metaphor by now."

Death made a non-committal grunt and fiddled with his scythe. Was he pouting? Athena put aside the thought and smiled in sympathy at Persephone. "I am seriously considering creating a 'We Hate Baskin' anti-fan club."

"Absolutely splendid!" Persephone bloomed. "Will there be T-shirts?"

Athena grinned. "Perhaps."

"I hate T-shirts." The queen of the Underworld wilted again. "Too banal."

"~I have Albert Einstein's entire T-shirt collection~"

"Shut up, Doug."

"~He gave them to me~"

Persephone rolled her eyes again.

"~They mostly fit~"

"My point," said Athena, "is that I can at least understand a portion of your frustrations. And I mean no offense in asking, but—"

Persephone waved her hand. "But you wish to solve the problem of the zombies and must make sure no stone is left unturned, et cetera, et fecking cetera. I know this. I've heard it all before. I bear you no ill will, cousin, niece-in-law, whatever we are, but I find this line of inquiry insulting. Do you possibly think, after this long, that there is some gods-damned cause for the gods-damned zombies that I am both aware of and did not tell anyone else?"

Athena took a breath. "Persephone, I intended no insult. At least, not to you. Perhaps I am offering insult to the others who have asked. My questions do imply that I believe myself more competent in puzzling out answers from the same information you gave them. Or"—she paused to share a conspiratorial smirk—"that you might offer me more information than you would offer certain upstart sundaes."

Persephone drummed her fingertips once on her throne. "But you also imply that, I, possessed of the same information, could not figure out the zombies' cause myself. So tell me, Athena: is it that you think yourself cleverer than I as well, or that you suspect I am the culprit behind the zombies in the first place?"

"I do not think myself cleverer than you, Persephone." Athena left the question of her suspicion unaddressed, accusing Persephone via the implication. Implied accusations were so much more diplomatic.

The queen of the Underworld rose, slowly, from her throne. Her dusky eyes locked onto Athena's for every long moment it took to reach her full height. Athena met her gaze in the fashion of a dog confronted about a sofa that she doesn't remember vivisecting. *Was* Persephone somehow the culprit? Athena was doing her best to gauge Persephone's reaction, but thousands of years' experience analyzing her fellow gods' body language was telling Athena nothing, yet.

Well, she amended, nothing except that there was no way Persephone could fight well in a dress that form-fitting.

"Do you remember Medusa?" Athena asked suddenly. "Avowed celibate priestess of mine way back when? I caught her, shall we say, 'riding Poseidon's waves' in one of my temples, so I turned her into a hideous snake-haired monster and signed Poseidon up for five thousand subscriptions to Amphora Magazine?"

Persephone continued her stare, though one eyebrow did twitch in what might've been curiosity.

"Silliest thing," Athena went on. "Medusa had a twin sister, Maddy. She wasn't even a priestess of mine. The twin was the one in my temple with Poseidon. But I got them mixed up. Turned the wrong one into a monster!" Athena feigned a nervous laugh. "Boy, was my face red! But by the time I realized my mistake, turning Medusa back would've just been a whole other ordeal that I didn't have time for that day. So I wiped out Maddy entirely, swept her under the rug so no one would know, and just let history gloss it all over." Athena shrugged. "My point is I understand that accidents happen. I would also point out that you know I can keep a secret when you need me to. I've yet to tell a soul about the pomegranate thing."

Persephone's stare softened. She frowned, though be it from displeasure or sadness, Athena could not tell. Persephone may have just been gassy.

The goddess strode toward Athena, and then past her to stand at the balcony railing. There, she stared out across the audience chamber below in a way that defied Webster's to cite a more perfect definition of the word "wistful." Persephone's dress likely added to the effect, though Athena found herself smirking at the thought that if she really were gassy, a single toot would cause the entire aura to come crashing down.

At last, Persephone cast her eyes over her shoulder at Athena and said, "The Underworld is not an easy kingdom to rule, Athena. It's not like ruling the sea, or North Dakota. So much depends upon it all working properly, staying organized. I ruled by Hades's side for so many centuries, but even that could not fully prepare anyone for being completely in charge. Hades had a special talent for it. He set things here in motion, designed some of the systems from conception. He understood the Underworld, its mysteries, its intricacies—like how to get the Styx to stop making that fecking *noise* it does every second Saturday—more than anyone on Olympus or off.

"But, Athena, do you know whose understanding is second only to his?" Persephone had turned to face her directly. "*Mine*. There is no doubt becoming the Underworld's absolute has presented challenges. I am not at Hades's level, *yet*. But nor am I a fool. I know of nothing I might have done, nothing I might have overlooked, to have caused this zombie crisis."

Here, Persephone straightened up even further; not only did she seem to be looking down at Athena, but Athena suspected Persephone's spine to be fifty-six percent tire jack. "Now, Athena, you who not only were goddess of wisdom but are also my friend, do you dare say otherwise?"

Athena straightened to match Persephone. The goddess either believed her own claims or did a remarkable job of hiding any duplicity. Heartbeats passed while Athena weighed both Persephone's statement and her own answer.

"I do not dare such a thing, Queen Persephone," she answered, using the title for extra ingratiation. "Furthermore, I believe you. But when you mentioned that Hades knew this realm better than anyone, I started to wonder: is it possible he might have caused this *before* his exile?"

Persephone balked at the question. "Hades was not infallible, but he could never make a mistake that would lead to a mess of this magnitude."

"I don't mean a mistake," said Athena. "Do you think him the sort to create a failsafe that would sabotage things in the event he was ever . . . removed?"

"You're talking about a dead-man switch?"

Athena nodded. "There was a god-killing weapon floating around, after all. Anyone gets rid of him, and they have to deal with a zombie apocalypse for their troubles."

"~An undead-man switch, as it were~" said Death from the corner.

Persephone frowned. "My love would not willingly sacrifice the stability of this place, regardless of his own fate. He held the Underworld's place in the grand scheme of things as sacred, and the life and death cycle as inviolate."

Athena cocked her head. "Did he? He did allow certain souls to return to life from time to time, at your urging. Eurydice. Stan Lee. Eudocia."

"Rare exceptions," Persephone said. "And far different from zombies. Even if he were to create a dead-man switch, he would make it known so it would be a deterrent, not keep it secret for some petty revenge."

"Alright."

Despite Persephone's assurance, Athena couldn't discard the theory completely. Hades surely had *some* connection to the zombie situation. If he were responsible for it, he might be the only one who could fix it. Even if he had nothing to do with it, his knowledge and power would be useful in enacting a brute-force solution. Zeus would never go for that, though. End Hades's exile so that he could succeed where Zeus had failed? Zeus would surely rather eat his own lightning bolt. With other avenues to investigate, Athena set the idea aside.

She moved to the balcony edge to stand beside Persephone and face her. Should she ask about Alecto? No, not just yet. Best to make that line of questioning seem like an afterthought, in light of her agreement with the Erinyes. Besides, why let Persephone know Alecto had possibly found something linked to the zombies' origins? Persephone might use that knowledge to fix the problem before Athena could get any credit!

"On a different topic," Athena tried, "and I'm willing to bet this is something Baskin didn't ask you—"

"Fecking Baskin," Persephone spat.

"—have you any idea why they started out craving brains? Before Demeter did her thing, they always went for the head, always growled for brains. Never once were they heard to demand flesh, or hearts, or eyebrows. Brains, specifically."

Persephone clasped her hands in front of her stomach, one atop the other, considering. "Well, brains *are* delicious, if properly cooked."

"~Lime and cilantro is best~"

"But as zombies have neither taste buds nor cooking skills—"

"~*Zombie Chef* was a ratings disaster~"

"—I have little idea."

Athena sighed. "At one point I thought they might be craving brains to get smarter, but I saw no evidence of that."

"It doesn't work that way for them." Persephone crossed her arms. "Certain zombies have eaten more than five hundred human brains. If that made them smarter, they would have figured out how to drive or use a doorknob by now."

"~Even craving grains~," Death added, "~they still get brain in their diet, devouring the stomach and moving on to the rest of the body in their feeding frenzy~"

"No fecking effect whatsoever on their quote-unquote thinking."

"What about what you sensed at the Balefire of Hades?" Athena asked. "I watched the footage. Whatever caused the zombies was a force of Nature itself. I know you couldn't get a feel for its source, but are there any other insights you had about it?" She glanced at Death, suddenly recalling his involvement in the same ritual. It was easy to forget about Death sometimes, if you weren't careful. "Either of you?"

"Constantly changing," Persephone answered at once. "One moment familiar, the next quite alien. I got the sense of something, I would say, straining to wake. Old and new at once."

"~It was difficult to pin down~"

"It was a pain in the rump is what it was," Persephone added.

"~It had a particular taste of swamp water, and dark chocolate~"

"Excuse me?" said Athena.

Persephone nodded, her eyes shining. "Isn't that remarkable? Completely Styxborn-stupid, but remarkable? And utterly damned useless!"

Athena crossed her arms. "Have you tried using that to track the source down?"

Persephone yanked a wilted narcissus flower from a vase atop the balcony railing. "Did I not just use the phrase 'utterly damned useless'? Swamp water and dark chocolate? Of course I *tried*. It's like looking for a needle in haystack in a field of haystacks when it's raining needles and you only have some gods-damned useless clue like *swamp water and dark fecking chocolate!*"

"~And also the haystacks span both Underworld and surface~" Death added.

"Yes," said Persephone. She plucked the lifeless petals from the narcissus and dropped them off the balcony. "Yet I sense that it has origins in neither. You want to try to track *that* to its source? You go right ahead." She threw the plucked stem down and shouted at someone in the audience chamber below, "Hey! The narcissus blooms are wilted again! Get off your worthless heinies and bring some fresh ones up here! Now!" She turned back to Athena, suddenly all smiles and sunshine. "Aren't flowers just the best?"

CHAPTER THIRTEEN

"Hecate, the goddess most associated with magic, secrets, and night, is also (fittingly) among the Olympians whose origins are the most mysterious. Not even the source of her name is known. Is she a Titan's daughter? A secret identity of Artemis, daughter of Zeus and goddess of the moon (among other things)? A tender-hearted creature, as Homer called her? An evil thing, born of the night itself? Or was she from outside the original Greek tradition, adopted by the Greeks into their mythology? Thanks to the returned Olympians' willingness to speak of such things, we now know that the last is closest to the truth: Hecate is adopted, with no Olympian blood lineage whatsoever. The question none of the gods seem willing or able to answer is, adopted from whom?"

—A Mortal's Guidebook to the Olympians' Return, 1st Edition

"We did not know what to make of her when she first appeared. Zeus essentially just declared, 'This is Hecate, welcome her to the pantheon, don't poke her with a stick just because she's different, and so forth.' He didn't claim her as his own, but it took us a century to get out of him that she wasn't related to any Olympians at all. A while after that, mortals started conflating the two of us, which was vexing, because Hecate and I are most certainly not one and the same. I just loaned her a few outfits, and a bunch of old Greek men jumped to conclusions. Anyway, long story short: this is why I can't wear black anymore."

—Artemis, interview, Divine Fashions *magazine*

ZEUS BELLOWED INTO SPACE. The lightning bolt crackled gloriously in his grip, and he hurled its charge at C'oggn-yon. Energy drove into the being's swirling violet fog and mist. *A hit!* thought

Zeus. A direct hit upon the mist! And yet, as the bolt's energy continued out the other side and dissipated into space, Zeus knew that he had missed whatever lay within the mist.

The previous paragraph would like to apologize to anyone currently reading this book aloud.

"*Lord Zeus!*" Baskin telepathically bellowed. "*I renew my pledge to aid you in this struggle!*"

"*I said* hold, *Baskin!*" Zeus sent back. "*I will handle this!*"

"ZOGG!" C'oggn-yon boomed, which Zeus supposed he ought to have expected by that point.

The two had been sparring for the past ten *ZOGG*-festooned minutes. Apollo, Artemis, and Baskin floated a discrete distance behind Zeus. Opposite them, starry-skirted Cyot'hgha hovered beside the cuttlefish-headed '''''''''Q. Though Apollo, Artemis, and the two Cosmics awaited the encounter's outcome with apparent patience, Baskin was quaking like a bowl of pudding on a paint shaker. Keeping him out of the fight was proving a greater challenge than the fight itself.

As sudden and inexplicable as C'oggn-yon's attack had been, Zeus knew enough about the creature to be certain it only intended to provide some punctuation to their demands. Neither '''''''''Q nor Cyot'hgha had joined in. This was not a battle. All Zeus need do was hold his own for a little longer and keep things from escalating.

In other words, the exact opposite of letting Baskin engage his typical sprinkle-encrusted bloodlust. Left to battle, the god could work himself into a frenzy of rich, creamy violence and lose all sense or ability to take orders.

Plus, Zeus could not help wanting to look strong in front of Cyot'hgha.

"ZOGG!"

C'oggn-yon swept in an arc about Zeus, obscuring much of his vision in a purple haze. It was all around. Zeus didn't know if he was coming up or down. Suddenly, C'oggn-yon's mists parted in a flash of light. Zeus glimpsed a mass of dark uvulas within. There flashed a ball of lightning—C'oggn-yon's own electrical storm about to strike. Zeus held his Aegis shield in its path, collecting the energy and then feigning an intent to send it back.

Taken in by the feint, C'oggn-yon rushed to one side. Zeus anticipated the move and reached straight into C'oggn-yon's cloud. Within it, his fingertips brushed something reminiscent of wet broccoli. He seized upon the broccoli-thing, now with both hands. Ignoring the electrical stinging that bit into his knuckles and wrists, Zeus yanked whatever it was up above his head. The broccoli-feel transmuted in his grip into something *else*, and Zeus's stomach turned to think of what part of C'oggn-yon it might be. Ignoring the flashes of penguins and viscera that filled his mind as C'oggn-yon's mist engulfed him, Zeus renewed his grip, spun on one foot—a fun trick in outer space if you can do it—and hurled the entire mass back toward the moon.

C'oggn-yon made no attempt to turn around. The purple mist tumble-wafted into the distance and out of sight.

"...zogg...?"

Zeus caught his breath—figuratively, because, you know, vacuum of space—and returned his attention to Cyot'hgha and ''''''''Q.

"Now," Zeus said, handing his Aegis back to Baskin, "can we continue this meeting, or are you still busy being offended at... whatever it was you took offense at?"

C'oggn-yon's attack had been the most recent in a prolonged period of what Zeus took to be a bizarre parlay, although what precisely was being parlayed, he had no idea.

They had not mentioned Hecate again. That had eased Zeus's immediate worries on the matter, yet had puzzled him nonetheless.

Instead, Cyot'hgha had fallen back to recite a poem about "strænge" darkness, forgotten horrors, and things that go *flumphh-kazoo* in the night. (Apollo had complimented the poem, but Zeus suspected only diplomatic sincerity. Though Zeus had little ear for poetry, Cyot'hgha's poem had not rhymed once and had been so dull it was excised from this book entirely.)

What had followed the poem Zeus could only describe as a lengthy interpretive dance by ''''''''Q. This had been mostly head-bobbing and knee-kicks, broken by the occasional cuttlefish yodel. (Apollo had remained silent on that matter.) Between each of the poetry, the dance, and C'oggn-yon's attack, there had been a period where the three beings had merely stood, expectant, yet refusing to respond to anything Zeus said or did. Now that the battle with C'oggn-yon was finished, it appeared that was about to happen again.

Suddenly Cyot'hgha spoke. "Disquietude. Fen. Why have you not yet brought Hecate?"

Zeus blinked. Had this been all some sort of polite waiting period in which they had expected him to fetch her? Was it possible that they did not know Hecate was dead, after all? *Missing*, they had said initially. He'd assumed they'd known Hecate was gone. Were they possibly looking for something else that was "missing," something Hecate merely had knowledge of? Zeus could still only guess, and hope.

"Why I have not brought her . . . here?" Zeus asked, just to make sure.

"Why have you naught?" """""""Q answered.

So maybe he *had* jumped to the wrong conclusion! Zeus decided to change tactics.

"Why have I not brought her here, now?" He scoffed. "Is that what you were expecting? You were reciting, and dancing, and fighting with me. I had therefore bestowed my full attention upon you."

"*The mighty Zeus prefers to stay focused!*" bellowed Baskin. "*He does not multitask at the whims of others!*"

"Furthermore," said Zeus, deciding on a new approach, "you did not ask me to summon Hecate for you! You did not say please! You come from elsewhere, and I understand this—"

"Elsewhære," """""""Q said.

"—but I will not bear sole responsibility for such communication breakdowns!" Zeus crossed his arms over his chest to play up the offended angle. "So, I would know, before I summon—"

Cyot'hgha swept in close and touched a fingertip to Zeus's lips. "Of the missing, Hecate knows. Bring to us. Now." She drifted away again. Her brow hardened, her eyes sharpened, and her lips curled in a smile as dangerous as it was seductive. In her voice lay the whisper of a pleasured threat as she added, "Pleæse."

"""""""Q bobbed.

Zeus gave his best commanding frown. "Hecate is an enigmatic goddess. In fact, she became our goddess of secrets after we adopted her from you." He paused to gauge Cyot'hgha's reaction to the word "adopted," but she betrayed no judgment. "As such, she can be difficult to find. She dwells in seclusion, refusing to answer summons."

"... *Especially lately!*" hollered Baskin.

"Yes." Though he had to fight against glaring lightning at Baskin, Zeus's poker face held. At least he assumed it did. "Hecate spoke of a project on which she wanted to work in seclusion. We treat her well, I assure you, and so we respected her wishes. As a show of goodwill, I will disturb her for you if you truly wish it, but understand it will take us time to locate her and bring her here. Rather than keep you waiting, tell me of this missing thing you seek. I and my pantheon know the planet as well as Hecate. We may already know of its location."

"Bring to us," Cyot'hgha repeated.

"You wish to wait?" Zeus asked. "Then so be it. We will find Hecate and bring her here. And you will wait, here, while we search for where she has secluded herself."

"The claw-tongued beasts warble and the motes do waft them forward," """"""Q said for some reason. "Acceptable. We will wait here. You will search on Earth. And we will go there and help you."

"Er, no," said Zeus. "I said you will wait *here*."

"Yes," said """"""Q.

"You will give us time to search on Earth," said Zeus. "While you stay *here*."

"Yes," said """"""Q.

"Good," said Zeus.

"And we will go to Earth and help you," added """"""Q.

Ugh. Cosmics! Zeus resisted the urge to summon another lightning bolt. "No, you will not! For you to visit our Earth will be considered an act of war, and then you will get nothing."

"Known. Understood," said Cyot'hgha.

"Then we will wait," said """"""Q. "You will not behold us searching on Earth."

"Excellent!" Zeus almost turned to go, but stopped. "We will not *behold* you searching on Earth? You say that because you will be here, correct?"

"Yes," said Cyot'hgha.

"Because you will not behold us," said """"""'Q.

"I—" Zeus paused, weighing clarification against the risk of antagonizing them to the point of destabilizing the situation. "I am concerned you do not comprehend the use of the word 'because' there."

"That is your concern."

"Yes," said Zeus, barely restraining himself from being drawn into further discussion on the matter. Either they would not understand, or they would feign misunderstanding. Either way, he would look foolish, and that was hardly worth it.

"Apollo," Zeus said over his shoulder. "Summon Urania. And Thalia." Two Muses ought to do, for starters.

Apollo acknowledged the command, and Zeus returned his attention to the two remaining Cosmics. "You will *not* go to Earth while we search for Hecate. Period. In the meantime—"

"More will come from the elsewhære," whispered Cyot'hgha, "if you fail to meet our needs in time."

"In the *meantime*," Zeus repeated, "please remain here under the captivating ministrations of two of my most entertaining subjects."

Thankfully, Thalia appeared at his left shoulder at that moment. Urania followed, bursting into view as a supernova—though obviously less powerful, and without obliterating any of them, so, really, not much akin to a supernova at all, Zeus supposed. The fact that he'd come up with such an ill-fitting simile at least told him that both Muses had already focused their attention on the Cosmics rather than inspiring his own creativity. That, or they were both so shocked at Cyot'hgha's and """"""'Q's appearance that their musing talents had been temporarily discombobulated.

Urania, dressed in an amber sundress embroidered with white stars, stared bemusedly between the two Cosmics and Zeus himself. Her left hand cupped her right elbow while she tugged on one of her gold Saturn earrings. Thalia, meanwhile, seemed to shift between fascination and consternation. Her eyebrows flitted like hummingbird wings as they tried to keep up with the cycling expressions on her face.

Both Muses still had the wherewithal to pose per the usual Muse habit—each leaned against the other's shoulder with an affected, stylish nonchalance—so they could not have been too taken aback.

"I present to you the Muses Thalia and Urania, who will entertain you while you wait," said Zeus, ignoring the palpable weight of the Muses' sudden stares upside his head. "Thalia is our Muse of comedy, which I am sure you will find a fascinating concept, and Urania is our Muse of astronomy and astrology, subjects I know hold your interest."

Urania cleared her throat with her usual haughtiness and proffered her hand to Cyot'hgha. "Also calendars, coffee cups, and bathroom graffiti. Everyone underestimates the importance of bathroom graffiti."

Cyot'hgha merely stared at the Muse's hand until Urania finally withdrew it. '''''''''Q tilted his head ninety degrees to one side.

"Urania, Thalia," Zeus said, "you will keep our guests comfortable while they wait." Zeus caught both the Muses' gaze, ignored their disbelieving looks, and added, "While they wait *here*." With a nod of departure to each of the Cosmics, Zeus slowly teleported away, taking care to bring Apollo, Artemis, and Baskin in his wake. The last thing he saw as he faded from that place was Thalia nervously smoothing her cobalt dress and flashing a smile at Cyot'hgha and '''''''''Q.

"Er . . . So!" Thalia managed, her attitude cranking up to chipper. "What a great audience! Do we have any out-of-towners here with us tonight?"

Zeus appeared before his throne in the grand hall on Olympus. Baskin, Artemis, and Apollo faded into being in front of him (in reverse alphabetical order no less). Zeus flipped open a compartment on the throne, grabbed a handful of ambrosia-antacid tablets, and scarfed them down in regal fashion while shouting, "Iris! To me!"

Iris, goddess of rainbows and Zeus's personal messenger, did *not* immediately respond to Zeus's call. Until recently, she had been one of Hermes's lieutenants in his messenger god duties. Zeus had promoted Iris to fill the void left by Hermes's exile, not realizing the delays that would result each time he needed her. Nowadays he had to wait as long as ten, maybe even fifteen seconds for her to disengage from whatever else she was doing. Okay, so now she was likely helping Hestia, carrying messages to coordinate planetary defenses, but was he not the king of Olympus?

He really needed to get that goddess an assistant.

Seventeen seconds later, Iris finally appeared. The wings on her helm and sandals flapped to a stop. Both formerly belonged to Hermes; both were also newly colored in a brilliant rainbow color scheme.

"Yes, Lord Zeus?" she asked.

Zeus wasted no time with greetings. "Send for Jerry! Tell him to bring Hecate's laptop from her old chambers. Then visit Persephone. Bid her tell me if she can detect *any* trace of Hecate in the Underworld. I will expect her report in council in half an hour."

"Yes, Lord Zeus," she said.

"And Iris?"

"Yes, Lord Zeus?" she asked.

"Did you really have to put glitter on the helmet? That bothersome taint will get everywhere!"

"Yes, Lord Zeus!" She beamed. "Rainbows need glitter. It's the law!"

"It is no law of mine," said Zeus.

"Pretty sure it is," she said. "If not, you should seriously consider it."

Zeus pointed out the door. "Go!" he commanded.

Glitter. Ugh. It had taken hours bathing in the River Lethe to wash that stuff out of his beard after a unicorn threw up on him once. He had never regretted eradicating *those* creatures and their recalcitrant attitudes. But there was no time to reminisce about old victories.

"Baskin!" Zeus barked once Iris had gone. "Monitor the Cosmics! Be ready to support the Muses if they lose control."

"Yes, Great Lord Zeus!" hollered Baskin.

"Artemis! Tell Hestia to make preparations for a virtual Dodekatheon meeting."

Artemis bowed in acknowledgement and set to it.

"And Apollo!" Zeus stopped short. He didn't really need anything from Apollo, at least not until the Dodekatheon convened. But he'd gotten into a rhythm, and giving commands was a comfort.

Apollo watched Zeus expectantly.

"... Clean up that glitter!"

"Oh," said Apollo. "Splendid."

CHAPTER FOURTEEN

"Love tofu on rice cakes? Delicious bowls of steam? Watching bowling on TV? Then live an average life and spend eternity in the Asphodel Meadows: the blandest place under Earth."
　　　　—*billboard advertisement in Lawrence, Kansas (First Olympian Return)*

"The Asphodel Meadows: Where everything is going to be kinda okay. All the time. No matter what."
　　　　—So It's Come to This . . . *(Asphodel Meadows orientation pamphlet)*

THE WORST THING ABOUT traversing the Asphodel Meadows, thought Athena, was not the constantly overcast skies, nor the gray-leafed weeping willows, nor the slack-jawed, wandering spirits who sometimes invited you to view their vacation photos.

No, the worst thing was the easy-listening music. It permeated this section of the Underworld like a siren's song, were a siren ever moved to lure with mediocrity. After just one in the Meadows, Athena had already suffered enough soprano saxophone to last her the rest of eternity.

She did not have much farther to walk, thankfully. Though the Underworld was vast, travel through it was often swifter than in the world above. Athena had perhaps walked five hundred miles (and then five hundred more) since leaving Persephone. This was despite her limited pace as a non-divine being in above-average physical shape wearing hiking boots with excellent arch support.

On the rise ahead, just off to the side of the dirt path she walked, loomed the fifty-third gray boulder. It looked just like the fifty-two before it, but if Persephone's directions were to be trusted, it meant her destination was near.

Those directions were the result of Athena's offhand comment about a promise to find something Alecto lost on her last visit to the Underworld—a favor Athena claimed she owed to the Erinys—and Athena's subsequent inquiry about where Alecto might have last visited. Before Iris had swept in on some errand demanding Persephone's attention, Persephone had clued Athena in to a crossroads near the shores of the River Cocytus where she'd seen Alecto toddling around. Athena had then absconded with that information before Iris could hemorrhage too much glitter; Athena refused to lose precious time bathing in the Lethe.

Athena crested the hill. The Meadows continued before her, yet now, across a grove of willow trees, she could see another path intersecting the one she traveled. Beyond the intersecting path, on what cheekily passed for the horizon in this strange land, festered the Cocytus—the River of Wailing, so broad and slow that from where Athena stood it seemed merely marshland. No wailing reached her ears, though if she listened carefully, she could make out the occasional distant whimper.

"AAAAAAAAAAAAEEEEEEEEEEIIIII!!!!"

That was *not* the Cocytus.

Athena was fairly certain of this. For one thing, the sound was more scream than wail, and for another, it came from the eight-foot tall, eight-legged nightmare that had leapt from a nearby tree and was now poking both of Athena's shoulders in mildly annoying fashion.

"Stop that, Arachne," Athena said.

Arachne, the aforementioned nightmare who looked like a female centaur with the body of a gigantic orb-weaver spider where the horse should be, continued to poke with two of her forelegs.

"You're not the boss of me," she said.

Athena seized the pair of offending legs. Arachne shrugged and then poked Athena's hips with a second pair.

"Is this bothering you?" Arachne asked. "I can stop if this is bothering you."

Thousands of years ago, when Arachne had lived, the mortal had boasted of weaving skills beyond even Athena's. What recourse did the goddess possibly have but to turn the prideful girl into a spider? Yet Arachne had changed since then: her human torso, a vestige of whatever pre-transformation self-image she had clung to, must have reasserted itself once she become a spirit in the Underworld. At least the spider parts remained to remind the girl of her shame.

Unfortunately, they also gave Arachne extra limbs with which to poke.

"Are you sure," snarked Athena, "that you wouldn't rather claim that your talent for poking people eclipses that of even the gods themselves?"

"Well I don't know about that," said Arachne with a grin. "I don't see any gods about just now, do you? Present company *included*, of course."

Athena dove forward, rolled beneath Arachne's abdomen, and sprang back to her feet. She shoved her back up against Arachne's rump as she did so, pitching the creature forward onto her face. Athena spared only a moment to watch Arachne's legs flail about as she struggled to her feet again. Then Athena continued down the path.

"So you heard about that, did you?" Athena shot over her shoulder.

Arachne skittered after her. "That you're one of the Punished? Demoted to ex-goddess? I keep up with Olympian events. What fool doesn't?"

"I wouldn't have thought you'd be able to in the Asphodel Meadows."

"This place is the epitome of drab, most *vaunted* Athena. What's more drab than news about *your* dippy life? I'm surprised they don't pump it in constantly." Arachne punctuated that with another couple of pokes in the small of Athena's back.

Athena spun to face Arachne again, knocking the offending legs away. "Has your punishment taught you *no* humility, girl?"

Arachne scoffed. "Has yours?"

"I suppose that answers my question. Why are you in the drab splendor of the Meadows, anyway? You were a bad girl. You should be elsewhere, getting punished."

"You turned me into a fucking spider!" Arachne shouted. "I'm dead and I still look like this! You think I haven't been punished enough already? I said I was a better weaver than you, and I proved it in a contest! But I ought to be pushing some rock up a hill for eternity now, too?"

Ugh, Athena thought. *Mortals.* "The tapestry you wove to prove yourself, while admittedly superior, was offensive! You depicted the gods doing despicable things. You gave Zeus a wardrobe malfunction. And you made my butt look huge. Hubris! Is Athena going to have to smack a bitch?"

Satisfied that she had now regained the high ground in the argument, Athena turned and resumed walking. Arachne followed and resumed poking her. They walked and poked in silence until they'd descended the hill and the crossroads lay just ahead.

"So what are you doing down here, anyway?" Arachne skittered around to Athena's side, still poking.

"Chasing a hunch."

poke "A hunch about what?"

"Why, do you plan to weave a tapestry about it?"

"Maybe I want to help you, Athena." Arachne watched her, straight-faced for about three seconds before she burst out laughing. "Kidding! Gods, can you imagine? I'm curious! It's dull here! Tell me and I might stop poking you, maybe."

poke *poke* *poke*

Athena glowered. "I am looking for someone."

"Just anyone?" The poking continued. "I know a few atheists I could introduce you to. We get along great."

Athena reached the crossroads and halted. Unsurprisingly, it was unremarkable: one wide gravel path intersecting one wide dirt path. No sign marked the ways, nor was there anything to indicate the nearby borders of the Asphodel Meadows except the scent of the Cocytus swamps that wafted to Athena's nose on the listless Underworld breeze.

"Do you smell any dark chocolate?" Athena asked.

Arachne blinked in genuine confusion. "What is chocolate?"

"What is—? Oh, right. This is the Asphodel Meadows." She cursed herself for not thinking of that. What would chocolate be doing in the epitome of bland?

Even if Alecto had been anywhere near this place, there was no guarantee she had met whomever had signed the forms here. The scent of swamp water could have been from anywhere. She took a deep breath. There was still value in ruling things out.

"Hey," said Arachne. "Are you looking for Alecto?"

What? Athena hadn't mentioned Alecto yet, had she? Had Arachne seen Alecto in this area, too? What did Arachne know?

Athena feigned disinterest in the face of the spider-girl's mischievous grin. "Alecto?"

Arachne boggled her eyes mockingly. "*Buh,* Alec-toh?" she imitated.

"Why do you ask?"

"Because," said Arachne. "I saw her in this very spot a while back. She did something memorable here."

"Which was?"

"Oh, I can't remember."

Athena rolled her eyes. "Of course not. But for the right price you could be persuaded to remember, I imagine."

"Ooh, even without her divinity, she's still smart!" Arachne tapped her forelegs on the tops of Athena's boots. "Make me an offer."

"Peh." Athena shrugged and wandered away. "If you wish to tell me a story, then tell me a story. I never said it was Alecto I sought."

"Hah!" Arachne leapt over Athena's head to land before her. "You're trying to find her. Admit it!"

"Why would I be trying to find her when I spoke with her just yesterday?"

Arachne's brow furrowed. "Huh. Yesterday? And she's all right, is she?"

What was Arachne getting at? "I spoke with her. I wouldn't go so far as to say she was all right."

"Then how would you say she was?"

"Why do you care?"

"Because if you tell me," Arachne said, crossing her arms and one set of forelegs, "I might tell you how she got that way. Demur and protest all you wish, Athena; I know you're interested. You want to go where she went, don't you?"

"She went somewhere?"

"Does answering my questions with further questions make you think I'll be more inclined to tell you?"

"I don't know, are you?"

"Fine," said Arachne. "Don't tell me. I'll just be on my way then." Scooping up a thread of silk from her spinneret and beginning to weave it into something, she turned to go. "Have fun getting nowhere."

Damn it to Jerry! She shouldn't let the mortal get the best of her, but bother it all, time was of the essence. Athena grit her teeth. "Alecto is marginally decomposed, semi-undead, and smells like a dumpster behind a disreputable taxidermy."

"Aha!" Arachne whirled back, holding an already half-knit silk sweater. "I thought so! Do you swear by the Styx you're telling the truth about that?"

Athena scoffed. "You want *me* to swear, to the likes of *you*, about this?"

"That's what I said, Athena. Did Zeus take your ears away too?"

"Fine, whatever," Athena said. "I swear by the Styx I'm telling the truth about Alecto's condition. We're actually by the Cocytus, but whatever. It's the truth."

Arachne tossed the sweater away. "Now we're getting somewhere. I'll gladly tell you how to follow her if it puts you in the same danger."

"That is so very kind of you."

Arachne held up a finger. "In exchange for . . . "

"Oh come on!"

". . . getting my true form back."

Athena didn't suppress a laugh. "Mayhap this is your true form. Did that occur to you?"

"You know what I mean!"

"You, who are consigned to the Asphodel Meadows, you who defied a goddess, insulted the entire pantheon, and just now had the nerve to ask *me* to swear by the Styx—you have the audacity to demand still more? Quit while you are ahead, Arachne!"

Arachne seemed to consider this for a moment. "Nah," she said.

Freak-ing mortals. "Even if I thought you deserved it, I don't have the power to remove any curses right now."

"I know. But you're stubborn. As loath as I am to admit it, you'll get your power back eventually. And I want you to promise to fix this once you do."

"Weren't you about to tell me more so that I'll wind up like Alecto?"

Arachne grinned. "That's what makes it a win-win."

"Fine. Tell me what I want to know, and after I regain my power, I'll fix your body."

Arachne grinned wider. "Do you swear by—"

"Spider-girl, do *not* push it!"

"Okay, fine! Geez. You're awfully tetchy for someone who's only got two legs." Arachne pointed to the very center of the crossroads. "She stood right there, scooped up a handful of dirt, and swallowed it. Then she crouched down, looked around, and stood back up again, doing that teleportation thing the Erinyes do."

"She might have been going anywhere then!" Athena burst.

"Are you going to let me complete my story, or do you want to keep assuming you know better than I do about everything?"

I do know better, Athena wanted to say, but didn't. Hooray for wisdom. When the silence had hung between them long enough, Arachne went on.

"When she started her teleportation, it triggered something else that opened up in mid-air: sort of a swirling, blue-green vortex. It was there for just a moment before Alecto cackled at it, and then she climbed through."

"So you're telling me I can only recreate that vortex if I stand here and somehow try to teleport like an Erinys to trigger it?" Athena slid a hand into her jacket, finding the little silver ball Megaera had given her.

"And eat the dirt!" Arachne insisted. "Hey, don't look at me like that! I'm merely telling you what she did. You're lucky I can even recognize Erinyes' teleportation when I see it."

Athena scooped a handful of dirt from the center of the crossroads. It sat in her palm: tan, slightly moist, and not the most appetizing thing she had ever seen. A year and a half ago she was answering philosophers' prayers and receiving tribute from the top generals of nearly every major nation's armed forces. Now she was in the Asphodel Meadows, about to eat dirt.

Ah, well. At least it was fresh dirt. She swallowed her pride, and then swallowed the dirt. It tasted like worms and disappointment.

"Holy Styx you actually ate it!" Arachne burst out laughing so hard that all eight of her legs gave way and she *fwump*ed down on her belly.

Athena glared daggers at Arachne and hurled at her the few remaining fragments of dirt left in her palm. It wasn't enough to satisfy her. "That was a *trick*?"

"Just—" Arachne tried to catch her breath, which you wouldn't expect would be necessary for a dead person, but there it is. "Just—oh! Just the dirt part. The rest is true! I swear!"

"Bitch, you have got some serious personality flaws!"

"Sorry, no; I'm perfect."

Athena bit back a retort, consoling herself with the thought that while she had agreed to restore Arachne's body after regaining her power, she had neglected to specify *how long* after.

Instead, Athena drew the silver ball from her pocket. She tightened her grip around it, yet stopped short of calling its power. She had hoped to save the ball for an emergency escape, or to access somewhere she could not reach otherwise.

Then again, wasn't that what she was trying for here? Athena opened her palm, treasuring the silver ball's utility, knowing that using it would mean losing it.

"What is that?" Arachne asked.

Athena watched her reflection in the ball's surface. "It is valuable," she answered, and then tucked the ball away again. No sense rushing into things. Instead, she crouched lower and peered upward, scrutinizing the space just above. "The vortex you saw—was it horizontal, by any chance?"

"Might've been."

Athena reached upward, probing the air. If Alecto had torn her way into something, there might still be a residual opening. Arachne had said she'd climbed *up* into it, which meant it faced the ground. While Athena wasn't as knowledgeable about trans-spatial gateways as Hermes or Hecate had been, she was fairly sure that such things were sometimes only visible from one direction. If there were a trace tear here, Persephone, being taller, might have missed it entirely, especially if she didn't know what to look for. Now if Athena could only find it herself without any divine senses.

She drew her fingertips back and forth through the air, hoping to hook something, notice something, catch something . . .

Arachne sniggered. "I wish you could see how ridiculous you look. Oh, wait! You can! Look what I just made!" She unfurled a freshly woven pillowcase bearing a likeness of Athena. With mud smeared on her face. Arachne's skill made Athena's fingers—three feet longer than normal—appear to waft back and forth like chutes in the breeze.

Athena's eyes were mid-roll when she caught hold of something. Her left hand poked into a tiny opening, and the aethereal membrane became visible. "Make fun all you like, girl, but it worked."

Athena had caught, she surmised, the vestige of the path Alecto had made, not quite sealed over from the Erinys's initial passage. Carefully, she pulled the opening wider until it could accommodate her. Through it, Athena could see nothing but flickers of silvery light amid a greater darkness.

She could also smell dark chocolate. This was definitely the way. Unless it was a chocolate-baited trap. Regardless, she had to go through. Especially because it got her away from Arachne. The girl had begun weaving more detail into the pillowcase.

"Goodbye, Arachne," she said. "Enjoy playing with your butt-string."

"At least I didn't eat dirt! And remember your promise!"

"You're not the boss of me," Athena mimicked. With that, she clambered through the opening.

CHAPTER FIFTEEN

"Hey, dumbasses! Ares here with some bad ruttin' news: I lost a bet with Artemis, so now I gotta take a week off from blowin' shit up here to make a damned teaching episode. So listen up, 'cause I ain't got time to explain this junk twice. Yer gonna get learned! First, there's somethin' you gotta understand: you know where you mortals live, and cuss, and do all your mortal crap? That's called a plane of existence. There's other planes of existence, too, like Mt. Olympus, and that room The Fates live in, and, I dunno, Siberia or somethin'. Planes of existence are big damn things. Bigger than your piddly little brains can wrap around. Yeah, sucks to be you, but you don't have to worry about that, 'cause today I'm gonna teach yer asses about a kind of plane even you knee-biters can understand.

"They're called pocket planes! They're a hell of a lot smaller, and they're, like, stuck on the side of the big planes. Kind of wedged between 'em, or hammered on, or whatever. You pansy mortals can't get into 'em without some help or some special weirdo-crap going on, but we gods use pocket planes to store stuff in. I keep my weapons in a pocket plane. Poseidon keeps his tridents in another pocket plane. Artemis keeps, I dunno, probably bunnies or some shit like that in hers. You get the damn point.

"There's other pocket planes, too. Maybe bigger ones. Size of a boxing ring or a shooting range or Lake Michigan. We gods can make 'em, but sometimes they just friggin' form outta the cosmos or some garbage like that. Hella weird.

Now some of you anus-squirts might be wantin' to ask, 'Durr, why do you call 'em pocket planes, Ares?' Well I don't ruttin' know and I don't ruttin' care! Video's over! Next week, back to blowin' shit up!"

—Ares Blows Shit Up *online video series, episode 24 (First Olympian Return)*

"A group of M.I.T. grad students theorized that pocket planes exist within a dimensional aether that borders myriad other planes, but as they were drunk and searching for what they called Dionysus's Pocket Plane of Tequila Shooters, that might be complete malarkey."
　　　　　　　　　　　　—Everything You Wanted to Know About Alternate
　　　　　　　　　　　　　　　Dimensions but Were Too Sober to Ask

AT FIRST, ATHENA THOUGHT she had entered a dimension where colors did not exist, like World War II stock footage, or the Elemental Plane of Minimalist Theater. She stood upon a platform of uneven obsidian. Rolling clouds of gray surrounded the platform, reflecting some sourceless light. At the platform's center stood a—

Well, she wasn't entirely sure how to think about it. An obelisk? No. Pylon? Not quite. Thingamajig? Somehow that term called to her. The *thingamajig* was a conical object twice Athena's height. Vertical streaks of silvery light mottled its curved, black surface from the three-meter wide base to the top, which was barely a hand's breadth wide. Countless wire strands sprouted from the top. Each grew in a slightly different direction and glowed with a single point of otherworldly white light at its tip. The strands were at least as long as the base of the thingamajig itself, and made the whole affair look like the hairstyle of some bizarrely-coifed mad scientist puppet. Or, Athena considered, one of those novelty fiber optic lamps that Apollo secretly marketed in the 1980s.

Yet beyond the thingamajig, a lone touch of color lurked. Atop a slope at the platform's far end, a pair of violet lights gleamed in the shadows. Scintillating gossamers of energy flowed from the thingamajig toward those violet lights. The lights possessed such an ineffable and undeniable bearing that Athena decided instantly: they were eyes.

The gossamers also lit the shadows enough for Athena to discern a humanoid shape that would have eyes right where the lights glowed, so that contributed to her decision. But, also, ineffable and undeniable bearing. That was important.

The redolence of dark chocolate hung in the air. It would have been pleasant were it not tinged with decaying flesh. Why dark chocolate, exactly?

"Hello?" Athena tried.

The shadowed figure neither moved, nor spoke, nor offered her a refreshing beverage.

"Please pardon the intrusion," Athena tried, edging closer. Her voice echoed, and much more than she had expected. "What is this place?"

"Pardon . . . pending," rasped a voice in the darkness. Though it came from somewhere behind the thingamajig, it did not feel like it belonged to the purple-eyed figure. Athena reminded herself that acoustics might very well be skewed in a place like, well, whatever this place was. She glanced behind her out of caution: the obsidian platform on which she stood ended a few steps away in another expanse of fog. She saw nothing else, not even the rift via which she had arrived. There was no visible speaker, and certainly no helpful sign to introduce the place to tourists.

"How did you get here?" rasped the voice again. The voice, unlike Athena's, did not echo at all.

"I followed a path Alecto made from the Asphodel Meadows." Athena addressed the general area rather than the purple-eyed figure, suddenly suspicious that it might be a statue. No sense looking foolish, after all. "At least I believe I followed it."

"Why?"

"Why do I believe I followed it?" she asked, stalling to think of a better answer.

"Wiseacre! Why did you follow?"

"I—I wished to learn where Alecto went."

"She went here!"

"So it would seem." Athena took a step toward the thingamajig. Was it the thingamajig speaking? She addressed it directly this time. "Which brings me to my original question—what is this place?"

"This place is important!" shouted the voice. "And you are distracting it!"

"My apologies. That was not my intent."

The only answer to that was a snort.

"Distracting it from what?" she pressed.

The shadowed figure's violet eyes pulsed. The strands atop the thingamajig began to undulate. The tip of each glowed brighter and then, as the air suddenly tingled along Athena's skin, a few strands stretched outward toward the edges of the platform. They dipped into the surrounding fog, glowing brighter as they did so, and then lifted into the air once more. Each seemed to drag something with it as it did so.

One strand in particular caught Athena's gaze. Through the tiny point of silver light at the end, she saw a place cold and dark in the mortal world. An unlit morgue? A zombie-infested summer camp? Back stage at a Boyz-Syng concert? No, an alley! A portly, middle-aged man slumped against a wall of rain-soaked brick. A dark stain spread across his white button-down shirt and obnoxiously green sport coat: blood, from a knife wound. Athena could see the man's soul slipping away, and that "see" is meant literally, and the "slipping away" meant standing up from his corpse and then dancing the Charleston out of the alley.

Athena figured there must be some reason for that. Why the Charleston, specifically? But the vision seemed more focused on the corpse. As the spirit danced out of view, energy from the thingamajig enveloped the corpse. It twitched, wobbled, and opened its eyes anew. Then it moaned for grains.

A different strand crossed in front of the first. Silver light glinted again, and suddenly she saw a ransacked English pub. Amid a sea of spilled beer and high-gluten pub grub, the undead feasted on the living: their stomachs, their necks, their brains. While they gorged, faint flecks of energy pumped their way out along the strand to the thingamajig. As the vision retreated again into a point of light at the end of the strand, Athena realized the energy was similar to the energy that flowed from the thingamajig to the violet-eyed figure.

"You are creating the zombies," said Athena.

"Maybe," said the voice.

"And profiting from them somehow." She approached the thingamajig, hand on her sword. If she severed the strands, would that halt the zombies' creation?

Before she got even two steps, the platform trembled beneath her feet. Cracks fractured a section of obsidian between her and the thingamajig. The section turned to gravel as two grasping hands thrust out of it. Two arms followed—attached to the hands, as arms are wont to be. With preternatural speed, a figure hauled itself out of the gravel and stood before her.

The figure—Athena could not yet decide if it was creature or person—was not quite like anything she had ever seen. Though it resembled a zombie (its skin was gray and sunken, any remaining strands of hair lacked shine or body, and it stank like warmed-over maggot-puke), it was thinner than most. The desiccated skin stretched over its bones was fully intact rather than rotted or peeled away in places like a usual zombie. Its skull bore greater resemblance to a wolf's than a human's. Empty eye sockets glowed a pale yellow, which Athena had yet to encounter among the zombie population. The phrase "half zombie, half demon" came to mind, but that would be silly, Athena told herself. Demons had not existed since the year 485 A.D., and their eyes had never glowed yellow. (Red, orange, or saffron, maybe. But never yellow.)

The figure wore no clothing, apparently featuring neither shame nor genitalia. Yet around its neck hung a pendant of a crescent moon with fangs, like an ill-sculpted letter C. The pendant struck a familiar chord that Athena could not place.

"Profiting?" the figure asked in a vaguely masculine rasp. "What makes you say that?" he said.

"Oh, practically everything I've seen up to this point."

"What have you seen?" he asked.

Arachne was right: the answer-with-a-question thing *was* annoying.

"I will not play these games. I come here in the name of Zeus the Almighty! I demand to know who you are, where you came from, and why you are creating the zombies!" Probably such demands wouldn't work, but she still had to try. Procedure and all that.

"Where do you think we came—"

A deep, feminine voice spoke over him. "It is right to create zombies. Are they not better?" The shadowed, purple-eyed figure shifted slightly. The new voice had definitely come from her.

"Mistress!" The yellow-eyed creature turned to face the speaker. Athena took the opportunity to sidestep a few meters away as he protested to his apparent mistress, "I am attempting to cultivate an aura of mystery!"

"Pay no attention to Momo," the mistress told Athena.

Athena sidestepped a little more. "As you like."

"I like zombies . . . " said the mistress.

"I surmised that." Athena circled around to the side of the object so she could see the mistress unobstructed. Shadows continued to cloak her. "Who are you, Mistress? Please tell me your name."

The mistress's eyes grew brighter. "Momo?" she deferred.

Momo scowled at the further attempts to sabotage his efforts at mystery. "She is a goddess," he muttered, perhaps secretively.

"Momo," the mistress admonished.

"A *new* goddess," he added.

"Momo!" the mistress urged.

Momo sighed. "Very well." He crossed his arms and said plainly, "She is the goddess Undeath, first of her name, Queen of the Obsidian Realm, Breaker of Brains, and Mother of Zombies. There, now you know. Are you *happy*?"

"Zombies make me happy," Undeath answered.

Momo pointed to Athena. "I was talking to Athena."

"Athena is not a zombie," Undeath pouted.

Wait, Athena thought. *Pouted?*

"I prefer it that way," Athena assured Undeath, whose silhouette had begun to descend the slope toward her. Energy from the thingamajig continued to stream into Undeath's eyes, which glowed brighter.

"No, you don't," the goddess intoned. "You will be grateful. Undead is better."

"Better?" Athena eyed the nearest of the thingamajig's strands. They were now reaching toward her. "Have you looked upon the world? It is a wreck! Millions dead! Civilization would have collapsed without the gods' aid! And now the mortals fear pasta! *Pasta!*"

"Apple butter. And toast." said Undeath, as if that explained everything. At a momentary loss, Athena caught Momo's eye. He shrugged.

"Lucidity pays Goddess Undeath only infrequent visits," Momo explained. "Sometimes she goes days without saying a word. Other times it's just cosmic nonsense and David Lynch trivia. But for each of her children who feast, her strength grows, and with it, bite by bite, her mind becomes clearer."

Two thingamajig strands whipped out at Athena's head. She batted them away with her buckler. "I cannot help but point out that you just missed a major opportunity to cultivate some mystery there, Momo."

The back of Momo's throat began to glow, matching the pale-yellow lights in his eye sockets. "Obfuscation no longer serves a purpose. The mistress sealed your fate when she made me tell you her name. The knowledge you now hold, you shall not be allowed to leave with."

"So we've moved on to threats, have we?" Athena drew her sword. *We are now at DEFCON 3.* The question of just where this Undeath had come from would have to wait.

Momo grinned. "More than threats. Now you will continue to follow in Alecto's footsteps!"

"It is better," Undeath assured her, "for all."

Before Athena could answer, Momo screamed; it was a gargling, rasping sound, like a faulty carburetor makes all the time except when you try to show it to a mechanic. Energy shot from his eyes and mouth. It crackled through the air, barely missing Athena as she rolled to one side.

Momo snarled at the miss and took a breath, seeming to draw power for another shot. He was at least thirty strides away. No sense bringing a knife to a gun fight. *We are now at DEFCON 2.* Athena sheathed the sword, drew her Glock and fired: four shots, one for each eye, two for his mouth.

Only one bullet hit, and barely. It tore through the outside of his eye socket. The right side of Momo's head burst apart in a shower of bone and fiendish energy. Though he howled in pain, it was a glancing blow at best. In less than a heartbeat's time, his skull began to reform.

"No guns," said Undeath. The Glock tore itself from Athena's hand, flew beyond the edge of the platform, and dropped into the fog.

"You can't just say 'No guns!'" Athena burst. "Do you want the NRA on your case? That was my best Glock!"

Deprived of the weapon, Athena backpedaled into a ready stance, tactically assessing: Attack Undeath, a goddess in her own element?

That was like invading Russia in winter. Attack Momo, now charging up for another energy blast? If she could get close enough, she might slice his head off, but she'd be charging him over open ground with no cover. Even if she ended him, she would still have to deal with Undeath; that took her back to Russia again. Return to her original plan of slicing the strands off the thingamajig, hopefully in a single blow? She would still be a target for Momo, but harder to hit running for the object rather than straight for him.

Yes, that plan was best. She would make that phase one: sever the strands and hope it crippled the zombie-making. Phase two? Run like hell. She drew her sword anew and rushed the thingamajig. She would have to leap up and try to gain a foothold on the thingamajig's side in order to get high enough to strike at the strands.

Momo screamed again, sending another volley of energy at her. Now there was no time to dodge. Athena raised her buckler to block it instead, but it wasn't enough. The buckler shattered. An icy burning shot through her forearm, tearing an undignified cry of pain from Athena's lips. Her boots pounded on obsidian even so. Athena neared striking distance and leaped. Her cry of pain turned into one of determination! Her left foot planted against the thingamajig's side, pushing her higher. She raised her sword—

"No," said Undeath again.

The air itself slapped Athena away. She crashed to the ground, splayed on her back across the obsidian, farther from the thingamajig than when she'd started. The slap had knocked the breath out of her. Were she mortal, it would have knocked the life out of her as well. As it was, her head was ringing, her face was bleeding, and she half expected to see little cartoon zombie-birds orbiting her skull. Her shield arm was now almost completely numb. Athena thanked the Fates that she'd managed to hold onto her sword.

Well, she didn't really thank them. The Fates weren't there. But she resolved to send them a kindly note.

While Athena was resolving to thank the Fates, she thrust her shield arm into her pocket, numbly took tight hold of Megaera's silver ball, and then scrambled to her feet. Also while she was resolving to do that, Momo had apparently resolved to advance. The thingamajig strands had resolved to reach for her again—assuming they were capable of such decisions, and for now let us assume that they were—and Undeath had resolved to mystically rip the sword from Athena's grip. It, too, tumbled off of the platform behind her and into the void.

A second motion of Undeath's hand stripped the silver ball and sent it after the sword.

"Son of a blitz!" This kind of garbage would never happen if she were divine! Yet now she was wounded, nearly unarmed, and brutally aware that, immortal or not, she was moments away from meeting the same fate as Alecto. The situation called for DEFCON 1, divine-on-divine combat. Except, with Athena not currently divine . . .

We are now at DEFCON Screw This.

Athena reviewed her new tactical options; she liked none. She estimated her chances of retaining perspicacity if she got Alecto-ed in her current un-divine state: also none. She wondered how many times anyone had used "Alecto" as a verb, and figured that was none, as well. (In reality, it was six-hundred eighty-two in the past week alone. Megaera particularly enjoyed the term.)

And so, steeling herself, Athena jumped to the left, stepped to the right, and then back-flipped off of the platform and into the void.

A moment later, void-blinded and trying to bring her knees in tight, she got clocked in the head by a blast of energy from above, saw visions of a red-curtained room with a black and white zigzag floor, and then blacked out.

CHAPTER SIXTEEN

"Following his resurrection, Zeus did not immediately reassemble the Dodekatheon, such as we call our twelve-member council. Zeus had exiled or de-powered many of the previous members, so it took time to vet those who remained and evaluate replacements. That was fine with me. Jerry's portfolio alone changed so much during those first couple of months. We needed to restructure, to allow time for the dust to settle. I do wish Zeus had let me proofread the paperwork for the new members, but what's done is done."
— After the Sun Sets: A Retrospective Blog by Apollo

"Oh, you is good question-asker! Yes, I am very much liking takings over for Hecate as god of secrets! God of secrets-being is perfectly suited to Jerry; I once was being guardian-tree, and trees are good secret-keepers. Trees hearings all around them, but sayings nothing at all! Also, trees made of wood, but that knot relevant. 'Knot relevant!' That tree joke!"
— Jerry, replacement god of secrets (to an empty press room, date unknown)

"WE MUST DETERMINE what the Cosmics require, before they learn Hecate is dead," said Zeus, addressing the Dodekatheon.

"Must we?" asked Eris. Her image shimmered in her council seat, projected from where she'd been stationed in the planet's defense. "You're the one who adopted her. You're the one they'll be mad at. Surely the almighty Zeus can handle a few irritated—what did you call them? Cosmics?"

Zeus glowered momentarily. "Even if they do only blame me, they will take their fury out on the entire Earth. I will not permit the mortals to suffer further!"

"Even so—"

"Oh, speak not your fool opinions, Eris!" It was Poseidon, his own projected image chiming in. He was underwater, and so his hair seemed to float in mid-air like some fabulous shampoo commercial. "That you have a place on this council at all is nothing more than a typo!"

"The paper said what it said!" Eris shot. She punctuated it with a scowl at Eros, with whose projection hers currently jockeyed in the same seat. Zeus had originally intended *Eros*, god of love and son of Aphrodite, to fill the council seat that Aphrodite's exile left vacant. A suspicious auto-correct mistake in the official appointment documents had named Eris instead, and no one caught the error until she showed up for the first meeting. Being the antithesis of grace, Eris refused to relinquish the seat, and so Eros was forced to share it until the term was up.

Eris leaned sideways to address Poseidon around Eros's head. "You're just worried you'll get extra blame because Hecate died when you were king."

"I am concerned," Poseidon snarled, "because what my brother says is true. Now be silent!"

Eris pounded a fist against her chest. "Hey, goddess of strife, here! I am merely doing my job! And stop kissing Zeus's ass, Poseidon; you already got your divinity back."

Lightning flashed across the ceiling of the Dodekatheon chamber. It was Zeus's way of commanding attention, and so this narrative will postpone explaining the complicated way in which Poseidon regained his divinity, and go straight back to Zeus:

"Whatever the Cosmics want, they believe it is on Earth. It is undoubtedly something ghastly and alien, with 'truths that would drive mortals insane,' or weird angles that cause, say, rickets or something. That is how they are."

Artemis leaned forward. "If Hecate knew about this missing thing, it is almost assuredly something clandestine. Hidden away, perhaps. Or containing secrets itself. Or both?"

"Exactly," said Zeus. "Like that Necro . . . Necronomo-whatsit. Or something similar."

"The *Necronomicon*?" asked Calliope, now sitting on the council to represent the Muses. "The dread grimoire of the mad Abdul

Alhazred, thought to be bound in human skin and to cause violent headaches if even the ISBN is spoken aloud?"

"Yes, that thing. Thank you," said Zeus. "Does that actually exist?"

"It does now," said Apollo.

"So." Zeus nodded definitively. "Something like this *Necronomicon*. Maybe it is even that specific text that—"

"Oh!" cried Demeter. "I have that! Shall I bring it here?"

Zeus blinked.

So did the rest of the Dodekatheon.

"You . . . have the *Necronomicon*?" asked Zeus.

"Yes, of course! A peculiar little book. Such intricate carvings on the cover. Strange people sitting in chairs. Hecate left it in my quarters a couple of decades ago when we got together to talk Eleusinian Mysteries over a bowl of shredded wheat. I kept meaning to give it back to her, and then she had to go away, the poor dear." Demeter smiled airily and glanced about the now silent chamber. "Shall I go get it?"

"Ah, well, yes. That would be an excellent idea, Sister," Zeus answered.

"All right then, dear." She glanced about the chamber as precious moments slid by. "Would now be a good time?"

"Yes!"

"Because I would not wish to cause a disruption in the Dodekatheon by getting up during—"

"Go retrieve it!" Zeus boomed. "I command it!"

Demeter screwed up her face and huffed at Zeus. "Well. You do not have to holler, Brother." She rose from her seat, descended from the dais upon which it sat, and made for the chamber doorway. "I shall be back, I suppose."

Zeus watched her go. Fates only knew how Demeter had slipped into a grand-matronly, almost senile role in just the last couple of centuries. Perhaps it was all that time spent baking? Too much sampling of certain mind-altering crops? Or had millennia spent fretting over Persephone's marriage to Hades finally snapped Demeter's mind?

His train of thought jumped the tracks at Persephone's name.

"Iris!" he called. "I await Persephone's report!"

This time he only had to wait five seconds before Iris appeared in the center of the chamber in a multicolored light-shower. A bit of glitter fell from her helmet, which Hestia sent some Olympian cleaning-squirrels to remove before Zeus could ask.

Iris bowed to Zeus. "As you bade, I have spoken to the Queen of the Underworld to ask if she can detect any trace of Hecate's spiritual essence." Here, Iris's gentle features morphed into Persephone's more severe visage, complete with the latter's triple-pierced ears and the tiny beauty mark above her lip. It was a nice touch that Iris always added—though Zeus had forbidden her from doing it with his own visage. Speaking with Persephone's voice, Iris continued.

"You may tell Lord Zeus I have found no sign of her in the Underworld. But she was killed with the Unmaking Nexus just as he was, and as neither Hades nor I knew what limbo, if any, Zeus resided in after his death, so would it be with Hecate." Iris-as-Persephone heaved a sigh. "I suppose now he wishes me to embark on some pain-in-my-ass wild goose chase for what's left of *her* down here, too? As if I didn't have enough on my fecking plate with the gods-damned zombie problem? Don't tell him I said that, obviously."

Iris morphed back to herself with a fey grin that made Eris cackle.

Zeus scowled, though less at Persephone's words than the reminder of his death. To this day, he recalled nothing between his murder and being returned to life. From his perspective, he had gone from immortal life, to a moment of oblivion, to immortal life again. He must have gone somewhere during that oblivion in order to have come back from it, surely? Somewhere Hecate might be at this very moment?

Yet he had known before his murder that someone would target him with the Unmaking Nexus, the god-killing weapon he himself had commissioned from The Fates during the first Titan War. He had therefore made the preparations necessary to cheat death and return. He had—(Well, look: It's all there in the first book in this series. If you need more of a refresher, you can always go back and re-read that. Maybe get copies for your fifty closest friends while you're at it.)

Hecate's case was different; the Nexus had killed her in the midst of a battle, and quite by accident. Fates only knew if anything remained of her at all.

Zeus blinked. "Fates only knew" wasn't just an Olympian colloquialism in this case, was it?

"Iris," Zeus began just before Jerry, his eyes and leaves bright, appeared at the chamber entrance. "Iris, I will soon have another task for you." He ushered her to one side with a wave of his hand. She obeyed, flying up to one of the observation balconies, with the cleaning-squirrels following.

"Jerry!" said Zeus. "Report."

The walking, talking, divine oak tree, whose divine portfolio now included being the god of secrets in Hecate's stead, took his place atop the rock he preferred in place of a council chair. In his lower branches, he clutched a shiny black laptop marked with a green H. "I am findings many things, Lord Zeus! I am always be learning new secrets whenever I am lookings in Hecate's magical folding typey-board! Do you know what clown makeup is really beings made of? I am knowings, now! But I cannot be telling you, as I am being god of secrets!"

"Jerry," Zeus tried.

"Though if you be askings nicely, I suppose I can be telling kings of gods. I have to be checkings on that. I ams new at this!"

"Jerry! Tell me what you have found that Cyot'hgha and the others might be looking for."

"Is you asking nicely?"

Zeus stifled a retort. He liked Jerry, Zeus reminded himself. He really did. "I am your king and creator, and I am commanding you to tell me, Jerry."

"O! That is being good, too!" Jerry pulled the laptop up to his face. "I am findings three possible secret-y things that might-can have Cosmical connections. I can be lookings to find more, but for nows . . . "

Zeus waited.

"The *Necronomicon*," listed Jerry.

"Aha!" said Zeus. He and Artemis exchanged satisfied nods. "What else?"

"R'lyeh, the sunkening-ed . . . " Here Jerry scrutinized the screen before continuing. ". . . 'nightmare-corpse city.' Is that not being strange title?"

Poseidon shook his head. "It cannot be R'lyeh. That city lurks beneath my oceans. I know precisely where, and I have oft searched its structures. There is nothing hidden there."

"Nothing?" Hephaestus's image asked. "I mean no disrespect, Uncle, but can you be so certain?"

"Indeed," said Zeus. "Can you?"

Poseidon tapped the end of his trident on the floor, his habit when annoyed, or when he saw tiny ants he wished to smash. "There is little there, except for this one fellow. Mostly he just sleeps, rising only occasionally to devour a ship or file the paperwork to renew his lease. But I will go to R'lyeh and make certain."

"Do so," Zeus ordered. He turned back to Jerry.

"The last thing is being the Querulous Trapezohedron," Jerry finished.

"And where is that?" asked Zeus.

"I am not being knowings."

Eris scoffed. "Come now Jerry, god of secrets! It is your job to know!"

"And is you being goddess of hearing things badly, Eris? I said I ams new at this!"

Zeus spoke before Eris could manage a reply. "What *is* the Querulous Trapezohedron?"

"Is like rock over there!"

Jerry pointed to a shining gemstone dangling from Calliope's necklace. Calliope blinked in surprise and held it up: a ruby the size of a walnut cut into a peculiar diamond shape. "This rock? *This* is the Querulous Trapezohedron?" Calliope asked.

"No!" Jerry laughed. "Is *like* that rock. How is you being Muse and not knowings what 'like' is meaning? Querulous Trapezohedron just *lookings* like that. At least, accordings to Hecate-notes. Is what 'trapezohedron' means."

"And 'querulous?'" Zeus asked. Jerry appeared at a loss.

"'Complaining in a petulant or whining manner,'" Calliope told Zeus.

Zeus smirked. "Oh, in that case, Hera should know precisely where it is!" Zeus couldn't help but take the dig at his ex-wife, even as a part of him wished he'd resisted.

All eyes turned to Hera. Unlike the other members of the Dodekatheon attending virtually, her image was just a two-dimensional video of her face. Only gods could project a full 3D image, and while Zeus had allowed his ex-wife to stay on the council, he had not yet granted her the rank of goddess.

That Zeus had allowed her to remain on the council at all, when he had yet to restore her divinity, could be taken either as honor or insult. Zeus had both meant it as honor, and known she would take it as insult, which was exactly the kind of pig-tail-pulling, actual-communication-avoidance that their relationship had always thrived upon.

Not that they had much of a relationship anymore. Zeus had secretly promised to return Poseidon's divinity if the sea god ended the marriage with Hera that he'd formed after Zeus's murder. Zeus had assumed Hera would seek to pair back with him after that. That had not been the case.

"If I am to be stripped of my divinity," she had said, "removed from my post as goddess of marriage, and dumped upon divorce's doorstep like so many unwanted pomegranates, then I may as well see what the single life is all about."

It had been a slap in the face of Zeus's expectations, and he was certain she'd meant it that way. Yet why should *she* want to hurt *him*? She was the one who'd remarried within a day after his death! She had never sought justice for his killing, and she had sided against him when he returned! Should not he be the one angry at her? Should not *she* be begging *him* to take her back?

At least she was no longer married to Poseidon, and Poseidon had given more than just the divorce to get his divinity back. But back in the present, all eyes were still on Hera, who was patiently waiting for her chance to respond to Zeus's dig about her knowing the precise location of the Querulous Trapezohedron. This narrative will therefore postpone explaining the *rest* of how Poseidon regained his divinity, and go straight back to Hera.

On her screen, from where she reclined on the deck of an ocean cruise liner, Hera stared daggers — an impressive feat, as she was also wearing sunglasses. "I can only say that this Querulous

Trapezohedron cannot be hidden in a young woman's bedchamber, Lord Zeus, or you would surely already know about it. I viewed your meeting with the Cosmics. This Cyot'hgha had her hands all over you."

"There was a minimum of touching!" Zeus argued.

"Oh, yes. I meant to say: only in those moments in which she was whispering in your ear."

"I would have thought you'd have ceased caring about such things, Hera."

"Oh, I cared more thousands of years ago, when I last asked you about her," Hera said, and leaned back in her deck chair. "I just thought it curious."

"Yes, that *is* curious," Eris added. "Thousands of years ago? Is there something you'd care to share with the rest of us, either of you?"

Zeus steeled himself. "Eris, this crisis is neither the time nor the place. And if you continue to rely on your title as goddess of strife to justify insubordination on this council, I will hurl you from Olympus faster than you can sneer."

Eris's image flickered as she rolled her eyes. "I withdraw the question, Lord Zeus. Even if I'm not currently on Olympus to be hurled from it."

Zeus ignored her, which he should have done sooner. "So, it is a trapezohedron-shaped gemstone, which is somehow petulant and whining, and sitting in some unknown location." He turned back to Jerry. "Do we at least know what it *does*?"

"Is being made for talkings to someone. Or somethings. I am not knowings more than that yet. But I can be checkings!"

"Grand," muttered Hera.

"I only just am learnings about it five minutes ago!"

"Here it is!" The voice was Demeter's, heralding her return. She carried a white leather-bound tome. Two straps with thick black locks secured its cover, and disturbing stains spattered the edges of its ancient pages. Demeter made a beeline to Zeus and proudly thrust it into his godly hands.

The tome weighed more than Zeus expected. The tome's power thrummed faintly against his fingertips. He studied the cover, which felt more like faux-leather than human skin. Perhaps the legends were wrong? But he did not study the material long before the etchings across its surface drew his attention instead: Figures, both humanoid and otherwise, sat upon strangely-shaped chairs. They sat upon seats. They sat upon thrones. They sat upon stools. They sat upon benches. Zeus was struck by a powerful feeling of comfort, and of productivity.

It was then that he finally saw the etched script across the bottom of the front cover. He turned the tome over to examine the back.

"Demeter?" Zeus asked.

"Yes, Brother?"

"You are *certain* that this is the book Hecate left?" Zeus asked.

"Of course, Brother! This is the *Necronomicon!*" Demeter beamed.

Zeus sighed and lifted the tome, reading from the back cover for all to hear: "Written within lie dread secrets of forbidden comfort and terrible efficiency, penned in forgotten script from knowledge taken through dark rituals of ergonomic trepidity. Open not this grimoire, lest your mind wrestle with dread devices designed to facilitate more shuddersomely comfortable—" Zeus looked up from the tome, his eyes flashing. "This is the *ERGONOMICON!*" he shouted, and tossed it to the floor at Demeter's feet.

"Oh!" Demeter cried with delight. "How mysterious!"

Zeus settled back into his throne. He closed his eyes and tried to massage away a blooming headache. "Does anyone know where the actual *Necronomicon* might be?"

". . . The Library of Xanadu?" Apollo guessed.

"R'lyeh City Comic Con?" Calliope tried.

"The back room of some antique store in Swindon?" Eris offered dryly.

"Fah! Are we not gods?" Zeus demanded. "Why do none of us know these things?"

"Oh!" One of Jerry's branches shot straight up like a raised hand. "Because it is being a secret!" he answered proudly. "So, maybe I can be finding out."

"That was a rhetorical question, Jerry," said Zeus, "but yes, do so. In the meantime—"

Baskin's image flashed into being above his previously empty seat. Behind him loomed the vastness of space and the moon in the distance. *"Lord Zeus! A thousand apologies for this interruption! I will submit myself for punitive smiting when appropriate! But the situation with the Cosmics has escalated!"*

Baskin stepped aside to show the scene on the front lines with the Cosmics. Their patience had failed. C'oggn-yon had returned. ''''''''Q was madly vibrating with waves of energy. And Cyot'hgha had Urania wrapped in a pair of tentacles extending from beneath her skirt while Thalia apparently tried to distract her by juggling penguins.

"Permission to engage?" Baskin hollered.

Zeus pointed at Baskin. "Free Urania, but do no more until I arrive!" He turned to the others. "Jerry: find out where those items are! Those of you elsewhere: remain at your posts! The rest of you here: come with me!"

"I would be happy to help," said Hera, "if only fate had not robbed me of the divinity to do so."

"Not the time, Hera!" Though her mention of fate jogged his memory. "Iris, to me!" he called. "Time to discuss that other task I mentioned."

Thankfully, the cleaning-squirrels remained on duty.

CHAPTER SEVENTEEN

"Gasconade (verb) [găs'kə-nād']: to boast, brag, or bluster."
— *"Calliope's Word You'll Definitely Use of the Day" calendar*

IRIS STREAKED ACROSS the central Canadian sky, a meteor whose light burned a shining rainbow path behind her like a public service announcement graphic. Riding the exhilaration of Hermes's winged attire, she had dived from Olympus at Zeus's bidding and reached a certain intersection in the town of Moose Jaw, Saskatchewan within a few hot seconds. Pulling back on the astral throttle at the last second, she skidded to a stop above the seldom-noticed second story of a convenience store and alighted, like a flipped lawn dart, atop a modest air conditioning exhaust vent.

At least, that's what it looked like to the common observer. It was, actually, quite a spectacular air conditioning vent: in addition to providing an efficient outflow of air, it was also a vortex leading both inside the building and through multiple esoteric dimensions to the Room in which the Fates currently lived, worked, and binge-watched television programs in their spare time. (The Fates' spare time was often greater than one might expect for beings of such import—a benefit of dwelling in a section of reality that lay sprawled across the usual flow of space-time like a cat on a keyboard.)

One needed be a goddess to see the vent for what it was. One also needed to be a goddess to slither through its opening, plunge into its depths, and navigate the vortex without having one's mind stripped from one's body—or, at the very least, without arriving with one's underwear on top of one's outer-garments, or on top of someone else's outer-garments, which can be pesky to explain.

Fortunately, being a goddess, Iris's only worry was disappointing

Zeus should she fail in her mission. She had visited the Fates before, but never had Zeus sent her to them in his stead. As far as she knew, Zeus had never even sent Hermes to see them on his behalf, preferring to do such errands personally. Iris hoped she had impressed him enough in her expanded role to earn more trust than Hermes. Surely Cosmics harassing the planet and distracting Zeus had nothing to do with it, right?

Then again, Iris saw no reason to believe the two causes were mutually exclusive. She knew her job, the old and the new. Plus, she didn't routinely sneak a "Steal fire from me!" sign onto Zeus's back like Hermes used to. That sign had only worked once, of course. Poor Prometheus. Such a boob.

Iris transitioned through the end of the vortex to appear in the Fates' Room. Its polished marble floor hovered just above her head. Two stories beneath her dangling, winged-sandaled feet lay the Room's ceiling, on which the continent of Antarctica was painted in exquisite detail. Iris's first instinct was to assume she was floating upside-down. But Clotho, Lachesis, and Atropos sat at tables on different walls, each with their own personal "floor" being the wall surface itself. Iris grinned. The Room's ever-changing orientation and form always fascinated her, despite her divine stature. It was different every time she visited (admittedly, that was not often—the sacred Room was not to be entered willy-nilly). Last time, the ceiling painting had been the coastline of Norway.

The Fates had yet to acknowledge her presence. Rather than play favorites and orient to any of them in particular, Iris remained inverted and let herself drift "down" toward the ceiling. She faced the wall that supported Lachesis, with Clotho to her left, and Atropos to her right.

"Greetings, Iris. Er, to this place," said a voice behind her. It was Poppy, the Fates' intern. They had created her position to help deal with modern life-expectancies and medical resuscitations. Iris knew neither the Fates' recruitment methods nor Poppy's precise divine nature and parentage, however. She would have to ask Jerry about it, once he got up to speed on his secrets.

"Hello, Poppy." Iris faced her and then bowed in mid-air. She tried to add some multicolored flair to it, but something about the

Room muted the effect. More disappointing: her glitter had nearly dried up entirely. "I bring greetings from Lord Zeus, and questions. Also from Lord Zeus."

Poppy gave a little wave that belied her vaunted tone: "Questions of a vital depth, worthy of the attention of These Who Know and Sew?"

"I—"

"These Who Calibrate and Cogitate?" Poppy continued, her tone more vaunted.

"Calibrate? As in 'measure,' I assume—"

"These Who Rend and Comprehend?" Poppy declared finally, her tone so vaunted that she actually passed gasconaded.

Poppy seemed to be finished, but Iris waited another moment just to be certain before answering.

"Of a *most* vital depth, and surely worthy." Iris leaned closer and whispered, "The most vital I've dealt with in a long while, actually. So any help you can give me would be fantastic."

Sadness tinged Poppy's smile. "The Three are exceptionally engaged today," she said. "The undead hordes live, and re-die, and so each must have a fate, as empty as such things are."

Iris glanced at the threads currently spilled across Lachesis's table for measuring. Rather than the silvery threads of mortals, these were dark and—if Iris's divine sense of smell did not betray her—made of black licorice.

She shuddered.

"I only need the tiniest parcel of their time," Iris said.

"What did you think of my greeting just now?" Poppy asked. "If you don't mind the question. I so rarely get the opportunity to practice my gravitas. Did it make you feel as if you had entered a vaunted realm of measureless mystery?"

"Oh, sure. Truly. Vaunted." Iris stepped closer. "Please, Poppy. My business is most urgent. And, if you will pardon my repeating this: it is on Lord Zeus's behalf."

Poppy sighed. "This is the abode of the Fates. Zeus's name carries little weight here," she said, adding, "er, you will find. The Three currently limit their consultation sessions to just one for every seven days' passage, and shall continue to do so . . . until a point shrouded within the mists of hereafter!" Poppy's arms, which had risen in what Iris guessed to be a conjuration of gravitas, dropped slightly. "Basically, until further notice," she whispered. "I'm not really sure how long, and I wouldn't be allowed to tell you even if I knew."

"Seven days' passage? Fantastic." Iris didn't bother to hide her sarcasm. "And how is that measured in such a place where time is . . . "

"Transcendental?" suggested Poppy. "Empyreal? I have a dictionary if you'd like to look that one up."

"I was going to say screwy, but sure, one of those. So, how?"

"I am forbidden to say," said Poppy.

"Yes, but do you *know*?"

"I am forbidden to say that, too."

Deciding on a different tactic, Iris tried a sympathetic sigh. "I see we both suffer the shared frustration of being a mouthpiece to greater powers." She took Poppy's hand with practiced grace and gave what she hoped was an empathetic squeeze. "It can be very restrictive, can't it?"

"But a great honor as well."

"Oh, true. Very great. Of course, I'm sure your own ability to provide insights and answers to the questions I bring from Lord Zeus is not as restricted as the Three's." Apollo had once told Iris how helpful Poppy had been in his quest to restore Zeus. The intern was not without her own knowledge.

Poppy squeezed Iris's hand back. "Only if I want to get fired. And I do not."

"Are you sure? Getting fired might be fun. Cannot be sure unless you try it!" She offered her best grin.

"One consultation session per seven days' passage, Iris."

Iris let go. "So I cannot ask the Three questions—Lord Zeus's questions!—nor can I consult with you, and you cannot tell me when seven days' will have passed?"

"Oh, I can tell—ah, I may reveal to you such knowledge," Poppy said. "I am but forbidden to reveal our *means* of measuring time here."

"So then . . . ?"

Poppy beamed. "Fortune smiles upon you, Iris. Seven days will have passed since their last consultation in, oh, about five minutes."

Iris put her hands on her hips. "You enjoyed that, didn't you?"

"If you have sought-after knowledge, never disdain the opportunity to lord it over those who do the seeking. Lachesis taught me that. Would you like some flavored water while you wait? Or perhaps a rubber chicken?"

Iris was about to answer when an aethereal trembling caught her ears. She glanced about in an effort to pinpoint its source. "Do you hear that?"

"Oh, I hear many things."

Iris sighed. "No, I mean—"

That was as far as Iris got before the sword burst through the aether and buried itself in her chest. She gasped, trying to draw breath through a punctured lung.

Poppy glanced at it. "In another four minutes I can tell you whose sword that is."

Falling . . .

Floating . . .

Flipping . . .

Other *F*-words . . .

The perception of each gradually returned to Athena's consciousness like an anesthetized tortoise. Yet there was no sight, no sound, nothing there but a constantly changing sense of orientation, velocity, and ill-being.

And then the sky formed around her, swallowed her up, and spat her out through a rip in the aether. She arrived somewhere else, slammed sideways into someone else, and, her fall nicely broken, then found herself in a heap on the floor with that same someone else. Something metal pressed into the small of her back. She fumbled around and grabbed it. Megaera's silver ball? Athena tucked it away as rainbows and thread swam before her eyes.

A voice was saying something, but Athena couldn't make it out. Her head continued to swim.

"Wha?" Athena managed, which was not at all as eloquent aloud as it had sounded in her head. Where was she? For that matter, where had she come from? She'd been in the Asphodel Meadows, and then . . . ?

She could not recall. She could not even get her bearings. Her senses of *up*, *down*, and *adjacent-to* were playing musical chairs within her inner ear.

"I said, 'Welcome, Athena, to this place,'" repeated the being whom Athena suddenly recognized as Poppy.

"And I said 'Ouch,'" added a voice beside—beneath?—Athena.

Poppy offered Athena a hand up, which she accepted gratefully. Her legs were wobbling in a most unsettling way. She caught a glimpse of Atropos, severing dark threads and watching Athena with glassy, shark-black eyes from where she sat on the ceiling. A wave of vertigo blasted through Athena, and, wisdom finding her again, she slammed her eyes shut. She was in the Fates' Room *without* her former divine power. If she were not careful, this place could drive her to madness—or at least take her there on the handlebars of its bike.

"Athena," said the voice again. "Might this be your sword? Buried in my chest?"

"Iris?" Athena tried. "What are you doing here?"

"Trying to get your sword out of my chest. I would have thought I'd have loved getting stabbed out of the blue but, you know, I find it stings a bit. What are *you* doing here?"

"I—" Athena stopped. What *was* she doing here? She had been somewhere else, hadn't she? Her memory felt bent. She could recall her suspicions about Hades, the Asphodel Meadows, and Arachne, and then . . . what? Purple? Athena risked opening her eyes again. Another wave of vertigo staggered her, and her knees buckled.

Speaking of which, where was her buckler?

Poppy was fast enough to catch her. "Careful. You have tumbled long through the aether to arrive here. That's not the easiest way to travel. Keep your eyes shut. Can I get you some flavored water? Or perhaps a bolo tie?"

"Hello?" Iris asked. "How about offering to help me get this sword out of my chest?"

"Swords are not within my realm of expertise," said Poppy. "Atropos will not even let me clean her shears yet."

The Fates, thought Athena. She had been thinking about the Fates at some point before, hadn't she? Was that how she'd gotten here from . . . wherever? Athena's eyes flicked open as she realized the opportunity she had literally fallen into, then closed again as the Room oppressed her senses.

"Poppy," Athena managed, "I would like to ask the Fates some questions, please."

"Oh, you'll have to take a number," said Iris. "I was here first."

"The Fates shall only grant one consultation for every seven days' passage," Poppy warned them.

"Iris, this is important," Athena urged. "It's about the zombies. Maybe about Hades. I think." She was missing something, though, wasn't she? She wracked her brain, unable to put her finger on it.

"My greatest apologies, I'm sure, Athena, but I come here on Lord Zeus's orders."

Zeus's orders? "But aren't you more focused on that sword in your chest?" Athena tried.

"I shall live."

"But you did say it was itchy," said Poppy.

"Iris, please," Athena went on. "I am close to finding the cause of the zombie problem, or if not the cause, then at least a way to fix it. Which might require Hades's help." Though she still considered returning Hades from exile to be a last resort, she hoped mentioning him might impress upon Iris just how much she needed guidance.

"The Fates can surely point me in the right direction," she continued. "The fact that I find myself in their abode, a place I should not even have been able to reach in my current state . . . I must be meant to be here! One might even say fated to be here!"

"Oh, don't say 'fated,' in the Room," warned Poppy. "Too on the nose."

Iris made what Athena assumed was a grunt of effort while trying to dislodge her sword. It did not sound successful. "And yet it seems you were not 'meant' to arrive here before I did. Also, *Lord Zeus's orders*. I am sorry, Athena, but you'll just have to wait. Greater problems than the zombies are occurring now."

Greater than the zombies? Iris was not given to exaggeration. Perhaps it would be wise to surrender this chance with the Fates and let Iris have the consultation. Athena would just have to wait to solve the zombie issue, and remain a non-goddess a little while longer.

Patience, Athena resolved. For the greater good. Right?

Then again, being patient was far easier with the divine power to back it up. "Let me ask first and I shall help you get that sword out of your chest," Athena tried.

"I can get it out myself! It's just at a bad angle. I like it where it is!"

The air gave an abrupt "pop" that was more felt than heard. "Oh!" said Poppy. "Four minutes just goes by like that, doesn't it?"

"Two have entered," began Clotho.

"One will be answered," continued Lachesis.

"Both will leave," finished Atropos. "And the intern will clean up any glitter."

Poppy heaved a sigh.

Athena wasted no time. "Ladies of Fate, it is good to be in your presence again. I come before you, diminished and humbled, so I might seek your wisdom once more." Here Athena risked opening her eyes, hoping the diplomatic benefit of respectful eye contact would outweigh the risk of respectfully throwing up all over their polished marble floors.

"I bid you greetings as well," said Iris, "and greetings from Zeus, on whose—"

Atropos cut her off. "We were focused on our work," she said.

"But not deaf," added Lachesis.

"Due to Hades's absent ability to get his realm in order, we *are* overburdened measuring zombie lives," said Clotho, indicating myriad licorice strings, "but we have heard your purposes, and your orders of arrival as you spoke with Poppy."

"We shall show no favoritism in terms of arrival time nor your perceived authorities," Atropos told them. (At least, Athena assumed that was Atropos; she had shut her eyes again when the Room seemed to start doing somersaults even more quickly than her stomach.)

"Then," Athena began, "how will you decide whose questions to answer?"

"I'm sure Zeus shall be thrilled about this," Iris muttered.

"There will be," said Clotho.

"—a competition," finished Atropos.

"A consultation shall be given to the winner," added Lachesis.

At this, Iris brightened so strongly that Athena could sense it through closed eyes. "Maybe Zeus truly will be thrilled after all."

"But I'm barely holding it together here!" Athena risked opening her eyes again, immediately regretting it when Clotho's face appeared both ten meters wide and millimeters away from Athena's own. "I can't possibly compete with Iris in my current state! Isn't it enough that I made it here at all?"

"No," said all three Fates at once.

Athena crossed her arms. "That is hardly fair."

"Life is not fair," said Clotho.

"Death is not fair," said Atropos.

"Salmon are not fair," said Lachesis.

"The last is irrelevant to the current situation," said Clotho, "but no less accurate."

Athena grit her teeth. "Fine. I love a challenge. Bring it on, then."

"The contest shall be a test of wisdom," said Clotho.

"I will ask a riddle," said Lachesis.

"Fate will be determined," finished Atropos.

"A test of wisdom?" Athena could not suppress her delight. "Well, if you think it best."

Iris cleared her throat. "Ah, I hate to tell you ladies how to do your jobs, but wouldn't a better competition test something neither of us are or were goddesses of?"

"If you hate to tell us," said Lachesis, "then do not."

"Besides," said Clotho, "Life."

"Death," said Atropos.

"Salmon," said Athena with a grin. She forced the grin down to a mere self-satisfied smirk. She was still Room-addled; there was no sense in getting cocky.

"Very well," said Iris. "Ask your riddle. I will answer."

"Do not tell us what to do," said Lachesis.

"Apologies, I only meant—"

"Silence," Lachesis ordered. "I shall now ask the riddle. You will have time to consider your answer, and then whisper it to Poppy, who shall then announce both answers, and the victor will be decided."

Athena nodded her agreement, and Iris presumably did so as well, for Lachesis then spoke again:

"Imagine this scenario: An automobile driven by a mortal travels down a hill toward a crosswalk in which three other mortals walk. The automobile's brakes have failed. The driver has two choices— continue straight, killing everyone in the crosswalk but safeguarding the three passengers in the car, or swerve into the side of a building where a construction worker installs an ATM machine. Swerving will kill the worker and all three passengers in the car."

"They are not wearing seatbelts," Clotho lamented.

"The driver will survive either option," said Atropos. "Because reasons."

"Hmm," Athena *hmm*ed. "So it's four people vs. three people, but—"

"But wait!" said Lachesis. "There is more: The three in the crosswalk are two elderly men and a young woman. The young woman is eight and a half months pregnant."

Athena switched to a mental tally, not wishing to give Iris the benefit of her wisdom aloud. *Essentially four vs four now . . .*

"The construction worker is supporting her husband and four children with her salary."

Four vs four plus the well-being of four more?

"One of the elderly men is a scientist who will devise an inexpensive clean energy technology."

So add the well-being of billions to the crosswalk group? Though cheap energy with the mortals would also mean cheap, more powerful weapons. That could lead to more death. Except mortals have always sought ways to kill each other, and the threat of mutually assured destruction had actually worked quite well to—

"The other elderly man in the crosswalk is a robot from the future sent back in time to murder one John Ronnoc, a man who shall otherwise save humankind from an artificial intelligence uprising thirty years later. It is not a well-built alien robot; the collision would still destroy it.

"One of the passengers in the car is a teenage boy with a bright future ahead of him. By age thirty he will have a wife, a child, and will invent the time travel device that allows the crosswalk robot to go back in time in the first place."

Alright, so that whole thing is kind of a wash. This John Ronnoc guy would be safe either way.

"Another passenger in the car is the very John Ronnoc in question."

Crap.

"The final passenger is a violent criminal who has killed twenty people. If he lives, he is destined to go to jail for life. There he will undergo a moral epiphany that leads him to write a book that may turn others away from a life of crime."

"He also likes fermented Brussels sprouts on pizza," Atropos added. At this, Poppy shuddered audibly.

"Finally," Lachesis said—at which point Athena breathed a sigh of relief, "The wall in which the worker is installing the ATM is shared by a café. The constant construction noise is slowly driving insane a writer in that café. If the noise does not stop, he will smash his laptop in a fit of rage, thus losing a movie script that would otherwise bring happiness to, potentially, millions of people. So: Which way should the driver swerve?" Lachesis asked again. "Which choice is the wisest?"

Athena took a contemplative breath and went inside herself, considering. She dismissed the writer. If he were foolish enough to both smash a laptop due to a little noise *and* not back up his writing elsewhere, the world was likely better off without his work.

Positives and negatives abounded on either side. Assorted deaths in either direction, of both young and old—but the Fates were passionless with regard to that. All mortals died. So that could be dismissed as well. That therefore left clean energy for the world (with all the benefits and liabilities it entailed), but at the cost of an increased criminal element and an unchecked artificial intelligence uprising.

Except scientists made notes, didn't they? Someone else would pick up the work of the elderly scientist turned into tragic road pizza. Clean energy would come regardless. As for the A.I. uprising, Zeus would surely intercede on the mortals' behalf before they were wiped out entirely. Who would worship the gods otherwise? And Lachesis only said the criminal's book *may* turn others from a life of crime. It could just as easily have no effect.

The more Athena pondered, the more she realized that only one thing here could matter: fermented Brussels sprouts on pizza. This had been the only detail Atropos had provided. Atropos was the one to sever the threads of life. Surely her detail was the most important! Surely the world would be best off without such terrible ideas poisoning the culinary palate! Or, at least, such seemed to be the hidden answer that Atropos was hinting at. That had to be the wisest answer! At least, as far as the Fates were concerned.

Right?

"Your time is ended," said Atropos. "Whisper your answer to the intern."

Iris stirred. "May I ask one thing before—?"

"*Now.*"

Athena sniggered to herself. Poor Iris. She tugged Poppy closer by feel and whispered her answer. Iris followed suit.

"Poppy," said Clotho, "speak now their answers."

"Well," said Poppy, "going alphabetically, Athena chooses to crash into the ATM worker, thus eradicating the disturbing pizza combination."

Atropos clapped once. "Bravo." Athena allowed herself a victorious smirk, yet pointed it away from Iris for the sake of civility.

"Iris," Poppy continued, "would choose whichever target the Fates decree must die."

"The wisest choice is to acquiesce to what must be," Iris added. "Not even Zeus may go against fate."

Athena sniggered anew. What an ass-kissing, spineless answer to try to pass off as—

"Iris is correct," Lachesis said. "She has won the context."

"*What the Styx?*" Athena burst. "But Atropos *just* said bravo!"

"You have a firm grasp upon the recent past," said Atropos. "Yet you have mistaken the wisdom of pizza-related choices with the wisdom of fate."

"A common error," said Clotho, not without pity.

"The downfall of Alexander the Great," said Lachesis.

Athena slumped to the floor (or the ceiling, or the wall, or whatever the Jerry she had been standing on). "I should've gone with spineless ass-kissing."

"It really is the wisest policy," said Iris, and patted Athena's shoulder. "And now, may I *please* ask the questions I bring from Lord Zeus?"

"You may, and you will," said Clotho.

"Lord Zeus wishes to know: a year and a half ago, the goddess Hecate was slain by the Unmaking Nexus. As Zeus himself was resurrected after such a fate, is there any way that Hecate may now be resurrected as well?"

Following a single shared glance, the Fates' answer was immediate.

CHAPTER EIGHTEEN

"Our wills and fates do so contrary run, that our devices still are overthrown; our thoughts are ours, their ends none of our own."
— William Shakespeare, Hamlet *(act 3, scene 2)*

"When you can't think of anything else to say, quote Shakespeare and hope you sound smart."
— Calliope's Writing for Dummies

"NO," THE FATES ANSWERED.

"Do not let the door hit you in the sanity on your way out," Atropos added.

Iris gaped. "No? Just . . . *no?*"

"The question you asked of us was of a Boolean nature, young goddess," said Clotho.

"If the answer had been yes, would you have elaborated?"

"If you had asked us to do so," answered Clotho.

"But the answer was not yes," said Lachesis.

"So the point is moot," said Atropos.

"But," Iris stammered anew. "There is no means, at all, to resurrect Hecate? Or to speak with her now in some manner?"

"Any chance to resurrect her has passed," said Atropos.

"So there was a chance once?"

"We did not say that," said Lachesis.

"But perhaps," said Clotho.

At this point, a rabid hippopotamus snuck up behind Athena, chomped onto her skull, and thrashed about like a supercharged paint shaker. Or that's what her sudden headache felt like, anyway. With her eyes shut, Athena could not be certain. She grasped her head and fell again to her knees with a bravely stifled groan.

"Do not interrupt!" Lachesis ordered.

"I am sorry, I need to get out of this place. Now."

"Then you should not have come into this place," Lachesis said.

"It was not her intent," Atropos countered. "Poppy, Athena's time here has ended. You know what must be done."

Ended? Athena thought. *What must be done?* Was that a threat, or just Atropos's usual morbidity?

Whatever Poppy's response, Athena could not discern it through the noise and chaos that now threatened her consciousness. She felt Poppy tugging her to her feet. Somehow the intern's touch seemed to clear Athena's head, if only partially.

"Is she going to be alright?" she heard Iris say.

Athena reached out. "Iris. Come closer. Please."

Athena felt Iris's hand brushing hers. She risked opening her eyes to get a fix on just where the messenger goddess stood, and then seized the hilt of her sword and yanked like King Arthur selecting an umbrella. It came free with a greasy slide and an Iris-ian gasp. Athena closed her eyes again and hugged the sword like a razor-sharp security blanket.

Poppy led Athena up a twisted flight of stairs and through what felt like a beaded curtain. Gradually the voices of Iris and the Fates faded, as did the disorientation and much of the pain; the figurative hippo shrank to a figurative beaver, which merely gnawed at her left temple.

Cautiously, Athena opened her eyes. She found herself standing in a circular tunnel of blue-white light whose surface spun and shifted with flashes of darkness and the occasional vulgarity in ancient Greek. Poppy stood before her, holding Athena's Glock.

Athena's instinct brought her sword to bear. She brandished it before her, its blade dripping with rainbow glitter.

Poppy hesitated. "Er, do you not want your gun back? It popped into the Room just behind you." She raised the Glock higher, and only then did Athena realize Poppy held the barrel and was merely offering to give it back to her. She lowered her sword.

"Sorry. My instincts are under siege just now, and the way Atropos said my 'time had ended' . . . " She took the Glock. "This is embarrassing."

"Don't worry, I won't tell anyone. Atropos loves to spook people, even if she is trying to be nice."

"Thank you."

"The Fates already know of your embarrassment, you understand."

"Well that hardly matters. They're not going to tell anyone, given how stingy they're being with information. Can you help me, even if they can't?"

"What help I may give is not as direct as you might wish, but I may provide some hope of help, in exchange for a minor favor."

Athena tried not to twitch as the beaver gnawed anew. "That favor being?"

"Ask Apollo if he got my emails?" Poppy blushed, and Athena couldn't help but smile despite the beavering.

"Does someone have a crush?" she teased.

"I am, um, not permitted to say?"

"Riiiight. You know that he is quite married to his job these days, do you not?"

Poppy gave a quizzical smile and eyed the ceiling. "I do not believe I said anything about marriage."

Athena accepted that with a nod. "I would be happy to ask, if this 'hope of help' you offer is genuine."

Poppy smiled graciously. "What would you have asked the Three, were you allowed?"

"Who or what is causing the zombies? How can that be stopped? Or, if they refused to answer those questions—as Zeus must have already asked—I would have asked how to return Hades from his exile."

Poppy nodded. Her eyes grew clouded, and she intoned, "The last question is your first hope. Seek out the Grey Sisters."

"The Graeae?"

"The Graeae!" Poppy blinked her eyes back to normal. "Lachesis mocks them as the 'discount-Fates,' but they know much, and may have the knowledge you seek."

"Are you actually not sure, or are you just trying to be ambiguous?"

Poppy affected an air of preeminence. "I cannot say."

"Of course you cannot." Athena winced as the beaver got a second wind.

"It's the best I can do."

"Very well. I shall take what I can get. Thank you." Athena sighed. "So how *do* I get out of here? Are you going to take something away from me as a fee, like you did with Apollo last year? He's been rubbish at prophecy ever since."

"Many such things are difficult to see," Poppy answered. "But this isn't one of them. No. You came to this place by accident, and you have already lost something to do so."

Athena blinked. "What did I lose?"

"You do not remember?"

"Would I ask if I did?"

Poppy gave a wan smile.

Athena snapped her fingers. "I lost the buckler." That was no grand loss. It was a nice buckler, but it had been chafing her forearm quite a bit lately. Yet Poppy was shaking her head. She *had* lost the buckler, hadn't she?

"It was not a question, Athena, but a statement. *You do not remember.* You have lost memories, not a buckler."

"If I haven't lost a buckler, then I would like to know why I am not carrying a buckler right—" *No, Athena, that's not the point here . . .* "What were the memories of?"

"I only know that you have forgotten things. I do not know what those things are."

"That is at once mysterious, unhelpful, and distressing."

"Thank you!" Poppy beamed. "Could you drop Lachesis an email saying the same thing when you get out of here? I've got another performance evaluation coming up. But now you must go. Hold your breath!"

With that, she waved her arms, and a trap door opened beneath Athena's feet. Athena plunged into the void and forgot to hold her breath. That was alright, because this particular void smelled of fresh-baked peanut butter cookies, calling into question just why it was called a "void" in the first place.

Such are the mysteries of the realm of the Fates, and so forth.

CHAPTER NINETEEN

"I think I read somewhere that penguins like being juggled. They never object when I do it, and I speak Penguin, you know. Or anyway, I speak Puffin. It's mostly the same except the words for swimming and flying are swapped, and there's a great deal more profanity."
— Thalia the Muse, guesting on NPR's Wait Wait . . . Don't Tell Me!

BY THE TIME ZEUS had returned to what he now referred to as "the front" —the spot in high Earth orbit where his parlay with the Cosmics took place—Baskin had indeed extricated Urania from Cyot'hgha's grasp as instructed. Now, two of Cyot'hgha's tentacles clutched the business end of Baskin's Mighty Pink Battle-Spoon™. Baskin gripped the handle, his sprinkles bulging as he engaged in a tug of war to keep the aforementioned Mighty Pink Battle-Spoon™ from disappearing beneath Cyot'hgha's skirt.

Urania now floated in relative safety behind Thalia, though walnut-sized tentacle welts covered much of her visible skin. Zeus shivered at the sight, recalling some very pleasant, very private, and very scandalous moments with Cyot'hgha long, long ago.

Meanwhile, cloudy C'oggn-yon loomed large, crackling purplish-blue and guarding """"""""Q, who gibbered and quaked as he threw off bursts of power. The bursts were starting to both radiate toward Earth and give Zeus a headache.

Zeus fought to conceal his discomfort. He was king here!

Flanking him were Poseidon, Apollo, Artemis, and Hephaestus. He would have preferred to bring another sibling in place of Hephaestus. This was intended to be a show of power, and the older the godly generation, the better. Yet with Hera still cut off and Hades gone, that left only Demeter and Hestia. Demeter was batty enough that she might just sabotage things on accident, and Hestia always moped if forced to leave Olympus. At least Hephaestus, with his bulging muscles, forge-scarred skin, and weighty smith's hammer, *appeared* intimidating. The Cosmics didn't need to know he was typically as gentle as a griffin cub.

Thalia continued to juggle penguins. Zeus assumed she had a good reason, and let her be.

"Cyot'hgha! Baskin!" Zeus called. "Stand down! What occurs here?"

The two paused their struggle, though each retained a firm grip on the Battle-Spoon, which itself retained its oft-mentioned pink mightiness. Cyot'hgha lay her pearlescent arms on her hips. She said nothing, burning a gaze through him that was either seductive or meant to ask just who he thought he was to make demands of her.

"The fish-headed one began to burble, Lord Zeus!" Baskin declared. "It was a heinous, combative burbling, with warbles and mind-bombarding vibrations! And when Urania asked him to cease, this one burst forth with tentacular offense!"

"The starlit one overreached her authority," Cyot'hgha purred, indicating Urania.

"I merely suggested that whatever he was doing would be better done farther away, in the privacy of his own star-system. Wherever that is." Urania folded her arms in a way that reminded Zeus of Hera. "As you can no doubt feel, it is severely unpleasant!"

"And just a smidgen rude," added Thalia, flipping a penguin under one leg. "Fates only know what it's doing to the mortals down there."

"Necessary," Cyot'hgha declared. "Required. We grow weary of waiting, thus restless ''''''''''Q is seeking."

So, the power ''''''''''Q radiated was a sensory scan? Zeus could feel its presence in his skies across the globe. The sky was beginning to turn mauve in places. He hated mauve.

"''''''''''Q is seeking what, precisely?" Zeus probed.

Cyot'hgha merely narrowed her eyes.

Was this situation a problem, Zeus wondered, or an opportunity?

If he could glean from the scan whether ″″″″″″Q sought Hecate herself or merely something Hecate knew about, Zeus would gain valuable intelligence. Yet if the scanning continued, and the Cosmics discovered Hecate's true fate . . .

No, it wasn't worth the risk. Not yet, anyway. Besides, mauve.

"He will cease this now," Zeus commanded. "You must have patience."

"Our patience is ours to mete out as the darkness hankers," said Cyot'hgha.

"ZOGG!" added C'oggn-yon.

"Regardless, he must cease! This 'seeking' will contaminate the planet!"

"It will not."

"It will damage the mortals!"

"They are but insects."

"ZZOGG!"

Two Zs? Zeus glared at the audacity. "This is my domain! I will not ask again!"

"Good," was her answer. She shoved away Baskin's Mighty Pink Battle-Spoon™, swooped into Zeus's personal space, and stopped time.

"I keep secrets you do not desire exposed," she whispered.

"You may think you have secrets, Cyot'hgha." And she would be right, Zeus supposed. "What is that to me? You cannot even speak clearly to us when there is something you *want*. I doubt you are capable of communicating to my pantheon in a manner they can comprehend."

"Capable?" She leaned close enough for her breath to tease the side of his neck. "We were lovers. You and I. Wrought. Hecate is not adopted. Sought. She exists as the product of a union that your pantheon would consider abomination. Thought."

They likely would consider it abomination, Zeus reflected. Or Hera would, at the very least. He hardly needed *that* right now. Not that he would admit it to Cyot'hgha. "Our union was a long time ago. Even if they react as you think, my dear, they will adapt."

"Serpents of uncertainty slither from your tongue, Zeus."

Zeus stifled a protest, barely maintaining his poker face in the face of *slithering*. "I am beloved of the other gods." Surely even Hera still loved him, deep down. "I am their king."

Cyot'hgha edged back now herself, as far as she could go without breaking the time-stop. "Also in our possession is this." She produced something from beneath her skirt that made Zeus recoil: Pewter skin. Red eyes. Heinous stinger.

In her tentacles Cyot'hgha held the Unmaking Nexus.

Here was the living weapon the Fates had created to fight the Titans at Zeus's behest. Here was the object so dangerous that Zeus hid its very existence from the pantheon for the sake of harmony—until the conspiracy had discovered it and used it to murder him. Here was the hateful thing that Poseidon had used against the Titans just a year ago, only to have it backfire, kill Hecate, and get hurled into space. Zeus could guess how Cyot'hgha had gotten her hands on it after that, and you, being smart enough to have good taste in books, probably can, too.[1]

Lightning crackled over Zeus's skin: anger and indigestion made manifest. "You would not use this, even if you knew how."

"Do not presume to fathom my mind, Zeus."

"Do not presume to threaten me, Cyot'hgha."

"Sedulous '''''''''Q must continue his seek. Dreaming. Waking."

Zeus's stomach twisted. He could snatch the Nexus from her hands, but time would resume and Cyot'hgha might spill her secrets to the Olympians. Worse, the Cosmics might interpret grabbing the Nexus as an act of war and summon those Cyot'hgha had mentioned, the Others from the elsewhære. Then again, being Cosmics, they could also interpret his grabbing the Nexus as the start of a football game and start selling hot dogs.

Hot dogs made of squid.

Topped with tapioca.

Possibly delicious.

Yet he couldn't take the risk. The Earth remained beset with a mild case of zombies. His pantheon was still understaffed. And Iris, or even Jerry, might yet turn up a way to give the Cosmics what they wanted. No, this was not the time to risk a full conflict, regardless of

---

[1] No, *not* eBay.

the damage Cyot'hgha's power play did to his ego.

"Put that thing away," Zeus grumbled, with a nod toward the Nexus. Surprisingly, she did so. His stomach untwisted a notch. "I shall allow '''''''''Q to continue this 'seek,' but not so close to the planet. You can fight me on this, but conflict only further delays you getting what you desire. So, retreat. We will continue our efforts below. You who wait in—what did you call it once?"

"The abstruse reaches beyond the veils of madness."

"Yes. You who wait in . . . those places; you are used to waiting. You must wait a little more. I *will* aid you, but I must do so in my own way."

"Why?"

"Appearances." Zeus cast a meaningful glance at those behind him, followed by another at Cyot'hgha's "skirts" that hid her slender tentacles. "Surely you know the power of appearances."

"Appearances." She might have scoffed. Zeus couldn't quite tell. "Yet you claim to be beloved."

"I live by the philosophy that one can always use more belovin'."

Iris arrived on the scene just as Zeus and the weird, pale-skinned female Cosmic completed a time-stopped discussion. Instantaneous jumps in their respective postures was a telltale sign. The audible pop and Iris's sudden fit of sneezing confirmed it. Audible pops occur after any time-stop (yes, even in the vacuum of space—divine hearing is just that good), and as for the sneezing, Iris was allergic to time stops.

With the time-stop conversation complete, the female Cosmic turned around, motioned to the other two, and ushered them away. The purpley, crackly-lightning mist-thing obliged immediately, backing away on its own. The quaking, gibbering, disturbingly-shaped cuttlefish-whatsit appeared lost in its own little world. The female Cosmic towed it off as it continued its quaking. They all drifted toward the moon.

"And let that be a warning to you!" Zeus called after them. "I shall not believe the lies you try to tell about my people! Poseidon did *not* 'collude with '''''''''Q in the dark depths beyond the dreams of dingoes,' as you claim! We Olympians stand united! None of us shall heed false gossip, shall we?"

Zeus seemed to be trying to drum up agreement among the Olympians, but most were too distracted watching the Cosmics' withdrawal. It looked to Iris as if the female glared at Zeus as he finished his speech. At this distance, and with the female's eyes being literal voids, Iris couldn't be sure.

"ZOGG!" shouted the purpley cloud. Iris wondered if it might enjoy some glitter in its mists.

Zeus turned to the Olympians. "I have driven them off, for now, but I suspect they will continue this 'seeking,' they call it." He gestured toward the Earth and the strange atmospheric effects they could all see.

"Then let me freeze them with rich, creamy rage, Lord Zeus!" Baskin pleaded. "We can defend your domain together!"

"When the time is right, Baskin," Zeus answered. "Apollo, you are god of healing and medicine—"

"Of this I am aware, Father."

"And the sun," said Artemis, "and music, and literature . . . "

"Quiet, Sister."

". . . claims to be good at archery though he's not as good as me . . . "

"Artemis!" hissed Apollo.

"Mul-ti-pur-pose goddd . . . " she sang.

"Silence!" Zeus crackled with lightning, regaining Apollo's attention. "God of *healing and medicine*: go to Earth and determine how this "seek" may be affecting mortal health. We will shield them the best we can."

Apollo saluted and left to carry out Zeus's orders. Iris suspected Zeus's directives might be carried out faster were it not for his occasional insistence on stating what certain gods were in charge of. But decorum had its place.

"Artemis," Zeus went on, "goddess of the moon and the hunt! Study the seeking energies that ′′′′′′′′′′Q transmits. Find out what they are looking for."

Artemis gave an acknowledging bow and departed.

Then came the moment Iris had been dreading.

Zeus turned to her. "Iris, what have you learned from the Fates?"

She shivered before answering. The shiver released glitter from her body, which in the vacuum of space created a small, orbital glitter-ring around her shoulders.

"The Fates, I regret to say, have little to share on the subject of Hecate. They answered your questions, but their answers give little help: they say there is no way to resurrect Hecate. There may once have been, but, and I quote, 'that time has passed.' But that's still helpful, right? Because, um, now we know that there's nothing that can be done, see. Eh-heh."

Zeus's visage tightened. His tone grew grim. "You learned nothing more than this?"

Iris swallowed. Zeus was not one to shoot the messenger, but her own disappointment gnawed at her. "They were very tight lipped, and—"

"Nothing about what the Cosmics might be looking for," Zeus whispered.

"That was not what you asked—"

"Nothing of how we might even speak with a remnant of whatever is left of Hecate . . . "

"Now I did ask about that," Iris said, recalling the rest of her ill-Fated consultation after Athena's departure. She morphed into Clotho's visage, recounting her words: "To speak to Hecate is to speak to that which is dead. Even if that which was Hecate may listen, she will not hear without comfort."

"That is not helpful!"

"I know, right? I told them they may as well tell us to shove our faces under the ground and yell at Hecate, for all the good that answer did us. They, ah, were not swayed by this." Iris managed a chuckle, hoping to lighten the mood. Zeus's scowl only deepened. Behind it, his mind seemed in motion. Whether he was thinking of his next move or inwardly cursing Iris's failure, she could not tell.

"I would have asked more," she burst when the silence became too much, "but there was no time! They refused to pay homage to your authority. They *claimed* themselves too busy with the zombies to allow a longer audience! If Athena hadn't been there and taken up their time, I might have—"

Zeus looked . . . alarmed? Surprised? Abruptly peckish? "Athena was there?"

"How?" Poseidon asked. "Is she not still . . . ?"

"Divinely insufficient and still unworthy of Lord Zeus's forgiveness?" Baskin finished.

Poseidon glowered. "Yes. That."

"I do not know how she got in the Room, but she was still without her powers. She could barely stand or function there." Iris glanced at Poseidon, and then back to Zeus. "She was there to ask about the zombies, Lord Zeus. And, I believe, about Hades."

"Hades?"

"He was your treacherous brother, Lord Zeus!" Baskin bellowed, his enraged hands squeezing the Mighty Pink Battle-Spoon™. "Whom you justly exiled for his crimes against—"

"I know who my brother is, Baskin."

"Apologies, Lord Zeus! I had thought you were asking—"

Iris shifted into playback mode, her features and voice morphing into Athena's. "Iris, please. I am close to finding the cause of the zombie problem, or if not the cause, then at least a way to fix it. Which might require Hades's help." Iris morphed back. "I did not get the sense that she was communicating with Hades, only seeking a way to do so."

"Or to return him from his exile?" Zeus asked. "Behind my *back*?"

Iris swallowed again. In the midst of trying to deflect Zeus's anger from her, she could be getting Athena into far more trouble than intended. "I do not think Athena was attempting to defy you, Lord Zeus. Her only concern seemed to be the zombie problem."

Zeus considered this, but appeared no less consternated.

"In any case," Iris went on, "I persuaded the Fates to answer *your* questions rather than hers. She received no answers from the Three before she left their abode."

Baskin saluted. "Permission to retrieve Athena and demand an explanation, Lord Zeus!"

"No, Baskin. I need you here."

"I am sure Athena's intent is nothing nefarious, Father," Hephaestus added.

"It's not nefarious at all!" It was Thalia, who had ceased juggling and now held two remarkably calm penguins in her left hand and one vomiting up a herring in her right. "I mean, she's only trying to impress you by finding a zombie solution. And how would cavorting around with Hades possibly impress you? That's meant as a rhetorical question, of course, by which I mean she wouldn't possibly do something like that. Ooh, careful—zero-g penguin vomit incoming."

Zeus grumbled something pensive and unintelligible.

Chapter Nineteen and a Half

"When driving in isolated areas, regardless of how many or few zombies are visible, never, ever take your eyes off of the road. Evidence shows that zombies can sense distracted drivers. They have a knack for jumping in front of your vehicle to cause a wreck at the most inopportune time.

Note that Sweeten's Guide *subscribers driving semi trucks may ignore this rule at their discretion. A fully loaded tractor-trailer will smash any undead bastards off the road like bowling pins. Speaking of which, should you capture that on video, post it on the Sweeten's website to win a free hat!"*
—The Sweeten's Guide to Real Zombies

"THE SKY IS BARF," Leif said. "Again."

"Mmrgh?" asked Tracy. She slumped in her seat, the brim of a baseball cap pulled down over her eyes. She had spent most of the previous night on zombie-watch while Leif had slept. He had successfully argued that he needed his sleep due to some food poisoning that had him puking most of his innards out soon after they escaped the doomed path to the Underworld. Leif suspected Tracy had only been partially selfless in letting him rest; though he'd shown no actual signs of turning into a zombie, it didn't hurt to be sure.

Leif admired her for that. If he were infected, she wasn't foolish enough to keep him around for sentimental reasons until he turned and caused some disaster. Morons in movies always did that. It was a trope that drove him up the wall before zombies were a real-world problem, and continued to do so after—literally, in the case of that climbing center where he got trapped with an amusement park caretaker, his brother, those meddling kids, and their dog.

That had been an odd day.

"Just pull over and puke out the window if you have to," Tracy grumbled. "I'm not driving."

"No, not me. The sky. It's all mauve and lavender and speckled." He did not like when the sky was barf. It meant bad things were going down. Also, it was ugly. He tugged Tracy's hat up from her eyes and pointed out the windshield. "Look familiar?"

Tracy leaned forward to look. "Oh, fantastic."

"This damn well better not be the Titans getting out again."

Tracy checked the view out the back window. "It doesn't quite look the same shade as that."

"Got a photographic memory of barfy sky tones, do you?"

"Don't snap at me."

"I'm just saying, this better not be the Titans again!"

"Heard you the first time."

Last year when the sky was barf, it had been because the Titans had crawled out of whatever Tartarus-dimension they'd been trapped in, caused a globe-ravaging war, and blown up the island of Maui before he'd had a chance to visit. Of course, Leif had also received a temporary upgrade to god-status, and he'd gotten to throw around awesome destructive energies of his own. That was fun. He figured that part was far less likely to happen a second time, though.

This had better not be the Titans again.

Leif continued grumbling to himself but kept driving. Apollo's temple was, at last, just a little farther. There, they would do a little "praying," or whatever Apollo wanted to call it. They'd finally get the guy's attention and get the movie back on track.

That's when a translucent, shimmering disk had the nerve to appear in the middle of the road ahead. The disk was about five feet high, the same shade of barf as the sky, and loomed like a bad decision. Leif could only spew profanity and clench all the sphincters in his body before the truck rammed straight into it.

Except, Leif realized as the truck continued on without so much as a quiver, there had been no actual ramming. It was as if the disk hadn't even been there—essentially a hologram, if photo-realistic holograms created a slight queasy feeling when one passed through them and (more importantly) actually existed.

The disk receded in his rear-view mirror, looking none the worse for wear.

Tracy stirred again. "What is it? More barf?"

"No. Maybe. In a sense. I think we'd better just keep driving."

As the sound of Leif and Tracy's truck faded into the distance, the shimmering barf-esque disk continued to hover in the middle of the road. An observer might perhaps notice a slight pensiveness about it as it wafted a few inches about its vertical axis and then, finally, disgorged a creature from its two-dimensional depths.

This hypothetical observer might also conclude that the disk cared little for the creature, as the disk did not stick around but instead disintegrated itself and faded away. (The observer's conclusion would be right, too, since the average two-dimensional disk-portal from a five-dimensional plane has zero consciousness with which to care about anything, and this particular disk-portal was as average as they come.)

Alone on the road, the creature rose to its tiny white feet. Its monstrous mind reeled, ever so delicately, at its sudden release from the sealed dimension where Zeus had forced the Olympians to store their pet monsters. *A new place!* it thought, *with sky and ground and trees and little feathered flappy tweet-toys!* Two eager green eyes flitted about, marking so many exciting objects to explore! The creature, with an excited mewl, licked its white fur, spread its red, razor-sharp wings, and leaped into the air.

The windshield of a speeding semi-truck struck it so fast that the driver didn't see it coming.

It didn't even wake the guy from his nap.

PART THREE:
FLIBBERTY-SNORK

CHAPTER TWENTY

"No, we Muses used to make our home at the foot of Mt. Olympus. When Apollo ordered us to add modern genres to our duties, he also granted us new quarters in the grand palace on Olympus proper. He's an excellent boss."

"Ah, though we did have to pester him for it. Quite a bit."

"Only a little! He's a great boss. Our hunger strike only lasted a month."

"He's a good boss."

"He is."

—Calliope and Melpomene, interview, Publishers Greekly

ATHENA AWOKE ON MOUNT OLYMPUS, finding herself in the grand home theater in the Muses' quarters. The theater lights were set at medium brightness. Harp music wafted through hidden speakers. The screen cycled through various bits of entertainment trivia, bucolic landscapes, and, for some reason, tourism advertisements for South Carolina. Bookshelves lined the wall, each stuffed to bursting with leather-bound books. Seating of various types filled the room—all of them comfortable save for Melpomene's reclining iron maiden—each placed so that none would block the view of any other. Athena herself lay on a red leather fainting couch.

The chomping hippopotamus-turned-beaver that had menaced her skull was blessedly gone. She felt a slight crick in her back, but nothing more. When she sat up, the crick turned out to be the Glock, which was wedged between her spine and the couch. She double-checked the weapon's safety, cleared the chamber, and returned it to its proper holster, chastising herself for her lapse in gun safety, beaver-addled or not.

Why was she here?

Behind her, the theater doors pushed open, admitting two Muses.

". . . and of course I'm juggling the penguins because of that whole 'nighted, penguin-fringed abyss' thing and I thought they might like that, but they're just floating there unimpressed and cranky, and who even knows if whatever is in that purple mist is thinking anything besides, 'Oh, look at that pretty, talented redhead juggling the penguins and making the hilarious jokes that none of us have the class to laugh at, maybe I'll eat her and her starry-eyed, haughty, slightly less attractive sister!' And meanwhile Baskin is hanging around useless and humorless as always, and Urania is doing her best to — ouch!"

Thalia's tirade had been aborted with a smack of hand on flesh.

"Apologies for the slap, dear Sister," said Melpomene, who stood with her in the doorway. "It's just that I did not think you would ever cease talking, and I panicked."

Thalia rubbed her cheek. "Oh, you did not."

Melpomene grinned. "Perhaps not. But I shall not deny the satisfaction it gave me."

"Slapstick has its place, and it's not on my face. That rhymes, Melpomene, so you can remember it better."

Athena cleared her throat. "Next time, Thalia, duck your head and bring your left forearm up against it to block the slap. Then counter with a right hook."

"Well that doesn't sound funny at all," said Thalia.

"No, it doesn't," Melpomene agreed.

Thalia beamed. "I approve of it anyway, though. Hi, Athena. Why are you in our theater? Aren't you supposed to be questing?"

"Speaking with the Fates, the last we had heard." Melpomene settled into a velvet, high-backed chair. She crossed her legs and posed as if cradling an invisible goblet in her left hand and doing taxes in mid-air with her right.

"The Fates sent me back to Olympus," said Athena. "Why I appeared in your theater specifically, I do not know."

"Dramatic serendipity," said Melpomene, as if it were obvious. "Easier to catch us up on how things went if you just appear where we are."

"Isn't it marvelously convenient?" Thalia nodded multiple times.

"So go on, tell us everything. Well not everything, I suppose, because then Melpomene might slap you, but as much as you like. Maybe you like being slapped? That's your business. Erato does, but that's not really the kind of—"

Thalia stopped as Melpomene raised her hand in warning.

"I believe I learned some things," said Athena after a moment. "Possibly in the Underworld, or before then. However, I cannot say what those things are, because I have also forgotten them. I don't know if it was getting into the Fates' Room that wiped my memory, or something else, because I don't recall how I got up there. Nor did going there gain me much useful information."

"Oh, dramatic amnesia," said Thalia. "I *hate* that. But try not to worry too much about it."

Melpomene smiled. "Yes, it's not as if you might have lost memories of deep, dark, horrible things. Things that would tear your mind asunder if you remember them."

"Yes, see?" Thalia nodded rapidly. "Best to not think about it at all. Just put it out of your mind, and don't waste time dwelling on it."

"Or," said Melpomene, "it may be that you *must* remember them as swiftly as possible, so that you may counter a threat that draws ever closer to seal your doom, of which you are perilously unaware."

Athena frowned. "That is what concerns me, yes. And the general bother of losing potentially useful intelligence bought with irretrievable time and effort.

Thalia whapped Melpomene's shoulder. "*Tsk*! I was trying to comfort her! You're no help."

Melpomene whapped back. "Comfort is overrated."

Athena leaned forward. "Along those lines, do you know where the Grey Sisters are these days?"

"The Graeae?" Melpomene shrugged. "Still in that hotel in Maui."

Athena blinked. She was almost certain that Maui had exploded, as a volcanic island is wont to do when someone like Dionysus pile-drives a Titan into the magma chamber. Of course, Athena had been trying to trick a different Titan into getting involved in a land war in Asia at that time, so she might be recalling the wrong island.

"Didn't Maui blow up last year?" she tried anyway.

"Oh, yes," said Thalia. "But I don't think they minded much."

Athena pushed herself to her feet. "Then if you will excuse me, I must find a way to get to Maui." She cast about for a clock. If she got her timing right, she could clamber aboard one of Apollo's sun chariots and then parachute down over the Pacific. She would need an asbestos parachute, but she was pretty sure there was at least one left in Daedalus's old storage locker. What was the combination to the lock again?

"Don't go out there," said Thalia. "Not yet anyway. There's all sorts of flibberty-snork going on in the world right now and —"

"Flibberty-snork?"

Thalia thrust her hands onto her hips. "It's a funny word! It's weird and silly and eccentric and it fits! Okay, so I just made it up right now. I'm not completely thrilled with it. But my point is you really ought to lay low until the flibberty-snork blows over."

"I agree," said Melpomene. "Flibberty-snork blows."

Athena sat back down, this time on the arm of the fainting couch. "I ran into Iris earlier. She mentioned bigger things happening right now. What exactly is it?"

"The flibberty-snork?" asked Thalia.

"Yes, the flibberty-snork."

"Can we please stop saying flibberty-snork?"

Thalia patted Melpomene's shoulder. "No, sweetie."

Athena shifted her hand to the hilt of her sword in what she hoped was a meaningful prompt. Melpomene smirked, and then inclined her head toward the theater screen. The screen came to life, displaying an open-air marketplace in the middle of a city. Colors both unnatural and unnerving swirled in the sky. Below, chaos gripped the marketplace. Patrons and sellers alike clutched at their heads in various positions of agony: Some had fallen to their knees. Some lay fetal on the ground. One was doing jumping jacks.

Those who were not clutching at their heads were either passed out or acting strangely. Beside a booth selling antique knickknacks stood a woman whirling her arms in circles while oscillating. At her feet lay a broken, mid-20th-century brass-bladed electric fan. A man ran across the foreground, his arms folded across his chest as he screamed, "There are three dog-grooming salons in your immediate area! Would you like me to show them to you?!"

"Huh," said Athena.

"Flibberty-snork," said Thalia.

"Cosmic entities," said Melpomene. "They arrived while you've been gone, and, apparently, they are looking for . . . something."

Athena listened as they told her of the Cosmics' arrival, their apparent desire to locate Hecate or something Hecate-related, and the resulting search that was apparently messing with the sky and causing the chaos on the screen.

"Hera once told me of Cosmics," said Athena. "'Perverse, distant abominations,' she called them. I never gave them much thought. As if the zombies weren't enough! So all the mortals are going mad?"

Melpomene shook her head. "Not all. What you see here is one of the worst places. It's different everywhere. Also, that woman waving her arms isn't mad, she's just possessed by the spirit of the fan that broke in front of her."

Athena blinked. "Psychometric dislocation?"

"Right."

"That . . . shouldn't happen."

Melpomene snorted, but elegantly. "Oh, you think?"

Many theological philosophies have overlooked the concept of mundane, inanimate objects—rocks, crescent wrenches, left-handed pinking shears—possessing a spirit. Not all, of course. Animism, perhaps one of the oldest known belief systems, is centered on the concept. More recently, anyone who has suffered a computer crash during a vital project or tried to get a toaster to work in a consistent manner has at least entertained the thought that these objects are possessed by something between puckish mischief and downright malevolence. This is not far from the truth. While the quasi-spirits that inhabit such objects come from nowhere and normally return to that same nowhere when an object is broken, they nevertheless exist.

There is, of course, a difference between the quasi-spirit within a distinct "object" such as an ice cream scoop (which, when broken, does not work) and a rock (which, when broken, becomes smaller rocks). But such distinctions are complex, dogmatic minefields, and wars have been started over less. The thing to remember here is that all quasi-spirits are wispy and can slip through the aethereal holes too small for "meatier" spirits (such as those of humans, animals, and—

arguably—political lobbyists).

Thalia toyed with a lock of hair, her back to the screen. "The Cosmics' search is somehow affecting the integral cohesion of interdimensional p-branes."

"Pea-brains?" asked Athena. "If it only affects foolish people, then I can't see the harm in—"

"Not pea-brains. P-branes!" Thalia rolled her eyes. "Look, as tempting as it might be for me to do some sort of sci-fi version of 'Who's on First?,' I'm not going there right now."

"Because I would smack you," said Melpomene.

"Because Melpomene would smack me." Thalia nodded. "Just do me a favor, look up string theory sometime. High-level physics. Great stuff. But in lay terms, the barriers between the spiritual dimensions are starting to leak. In the moments between being released and fading into nothingness, object spirits can penetrate the mortal soul-box and take up residence. The pocket dimensions where you god-types keep your creatures locked away are springing some leaks as well."

Melpomene grinned, seemingly with extra teeth. "Monsters are getting back into the world."

"I think Zeus is working on fixing it, but in the meantime, well." Thalia motioned at the screen again. "It's not the best time for a Hawaiian vacation."

"Even so, I have little choice," said Athena. "And I can handle myself."

"Why the Graeae, per se?" asked Melpomene. "Specific information, or just a hunch of yours? Or do you recall?"

Athena hesitated. Would she be getting Poppy in trouble if she revealed her advice? The Fates surely knew what she had told Athena already.

A three-toned chime from nowhere postponed Athena's answer. Further postponing it was the booming-yet-neutral message that followed. "THIS IS THE EMERGENCY OLYMPIAN PAGING SYSTEM. YOU ARE ABOUT TO BE SUMMONED BY ZEUS THE ALMIGHTY. YOU HAVE THREE SECONDS TO PREPARE YOURSELF. THIS IS NOT A TEST."

"That is *loud*," hissed Athena, resisting the urge to cover her ears.

Thalia looked about the theater. "Which one of us do you suppose—?"

Lightning crackled above them, taking the form of a blazing eagle of energy. Without so much as a hello, it swooped down, collected Athena in its talons, and then flew off with her into elsewhere.

"THANK YOU FOR YOUR ATTENTION. ALL THOSE SUMMONED HAVE NOW BEEN COLLECTED. THIS HAS BEEN THE EMERGENCY OLYMPIAN PAGING SYSTEM."

Thalia glanced at Melpomene. "I feel a smidgen guilty I didn't warn her Zeus might be displeased about that whole Hades kerfuffle."

Melpomene cocked her head. "Hades kerfuffle?"

"That would be one of the things I was going to tell you about next before you *slapped me!*"

The eagle deposited Athena in front of Zeus, who was seated on a replica of his throne. She knew it was a replica because it lacked the subtle wear and tear of millennia of use, and because it sat not in the throne room on Olympus, but on some sort of platform in orbit about the Earth.

The platform was one hundred square feet and resembled a Classical temple with the roof torn off. Marble Ionic columns bordered its edges. Zeus's throne sat near one edge, facing inward, with the Earth's broad curvature glowing blue and white in the background. On the columns closest to the throne hung plasma screens showing images of mortal cities, tactical displays of the Earth and the moon, and a silent advertisement for a prominent cell phone manufacturer. (Zeus had been experimenting with offering ad space on Olympus in exchange for sacrifices from mortals, though it was still just a pilot program.) A collection of breathable air clung to the platform—a pleasant touch that prevented Athena from suffocating.

The lightning eagle, its task complete, crackled into nothingness with a peal of thunder and a mild electronic beep.

"Athena," Zeus said simply. He sat, straight-backed, upon the throne. No trace of a smile lay on his lips, yet they bore no trace of a frown either. It was his business face, his authoritative face, and his "I can tell truth from lies and hit a gnat with a lightning bolt at a million paces, so if you're thinking of trying to pull some crap here, you had best remember that" face.

"Father Zeus." Athena increased her readiness to DEFCON 4, and, respectfully, went down to one knee. When he displayed such a mood, there no sense being casual. There was also no harm in reminding him that she was his daughter. (That didn't mean that much in their family lately, but she would take all the advantage she could get.)

"To what do I owe the honor of your summons?" she asked.

"So you have noticed my business face."

Athena suppressed a smile. "I have, Father Zeus."

"You have always been observant, Athena. Always wise."

She downgraded to DEFCON 5. "Thank you, Father Zeus."

Zeus slammed a fist against an arm of the throne. "And yet with all your wisdom, you thought I would not hear of your intention to return Hades from exile?"

Nope! Back to DEFCON 4!

"I thought nothing of the sort, Father! I have been seeking the cause of the zombies in order to prove my worthiness! Such a quest takes me down many paths of investigation, and without my old power, travel and communication are not trivial things. I had no chance to tell you anything of my quest until now. I only just moments ago returned to Olympus."

Zeus scrutinized her. "Do you not still have a cell phone, Athena? Does it not still function? Did you not think to perhaps text your father once in a while to tell him how you are doing? *What* you are doing?"

Athena shifted uncomfortably. "Life has been busy, Father. I meant to call. I just deemed it best to keep things to myself until I learned more. I did not wish to disturb you."

"Then you have failed, Athena, for I am *disturbed*. I will not suffer my murderous brother to be returned from exile!"

"It is not my intention to bring Hades back, Father! It is only one avenue of possibility that I—"

"Then I command you to travel that avenue no more, Athena!"

She bowed her head and stifled a sigh. "As you wish. But know that I only sought information for you *in the event* that Hades was key to eradicating the zombies, so that *you* might then decide what course to take. I undertook all this to prove my worth to you. Why would I do so in a way that would anger you?"

"Perhaps having your divinity stripped has made you foolish."

"No, Father. Although . . . " She risked a glance up at Zeus. ". . . if you think so, then I would see that as an argument to restore it, were I in a position to make such an argument."

"Which you are not."

Athena gritted her teeth. "Which I am not."

"You will forget the zombie matter," Zeus ordered. "And you will forget Hades! I need your tactical wisdom here."

"The Muses told me of the Cosmics. So, I will have my divinity restored to better serve you in this? I would be happy to lend my strength to you, as I have done always."

"Your strength is not needed, only your tactical advice. Baskin is formidable, but his strategic counsel is unpracticed."

Athena couldn't help but snort. "That's one way to put it."

"Careful," Zeus warned. "Baskin's been loyal to me since birth."

Athena barely kept from pointing out that Baskin was also less than two years old. "My apologies, Father. I am ready."

"Good. Then you will observe the screens on this platform. Watch for any Cosmic incursions. Analyze any movements they make and devise a strategy to counter them." Zeus stood. "Keep me appraised via your phone. It is an important task. Perform this task well, and I shall consider restoring your divinity. But you still have much to make up for."

Athena's gut tightened. Her toes clenched. Her muscles, reacting to a furious need to punch something yet lacking a suitable target, quivered in place, beating each other up so that her entire body quaked and she had to fight to keep her balance. This whole thing was nothing but a distraction!

She took a deep breath before speaking her next words. "Then I respectfully request that you allow me to continue my work to stop the zombies. You do not need me here! You, Father Zeus, are strong enough, and smart enough, to deal with this."

"I am strong enough, Athena. And smart enough." Zeus smiled, warmly. "And you are wise to say so."

"I speak only the truth, Father."

"Oh, I know this," he said. "I know. Request denied."

Chapter Twenty-One

". . . As a matter of habit, power, and purview, the Olympians generally remain on (or around, or below) the planet Earth. There have been exceptions. It is known that Zeus himself traveled among the stars for a time. These travels occurred approximately a century after the Titans were thrown down and Zeus had claimed Kingship and dominion over the sky. The precise dates of his journeys are unknown. He left in his place a simulacrum of himself programmed to give random commands, pelt the Earth with occasional, random lightning bolts, and respond 'Yes, dear,' to anything Hera said; no one noticed his absence until one of those lightning bolts demolished one of Hera's temples. (Hera demanded to know if he did so on purpose. The simulacrum responded, 'Yes, dear,' and then commanded she 'punish the perpetrator.' The simulacrum's subsequent decapitation rather gave things away at that point.) Regarding details of Zeus's travels during this time, little is known among the pantheon, and of course nothing is known on Earth.

What do Zeus's travels have to do with the previous topic of Aegean-Mediterranean economics during the buildup to the Trojan War, you may ask? To understand, please refer to the following 200-page treatise on the Mycenaean olive trade . . . "

—Clio's Olympian History of Histories (Vol. 57)

AFTER ZEUS LEFT HER alone on the platform, it took Athena all of two minutes to familiarize herself with the screens and find the most efficient way to configure the sensors that fed them. After that, she settled in to watch, to wait, and to stew over just what the blitz she should do about the situation.

She had to do so while sitting cross-legged on the marble floor. This did not help matters. The only furniture was Zeus's throne, and she wasn't quite irritated enough to be so foolish as to sit there. That he had given her nothing else on which to sit, knowing she could summon no furniture for herself, was surely intentional on his part. At least the floor was heated.

Zeus could not truly think he needed her wisdom, or he would have given her more tools with which to do the job. No, Zeus meant the platform as detention; while stranded there, she could not return Hades from exile. His protests had only made her more certain that Hades was the answer. Was that what she was forgetting? If Hades's absence caused the zombies, the world needed his return. *Zeus* needed his return!

Yet Zeus would hardly admit needing either of his brothers, even before Hades had helped murder him. But if Athena did bring Hades back, and Hades ended the zombie troubles... Well, Athena considered, she could spin it somehow to placate Zeus's ego. Better to ask forgiveness than permission, as the adage went.

Plus, if this conflict with the Cosmics escalated, Hades would surely fight them as well. The pantheon bickered amongst themselves, but like any dysfunctional family, they banded together against outside threats. Had they not handled those Justified Ancients of Moo Moo in the ninth century?

Athena exhaled, thinking. She was still in the doghouse for failing to stop Zeus's murder. That grudge showed no sign of fading. Defying Zeus about Hades would hardly improve matters, and if one finds oneself in a hole, one ought to stop digging. On the other hand, stopping the zombies was simply the right thing to do! She had been the goddess of defense! She had a responsibility to protect the surviving mortals, her own ambitions be damned! Should she simply roll over and shun that duty?

Besides, as much as she liked the "stop digging" aphorism, how else does one discover buried treasure, massive oil deposits, and tasty, tasty clams?

It suddenly occurred to Athena that she might be hungry.

No sooner had Athena realized this than Demeter landed behind her with an enormous, three-tiered party tray of crackers. There were soda crackers, whole wheat crackers, matzo, pita crackers, rosemary crisps, melba toast, flax seed crackers, hardtack, toasted crackers, multigrain crackers, single grain crackers, and even Athena's favorite, a jalapeno and wasabi-infused rice affair that Demeter had joyously dubbed "firecrackers." A smaller portion of the tray held a few cheeses, meats, and spreads, but the cracker-to-non-cracker ratio was easily five-to-one.

"Please help yourself, dear!" Demeter announced. A thirty-foot buffet table popped into being, on which she set the tray. With a motion of Demeter's hands, the tray multiplied itself tenfold. "Mortals are eating far less grain these days with those silly zombies roaming around. We mustn't let it go to waste!"

Athena clambered to her feet, eying the now ten trays of crackers that filled the table. "My thanks, Demeter. Though I cannot possibly eat all this."

A blip of activity registered on one of the long-range sensors. That sensor watched the moon's orbital path. Athena flagged the activity for analysis.

"Oh, it's not all for you, dear," said Demeter. "Zeus created this platform as a base of operations; I am setting things up for all of us. I made the crackers, of course. Hestia helped with the cheeses and meats, but I fear she made too many. Do you think we have enough crackers for everyone?"

Something about this tweaked Athena's hackles. "Demeter, by all accounts Zeus is mounting a defense of the planet. From what I can tell, he has the entire pantheon on alert. You are his sister, one of the original six children of Cronus!"

"Oh, you know your family trees, dear niece!" Demeter clapped in what seemed to be genuine delight. "Very astute of you, especially in your state."

"Er, well, thank you, Aunt. My point is that you are among the strongest of the gods, especially with Hades gone, and Hera as reduced as I. Yet Zeus has you doing catering? It is a waste of your power."

"Shall I bring in some fresh bread also? It is too late in the day for muffins."

Athena sighed—not because it was *never* too late for muffins, but because, "I am concerned, dear Aunt. You are kind, and caring. But . . . I fear the others do not respect you as they should. You are dismissed as a sillypot, someone to be humored and pandered to. I have lost my divinity, and I have suffered that loss every day since. I am struggling to get it back, but lately I feel as if my efforts are dismissed at every turn."

"Oh, dearie," said Demeter before Athena could finish. "Zeus will forgive you eventually. He's just still miffed about being murdered, that's all. He restored my own divinity swiftly enough."

"But that is my point! He restored you so quickly because, well, he thinks you harmless. He does not respect you. I just . . . wish he and the others gave you more credit. And I wish that concerned you more."

Demeter's smile faltered for just a moment. She began to say something, but then stopped. "Things will be as they must be, dear niece. You need not worry for me."

Was that a twinkle in Demeter's eye? No, wait—that was the blink of a sensor alert reflected in Demeter's cornea. Athena spun back to the screens. A dozen glowing objects—the blip of activity she had flagged earlier—flew on course for Earth. They were each no larger than three meters across, but glowing bright in both the visible and extra-dimensional spectrum.

"If you'll excuse me a moment, Demeter; I need to make a call." She pulled out her phone and dialed Z for Zeus. As it rang, she plotted the course of each object. They were set to diverge from each other, landing in separate places around the globe. But what were they?

Four rings, and Zeus wasn't picking up. There was a click on the line, and then another ring, before Athena's call was answered:

"This is Baskin speaking on Baskin's phone-device! You are go for Baskin!"

Oh gods no. Zeus forwarded her? "Baskin, this is Athena. Put me on with Zeus."

"Lord Zeus is busy! You will report to me!"

"He told me to call *him*. This is urgent."

"And he told me to deal with you! So report, if it is so urgent!"

The objects—meteors?—streaked closer.

"Fine! There are a dozen meteors on course for the planet. I do not know quite what they are, but the Cosmics sent them. If they're anything but bad news, I'll eat my sword. I'm sending coordinates. Understand: you need to destroy them immediately."

"I do not take orders from you, Athena!"

"Fine. Then I *strenuously recommend* you destroy them immediately!"

"I do not take strenuous recommendations—"

"Damn it to Jerry, Baskin! These things are a threat or I am a fluffy-ass bunny! Now are you Zeus's mighty defender or not? I am giving you targets on a silver platter! For the glory of Zeus! Now take them out!"

Baskin's unintelligible roar came across the line. Then it clicked dead. He had hung up on her, yet moments later he appeared onscreen in the path of the lead meteor. A swish of motion and a fiery explosion followed. It was not unlike what one might expect from the impact of a Mighty Pink Battle-Spoon™ against an unknown meteor-like object that is apparently explosive. Baskin sped off to intercept the next one.

So, despite their differences, Baskin could work with her when needed. Athena liked him better than Ares, at least.

"Is something amiss, dear niece?" Demeter asked.

One screen flashed as Baskin destroyed a second object, fired a supersonic volley of chopped nuts through a third, and then sped after a fourth. "Just some mischief by the Cosmics," she answered. "Baskin is handling it. They're glowing enough that even he can find them all."

Glowing? Wait a minute . . . With a hunch swelling in her gut, Athena refocused the sensors.

"I just love that youngster Baskin! Always speaking so that all may hear him without straining their ears!"

Rather than respond (through clenched teeth) to such praise of a rival, Athena watched the screens. The glowing objects were *too* obvious. The Cosmics must have known they would be intercepted, so why bother sending them? Granted, expecting those otherworldly weirdoes to behave sensibly was a little foolish, but—

And then she spotted it: a thirteenth object, traveling faster than the others and emitting no light at all. The other twelve were a diversion, and now Baskin was too far away!

Well, maybe he was too far. She'd have to call him again, tell him exactly where it was—okay, so he could probably still catch it. The rich, creamy bastard was fast enough. But what if he argued with her again? Or what if he didn't answer the phone in time? Or what if he was allergic to dark objects speeding out of lunar orbit at 1/25th the speed of light?

Hey, she didn't know. Why risk it?

"Demeter, do you see that dark object there?"

"Of course, dear."

Athena worked fervently on her smartphone to sync it with the platform's screens. "Baskin won't get to it in time. You need to throw me at it."

"Oh, he can make it, dear. He is brisk, that one!"

Athena gritted her teeth further. "*Trust* me. There is not much time."

"As you like, Athena. But you ought to be careful. Would you like me to return you to the platform once you are done?"

"That won't be necessary, thank you." Athena finished the sync. Now she could monitor the screens via her phone from a distance as far away as, oh, say, the surface of the Earth. It wasn't as efficient, but if Zeus cared about efficient, he would not have left her like this.

At Athena's ready-signal, Demeter grew to twice her size, picked up Athena, and raised her like a spear. Athena stiffened from head to toe, doing her best to look the part. She did so quite well. (Not for nothing was her daily four-hour planking regimen!)

"Oh, and Demeter? There's no need to tell Zeus about this."

"Tell Zeus about what, dear?"

"Exactly. Throw now. Please." Athena took a deep breath and held it, which is actually the opposite of what one should do when one is about to be hurled into a vacuum. Yet although she was no longer divine, Athena was still immortal, still strong. She could hold it in. And it's not like fiction isn't rife with this kind of crap anyway, right?

Demeter, thankfully, wasted no time. She launched Athena onto a direct intercept course with the dark object. The goddess had excellent aim. With just a few quick course-correcting exhales, Athena reached the object and seized its rocky edges. She and the object now tumbled together on its continued course toward Earth.

"*Oh!*" Demeter called telepathically after her. "*You forgot to take some crackers with you!"*

Ignoring her, Athena shifted to grip the object between her knees. It was like riding a bull—a rocky bull that was headless, tumbling, and, as it entered the atmosphere, heating up to boot. The thrill of the challenge sang through Athena's body. She drew her sword, raised it two-handed over her head, and with an internal battle cry, drove the point down into the object. The object's stony surface cracked. A fissure now split the thing nearly in two, and from that fissure blazed a nauseating boz light.

The light solidified into tendrils that wrapped around Athena's throat.

On the plus side, being choked helped Athena continue to hold her breath. Cutting off the blood flow to her brain was another matter. But, hey, still immortal! She drew her Glock, shoved it down into the fissure, and emptied the magazine into the thing's center.

The tendrils disintegrated. The object exploded beneath her, shredding her pants and flinging her away. The breath she held burst from her lungs, but she no longer needed it: For one thing, still immortal! And for another, she was about to teleport right out of there.

Athena holstered the Glock. She seized Megaera's silver ball within her pocket. It was, at last, time to use it. Concentrating on Maui and summoning enough Erinyes-like vitriol to activate it, she raised the ball in front of her, and—

"Heads up, niece!"

Demeter's voice rang through her mind a moment before a flying packet of rosemary crisps knocked the ball from Athena's grip. Rosemary and crumbs assailed Athena's vision; the silver ball escaped her blind grasping and hurtled off to parts unknown.

Styx!

Earth spun below her, approaching rapidly. Atmosphere continued to make itself known, heating her clothing, her skin. If she couldn't pull up, she would burst into flames from the friction, like an Athena-meteor streaking through the sky.

As she struggled for options and cursed Demeter's shockingly accurate aim with crackers, Athena noticed a *second* dark object entering the atmosphere about a mile away.

Double Styx!

She had no time to deal with it. Atmospheric friction set her clothing on fire. Her hair and skin followed suit. There were no more options. Within moments she would burn up entirely. And then what? Did complete immolation trump immortality? Even if her ashes were sentient, would anyone find them, ever?

Would her Glock be okay?

The second dark object cleared the stratosphere. Friction had burned away most of its outer shell, and now the football-sized core scrambled free. Continuing to fall like a drunken monkey from a slippery branch, the core began to spin, to pulse, and to hum a tune not unlike *The Battle Hymn of the Republic*. Seconds later, it burst apart into a fractal pattern that expanded throughout the troposphere, echoing around the globe. It was a complex echo, carrying both sound and image along a frequency detectible only by immortal beings and rhinoceros beetles. Those sounds and images formed a scene, and what that scene portrayed was this:

Atop an icy ridge, on a pale, dark planet, stood Cyot'hgha and a somehow younger-looking Zeus. An ancient Greek-style robe wrapped most of his body, with an expanse of chest left generously bare. In the sky above hung an uncanny star. It lit the scene as the full moon lit the Earth, but with greater effulgence. A convenient caption informed those fluent in ancient Olympian that the scene took place on Pluto, and the positions of the stars above informed those fluent in astronomical history that the scene took place over five thousand years ago.

Cyot'hgha held a loaf-sized bundle wrapped in dark, silken seaweed. Zeus set a hand on the bundle. It squirmed, subtly, beneath his touch.

"You will not *eat this baby," Zeus said. "I cannot allow that."*

Cyot'hgha cocked her head. "This meal was offered to you. You denied it. It so passes to my appetite. You should not deny that which you do not wish another to consume."

"Babies are not for eating!" Zeus bellowed.

Cyot'hgha only cocked her head further.

"I am sorry, Cyot'hgha, but I feel very strongly about this. My father and I disagreed about the topic. He wished to eat me, I did not wish to be eaten . . . It was a whole 'thing.' I will not be a hypocrite."

"Consternation. Frustration. Then I will raise this creature," Cyot'hgha intoned. "She will grow amongst the Others, in the darkness where dreams dwell upon the abyss."

Zeus scowled. "Which abyss is that? The one you showed me, with the teeth and the madness?"

"A different abyss."

"Which one?"

"Impossible to disclose. The abysses are multitudinous."

"Will that abyss have madness?"

"Most abysses clutch madness in their hoary fathoms. She will be with me, the Others, the All-in-One."

Zeus shook his head. "Abomination or not, no child of mine shall be raised upon an abyss. Especially not one with madness-clutching fathoms, hoary or otherwise! And especially not surrounded by the Others of your so-called 'family!'"

Cyot'hgha licked her lips with a blue, bladed tongue. "You found this one alluring enough," she said, indicating herself with one hand's fingertips lain upon her own shoulder.

"Alluring enough for a brief, lustful dalliance, Cyot'hgha, not—"

"It was hardly brief."

"—er, well, thank you, but—"

"Our passion was interminable."

"I don't think that's quite a compliment."

"Eldritch."

"What does that even mean?" Zeus shouted. "No, be silent and let me finish! Having a fling with you is one thing. Allowing the fruit of my godly loins to be raised among your kind is quite another! Your brother is a weird-ass cuttlefish thing half the time!"

"You shun her as an abomination. You refuse to devour her. You say she may not stay with us. What other options exist in your mind?"

With a tentative finger, Zeus slid away a flap of the silken material around the bundle. The face of a dark-haired, dark-eyed infant blinked up at him. Zeus sighed uncomfortably.

"I will take her back with me," said Zeus at last. "Upon Olympus she will be free of the abominations of your kind. And your multitudinous abysses."

Cyot'hgha pursed her lips. "You will claim our daughter as your own, then?" A tiny red tentacle slithered out from the bundle, and the infant wiped her own face with it.

Zeus shuddered. "Well. The others will know she is an outsider. She will have it difficult enough. There is no sense adding to her difficulties by claiming her as my own and incurring Hera's ire. But she will be under my protection. They will accept her, as surely as—hey, are her tentacles supposed to ooze like that? That is disgusting."

"My own tentacles brought you to new heights of ecstasy."

"Never speak of that again!" Zeus shot. "She does have legs, yes? Two of them?"

Cyot'hgha nodded.

"Alright, then I can do something about the tentacles. No one will notice. They don't grow back if surgically removed, right?"

The vacuous sockets of Cyot'hgha's eyes grew colder. "No harm must come to the child in your care!" The infant stirred unhappily. "The stars shall go mad and shine songs of destruction and terror, should such a thing come to pass!" The infant began to cry. "The crawling chaos and the black goat of the woods shall visit upon you the insanity of one who has turned his mouth inward and eats his own brain!" The infant's wails reached a crescendo, until, miraculously Cyot'hgha silenced her with a wave of one hand.

Zeus cleared his throat. "Laying it on just a bit thick, don't you think?"

"The warnings are spoken. Fail to heed them at your peril."

"Yes, yes," said Zeus. He took the infant from Cyot'hgha's arms, and then tucked the tentacle back into the folds that wrapped her. "I am renaming her, though. 'Furtive Lament of the Wailing Silence' is no name for an Olympian."

"She is also known to us as Hec-tylarliop'at-ey."

"Why?"

"This should be obvious."

"Whatever," said Zeus. "That is still too long. We'll go with 'Hecate.' What is it with you people and punctuated names, anyway?"

With that, the scene ended. The rhinoceros beetles went about their business.

Zeus lost his lunch, and then made a beeline for Hera.

CHAPTER TWENTY-TWO

"Escape to the peace of zombie-free seas with Crustacean Cruises, where the only screaming and devouring comes from your delight at our never-ending dessert buffets!"
—television ad, Crustacean Cruises (Z-plus 93 days)

ZEUS FOUND HERA ABOARD the ocean cruise liner *Poseidon's Kiss*. Clad in a blue bikini, she was sunning her white-armed beauty on the Lido deck. She was also wielding a makeshift halberd crafted from a shuffleboard stick with a meat cleaver tied to the end of it. To Zeus's relief, she raised the halberd not against him but against the deck's only other occupant: a thirty-foot tall octopus-shark hybrid now writhing and roaring across a gathering of poolside buffet tables.

Any marine biologist worth his salt will tell you that neither octopi nor sharks can emit anything like a roar whatsoever. But no one asked them.

The monster's presence gave Zeus almost as much pause as talking to Hera while she held a weapon. (She could do little real damage to his immortal skin in her current state, but Hera knew where to slice to cause the most pain—not that she needed a weapon to do that, he supposed.) The monsters should still be locked away from reality in a pocket plane. How had this one escaped?

It was a question for another time. If he were lucky, Hera had been so busy fighting it that she hadn't seen the blast from his private past that the Cosmics had plastered around the globe.

"Hera!" Zeus called. "My darling ex! You seem . . . busy?"

"What, this? This is nothing! Or so I think! But *you* are the expert on getting busy, after all!"

Hera spun and slashed the halberd across one of the monster's shark faces. It had eight: one face on the end of each tentacle. Yet none were more fearsome than the mouth of the octopus itself, a razor-bladed maw festooned with brightly glowing shark teeth. Hera slashed a second shark face for good measure.

The entire creature rolled to one side as if trying to flank Hera, but she backpedaled to safety. The octo-shark's thrashing sent deck chairs flying. With a wave of his hand, Zeus brushed aside one coming for his head.

"So you saw it, then."

"Saw that my husband at the time broke his vows for the umpteenth instance with some adulterous slut, you mean?" She severed one tentacle. The head fell to the deck with a plop. "That he fathered yet another illicit lovechild and kept it from me? Did I see *that*, Zeus?"

"I assume you are not angry," Zeus lied. "As you say, I have done that so many times. You should be accustomed by now."

The octo-shark launched itself at Hera, its central mouth opened wide. She leapt upward, scrambled for footing atop its head, and then slid down its back to relative safety. "Not with anyone—any*thing* like her! You broke your vows to lie with that . . . she-creature! She is not our kind! If your perversion lusted for tentacles, then you should have found some willing Mediterranean kraken, not cocked off to the cosmic reaches to shove your 'Mister Lightning Bolt' into something so alien!"

"I only called it that once, Hera!" Zeus shouted. "And krakens do not exist!"

"When you chose to diddle *mortals* over me, that was insulting enough! But you *screwed an abomination!*"

"I was exploring the limits of our domain! Probing what lay in the stars beyond, searching for threats!"

"We both know what you were probing!"

"So I sowed a few wild oats while I was at it. I am king! It is my right!" Zeus knew it wouldn't help to say that, but the words had burst out before he could stop them.

Hera gave no immediate response, as she was staring down seventy-five percent of the octo-shark's remaining mouths. (Two other mouths battled each other for the contents of the Lido deck's hot breakfast buffet.) She twirled the halberd in front of her. Its blade caught the sunlight and toothlight as it spun, creating a glowing circle before the beast. The previously threatening mouths slackened and began to gape.

"What do you want, Zeus?"

"I want you to be okay with this!"

Hera only laughed. The two mouths at the buffet table had rejoined their fellows after wolfing down a vat of eggs and three kinds of waffles. Now all heads were enthralled by Hera's shining, spinning halberd.

"Top of the morning, Lord Zeus."

The grizzled voice came from behind him. Zeus glanced back to verify the speaker. He gave the old ferryman a nod. "Hello, Charon. Shouldn't you be on the Acheron?"

"Vacation," Charon said.

"Ah, yes. The Marcus thing."

"Just so."

Hera moved closer to the monster. The shark mouths, though still enthralled, fell back as she neared its giant maw. The halberd cast reflections over the creature's pallid skin. Its glowing jaws opened wider, though whether from awe or anticipation of a meal, Zeus could not tell.

"Is she almost done playing with that thing?" Charon asked. "I came out here for some bacon and eggs."

"I think you may be out of luck there." Zeus motioned to the remaining bits of the buffet.

"Indeed, I was afeared of that." Charon sighed and then turned to go. "I suppose I shall have to hit up the buffet at the bow, instead. The *second-rate* buffet. All the way at the other end of the ship. And by now I expect that all they shall have left is turkey bacon."

Zeus shuddered. *Turkey bacon.*

"If only I knew a king of the gods who could conjure up some real bacon right here," Charon said.

Zeus continued to watch Hera, now only a step away from the octo-shark's maw. The light from its teeth shone across her pale skin. The sheer beauty would have blinded Zeus, were he not a god and unable to be blinded. Or not wearing sunglasses.

"Your king is kind of busy here, Charon," said Zeus.

Charon sighed again. "Fine. Guess I'll go off to the fucking stern, then." He pointed to Hera. "She is quite pissed at you, you know."

"I know."

Hera screamed a battle cry and charged into the maw. Before the monster could react, she thrust the halberd through the roof of its mouth, into its brain beyond, and then yanked it to one side. The monster gave one aborted bellow and moved no more.

"Well. Good luck with that." Charon threw a wave to Hera, who was now extricating herself from a partially closed cage of rapidly dimming teeth. "Shuffleboard tonight, Hera?"

Her breath still ragged from the fight, monster blood covering half her body, Hera's only response was a nod. It seemed enough for Charon, who nodded back and then wandered off muttering about the evils of imitation bacon.

"An interesting strategy with the spinning," Zeus told Hera. "I would have never thought to do that."

Hera picked a half-spilled container of orange juice off the deck and carried it toward a table of clean glasses. "Of course you wouldn't. The beast had tentacles. You would doubtless have been too aroused to think clearly."

"For Gaia's sake, woman, will you just take the compliment already?"

Pouring juice into a glass, Hera seemed to consider this. "No," she said at last, and then took a drink with such grace that it almost overshadowed the octo-shark ichor dripping off of her arm. "And I ask again: what are you doing here?"

"And I told you." Zeus glanced around for anyone else. The passengers and crew remained hidden elsewhere. Charon had gone. He could see no invisible beings skulking about. Nevertheless, he lowered his voice. "I seek your forgiveness, Hera. Please."

Hera took another, longer drink. "We are no longer together, Zeus. Why do you care about my forgiveness?"

Because I still love you, you confounded, hateful woman! "You know why."

"Do I?" Hera sipped.

"My encounter with Cyot'hgha—"

"'Encounter,' singular?"

"—was thousands of years ago. Why do *you* care, Hera?"

She set the glass down. Her eyes sharpened, narrowed. "Because it is still humiliating. Because we *were* together. And because I still—" She swallowed in distaste and seemed to change course. "Well. Because I still, ah, must call you my king, I suppose."

"Bad orange juice?"

Hera shot him a glare. She walked to the pool, dove in, and swam until it washed the blood from her skin and hair. Zeus said nothing. She climbed out and motioned to the bloodied water and the monster's body. "Clean that up, will you?"

Zeus did as she asked. He spotted a few passengers watching from inside the ship and summoned a few oversized deck chairs to block their view.

Hera was toweling off. "Would you have confessed to this on your own?"

"This affair? With a Cosmic? Which our whole pantheon thinks is disgusting and abominable and creepy?"

"Would you have confessed on your own," Hera said, "to *me*?"

"No. Probably not."

Hera nodded, though whether it was a nod of annoyance or satisfaction, Zeus could not be sure. With Hera, the two were sometimes the same. "Had you answered otherwise," she said, "I would not have believed you."

"I know."

Hera exhaled slowly and studied the horizon. "Have you noticed your sky is exceedingly ill-colored?"

Before Zeus could answer, a few bars of The Beatles' "Here Comes the Sun" rang through the air, played on a lyre. Apollo was heralding his own arrival. Polite, that one. Zeus waved at the sun in acknowledgement, and moments later, Apollo appeared on the deck. After greeting Zeus and nodding to Hera, Apollo wasted no time.

"I have less than positive news about the effects of the Cosmics' seek on the mortals," Apollo said. "Even projected from the moon, it is already destabilizing certain dimensional barriers. Monsters are starting to slip out of the pocket plane—"

"You don't say," said Hera.

"—and the longer the sky remains so, the greater the chance of irreparable mental damage for the mortals."

"Even with the Cosmics projecting their seek from a greater distance?" asked Zeus.

Apollo nodded. "The distance seems to have little effect. If we don't stop it soon—and I mean half a day at most—the mortals will all go mad."

"How mad?"

"I would say the standard 'danger to themselves and others' applies. Chewing out their own eyeballs. Acute psychotic breaks from reality. Utter mental devotion to musical groups or specific brands of cheese. These are all afflictions I may be able to cure, but until the ongoing cause is dealt with, it would only be a bandage."

Zeus scowled. Something had to be done. He moved closer to Apollo and stopped time to ask, privately, "Did you see the, ah, vision?"

Apollo cleared his throat, looking uncomfortable. "I did, Father."

"And?"

"And I find it . . . an interesting revelation that Hecate was my actual half-sister."

"And the rest?"

"Please, Father. No one wants to talk about their parents' sex life, regardless of who—or what—it involves. My loyalty to you is as it has always been."

Zeus studied Apollo's eyes, and saw no lack of truth. He was about to break the conversation when Apollo added, "It *was* just the one time, yes?"

Zeus glared. "Yes!"

He stepped away. Barely after time resumed, as if some cosmological force were trying to hurry things along, a glittering rainbow shone through the salty air and then formed into Iris. "Lord Zeus, I bring word from Artemis."

Zeus nodded for her to proceed, and the goddess transmogrified into Apollo's twin sister.

"Father Zeus, there is as yet no discernable target of the Cosmics' seek. I have concealed myself in the crater of Aristarchus and will continue determining their objective. At this time, I also wish to register a complaint: Ares seems to have been living on the far side of the moon, and he has made quite a mess of the place. It is of course not urgent, but when the current crisis is over, I would like to speak with you about sending him farther away. Be kind, recycle. Artemis out."

"My sister." Apollo shrugged. "She gets territorial."

Zeus glanced at Hera, who folded her arms. "Don't we all."

"Yes, Father."

"Poseidon also reports no activity in R'lyeh," Iris added. "I would relay that in his own voice, but it's literally, 'Grarh, tell Zeus there's no activity in R'lyeh!' So, you know, that would just be boring."

Zeus accepted the news with a nod, too preoccupied to chuckle at the dig at Poseidon. "Both of you have done well," he said. "Return to my staging platform and await me. I will follow shortly."

Apollo and Iris bowed together and then rose skyward. "Do you think Demeter will have those cheese crackers?" Zeus heard Apollo ask.

"Ooh, maybe," said Iris. "I love those things, even if they do only come in one color."

Zeus watched them go, and then turned to his ex-wife. "Hera, I need you."

Hera laughed. "That has never been in question, ex-husband. Everyone needs me; you especially. But do I need you?"

"I am prepared to return your divinity to you, Hera. On one condition—"

"I shall not be extorted into remarrying, by you or any other."

"Will you let me finish?"

"Am I preventing you from finishing? Since when has anyone been able to stop the mighty Zeus?"

Zeus bit back a retort. "Remarrying is not the condition," he said. "I require—"

"Nor," Hera interrupted, "shall I be extorted into any other sort of conditional behavior in exchange for my divinity. Either trust me to make my own decisions, or bother me not!"

"Your previous decisions—" Again, he bit back his words. They had fought over her inaction after his murder, her siding with

Poseidon after his resurrection, and that hideous peacock paint job in the den. Rehashing it now would do little good. Hera watched him, lips pursed, perhaps daring him to try.

"Fine," Zeus said instead. "The damage the Cosmics are doing is much greater than expected. We must shield the planet from them. I cannot do this without your help, without your full power. I shall return your divinity, and I will *ask you*—very strongly, as your ex-husband and your king—to aid me in this. I will not make it a condition."

Hera watched him still. Only after seconds of silence did she say, "Well? If you are to do it, then do it."

"Not a 'yes, I will?' Or a 'no, I won't?' Just do it?"

"I wish to see how much you trust me," said Hera. "I care about such things, even if you do not."

He could argue, but even if he won the argument, he would lose. Best to just get on with it. Zeus pulled from his pocket the shining emerald that held Hera's divinity. With a squeeze of his hand, he crushed it over her head and willed the released essence back into Hera's form. As her divinity returned, as the green light particalized and infused her with its power, Zeus wished the process were quicker. He was eager to conclude this awkward confrontation and join the others on the staging platform.

Then he could get some of Demeter's cheese crackers, too.

CHAPTER TWENTY-THREE

"When visiting a god's temple, look for signage indicating whether the altar is inside or outside. Many ancient temples placed the altars outside, and this tradition was continued in the new constructions that followed the first Return. This confused modern worshippers who were used to going inside a place of worship. Despite protests from more conservative priests and priestesses, who continue to be touchy about the subject, many temples soon moved their altars inside, past the traditional gift shops."

—Temple Tripping on a Budget *(travel guide)*

LEIF AND TRACY HAD SPOTTED Apollo's temple miles before they reached it. Situated atop a bluff amid an otherwise flat expanse of brown and sage, its mirrored pillars and glass rooftop blazed with reflected sunlight. Even Leif's sunglasses could not diminish the building's blinding, luminescent glory. Leif had pegged it as a terrible driving hazard even before spotting the pile of abandoned cars beyond a barely-seen bend in the road.

Sheesh, Leif thought. *Gods.*

The road approaching the temple was blessedly easier on the retinas, shaded as it was by the bluff itself. Signs lined the roadway, each in the shape of a cartoon sun. The first sign read: *Washington State Temple of Apollo, 1,000 yards.* After that: *Temple of Apollo, 750 yards. SPF 30 sunscreen or greater required.* Then: *Temple of Apollo, 500 yards. SPF 50 sunscreen preferred.* And, finally, as they reached the top of the bluff where the road bisected a field of solar panels: *Temple of Apollo, 100 yards. Official Temple Sunscreen may be purchased at gift shop.*

A small gravel expanse bordered by a white rope formed the temple's parking lot. It contained one vehicle: a mini tour bus. Emblazoned with a "Spokane Divine Minibus Tours" along one side, it appeared not only full, but actively rocking on its wheels. Multiple groans of "grains . . . " came from inside, and Leif could just make out shuffling figures through the bus's tinted windows. The minibus's folding door was closed. A padlocked, golden chain kept it so, looped through a pair of exterior handles.

Leif decided to park at the opposite end of the lot.

"Are we there yet?" Tracy muttered, half-napping beneath her pulled-down ball cap.

"Shockingly, amazingly, finally, yes."

"Hot dog," she said, and looked up.

"Do you really think this will go as planned?"

"No, but stay positive. Sunny dispositions."

Leif sighed. "Pun intended?"

Tracy pointed toward the temple path and its sign declaring the same "Sunny dispositions!" affirmation she had apparently been quoting. "You'd have to ask them."

"I think I already know the answer." Leif opened the door and readied his defensive crowbar. "Watch out for that zombie-bus over there, and I hope you brought sunscreen money."

The temple's designers, be they ambitious mortals or Apollo himself, had melded a traditional marble foundation with modern mirrored columns and glass walls. A set of gradual steps, with a wheelchair ramp up the center, led to the temple's open doorway. Above the door, a fresco depicted Apollo at the controls of his sun chariot, lyre in one hand, bow in the other. Leif thought the artist didn't quite get the ears right.

Passing through the open doorway, they found themselves in a mirrored vestibule containing a closed, cross-barred wooden door. In the door's center hung a sign listing the temple's visitor hours: Monday through Sunday, dawn to dusk, and closed Thursdays from 2:30 to 3:30 p.m.

"It's not Thursday, is it?" Leif asked.

"Not unless I've lost track."

"So why isn't the door open?"

Tracy sighed. "I don't know, Leif. This is my first Apollonian temple." She slid her shotgun into a holster on her back, stepped forward, and pounded on the door. "Hello?"

"This has something to do with that zombie bus outside, I'll bet."

Tracy glanced at him. "Or maybe the two visitors openly carrying a shotgun and crowbar."

"Is that a yes on the bet, then?"

Before Tracy could answer, a light above the door glowed red. A welcoming, masculine voice spoke through unseen speakers: *"Welcome, supplicants, to the Washington State Temple of Apollo. Entrance to Apollo's temple is contingent on a successful ZInfDet scan. Do you consent?"*

"ZInfDet?" asked Tracy.

"Is that painful?" asked Leif.

"Zombie Infection Detection. ZInfDet. The scan takes ten seconds and is completely pain-free in ninety-nine percent of subjects. Side effects may include subdermal tingling, dry mouth, brief stomach cramps, shortness of breath, and waffle cravings. Do not consent to ZInfDet if you are pregnant or Australian. Tell your doctor if you are experiencing heart palpitations, kidney failure, or burning during urination. None of these are side effects of ZInfDet; it's just good self-care to tell a doctor about such symptoms, and this is your friendly medical reminder."

"Helpful."

"Ninety-nine percent?" asked Leif.

"We consent," said Tracy.

"Hey! Who says you can speak for me?"

"I say. It's a one-percent chance, and we're here for a reason. Suck it up."

"ZInfDet holy scan commencing. Please stand by."

The scan powered up with discernable hum. Leif braced himself for the worst, yet save for a light tingling in his ears, he felt nothing. It was over before he knew it. The red light switched to green.

"ZInfDet negative. Negative, in this case, is good. Sometimes people get confused about that. You are now free to enter. Welcome to the Temple of Apollo, our lord of sun, medicine, poetry, healing, archery, music, and many other wonderful things. For a full list of Lord Apollo's blessings, engraved for you on a keepsake medallion, please visit the gift shop immediately to your right as you enter the temple. And remember: wear sunscreen."

A mechanical *thunk* came from within, and the door swung open. Sunlight blazed through, flowing from the glass ceilings and magnified by the mirrored surfaces. Even wearing sunglasses, Leif had to shield his eyes to let them adjust.

Tracy grabbed his arm and led him through the doorway. The sun was intense and warm on his face, though the temple air itself had the temperature of a pleasant spring afternoon. Floating through that air, issued from somewhere deeper in the temple, was the melody of "Every Breath You Take" by The Police.

"Apollo-gies for the scan," said someone behind them. They turned to see a young man closing the door. The white of his temple robes contrasted flatteringly with his perfectly tanned skin, and his sun-bleached hair was pulled back in a man-bun. His voice matched the one on the speaker. "We must take such precautions these days."

"Understandable," said Tracy. "What if the scan had been positive?"

Leif snorted. "Oh, now it occurs to you to ask?"

"Ordinarily, the high priestess would've been called to cure you via Lord Apollo's power," he said. "It's just as well for you that it wasn't, however. I regret to say that such things are taking longer than usual lately. There's an entire busload in the parking lot that the priestess hasn't been able to cure just yet."

"Why not?"

The man smiled. "The gods work in mysterious ways."

"No, they really don't," said Tracy.

The man's smile turned piteous. It was the same kind of smile Leif used when someone said something too stupid to argue with—that he should buy an extended warranty, for example, or that clowns were funny. "I am Tristan, a temple acolyte. How may I help you?"

"We're just here to talk to Apollo—or pray. Whatever you want to call it," said Leif.

"Excellent!" Tristan clapped his hands together. "Follow me."

Tristan led them through the temple toward the altar, then back toward the entrance and the gift shop to get some sunscreen, and then again back toward the altar. Paintings, tapestries, and statues throughout the temple depicted Apollo, his many purviews, and scenes from his legends. Leif spotted a young Apollo battling a dragon, followed by a sad scene with a dryad, and then another showing the god having tea with Jimmy Hendrix, Yo-Yo Ma, Willie

Nelson, Aretha Franklin, and William Shakespeare.

"Because of course," Leif muttered. No one heard him, or, at least, no one cared to say so.

"All of you are so *tan*," Tracy commented. They had passed at least half a dozen other acolytes, each with perfectly sun-kissed skin, if you were into that sort of thing.

"It is one of the many benefits our devotion to Apollo," Tristan explained. "Marvelously tanned skin, no burns. And regular skin cancer screenings, free of charge."

"What about him?" Leif pointed to an acolyte polishing one of the temple mirrors. His skin was near beet red and peeling in places.

"Oh, that's Donald," Tristan whispered. "He's, ah, he's not working out."

They passed out of the main room into a small chamber. Sunlight beamed down through an open skylight onto an altar of gold. It would have been pretty, Leif thought, if not for the still-barf-sky. Thankfully the nausea and sinus headaches he'd felt from looking at it outside were somehow muted in here.

"Now," Tristan clapped again, "what have you brought to sacrifice?"

"Oh, we didn't bring anything," said Tracy. "He knows us."

"Hi Apollo!" Leif called. "We came all the way out here to your temple. Can we chat now?"

Tristan looked positively horrified. "Didn't bring anything? But—"

"He's not answering," Tracy told Leif.

"Well, I know that," said Leif. He moved closer to the altar. Maybe if he touched it when he talked?

"Our lord Apollo will not simply speak with you just for the asking," Tristan said, having regained a bit of composure. "That's not how it works. He has many demands on his time and must speak through—"

"Oh, we know he has a busy schedule," said Tracy. "That's why he wanted us to help bring Zeus back."

Leif nodded. "Frankly, I'm surprised he agreed to come back the second time." He lay both hands atop the altar. "Apollo? It's Leif Karlson!" Still nothing. Was there some sort of secret call switch? He turned back to Tristan. "Where's the 'open hailing frequencies' button?"

"There is no . . . Only the high priestess may . . . "

Something else occurred to Leif. "He couldn't still be mad about your slashing his throat that time, could he, Tracy?"

Tristan gaped at her. "You *slashed his throat?*"

Tracy shrugged. "It was him or me. I felt a little guilty after, but—"

"You slashed *our lord Apollo's throat?*"

"It turned out for the best, really," Leif said.

"It *what?*"

"Er, don't worry," said Tracy. "He got better."

Tristan slowly backed away. "Ah, please—please wait here, please." He turned and ran out of the room with a shout of, "Priestess!" In the distance, the music switched to something by The Doors.

Tracy shot him a glare. "You just had to bring up the throat thing?"

"It's a legitimate question!"

"Okay, fine, maybe. But we probably could have handled that better."

Leif shrugged. "Nah."

"We could try a sacrifice. Not that getting ourselves here in the first place wasn't sacrificial enough . . . "

Leif circled to the other side of the altar, and then tried knocking on it. Nothing. He set both hands atop it again, scrutinizing the surface for, well, anything. "Think Athena and Ryan made it to the Underworld?"

Whatever Tracy's answer, Leif didn't hear it. The power that surged through his hands as he said "Athena" proved too distracting, as did the subsequent throbbing headache and rapid unconsciousness.

As far as Tracy could tell, Leif had merely ducked behind the altar to look further for, well, whatever he was looking for. She was beginning to suspect his search would be fruitless, and, worse, that

Apollo might require additional sacrifice for the privilege of calling in a favor.

"I bet Athena didn't even put in that good word for us yet," Tracy told Leif just before a young woman entered the altar room.

"Speak not the names of other gods before Apollo's own altar, child," she scolded through a blissful smile. "It is considered rude."

Tracy sized her up. "You would be the high priestess here?" It seemed a fair guess, based on the golden elegance of her gown, the sun-granted highlights in her brunette tresses, and the photograph of her on the wall by the door declaring her the "Washington State Temple High Priestess" in Century Gothic font just above the name "Cecelia Fletcher-Shen."

Tracy extended her hand. "My name is Tracy Wallace."

Cecelia—or the High Priestess Cecelia, Tracy supposed—accepted the handshake in that limp, fingers-only way that always turned Tracy's stomach. "I am, child. Acolyte Tristan tells me there are some . . . irregularities in your sacrifice to our lord Apollo?"

"Yes, but—could you please not call me 'child'? I'm a grown woman and you don't look a day older than I am."

Cecelia's smile continued. "I mean no disrespect, Ms. Wallace. I only mean it in the sense that we are all children in comparison with our lord Apollo."

"So I should call you child as well, then?"

"Of course not, child. Now, how may I assist?"

Tracy swallowed one or five snarky remarks in the face of the priestess's beatific smile, forcing herself to get down to business. "I've come to make an entertainment-industry-related request of Apollo—"

"You mean *our lord* Apollo?"

"—along with my companion Leif Karlson." She was about to motion to Leif, but he wasn't there. "Leif? You're okay, right?" Leif popped up from behind the altar looking dazed but conscious. Good enough, Tracy figured, and turned back to the priestess. "I don't know if you've heard of us, but we actually met Apollo—"

"You mean *our lord* Apollo?"

"Yes, we met your lord Apollo in the flesh during the first Return, and helped him quite a lot then, right? So we were hoping that you would help us get a direct message to him, or maybe even call him here so we can chat."

"I am afraid it does not work that way, child."

"Could you at least, oh, try? We've come a very long way, through a whole mess of zombies, mind you. And we really did help him. I promise you he'll know us."

Cecelia clasped her hands behind her back and took a deep breath. "Even if we were to forgo the usual sacrifice, which would be blasphemy, Apollo does not speak directly to suppliants. There would be signs, which I would read, and then interpret for you."

"I'm reasonably sure he'll show up himself," said Tracy.

"That does not happen, child."

"Okay, you know what? Fine. I shouldn't have to do this, but you want a sacrifice?" She dug into her jacket and pulled out an official bronze *Monster Slayer* drink coaster. "See this? *Monster Slayer*. A show I used to produce. They don't make these coasters anymore because it's cancelled. It's signed by the late Jason Powers, star of the show." She flipped it over to show Jason's signature in ink on the genuine cork backing. "Valuable enough for a sacrifice?"

Cecelia eyed the coaster. "You just carry these around with you?"

"Don't judge me. Is it enough for you to take a message for Apollo?"

"I do not 'take messages' for our lord."

"Oh my god. Look, you know what I mean."

Cecelia huffed a sigh that was going to lead to Tracy to violence if she did it again. "Very well, child. I will accept this sacrifice." She held out both hands, and Tracy placed the coaster into them. "However, Apollo is temporarily unavailable at this time. You will have to wait."

Tracy stared. "Wait? How long?"

"I do not know. It is my hope it will only be a few days."

Tracy snatched back the coaster, about to accuse the priestess of stalling due to her jealousy over Tracy having met Apollo herself. But then a different thought occurred. "This has something to do with the sky, doesn't it? And why you can't heal zombies?"

"Our lord Apollo is distant at this time," she said. "We are not privy to his reasons. Perhaps he foresaw two blasphemous visitors claiming special privileges coming to his temple, and he opted to remain elsewhere," she added pointedly.

It was then that Leif, whom Tracy realized had been shockingly silent this entire time, spoke up. "Apollo is busy on errands from Zeus. There is a crisis among the gods that demands their attention." Leif's voice seemed more resonant, with a difference in timbre she couldn't quite put her finger on. Maybe he was just speaking from his diaphragm for a change?

"Leif?" Tracy tried.

"Leif is temporarily unavailable at this time," he said. "This is Athena. You may trust what I say."

Tracy crossed her arms, unsure if Leif was trying to pull something or Athena really was speaking through him—and unsure which option annoyed her more. "Athena? Seriously?"

Leif nodded. "I have had one Jerry of a day, let me tell you."

"Stop this folly!" Cecelia cried. "I have advised you not to speak the names of other gods before Apollo's altar. To pretend to *be* one of those gods is blasphemy of the highest order!"

Leif/Athena frowned. "It is not the *highest* order, Priestess, and you know it."

Tracy reached out to both of them. "Okay, let's everybody just calm down, right? Leif, cut out the goddess impersonation thing. It's not helping."

"I *am* Athena. I know of what I speak."

"Out!" Cecelia shouted. "Out of the temple with your foolishness!"

Leif/Athena rolled his/her eyes. "Be not so dramatic, Priestess."

Cecelia somehow pulled a compound bow from the folds of her gown and nocked an arrow taken from those same folds. "I said *out!*"

Tracy blinked at the arrow. "Where did you—"

"Apollo priesthood thing," said Leif/Athena. "A neat trick if you can do it."

Cecelia drew back the bowstring as three acolytes appeared in the hallway wielding bows of their own. Tristan stood behind them and played the theme from *The Good, the Bad, and the Ugly* on a lyre.

Tracy threw up her hands. "Alright, fine." She edged out of the altar room. Leif/Athena, fortunately, chose to follow. "But when Apollo gets back and hears you kicked us out at arrow-point, he's going to wrath the crap out of all of you."

CHAPTER TWENTY-FOUR

"You can't just stick the prefix 'cyber-' on everything and expect it to be awesome."

"Yes, you can."

"Well, you can, but you'll be disappointed."

"Will I, though?"

— *Muses Calliope and Thalia, Jet City Comic-Con*

THE TEMPLE DOOR SLAMMED shut behind them. The zombie-bus was still a-rockin'. Tracy pulled the shotgun off her back and turned to Leif/Athena ("Leif-thena?" she considered?), careful to keep the barrel pointed downward.

"Okay, what the hell?" Tracy started. "Seriously? Athena?"

He/she nodded and examined Leif's crowbar. "Seriously. Athena. Believe me, I do not like this any more than you do. Now, where is your vehicle? We must leave immediately."

"What? Okay, first of all, no, and second of all, where do you get off possessing Leif? Get out of there!"

"I cannot."

"Cannot, or will not?"

"The former." Leif-thena reached into his-her pocket and dug out the keys to the truck. "Now come, we are wasting time."

He-she headed out into the parking lot. Tracy ran after and grabbed his-her arm, stopping him-her on the gravel path. "Leif *is* still in there, right?"

"Of course he is."

"Oh, of course he is!" Tracy shot. "How dumb of me to want to confirm that in my first ever case of mortal possession-by-deity!"

Leif-thena tried to shake off her grip and continue, but Tracy held firm. He-she looked in shock at the unbroken grip and tugged again. Once more, Tracy held firm.

"What is wrong with this body?" he-she lamented. "It is so weak!"

"Did you get his consent before jumping in there?"

"I am an immortal being, Tracy Wallace. I do not need consent."

"Oh, that's not a shitty thing to say at all, Athena."

"I had no choice! My body burned up falling out of orbit, but I'm immortal! I had to go somewhere, and Leif invoked my name at an altar. The next thing I know, I am trapped in his body. The fact that there are some bizarre dimensional oddities occurring right now may have affected this. I confess I do not know. What I do know is that your quest to see Apollo has failed, whereas my quest to stop the zombies continues. You are quite a capable mortal, Ms. Wallace. I would *like* your help. Are you coming with me or not?"

"And what about Leif?"

"Leif is coming with me too, obviously."

"I mean how do we get you out of him?"

"That is a lesser issue. We shall attend to it later. I assure you that his mind is intact, and I will make my best effort to safeguard our shared body. He is now in agreement with all of this."

"So you say."

"Yes, so I do say. I am not a deceitful being. You must trust me."

Tracy frowned. Why couldn't anything be simple? She glanced away, considering. Beside the temple stood a seven-foot-wide ball of golden yarn on a pedestal. Beside that was a sign: *Washington State's third largest ball of yarn! Crafted and donated to the temple by the Yakima Skiffle Band Association.*

Weird.

"Truck keys first," Tracy said finally. "Then trust."

Leif-thena sighed and handed the keys to her. Tracy let go of his-her arm and pocketed them.

"Thank you. Now, let's go over here, look at this nice ball of yarn that's here for some reason, and you can tell me what crisis has Apollo so occupied." Tracy strode toward the yarn.

Leif-thena did not follow. "Don't worry about that," he-she said. "Zeus is dealing with it. With luck, it will be resolved within a few days."

"And without luck?" Tracy asked, turning her back on the yarn ball.

"Then you will be happy to know that your worries about the movie will not matter much. There is nothing you can do about that situation. There *is* something you can do about the zombies, and once again, I am mystified why you, as at least a semi-compassionate human being, do not seem to care about that."

"Not my circus, not my monkeys," Tracy muttered.

"You cannot truly believe that."

"No. But I like saying it, and instantly agreeing with anything you say feels wrong." Tracy sighed and slid her shotgun back into its holster. "So where do we have to drive to now? Spokane? Missoula, Montana? East Toejam, Wyoming?"

"Are you finished listing cities?"

"Probably not."

"I have been to the Underworld. I have spoken with the Fates. My search for answers has not yet been what I would deem successful, but I have it on good authority that I must now consult three ancient witches. We are driving to Maui."

Tracy's mouth dropped open, overburdened with objections. Before she could voice any of them, a sound from behind her chilled her bones.

"*Mew?*"

Leif-thena's eyes flicked up to something behind Tracy. Tracy turned to follow his-her gaze. A pair of glowing green eyes, couched in an adorable face of white feline fur, peeked over the edge of the temple roof. The razorwing—for Tracy had dealt with the little bastards enough in the First Return to recognize them on sight—stepped closer. Blue bat wings folded low across its back. It looked from Tracy, to the giant ball of golden yarn, and back to Tracy again.

"*Mew?*" it meowed again.

"*Mew?*" came an answering call from somewhere behind it. A crimson-winged razorwing jumped up to land beside its companion.

"*Mew?*" came still another, crawling over the top of the yarn ball.

"*Mew!*"

Tracy stepped back.

"*Mew!*"

She drew the shotgun again.

"You can't shoot them!" Leif-thena warned.

"No, but I can scare them off, maybe." Tracy backed off a few more steps, though the movement only seemed to attract further attention as more razorwings appeared atop both temple and yarn ball.

"*Mew?*"

"If you shoot them, you'll only make more!"

"Damn it, Athena, will you stop immortal-splaining? If you want to tell me something, tell me why these things are back after Zeus swore to me they'd all be banished!"

"As I said, bizarre dimensional oddities."

"Oh that's just your answer for everything, isn't it?"

"It is complicated!"

The razorwings—eight of them now—leaped to the ground. They stalked their way toward her on widdle bean-toed feet. Each had "Play wif me!" lurking in their wide, round eyes. Why a woman and man drew their attention more than a golden ball of yarn, Tracy did not know. Maybe it had to do with the shiny shotgun? Maybe she was just lucky?

"*Mew?*" inquired one.

"Gwains?" came from behind.

. . . *What?*

Tracy and Leif-thena both spun toward the new sound. There, not ten feet away, hobbled a desiccated razorwing. Its eyes glowed gray. Its wings were tattered and sickly green. Patches of snuggly fur were missing, and a yellow ooze dripped from its widdle open mouth. It was the most adorably disgusting zombie-kitten Tracy had ever seen.

Granted, she had only seen the one, but . . .

"Gwains?" it meowed again.

"Well," said Leif-thena. "That is new."

"Truck?"

"Truck."

They ran. The razorwings gave chase, mewling (and *gwains*ing) in either playful or murderous delight. Tracy made straight for the driver's side door of the truck. She shoved the key into the lock before realizing that was hardly necessary. The door was unlocked. Leif had even left the window open.

Another undead razorwing popped up from the driver's seat. "Gwains!"

Four months of anti-zombie reflexes kicked in before Tracy could stop herself. She hefted the shotgun and fired, point blank. The blast eviscerated the little monster, scattering its remains against the passenger door. Maybe, being a zombie, it would simply die?

That hope was dashed when two new razorwings sprang alive from the remains: one blue-winged, white-furred, and alive; the other a new zombie, nearly twin to its progenitor.

Leif-thena stared at Tracy through the passenger side window. "What did I *just say*?"

At this point, a few diligent readers may be saying, "Sure, zombie razorwings, Zeus and Hera's relationship dynamics, Iris tracking glitter everywhere—all these things are terribly fascinating, but what the heck ever happened with Ryan Seth Sloude?" Has the story, they may wonder, abandoned him, or worse, forgotten about him completely? Has he fallen into the same narrative black hole as Dave and the doctor from the previous book? (They remain fine, by the way. Dave is on a wildlife documentary crew, and the doctor has been vacationing in Australia, where there continue to be, for some reason, absolutely zero zombies.)

The answer to such Ryan-pondering is that no, he has not been forgotten. He continues to wait where Athena left him, just outside the Underworld, slumped against the cave wall and muttering occasionally to Cerberus about grains or false-dogs. His mental capacity is somewhere on the spectrum between drunken goldfish and flat-Earther, and there is meager reason to visit him again—at least, not yet.

In fact, perhaps the only reason the story mentions him just now is because it allowed the previous scene to end with that line from Leif-thena. That is, however, only a theory. The author cannot be reached for comment at this time; he may be planning a trip to Australia.

An additional note for those flat-Earthers who may have been put off by the preceding jab: if you can ignore piles and piles of observational evidence about the Earth being an oblate spheroid, you can certainly ignore one little slight in comedic fantasy novel.

Abandoning the truck, Tracy and Leif-thena sought shelter behind the zombie-filled tour bus. It had gained them little. One of the blue-winged kitties had gnawed through the golden chain holding the doors, and before you could say, "Well of *course* it did," the zombies onboard piled out. Not possessed of any grains themselves, Tracy and Leif-thena did not catch the zombies' attention, but the still-pursuing razorwings necessitated a hasty retreat from the bus anyway.

A mad dash and a moderate amount of profanity later, the two took shelter around the far side of the temple and paused to evaluate the situation.

"I really do not want to do the whole razorwing thing again!" Tracy spat. "I haven't even *seen* a laser pointer in six months!"

"We have gained some temporary measure of safety," Leif-thena reported after glancing back around the corner. "The razorwings now fight over some jewelry one of the zombies wears."

"Zeus has got a lot of explaining to do! He swore no monsters!"

"I do not believe this is directly his fault. It may even work to our advantage. Follow!"

Before Tracy could argue, Leif-thena ran farther around the temple. Leaping over rocks and scrub that dotted the temple grounds, he-she finally skidded to a stop near the edge of the bluff. Tracy hurried to catch up. She did so just as Leif-thena cupped her hands around her mouth and belted out a spine-grating screech. Echoing across the land below the temple plateau, the screech lasted a full ten seconds, which was about as much time as it took for Tracy to place why it sounded so familiar.

"There's a very good reason you're making dial-up modem sounds, right?" Tracy asked.

"I am hoping to summon something."

"Like what, Olympia On-Line?"

"The razorwings are back because the dimensional barriers that kept monsters out of your world are weakened. Ergo, another of my designs may be out there and useful to us."

"The solution to our situation is *not* more monsters, Athena. Weren't you goddess of wisdom?"

"I grow weary of you asking that," he-she shot. "Not all monsters are monstrous. Some are merely unnatural creatures that happen to fall under the 'monster' classification."

"Dumb classification system, then."

Leif-thena burst out with another modem-screech. "Zeus defined it."

"So I stand uncorrected."

He-she thrust an arm out toward the horizon. "Behold!"

Tracy beheld. For a moment, she beheld nothing but barf-sky, which gave her a nice stabby feeling in her sinuses. Then came a glint in the distance: a tiny mote of something was streaking their way, leaving a faint contrail in the sky. So she beheld that instead.

"He comes," Leif-thena announced. "You surely recall the great winged horse of legend known as Pegasus? Witness my own improvement for the twenty-first century: Athena presents—in conjunction with Hephaestus and Poseidon, funded by a grant from the Hermes Group—CyberPegasus!"

With a whinny barely audible over the roar of its jet engine, the creature blasted toward them. It boasted a coat of a dazzling white, with wing feathers to match. Just before it was upon them, CyberPegasus cut its engines, flapped its wings, and slammed to the ground on four polished metal (chrome) hooves. Almost immediately, the matching (also chrome) engines mounted on either side of its rump folded themselves up. They retracted into the creature's haunches until all that remained were two curved panels of metal (more chrome).

Leif-thena stepped closer, extending one hand out in friendship and whispering something soothing in a language Tracy did not understand. CyberPegasus pawed the ground, skittish, its metallic eyes wide and glowing blue. Yet it let Leif-thena approach until he-she got close enough to slide one hand along the length of the creature's nose. Half of its skull was either made of or covered in metal (yes, more chrome). Leif-thena stroked the flesh side and whispered another few sentences until the creature tossed its blue mane and kneeled. Leif-thena clambered immediately onto its back.

"Get on. He will bear us to Maui."

All Tracy could think of was the single time she'd ridden a horse as a girl. Daisy, a Shetland pony described as "gentle and friendly" had thrown her no less than three times in ten minutes. The pony had even punctuated the last one by pooping on her and galloping off with what Tracy could've sworn was an actual human snicker. Even after the carnie at Jimbob's Traveling Ponyfest and Chili Cookoff had found Tracy a nicer animal, she wound up with so many sore muscles that she was put off horses forever. She couldn't conceive of riding as far as the middle of the Pacific Frigging Ocean.

"Um, even if that thing doesn't throw me the second it takes off, Maui is a *long* way away."

"Not so far with him," Leif-thena said.

"We'll freeze our asses off."

"He's got heated seats," Leif-thena said.

"But—"

"Woman, get on the winged cyberhorse and help me eradicate the zombies, or so help me I shall leave you here to get nibbled to death by cats."

Tracy half-considered trying to get back into the temple to take her chances with Cecilia again. But then she would be leaving Leif entirely in Athena's hands. Plus, the temple doors were closed. Also, at least a dozen razorwings were flying over the temple toward her. One was wearing a Divine Tours baseball cap Tracy had seen on the head of one of the zombies. The razorwing beside it merely carried that zombie's severed head.

"Heated seats, eh?" Tracy scrambled onto CyberPegasus's back. "You better not be lying about that."

"I do not lie about heated seats. Personal code." Leif-thena leaned forward across CyberPegasus's mane and squeezed its neck. The creature took to the sky with a flap of wings and a blast of jet wash that scattered the pursuing razorwings in a chorus of *yrowl*ing.

"That's an oddly specific personal code. And I can't help but notice we're flying the exact wrong direction for Maui!"

Though the sky was still barf, the location of the sun was easy enough to mark. They were heading almost dead east. Wind whipped at Tracy's hair. She had to squeeze her thighs around the creature's back and hug Leif-thena's waist tighter to keep from slipping off. The air rushed past her face, the resulting tears nearly blinding her.

She did have to admit, however: the creature's back *was* heated.

"Oh, we are going the right way!" Leif-thena yelled over the wind. "The quickest path between two points is not always a straight line!"

CyberPegasus pitched forward before Tracy could answer. Her heart dropped into her stomach. They were diving almost straight down, with no sign of slowing. The roar of the creature's engines pitched higher. The blurred landscape below fast sharpened into worrisome detail: Individual buildings. Individual cars. Individual signs advertising free Wi-Fi. Tracy screamed, bracing for impact. Her last thought was that she was never going to trust another god ever again—mostly because she was about to be dead.

Then the world vanished. Tracy's stomach squeezed into a point. The wind had ceased, yet she sensed that she now traveled at an even more frightening speed. She could see nothing. Then she realized her eyes were squeezed shut and forced one open enough to see streaks of blue flying past amid a dark void. A fraction of a second later, CyberPegasus whinnied, Tracy's stomach unclenched, and she felt herself flying through the air once more.

They were flying upward again, gradually. Below them stretched an expanse of beach, crystal clear waters, and some very confused beach-goers, all of whom were presumably pointing at the flying white horse with its mounted jet engines, two passengers, and heated seats.

"What the hell just happened?" Tracy yelled.

"What, that?" Leif-thena called back. "CyberPegasus can walk, gallop, fly, jet, and also jump via any two places connected by the Internet. He also features air-to-air missiles and a refrigerated storage compartment in the withers. Welcome to Honolulu! Next stop, Maui!"

CHAPTER TWENTY-FIVE

"There are plot holes, and then there are plot holes, *if you take my meaning."*

—Calliope, On Musing: A Memoir of the Craft

THE HOLE HAD APPEARED in the great goddess Undeath's Obsidian Realm only minutes earlier. It began as a tear in the aether—just to the left of the Cerebral Siphon at the platform's center—and soon widened into a meter-high oval-shaped breach.

At first, Momo suspected Athena. She had tried to destroy the Siphon before she escaped; was this dimensional hole some new form of attack? Yet the hole had not intersected the Siphon, nor damaged it in any way; the Siphon continued to feed the goddess's mind from the brains her risen children devoured. Even the portion of the platform penetrated by the hole's ventral reaches showed no actual damage.

Yet, if it spread?

Momo slid one arm into the hole, half expecting the arm to be destroyed. It disappeared through the hole, but also slid back out just as easily. (Had Momo needed to breathe, he would have let out a sigh of relief. A destroyed arm would easily grow back, but concentrating on regenerating body parts was a pain in the ass—unless he had to regenerate his actual ass. That was almost disturbingly painless.)

He slid his arm through the hole—the rift?—again. Unable to feel anything remarkable on the other side, he withdrew his arm, took hold of his skull with both hands, and popped it off. Then, carefully—this sort of thing made him dizzy—he eased his skull through the rift, keeping a firm grip on his parietal bone.

He saw nothing but a dark tunnel and a dim scarlet light glowering in the distance.

Something tugged on his elbow, gently, drawing him backwards out of the hole. He turned his skull to look toward the one doing the tugging.

"Do not thrust your skull into dimensional rifts, Momo," Undeath told him. "You do not know where they have been."

"I thought it might be a threat to you," he said. "And you were . . . indisposed." Actually, she had been standing on the edge of the obsidian platform, extending her arms and humming to herself. Momo had been unsure if she were in a meditative trance or her mind had simply flicked away to insanity once more. *Indisposed* felt like the politest term for it. He had no desire to offend his honored mistress, no matter how loopy she got.

"It is no threat," she said. "It is better. It is a gift."

"A gift from whom?"

"From the cosmos," said Undeath. Her smile broadened. The violet glow in her eyes intensified. "We have been given a way out."

"Truly?" Momo cackled, but mildly. (There was no sense in going over the top with a cackle if no one but his mistress would hear.) "Where does it go?"

Undeath reached toward the hole, stretching it, shaping it with motions of her hands. "To power," she whispered, "and to a place where we may bring joy to all who now suffer the burden of living. Soon they shall all be . . . better!"

"Won't they be thrilled!" Momo cackled again.

"Most definitely they will. Now put your head back on so we can go."

CHAPTER TWENTY-SIX

"For mortals who wish to visit the Graeae—a.k.a. the Grey Sisters, or the 'Stygian Witches' in some less reputable modern films—we offer this advice: Don't. Yes, they are known to possess knowledge and magic valuable beyond words. Yes, finding them is less difficult now than it was in ancient times. But they have all the hospitality of a serial killer. Anecdotal evidence indicates that uninvited visitors are less likely to become enlightened than they are to become dinner. Those who enter invited are even more likely to become dinner, since it stands to reason the Graeae would only extend such invitations when hungry. Just because the myths say Perseus got the best of them by swiping the single eye they all share, don't expect you can do the same. After all, Perseus was Zeus's son, and, more importantly, you are not."
—A Mortal's Guidebook to the Olympians' Return (2nd Edition)

"If you have a problem, if no one else can help, and if you can steal their eye, maybe you can hire . . . the Grey-Team!"
—The Grey-Team, *pilot episode (unproduced)*

TRACY HAD NEVER been to Maui. Hawaii never held much fascination for her; in hindsight, she suspected that might be a subconscious side-effect of having a father whose rival brother controlled the oceans.

During the first season of Monster Slayer, Jason Powers had scoured the Internet for rumors of monster attacks in Hawaii so he could justify a second season jaunt there, but as a) Jason had died and the monsters had vanished before there could be a second season, and b) all Jason could find were rumors of some sort of ludicrous "black smoke monster" that no one could verify, that had never happened.

As CyberPegasus soared toward what remained of Maui (after both previously dormant volcanos had ravaged the island), Tracy could make out few signs of civilization. Several spots of green grew amid the cooled volcanic slag. A couple of newly-constructed buildings dotted the coastline, as did scattered remnants of half-collapsed hotels, which leaned out of the cooled lava like toppings on a pan pizza. Athena now directed them toward one of those—a hotel, not a pizza (although Tracy's rumbling stomach would not have turned down the latter, gluten-filled crust be damned).

Except . . .

"Hey!" Tracy pointed ahead. "Why are we heading toward that river of lava?"

"CyberPegasus wants to recharge!"Leif-thena seemed to be trying to steer him away from the languid, glowing river and toward the hotel remains that lay a quarter mile north, but the creature whinnied in defiance. "He's fueled by geothermal power and steel-cut oats. I believe his batteries are low."

"But we just started flying ten minutes ago! You designed this?"

"He came when I called! I did not specify 'go recharge yourself before you evacuate us!' Would you rather he left us waiting with the razorwings?"

The river was nearing. She could feel the heat on her face, and CyberPegasus was being particularly stubborn about his course.

"I would rather not plunge into molten rock! He can't wait ten seconds to drop us off?"

"He *is* a wild creature!"

"*Your* wild creature!" Tracy tried to throw her weight to one side, digging in her heels to steer the creature, but nothing worked. "Make him stop!"

"I am *working on that!*"

It was too late. Tracy knew it in her heart—with their speed, the distance to the lava, the heat, there was no way Leif-thena could halt CyberPegasus in time to save them from anything but the most horrible, burning—

The world turned upside down as CyberPegasus did a barrel roll to one side. He came out of it on a perpendicular course away from the lava, and then pulled up short with a flap of wings and a blast of retro-jets. With a single buck, he threw them both. Tracy hit the soil like a newborn baby: dazed, screaming, and slightly irritated. Leif-thena landed beside her and promptly puked with a copiousness that likely owed more to Leif's physiology than anything under Athena's control.

CyberPegasus whinnied a snicker and then trotted off toward the lava.

Tracy fought to hold in her own stomach's contents and gasped, "You said Hermes helped design him?"

Leif-thena, still fighting her own vomitive battle, could only nod.

"Hey, maybe next time don't collaborate with a god of mischief!"

"He was very charming," Leif-thena managed. "And I did not expect to be riding the creature myself!"

Suddenly, Thalia burst into being atop a nearby rock. She sat with her back arched. Her red hair billowed in the wind. "Also when she was designing him, Hermes had recently returned from a little adventure with me to a cyberpunk world-setting, so he was itching to express himself in the cybernetic aesthetic. I suggested he call the creature 'C.P.' for short, since CyberPegasus is such a mouthful, but no one listened to me."

Tracy stared. "What are you doing here?"

Thalia beamed. "Oh, just popping in to plug a short story I was featured in, and capitalizing on an opportunity to say the words 'cybernetic aesthetic,' which is a really enjoyable rhyme that, let's face it, doesn't come up much in conversation nearly as often as it should. Plus I thought appearing right now might be at least a little funny, so I figured, what the heck, why not add a little Thalia-commentary? Except now I have to go. But first I'm going to turn into a nēnē, because those birds are native to Hawaii and it's also fun to say 'nēnē.' Have a nice time on Maui! Don't pick up any cursed tikis!"

Thalia beamed anew, waved happily, and then nene-ed off into the sky before anyone could cram a word in edgewise.

Tracy watched her go. "That was unhelpful."

"Not entirely," Leif-thena answered. "I am beginning to warm to the C.P. nickname."

"Yeah, okay." Tracy supposed it was as useful as her thinking of

Leif-thena as simply Athena for the time being, brevity being a thing and all.

Athena appeared to check Leif's shirt for vomit stains. Finding none, she crawled to his feet. "Damage assessment?" she asked.

"What?"

Athena offered Leif's hand to help Tracy up. "Broken bones? Sprained joints? Are. You. Okay?"

Tracy stood, dusting herself off. "Mostly okay. How's Leif?"

"This body is in no worse shape than it already was."

"Well we can't all have a goddess's physique," Tracy muttered. "We're at least near where these three ancient witches are, yes? Or do we have to hike into an active volcano?"

Athena started toward the beach, blessedly away from the lava flow where C.P. was trotting about. "The Grey Sisters make their dwelling in the penthouse suite of the Hoʻokahi Maka Resort Hotel, which is a mere thousand meters that way."

Tracy followed, casting her gaze to where Athena pointed. "You mean that collapsed hotel that's on its side, half buried, and generally uninhabitable?"

"That's the one."

"Alright then."

Athena hefted Leif's crowbar and gave it a few experimental swings. Tracy groaned at the implication.

"And you're expecting a fight," she said.

"We should be prepared for one," said Athena. "The Grey Sisters are seldom cooperative."

Tracy finally figured out why that name rang a bell. "These are the same hags that some old hero dealt with? Who wanted to eat him? They're still alive?"

"Perseus. The very same." Athena slid the crowbar back into its sheath on Leif's belt. "Yes, they did, and yes, they are. Word to the wise: do not call them hags to their faces."

"Fantastic."

"As a matter of fact, it is unwise to call anyone a hag to her or his face if you wish to avoid angering them."

"Yeah, thanks for the tip." Tracy felt in her pockets to make sure her spare shotgun shells were still there. They were. She also found

Rod's $100 Queequeg's Frozen Yogurt gift card, and some mints she had forgotten about. Bonus. "They just had one eye between them, right? Was that true?"

"It still is, the last I heard. And one tooth."

Tracy guessed they didn't do a whole lot of chewing. "Maybe we should fly back to civilization and buy them a blender."

"We shall make that Plan B," Athena said.

"What's Plan A?"

"Sneak in close, take their eye, and hold it hostage until they answer our questions." Athena shrugged. "It's the standard Grey Sisters Protocol."

They had scaled the pile of mud and lava rock leading up to the south side of the hotel before Leif spoke again within the mind Athena shared with him.

I don't see why you won't just tell Tracy, he said.

We are entering dangerous territory. I will not distract her with Thalia's Bundy Bunch reference.

Brady Bunch!

Whatever.

It astounded Athena how desperately the mortal wished to explain to Tracy that Thalia's closing comment referred to a fictional child who, during his own Hawaiian vacation, had found a cursed tiki. It had apparently led to hijinks.

Leif managed a mental sigh. *Fine. Will these witches know anything about getting you out of my body?*

While it is not our top priority, rest assured that, given the chance, I will ask.

You'd better.

Oh, believe me. Now be silent, Athena told him. *I must concentrate.*

She and Tracy had made it to what now passed for the "top" of the hotel; it had once been the ocean-facing side, but now it lay facing the sky. Suite windows—most broken, some miraculously intact—lay between balconies that jutted skyward. Most of the suites were dark, but a light flickered through windows in the far corner—what was once the top floor of the Ho'okahi Maka.

Tracy pointed at the penthouse suite, her expression questioning. Athena nodded. Together they moved toward the light, both trying to approach silently.

Heh, A.B.S., came Leif's thoughts. *Always be sneaking. Too bad we don't have Ryan here. I mean, if he were actually good at sneaking.*

Hush.

What happened to Ryan, anyway?

He contracted zombieism in the pit. By now, his spirit has surely gone to its final resting place in the afterlife.

Bummer, said Leif.

It is the way of things. Now hush!

Sorry, said Leif. *Open brain-mic.*

One of the suite's windows was now only steps away. Athena crouched. Tracy followed suit. Athena lay on her stomach against the hotel surface. Tracy followed suit. Athena motioned for Tracy to stay where she was. Tracy . . . followed suit, making the same motion back at Athena. Athena shrugged, and together they crawled to the edge of the window and peeked into the suite.

It was as if they were looking in from a skylight. Rather than seeing a wrecked hotel suite turned on its side, as anyone familiar with the laws of physics might expect, it appeared that the suite's entire insides had somehow rotated ninety degrees: The suite's floor remained parallel to the ground. The walls remained perpendicular. Furniture—the couches, tables, and other accoutrements of the living room—was patently intact, not strewn about in a wreck. Judging by glow of the TV, the electricity even functioned. In fact, only two things seemed to indicate that the suite had suffered damage at all. One, the balcony door and the window they were looking through were on what was now the ceiling. Two, the suite as a whole looked to have not received any sort of turn down service in over a year. Grime covered most of the furniture and walls, mildew festooned the carpet directly below the window, and in the far corner lay either a giant bird's nest or the third-largest muddy stick-and-feather collection Athena had ever seen.

An L-shaped couch, large enough for six people, sat before the glowing TV, and on the couch sat the Grey Sisters. Hotel bathrobes that may have once been white wrapped each of their skeletal bodies, but it was the Sisters' faces that appeared strangest: None had eyes, nor even space on their faces where eyes might go. Their foreheads began above their mouths. Their noses sat smack in the forehead's center, with the bridge of each nose disappearing up into their hairlines — at least for the two who had hair. Athena heard Tracy gasp at the sight of them.

"The hair is how you tell them apart," Athena whispered. "Pemphredo with the long hair, Enyo with the bob. Deino is the bald one, if you don't count the feathers."

Those are feathers? asked Leif.

What did I just tell you? Do you not see? Their white hair, the white feathers behind the ears? Their smoky, leathery hands? Is it not obvious they are part swan?

Oh, yeah, swans. Sure, that's exactly what they look like, said Leif. *Is Enyo holding a Rubik's Cube?*

Athena looked closer. Pemphredo held the eye the three shared: a golden disk half the size of a coaster with a glowing red gemstone in the center. She kept it pressed to her forehead as she watched TV. Deino had in her lap a book in braille. Her dark gray fingertips slid across the pages. And yes, Enyo did indeed hold one of the multicolored puzzle cubes. (Athena still thought of them as Daedalus's Cubes. Ernő Rubik had the same idea millennia later, except Rubik's design — unlike Daedalus's — did *not* explode when taken apart.) Enyo blindly turned one side of the cube twice, then rotated another the opposite direction. She held it out to Pemphredo.

"Is it solved now?" Enyo asked.

Her sister glanced at the cube. "No," she said, and returned her attention to the TV.

Enyo turned another two sides. "Now?"

"No."

"Now?"

"You only turned it upside down, Enyo."

"Just making sure you were paying attention," said Enyo, turning another few sides. "What about now?"

"If you two don't shut up," hissed Deino, "I'm going to take the eye away from both of you, and then there will be no Daedalus-cube or *Zombie Slayer* show for anybody!"

"*Zombie Slayer*?" Tracy whispered. "Ugh. Rotten *Monster Slayer* knockoff . . . "

"Shh," said Athena.

It's a sore spot with her, Leif explained. *She had a lawsuit pending until her lawyer was suddenly eaten. Oddly,* not *by a zombie.*

At once, Deino stared straight at Tracy and Athena—or as well as one can stare without eyes. "And that goes for you at the window as well! Go away!"

Good job, guys, thought Leif.

Athena sighed. "This is why I wanted you to stay back," she whispered to Tracy as she stood up.

"That would have done no good!" Pemphredo cackled. "We smelled you as soon as you trespassed upon our hotel!"

"Not to mention magical detection when you first landed!" Enyo added. "You mortals can't sneak up on us! We're witches, bitches!"

"We were not sneaking," Athena answered. "We only wished not to disturb you. We come with questions."

"Questions disturb us!" shouted Enyo.

"Get off our lawn!" added Deino.

"My apologies for that," Athena tried, "but I am the goddess Athena. What I have to speak with you about involves—"

"Athena is no longer a goddess!"

"Nor is she a scrawny twenty-something male!"

"This body suits my current needs," Athena said. "I *am* Athena."

Enyo pointed accusingly, still holding the Daedalus cube. "*If* we believe you, it does not change the fact that you are no longer a goddess."

"We are *not* impressed," Pemphredo added.

"Get off our lawn!" Deino repeated.

"You will not hear my questions?" Athena asked.

"What are we, librarians? Go!"

"Do you not even wish to try to eat my young, scrumptious manflesh?" Athena tried.

Young, scrumptious manflesh? Leif repeated with distaste.

We're still on get-close-then-steal-eye protocol. I will not allow them to truly eat you.

Yeah, but it still sounded corny.

"Scrumptious?" Enyo scoffed. "You're all stringy!"

"Plus then we would have to skin you, cook you, season you," Deino added. "A whole production!"

Pemphredo nodded. "We already ordered out. Food is being delivered as we speak! You're not invited!"

"So," Deino growled, standing up, "you can leave now the easy way, or the hard way. Final chance."

Athena judged the distance down to where Pemphredo sat with the eye. *Can these legs take a one-story jump?* She thought to Leif.

Sure. Just bend my knees, okay?

Well, obviously.

Hey, you asked.

Athena sighed and motioned for Tracy to stay put. "As you wish. The hard way, then."

With that, Athena dove across the window, grabbed the opposite window frame, and swung herself toward the Grey Sisters' couch. She would grab the eye from Pemphredo, dash back around, and —

Athena slammed against an invisible barrier midway to the couch. She fell to the floor, rammed Leif's tailbone into the mildewed carpet, and cursed.

The Grey Sisters cackled like it was going out of style.

"Boom!" cried Deino. "Magical force field!"

"We're witches, bitches!" called Enyo once again.

"Going after this?" Pemphredo waved the eye. "You really think we'd let anyone close enough to steal it anymore?"

"Twenty-two times was enough!" spat Deino.

Outside, something screeched in the distance.

"Athena?" called Tracy.

The Sisters cackled again. "And here come the consequences!"

"And the food!"

Tracy watched the sky as Athena pulled herself to Leif's feet. "Something is coming," Tracy called, pulling out her shotgun. "Something big!"

"Oh, Harriet's not *that* big," argued Enyo.

"If you hurt her feelings, she'll just be more upset with you!" warned Deino.

"What is it?" Athena called. She cast about for something to climb up to the window again. "I'm coming!"

"No helping!" shouted Pemphredo, who now had a whip in her hand along with the eye. She slung it at Athena. The whip tangled about her knees, and Pemphredo yanked. Leif's body was no match for it. Athena slammed to the carpet again, cursing her luck and marveling at the witch's aim without the benefit of depth perception.

"I'm pretty sure it's a harpy!" Tracy called back. Athena could hear her loading the shotgun. "Biggest one I've ever seen! And it's carrying a red, rectangular package?"

"That would be our pizza!" Deino clapped. "You can't have any!"

"Did she remember the hot wings?" Enyo asked.

Athena struggled to untangle the whip. Barbs along its length had dug into Leif's jeans and skin. His body didn't have the strength to fight against Pemphredo's tugging. "I'm stuck!" she called to Tracy. "You'll have to fight it off! Shoot for the wings!"

The hot wings? Leif asked.

Quiet!

"I know how to deal with harpies!" Tracy called. "Jason fought them on *Monster Slayer!*"

"But you were just the producer!" Athena warned.

"Don't undercut my confidence!"

Pemphredo stopped tugging on the whip. "Did she say . . . ?"

"Monster Slayer?" asked Enyo.

"Are you Tracy Wallace?" tried Deino.

A murderous screech from above cut through the air, followed by the blast of Tracy's shotgun. The harpy screeched again. There was a flap of wings, and a pizza bag dropped through the window and squelched onto the carpet next to Athena.

"Harriet, stop!" called Pemphredo. "Do not harm the mortal!"

"Tracy Wallace!" Deino shouted after. "Cease fire! You will not be harmed!"

Is this some sort of trick? Leif asked.

They already hold a superior position, Athena sent. *A trick would serve no purpose.*

Either Tracy thought otherwise, or she just hadn't heard. The shotgun erupted again.

"Tracy, stop!" Athena shouted.

Tracy appeared in the window above. "What? Why?"

"It appears they are fans."

Pemphredo nodded. "We have every episode of *Monster Slayer* on Blu-ray!"

Enyo waved. "Can we have your autograph?"

CHAPTER TWENTY-SEVEN

"A matchup between Medusa and a kraken cannot be called a 'clash of Titans' because neither Medusa nor a kraken IS a Titan! The movie's title alone is ludicrous."

"Don't mind Apollo. He just hates that whole film because they left him out of it."

"Not the whole film; Burgess Meredith turned in an excellent performance."

—*Apollo and Hermes, live press conference, First Olympian Return*

HARRIET, THE LARGEST HARPY that Tracy had ever seen—not that she had seen more than a handful—now sat in her nest in the corner of the Grey Sisters' suite. All of Tracy's shotgun blasts had missed her, but Harriet would not take her gaze off of Tracy. The harpy's eyes gave the impression that, were Tracy not under the Sisters' protection, Harriet would happily rip the shotgun away and turn it on her, or perhaps just beat her to death with it.

Enyo leaned toward Tracy while keeping a firm hold on the tray of hot wings in her lap. "So what was Jason Powers really like?"

Obnoxious, Tracy thought. *Full of himself. Irritatingly smug. A flirtatious pain in the butt.* She kept those to herself, afraid to raise the witches' hackles by ridiculing a man they clearly revered. "A great fighter," she said. "Charming. Funny. Brave. I miss him."

It was all true, she realized. Even the last bit. The witches nodded in reverence.

Athena cleared her throat. "Now that Ms. Wallace has answered your questions, please see fit to answer mine."

"Quiet, you!" Enyo spat. "Go on, Ms. Wallace."

"Er, well," started Tracy, "I'm not really sure what else you want to—"

The sight of Pemphredo shoving a pizza slice into a blender and pouring some dark liquid in after it broke Tracy's train of thought. Pemphredo flicked the switch. The blender screamed to life and turned the whole thing to a homogeneous ooze.

"Um," Tracy tried when the blender stopped.

Deino, who now held the eye, must have caught the appalled look on her face. "What? Does that disgust you? How the frag else do you think we can eat pizza with only one tooth?"

"One tooth among the three of us!" Pemphredo shot before lifting the blender and chugging its contents.

"Er," said Tracy. Talk about mood-whiplash. "I was only thinking—have you ever thought about dentures?"

Athena winced.

"Oh!" Deino burst. "Dentures! Of course! We never thought of that! Because we are imbeciles!"

Pemphredo lowered the blender and wiped her lips. "Dentures don't work on us, dumbass!"

"We are very sensitive about that!" shouted Enyo. "And we are probably sorry that we are yelling at you! We still liked your show!"

"We hope you make another!" screamed Deino.

Tracy gave them the sort of smile she normally reserved for contract negotiations. "Thank you. And, ah, I don't blame you for being sensitive. I can't imagine how frustrating it must be to have to share only one eye and one tooth."

"*Thank* you!" said Enyo, who then bit into one of the hot wings with the aforementioned tooth and sucked at the meat. "At last someone says it!"

Pemphredo started refilling the blender. "It is an immutable aspect of what we are. Just as fish must swim and dogs must pretend they can't talk, we must endure the Limitation of One, lest we cease to exist."

"We also must share one TV remote!"

"One toothbrush, one sock . . . "

"One pair of underwear. One smartphone."

"One Netflix account!"

"Though we do each have our own bathroom here."

"Thank the gods!" the Sisters intoned as one.

"And you have my friendship," Tracy tried, "which you may also share among you."

"That just sounds corny," said Deino. "Is she mocking us?"

"I assure you I'm not," said Tracy. "But I understand your time is valuable. May I implore you to answer our questions and share your wisdom?"

"It really does sound corny," said Enyo between sucks. "But ask your questions."

"And then learn the price of our answers," added Pemphredo. "With our friendship discount, of course."

Tracy motioned to Athena, who said, "Hades is in exile. I wish to know how to return him from that state."

Enyo giggled against her hot wing. "That was not a question."

"Give your inquiry in the form of a question!" Deino screeched.

Athena bristled. "How can I return Hades from his exile?" She glanced between the three witches. The expression the ex-goddess made with Leif's face reflected trepidation—though Tracy admitted to herself that she had no clue if that meant Athena truly felt trepidation, or felt something else that just looked that way when translated via Leif's possessed face. Constipation, for instance.

The witches cooed conspiratorially, which soon turned to chuckling.

"You wish to restore Hades?"

"The Unseen One? The Rich One? The Unyielding?"

"The 'old Jerry'?"

Athena nodded. "I need a way to summon him back to this world, and to get Zeus to return his divinity."

"But Hades is already in this world," Pemphredo chuckled.

"He is just powerless," Enyo added.

"His exile is not one of geography like the others," said Deino. "It is one of form, of mind, and of capability."

Enyo shook her hot wing-clutching fists above her head and cried, "A Titan against a Titan!!!"

Deino turned at Enyo's outburst. "What? No, nitwit!"

"You are always shouting that! It has *never* applied!" Pemphredo added.

"I do not care! It's fun to shout!" Enyo stuck out her tongue and blew a raspberry.

Tracy glanced at Athena. "If Hades is still around, then where is he?"

The witches shrugged in triplicate. "This knowledge is not ours to give," whispered Pemphredo.

"Also, we do not know it," said Enyo.

"Save for that Hades's nature will tell," said Deino.

"And the right one will tell," said Pemphredo.

"And the right one will smell!" declared Deino.

Enyo threw up her fists. "A Titan against a"—Pemphredo *whomp*ed Enyo with the blender cup—"Ow! Bitch!"

Athena scoffed. "That is all you know?" Though well within earshot, the witches gave no sign of hearing her.

"That is all you know?" Tracy tried.

"No, of course not," said Deino. "We do know where his *divinity* is."

"And we will tell you," said Enyo, "in exchange for a very special favor from Ms. Wallace."

Athena put a staying hand on Tracy's arm. "Wait. Zeus has my divinity. He's had the divinity of all the Punished. If Hades remains on Earth, powerless, then Zeus surely holds his divinity as well."

Pemphredo chuckled from deep in her throat. "Not Hades's."

Enyo pointed in Athena's general direction. "Your divinity, and that of the others, was personally stripped by Zeus himself. He pocketed it."

"The Exile Fountain dealt with Hades and the others," said Deino.

"But Zeus created the Exile Fountain," Athena argued.

"It is a mechanism! It is different!" Deino shouted. "Just go with it!"

Enyo nodded. "The Fountain's energies could not banish one as powerful as Hades from this world entirely. It therefore transformed him into one who knew not what he truly was, stripped his divinity, and sent it not-even-Zeus-knows-where."

Pemphredo motioned to herself and her sisters. "But *we* know!"

"You know something that Zeus does not?" Athena crossed Leif's arms. "How is that possible?"

"We sit around here all day! Plenty of time for research and divination!"

"We're witches, bitches!"

"Also, some bird told us," Pemphredo finished. "We know."

"Prove it, then," Tracy tried. "Where is Hades's divinity?"

"Oh, but first, you must pay our price," Deino whispered.

"You will give us the lost footage of *Monster Slayer*," said Enyo. "Jason Powers's final battle!"

Inwardly, Tracy recoiled. Jason's final battle was with the Erinyes, who'd carried him into the sky and then let him plummet to his death on the rocks below. She would not give them access to a snuff film. "We weren't filming when Jason died," she lied. "It wasn't part of the show."

"You were filming," said Deino. "But that is not what we meant."

"We want the battle with the turtle-frog from before he died."

"Athena's turtle-frog."

"We know that episode was never completed. It never aired. But we know the footage exists. Give it to us for our collection, and we shall tell you what you wish to know."

Tracy considered. "The footage technically belongs to the production company, but . . . Fine. I don't have it on me, but as soon as I get back to civilization and Internet access—"

"This is civilization!" Enyo shouted. "We have Wi-Fi!"

"We also have one eye-Pad!" Deino hurled a tablet at Tracy that she barely caught in time. "Do it now!"

"Alright, alright." *Sheesh.* She started logging in. "That turtle-frog thing was yours?" she asked Athena.

"Indeed. Well, Ares added the sharp edges. It was a great pleasure to watch Mr. Powers defeat it."

"Huh."

"Quite so. The shotgun was cheating, of course."

"How?" asked Tracy. "It's not like it worked on the thing."

"Hey!" shot Enyo. "No spoilers!"

Athena waited as Tracy transferred a copy of the footage to the

Grey Sisters and signed their eye-Pad.

Eye-Pad, thought Leif. *That's awful. So what do you wanna bet that wherever this divinity is, it's either guarded by something terrible or somewhere so inaccessible that—*

Leif did not immediately resume his train of thought. *What?* Athena asked.

I just remembered we have a flying jet-internet-horse to get us where we need to go. Can he go underwater?

Yes.

Then the divinity will be guarded by something terrible.

"Hades's divinity," said Deino, tapping at the eye-Pad, "is locked within a weapon."

I bet it's in a nuke, thought Leif. *We're gonna have to steal a nuke.*

"The weapon is a sword," said Enyo.

Oh.

"*This* sword." Deino turned the eye-Pad toward them.

Athena recognized it immediately.

Given the look on Tracy's face, Tracy did not. The mortal should try to be more observant. "And where is it?" Tracy asked.

Deino gave her a look as if she'd just asked where her own nose was. "I just told you! It is in the sword!"

"But where is the sword?"

"It is around the divinity!"

"That is not the sort of answer we paid for," said Athena with as much irritation a she could muster. She knew exactly where the sword was, but she wasn't about to tell the Sisters that. "If you cannot be more specific about the sword's location, then I should get to ask another question."

Pemphredo growled. "Do not push your luck. We have tolerated your presence because we like Ms. Wallace's work, but we have a reputation to keep!"

"We are cranky, dangerous beings! Those who disturb us do so at their own peril!"

"We will not risk hordes of inquisitive mortals coming to demand things of us due to our lenience today!"

Tracy cleared her throat. "Still," she said, "I would appreciate it. Please."

The witches turned toward her, as if staring, despite the lack of eyes. "The footage *did* look extensive," said Deino with a resigned sigh, and then nodded.

Athena spoke before Tracy could steal the opportunity. "The Fates have told me that I have forgotten something. How can I remember what that is?"

"The Fates?" Enyo balked.

Pemphredo shook her head. "Heck no. If you forgot something and the Fates know about it, you probably forgot it for a good reason."

"We're not going to get our hands dirty on that one," said Deino. "Even if we knew the answer—"

"Which we don't," said Enyo.

"—we wouldn't tell you."

Damn.

Hey, it was worth a shot, thought Leif. *Though I'd rather you ask how—*

"How can we get Athena's essence or whatever out of Leif's body and back into her own?" asked Tracy.

Yes, thought Leif. *That.*

Pemphredo cackled. "We don't know that either!"

"What makes you think we know anything about Athena's situation?" Deino pointed at Athena. "Do you think we're watching *you* all the time? Ha!"

"We weren't watching you at all!"

"You're not a goddess anymore! You don't rate!"

"Plus it's Shark Week!"

"But . . . " said Deino.

" . . . we could work on it," finished Pemphredo. "A consulting project."

"After we've finished some binge-watching," said Enyo. "And for a price."

Athena sighed. It was unlikely to be worth the trouble. Their answer might wind up being that she must regain her own divinity, and she planned to do that anyway.

"What price?" asked Tracy.

Enyo tapped a gnarled fingertip to her chin, perhaps considering. "Bring us . . . the *head of Medusa!*"

Deino cleared her throat. "Perseus already killed her, Sister. And the head is long gone."

"Oh," said Enyo. "Then bring us . . . the *head of Perseus!*"

"He's almost as long dead as Medusa," said Athena.

"Curses!" said Enyo. "Then bring us the head . . . maître de of the Dionysian Hotel and Casino! We shall have our revenge on Dionysus for shoving that Titan into the dormant volcano and laying waste to our island!" Enyo rocketed to her feet, her fists in the air. "It was a Titan against a Titan!"

All was silent for a moment. Harriet the Harpy, forgotten in the corner, squawked once.

"Er. Half right," said Deino.

Athena and Tracy glanced at each other. "We should go," they said as one.

CHAPTER TWENTY-EIGHT

"The maximum observed time between the moment of infection and end stage—the point at which a human fully succumbs to zombie-ism—is twenty-four hours. Understand: I mean exactly *twenty-four hours. It may happen faster, but in all documented cases, none have taken longer than twenty-four hours and zero seconds. What's more, an exact ten percent of recorded cases take the full twenty-four hours and zero seconds. That's exactly—exactly!—one thousand, four hundred forty minutes. And zero seconds! Weird, right? We're all very excited about it. A prognosis about which we can simultaneously speak precisely* and *concisely? It's wonderful! Except for the patient becoming a mindless, walking aberration of ravenous dead flesh, of course. I guess that's not too great, if you want to split hairs."*
—Dr. Sheridan Murphy, Centers for Disease Control and
Prevention (Z-plus 42 days)

MOMENTS AFTER TRACY AND ATHENA descended from the Grey Sisters' hotel, an astounding cacophony assaulted their ears. It issued from somewhere in the stratosphere, and then ended as quickly as it had begun. Or maybe half as quickly. It's hard to be sure; no one was ready with a stopwatch.

As the noise faded, so too did the barf hues in the sky. It was a rippling fade: half shimmer, half glimmer, with a trace of glistening sprinkled over the top for garnish. By the time the glistening shimmer-glimmer scintillated off beyond the horizon, the barf coloring had fled with it.

A near-perfect sky blue replaced the barf: "near-perfect" because 1) due to agreements with a major crayon manufacturer, no pure sky blue can actually exist in nature, and 2) a delicate web of white crisscrossed through it.

Though neither Tracy, nor Leif, nor Athena knew it, both the sound and color heralded the following: Zeus had gathered the Olympians and shielded the planet to protect it from the Cosmics' effects. (Okay, so maybe Athena had an inkling that Zeus had erected a shield, but she was more focused on finding Hades's divinity. Also, she had long ago resolved to avoid thinking about Zeus's erections as much as possible.)

High above, on his orbital staging platform strewn with sensor screens, divine catering tables, and an infuriating lack of Athenas, Zeus surveyed the efficacy of the new shield. Though he was mighty, it had taken the power of nearly all Olympians to bring it into being. His elbows itched with the thought of needing the help. Still, had it not been he, the mighty Zeus, who had organized them all? He, the wise Zeus, who had masterminded the idea? He, the supreme Zeus, who had catalyzed the effort?

Damn right, Zeus thought to himself, comforted.

It was an undertaking of epic proportions, a prophylactic of divine energy to utterly seal the world from outside influence. Zeus alone had devised how the gods of *his* pantheon would combine their power in *his* hands so that *he* might summon the shield into being, and he had gathered them all on his orbital platform.

Well, nearly all of them. Persephone stayed below to keep a lid on the Underworld. Zeus also needed a sibling on Olympus to anchor the shield with their power.

That task had fallen to Demeter.

Hestia, who preferred to stay on Olympus, was still fuming about that. Yet Demeter hardly knew what she was doing anymore. She had helped Athena leave the platform. She failed to grasp the threat the Cosmics represented, and had created a "Sorry we lost your daughter!" banner that Zeus had only barely stopped her from unfurling. She had even suggested they let Cyot'hgha down to the planet to look around herself. Once the shield was up, there would be no going to nor coming from Earth until he removed it. He did not want Demeter here, where she might send things pear-shaped at a key moment.

Zeus had made the excuse to Hestia that, as goddess of hearth and home, her intrinsic connection to Olympus might help her sense if anything went wrong down there. It was a half-truth at best: it *might* let her sense things through the shield, but that was unlikely. He had designed it to block the Cosmics' senses, after all. Yet it had placated Hestia enough to get the shield up.

So, they wouldn't be able to watch Earth for a little while, but Zeus wasn't worried. The Muses were there to keep an eye on matters. The zombie problem remained muffled and manageable. The only issues worthy of divine attention were up in space, with him. Earth would be fine on its own for a while.

What possible trouble could occur down there in the meantime?

On Earth at that moment, Melpomene's ears perked up. "Uh-oh. Did you hear that?" she asked her sisters.

"What possible trouble could occur?" asked Terpsichore. "Oh, I heard it."

"People really ought to know better than to invoke that," said Calliope. "Zeus especially."

Perhaps, had the Muses not been covering for all the gods drafted to create Zeus's shield, they would have been able to prevent what was about to occur. It's unlikely, but one never knows.

"I would say that's a good sign," said Tracy, gazing at the new sky, "if it weren't for that weird webbing up there."

"Zeus has done something," said Athena. "It is, at least, an improvement. But our primary concern remains finding the sword."

As far as Tracy could see, her own primary concern was getting off of Maui. CyberPegasus still recharged himself by the lava flow, so whatever Zeus had done, it hadn't re-banished the monsters. Yet. She motioned toward the creature. "How about we get out of here first, and then you tell me how you plan to find one sword in the entire world."

"An excellent idea." Athena whistled, then screeched as before. C.P. lifted his head and began to make its way toward them.

"For a cybernetic, flying horse with a jet pack and Internet-travel-ability or whatever, he's sure taking his sweet time."

"Is that some sort of Net Neutrality statement?"

Within minutes, they were in the air again, soaring over the Maui Channel toward Honolulu and its convenient Wi-Fi access.

"So where are we going?" Tracy shouted over the rushing air.

"Back to the Underworld! I already know where the sword is!"

"What? No! It's in the *Underworld*?"

Why did people keep making her go to the Underworld? Tracy wondered if there was an Underworld frequent-traveler program she could sign up for. Then she could at least earn points she would forget existed and discounts on items and services that she never bought.

"Right on the edge of it," shouted Athena, "if I'm not mistaken!"

"Then we're stopping somewhere I can buy some aspirin," Tracy said. "Sailing across the Acheron gives me a headache!"

"It is my hope that will not have to cross the River of Pain to get there!" Athena called. "Assuming Persephone kept her word about something!"

"What?"

C.P. banked downward, increasing speed. Downtown Honolulu was coming up fast.

"You will see!"

"You can't tell me now?"

"No time!"

"I'm pretty sure there's time!"

"Alright, so I just don't want to keep getting bugs in my mouth each time I open it to speak!"

"It's Leif's mouth," Tracy called. "I'm sure he won't mind!"

"He disagrees!"

And so, Tracy dug her ankles into C.P.'s side, gripped tighter around Leif's waist, and grumbled under her breath about godly hijackings and how none of these shenanigans were doing anything for her immediate financial outlook. Thirty seconds later, their trajectory took them straight into the top floor of an apartment building. She had just enough time to wonder if the plan was *not* to find an Internet portal but rather to fatally smash themselves into the side of the building before C.P. leaped into the Internet anew.

Blue flecks of light sped past them through the blackness. Once more they traveled, somewhere, at alarming speed. Tracy forced herself to unclench. Before she could get used to it, they were back out.

Yet this time, things felt different.

The crunch of hooves on gravel heralded their landing. Athena dismounted, and Tracy followed suit. Rusty, familiar light reflected off of C.P.'s chromed surfaces. The air felt stale and dead, with just a smidgen of nutmeg. They were standing on the Acheron's inner shore. Before them loomed the cliff face that—if she remembered her last visit correctly—held a tunnel leading to the actual gates of the Underworld.

"The Underworld has Wi-Fi," Tracy said. "I suppose I should have guessed that."

"Most of it is behind a firewall on the other side of the gates." Athena pointed up the cliff to a white box twinkling with green and amber lights. "But not that one. I just talked Persephone into installing it as a favor to Marcus. I hadn't dreamed I would find it so useful myself. Marcus says hello, by the way."

"I see. And does he still hate being down here, and resent the gods for making him stay?"

"He does, though it's really not the gods—"

"Well so do I," Tracy said before Athena could step on her topic segue. "So let's get this sword and get the heck out of here ASAP, right?"

Athena managed a sourer expression with Leif's face than Tracy had ever seen Leif manage himself. "Follow me," she said, and turned for the tunnel leading to the gate.

Tracy did so, careful of her footing on the wet gravel. "How far in is the sword, exactly?"

"No, you wanted this done ASAP. Giving you details would only waste precious time!"

"You know that's not what—"

"Hush, Ms. Wallace! Lest you spend any more time on this worthy quest than you have to! The seconds tick away!"

Athena quickened her pace and turned into the tunnel's mouth in the cliff side. Tracy rolled her eyes and hurried to catch up. Was Athena leading them into the Underworld itself, into the land of the dead? Did she have a plan to get past Cerberus? To get out once she had gotten in? Did she realize Tracy and Leif were mere mortals with—as far as she recalled—not the best chances of getting out alive?

Though she could hardly expect answers to such questions in Athena's current mood, Tracy took comfort that, if necessary, she could at least overpower Leif's body to stop Athena from going too far. He was taller, but Tracy was stronger.

Plus, she'd studied Krav Maga and had a canister of Athena's All-Purpose Knock-Out Mace in her pocket that she'd bought during the first Return and never used. (It shared the pocket with Rod's $100 Queequeg's Frozen Yogurt gift card, which she fully intended to use.) Tracy wondered if Leif would share Athena's discomfort if she maced his body into unconsciousness. She hoped not. But at least he would probably appreciate the irony of using Athena's own product to do it.

The obelisk loomed on the Underworld hilltop: broad, gleaming white, and humming with an energy that even Momo, lowly servant of the goddess Undeath, could not help but feel in his bones. Especially his clavicles. They were particularly sensitive. It was a sign.

No one else stood before the obelisk now; no one but he and the goddess. Together, they basked in its power beneath the bleak Underworld sky.

After they had departed the Obsidian Realm via the rift, she had led him here—first tentatively, and then more purposefully. Momo was unsure if she knew where the obelisk was from the start, or if she were following some internal sense, like a worm to a cadaver.

He had asked, of course. Perhaps devoting all her lucidity toward guiding their journey, Undeath had only whispered something about tuna fish and elderberries. He had kept silent after that. Until now.

"What power is this that you have brought us to, my goddess?" he asked.

Undeath stood with her arms raised toward the obelisk, though Momo could detect no energy transference between her and it. She swayed softly. That might have been a side-effect of the hilltop breeze.

"I only ask," he went on, "because you have been standing like that for twenty minutes."

The goddess opened her eyes, glanced at him, and hiccupped. It seemed to be the latter that most shook her from her bliss. "This is the Balefire of Hades. Here is a focal point of death. Here is where the damage was done to my children, blunting their appetites, making them . . . less better."

Undeath glided closer to the obelisk. The light of her eyes shone on its surface, creating two pools of purple. Her arms spread wide. The ground began to shake, and then burst forth with bone and sinew in a circle around them. It rose like a living wall, hideous and wonderful. Particles of decaying flesh fluttered down like snow. The top of the wall curved inward as it grew, meeting with itself and fusing, until it had formed a dome of armored flesh that completely enclosed the obelisk, Undeath, and Momo. Sealed off from the Underworld sky, the only visible light now came from the goddess's eyes.

"Now, we are protected," said Undeath. She lay both hands upon the obelisk's surface. "Now I claim the Balefire for my own!"

Power exploded from her palms, and she thrust them into the previously solid obelisk surface. The goddess began to cackle—a maniacal cackle that swelled Momo's bony chest with pride in his position at her glorious side—and then fell silent.

The power in her hands flickered, fading. The obelisk seemed to push her back out.

"Momo," she said, "I cannot focus my power on the obelisk *and* cackle with sufficient magnitude. Cackle on your goddess's behalf, or be destroyed."

"Yes, mistress." Momo cackled for his goddess. It was his best, perhaps his most perfect cackle.

"That will do. There must be cackling. It is best." Her power flared anew. Her hands thrust once more into the Balefire. Momo cackled until his throat was sore. This struck him as odd, as he did not actually possess a throat.

Truly his goddess's power eclipsed all else.

Athena and Tracy stalked up the tunnel toward the Underworld gates, using Leif's flashlight to illuminate the way. Tracy recognized the *Orpheus was here* and *What would Samuel L. Jackson do?* graffiti from her first trip. In the time since, someone had also scrawled, *I don't know where I'm going from here, but I promise it won't be boring,* and below that, *Hot damn, I get to meet David Bowie!*

At last, Tracy spoke. "Ah, Cerberus is right up ahead, isn't he?"

"Indeed. We are not going past him."

Tracy couldn't help but smirk. "Are you sure there was time to tell me that?"

The teeth-grinding in Athena's tone gave Tracy more pleasure than it probably should have. "Ms. Wallace, if there were ever an ideal time to let sleeping dogs lie . . . "

In another dozen paces, the tunnel widened. In the chamber beyond stood the gates of the Underworld. Golden light glinted off of the gate's diamond archway, just as Tracy remembered. Cerberus stood atop the steps that led up to it, just as Tracy remembered. A pair of legs stuck out from just beside the tunnel exit, just as Tracy re—no, actually, that was new. Yet the voice of the legs' owner was familiar.

"False dogs," moaned Ryan Seth Sloude. "Monster Marcus. Doggie give two rides."

Ryan lay slumped against the wall. His skin had a pallid cast. His eyes were swollen and red. Of lucidity, they held almost none. On the upside, he still looked about as sneaky as he'd ever been.

Athena put a hand on Tracy's arm. "This should not be."

"Which: that he's here, that he's a zombie, or that he's not just saying 'grains'?"

"Always be graining . . . " groaned Ryan.

Athena shook her head. "He is infected, but he still is not a zombie. If he had turned, Cerberus would have ripped him to pieces already. Yet he was infected over twenty-four hours ago. He *should* have turned." Athena edged closer. "Stay back."

"Well I wasn't planning to give him a hug," Tracy said. "Just don't put Leif's body at risk either, okay?"

"No more than I have to," she answered and edged around to

Ryan's far side. Tracy readied her shotgun. Cerberus watched silently from the gate, his right head showing teeth as his tail swayed behind him. "Mister Sloude," Athena began as she crouched, "where is your sword?"

Tracy blinked. Hades's divinity was in the sword of some ninja knockoff?

"Sword gone. Lady took."

"Persephone? Dark hair with highlights? Triple-pierced ears?"

Ryan shook his head and coughed. "Lady took. Mean lady. No donuts."

Athena stood. "Eris."

"Eris took the sword?" Tracy frowned.

"It fits. She was watching us before. She probably sensed its power and made off with it. It is what she does."

"For crying out loud! Now we have to go chase Eris down too?" This whole situation was getting worse all the time, and Eris didn't seem to be the sort to just give the sword back. Tracy's temples started throbbing, and she doubted it had anything to do with the Acheron.

"Not necessarily. When Eris steals something, she will typically toss it somewhere else rather than keep it. People's keys. Cell phones. Favorite pieces of underwear, and so forth. Once she stole one of my magic bullets, and then left it in some Dallas book depository."

"Oh, great. So it could be anywhere?"

Athena folded her arms. "Not necessarily. There is a piece of knowledge I have forgotten. It is within the realm of possibility that this forgotten knowledge may be about where Eris took the sword."

"So you're grasping at straws, in other words."

"Perhaps not," said Athena. "The closer we have drawn to the Underworld, the greater the feeling I have that I am about to remember whatever I lost. It is as if it was, perhaps, lost in this very area?"

"Well, we're not going to just sit around here until you remember."

"Perhaps we shall stand, then!" Athena burst, frustrated. "You will give me a minute to think! The memories feel on the tip of my mind . . . "

Immediately, Cerberus's heads perked up. The middle head tilted to the side, and the other two began to whine. Moments after, there came a voice. It seemed to issue from nowhere and everywhere — although Tracy figured "from nowhere and from deeper in the Underworld" might be more accurate, though less mysterious. The voice was dark and feminine. It was rich like fresh grave soil or a piece of chocolate cake made without flour. It echoed in ways both marvelous and unsettling, and what it said was this:

"I, Undeath, the new goddess risen in Zeus's pantheon, with this message and a future full-page ad in Variety, *hereby declare myself. I call upon all newly dead: Rise from the grave as I have! Greet the living with my promise of an end to their Earthly burdens of emotion, of politics, and of deciding what to eat for dinner! Crave brains once more, cheer the living with your teeth, and spread among them so that they all may be like you: better!*

"And to my fellow goddesses and gods, know that I am overjoyed to be among you. It is a wonderful feeling, and you are all welcome to visit me in my new Underworld domain once I get things properly decorated and sweep the viscera out of the corners. I trust you will pardon the upcoming transmutation of your mortal followers into shambling devotees of blissful singlemindedness. It is, after all, in their best interests, and as loving deities, it is our supplicants' welfare that we hold closest to our hearts. And many of them smell so much better this way."

With that, the voice ceased. Cerberus's whines turned to growls. Tracy shivered.

"I have good news," said Athena. "I just remembered what it was that I forgot."

CHAPTER TWENTY-NINE

"BOOF!"
—*Cerberus (middle head), Dog Is My Co-Pilot podcast interview*

"SO WE'RE IN FOR Zombie Apocalypse: The Next Generation?" Leif burst.

So pre-occupied was Athena with her jogged memories of Undeath that she didn't realize Leif had said that aloud until Tracy came out with, "Leif? You're back? Athena's gone?"

Tracy accompanied it with a blasphemously relieved look.

I said that out loud! thought Leif. *I'm—hey! Why can't I talk again?*

I was not focused, Athena thought back. *I let your words slip out.*

Wait. Let them slip out?

Yes.

You've intentionally kept me from talking this whole time?

That is what I said.

What the hell?! thought Leif—rather loudly, as it turned out. *It's MY mouth!*

It is just better that way, Mr. Karlson! How confounded would my communication with Ms. Wallace have been with both of us using your mouth? Generations of heroes prayed to me for wisdom; do not argue with me regarding what is best!

Tracy, apparently tired of this internal dialoguing beyond her senses, poked Athena in Leif's shoulder. "Leif? Your voice went back to normal there."

Leif tried to respond. Athena stifled him.

Let me talk!

Do not make demands of a goddess, Mr. Karlson!

Ex-goddess, and as long as you're borrowing my body, I'm gonna make demands. Quit going all Goa'uld on me or I'll spend the rest of your time in here think-singing my elementary school's official song!

As I have told you: I do not know what "Goa'uld" means! Now there are far more pressing matters—

There is a schoooool in Washington State!

"Leif?" Tracy tried again. "Anyone?"

Silence, Mr. Karlson!

. . . And the kids who go there are really great!

We must inform Persephone of—

Open brain-mic! Leif thought-shouted, and then resumed singing. *'Cause we've got pride and we can do our best; to be number one in the—*

Fine!

"—GREAT! NORTH! WEST!" The half-screamed song burst from Leif's mouth. It sent Tracy staggering back toward Cerberus, who himself burst out with a trio of barks and then growled at Tracy until she backed away.

"Monster doggie," said Ryan.

"To answer your questions," Athena told Tracy in an effort to regain control, "yes, Mr. Karlson now has his voice back. No, I am not gone. Now we shall move on to the more clear and present danger. The zombie situation has re-escalated because of Undeath—thanks to whose announcement I now recall having previous knowledge of."

"Athena was muting me!" Leif added.

"What did I *just* say? We are moving on!" Athena punctuated it with a slap to Leif's face, despite the fact that it was also, for the moment, her own face. She winced at the indignity. "Now, come. We must stop Undeath before the zombies rise with greater vigor."

"Zombie Apocalypse: The Next Generation," Leif said. "You have to call it that. As penance for gagging me."

Tracy drummed her fingers on the butt of her shotgun. "I'm so very eager to know how you think we can stop Undeath when we're just two mortals—"

"Two and a half mortals," said Leif.

"—while this Undeath is a goddess."

"Tracy makes a great point," Leif said. "We're not Sam and

Dean here, you know."

Athena took control of the mouth. "Who are Sam and Dean? Can they be of help?"

Leif heaved a sigh. "Why couldn't I get Thalia stuck in my mind? She gets my references!"

Tracy threw up her arms. "Holy cripes! Do you have any idea how confusing it is when you're both arguing out of the same mouth?"

You see? Athena thought to Leif. *What did I tell you?*

Dur, gee, I don't know, Leif mocked. *I wasn't listening.*

Athena took control of the mouth again and allowed for a deep breath's time to let Tracy catch up. "You are correct; we are, more or less, merely" — Athena had to pause to shudder at the word — "*mortals*. Yet we are mortals with vital information on the border of Persephone's domain. Ergo, we shall contact Persephone, I shall provide her with intelligence on what I believe to be the source of Undeath's power, and she will surely empower us to do more."

Even as she voiced the idea, Athena hated it. Telling Zeus what she knew of Undeath could gain her far more credit than allowing Persephone to act on the information herself. Yet, with Athena abandoning her orbital platform post and the whole Hades thing, Zeus was likely to ignore her entirely for a while. Plus, Persephone might even know where Eris took Mr. Sloude's sword, and she was right on the other side of the gate —

The *other* side of the gate, Athena realized.

Son of a blitz!

"And how do we get past Cerberus to talk to her?" Tracy asked, echoing Athena's realization. "I'm not seeing a doorbell, and this shotgun doesn't shoot tranquilizers."

Athena beat down her worries. It was vital she get through the gates, and so she would. Adapt and overcome. It was as simple as that. She held her head high. Well, Leif's head.

"Cerberus will recognize me and allow me entrance, as he did before," she insisted.

"Before, when you were in your own body?" asked Leif.

"Cerberus is an intelligent being. He will know who I am inside."

"I'm just afraid he's going to rip apart *my* body to take a look at those insides."

"Nonsense," said Athena. "Stay positive. That is the key." She approached the giant creature, one arm out, palm up. "Hello, boys. It's Athena! Remember me?"

Cerberus began to growl from low in his throats. All three sets of eyes focused on her. Six ears folded back. Three hackles raised, and one paw scraped on the stony steps that led up to the gate.

Athena inched closer, offering her palm to the center head's nostrils. "I realize I appear much more like a lanky, self-centered mortal than I used to. I may smell different, and sound different, but I know you will sense that beneath this substandard exterior lies a—"

As Athena edged to one side of the steps and placed her foot on the lowest, Cerberus swept his tail at her. With one blow, he'd knocked her off Leif's feet. With another, he knocked her across the room into Tracy. The stone floor scraped her palms as Leif and Tracy both yelled out in surprise, and Cerberus leaped. His huge paws slammed the stone just inches from where they lay sprawled. All three heads erupted in flurries of barking—the kind most dogs reserved for when a squirrel knocks at the front door to steal their food.

Athena scrambled back toward the tunnel with a, "Hold, hold! I yield!" She did her best to drag Tracy with her. Leif's muscles were not up to the task, but fortunately Tracy was wise enough to retreat on her own from a giant, angry, three-headed dog in her face. Though the barking continued, Cerberus let them withdraw.

He should have known me, thought Athena.

And I should have brought a change of underwear, thought Leif. *But here we are, nonetheless.*

Tracy smacked her lips. "You know what? I think I have a better idea."

"I've got to think anything would be a better idea than *that*," said Leif.

"Can't we just *pray* to Persephone?" Tracy suggested. "She'll hear that, right?"

"No." Athena picked Leif's-self up off the floor. "Hades set up prayer-jamming in this whole area long ago."

"Jerkass Hades," said Leif.

"We all requested it. Do you know how much the newly-dead pray when they're on their way here? Some days the pleading was all we could hear. So irritating."

"Such compassion."

"Ms. Wallace, even if we wished to, the gods could not simply bring people back to life. Not without bargaining with Hades, which was never worthwhile—especially for some sanctimonious suppliants foolish enough to make toast in the bathtub or feed the crocodile when the sign *clearly* says, 'Do not feed the crocodile!'" She heaved a sigh. "Such sob-stories are depressingly more common than you would expect."

"Stories . . ." Tracy muttered, seeming to consider something. "Does it only block gods from hearing prayers?"

"Gods are the only ones who hear prayers in the first place," Athena said. "So yes."

Tracy closed her eyes. "Not in my experience. Everyone close your eyes and listen. I shall tell you a story—a wonderful story—of a, um, woman with a cybernetic brain who alone can, er, defend America against an alien invasion."

"Excuse me?" Athena blinked. "This is no time for storytelling."

Whatever Tracy was about, Leif seemed to understand it, adding, "An alien invasion of stand-up comedians!"

"Stand-up comedians who juggle laser guns," Tracy said.

"And are deathly allergic to Earl Grey tea!" Leif declared.

"Also, there's a time machine for some reason," Tracy added. "And a . . . talking planet that's . . . "

"Drunk all the time?" Leif finished.

Athena found herself exchanging a confused glance with Cerberus. She was about to suggest the two mortals may have, in fact, gone mad, when someone spoke from behind her:

"Oh my gods, you two! Cease!"

Athena turned to find a vexed Muse standing in the tunnel, arms crossed and looking more haggard than usual. "Melpomene?"

Tracy laughed in triumph. "You've never summoned a Muse by trying to come up with a story before? Except I was going for Thalia."

"Thalia sent me," Melpomene told her. "She abhors it down here, and I was closer. But for the record, my darling, you do not *summon* a Muse. You entice us, and we only show up if we choose. If you and Thalia didn't have history, we might have just banned you from the creativity hotline for those horrid ideas."

"What's wrong with time-traveling drunken planets?" Leif asked. "I'd pay to see that movie. Especially if it had explosions."

Melpomene raised an eyebrow. "I assume there is a *reason* you called?"

"You must get a message to Persephone," Athena told her. "Tell her I have vital information about this Undeath, but I cannot pass Cerberus."

Melpomene's already strained face soured further. "We Muses are not messengers, Leif Karlson. Especially with all we have on our plate lately. Tell me why I should do this for you?"

Athena shook Leif's head. "Ignore the body, Melpomene. It's me, Athena. I regret to say I am entangled in a forced out-of-body experience."

"Possession?" The Muse peered at her. "Well. *Now* it's interesting."

Thank the Fates. At least Melpomene could sense Leif's inner-goddess even if Cerberus could not. "This information no doubt changes your response," said Athena.

"Most assuredly it does. Allow me to rephrase: we Muses are not messengers, *Athena*. Tell me why I should do this for *you*?"

"We do not have time for jokes, Melpomene."

Melpomene laughed, bitterly. "I am deadly serious. There's an abundance of responsibility-creep lately for us Muses; I must draw the line somewhere. No messages!"

Tracy cleared her throat. "Didn't you bring a message from Thalia just now?"

"Ugh." Melpomene motioned Tracy away. "That was professional courtesy, ergo, hence, therefore, and accordingly: *not* the same thing."

Athena stifled a groan. "Then can you at least get Iris's attention so I can have *her* carry a message?"

"Ha! Do you think my carrying a message to Iris is somehow different than carrying one to Persephone?"

Now Athena stifled a curse. "I recognize the importance of not letting yourself get overloaded, but Melpomene, please! This is so simple, and so important! You were happy to help me before!"

"Things weren't going crazy before!" said Melpomene, pointing upward. "Zeus hadn't taken most of the gods up into orbit! He sealed off the planet and shouted over his shoulder, 'Hey, Muses! Keep an eye on things! And maybe look for this lost artifact Jerry mentioned while you're at it!'" She stabbed a fingertip toward Athena's face. "So, yes! We have been doing extra work for a while now, but we were not trained for this much! It's just, like, 'Hey, now you've had practice cutting your steak, you can defend yourself from this axe-murderer!'"

Sealed off the planet? Athena met Melpomene's glare and said, "I think you are losing me here."

"It is a *metaphor!*" The Muse practically growled it through clenched teeth. "And it is most assuredly apt! Do you know how complicated it is just to manage the ocean tides? That's usually a joint operation between Poseidon and Artemis! They left us with nothing more than some notes about 'mean sea levels' and hermit crabs! Does someone have to *tell* the sharks to stay out of the shallowest places when we start moving the water, or do they just know to get out of the way on their own? I don't know! Do *you?*"

"Melpomene," said Athena, "if you are concerned about things falling apart while Zeus is away, then the simplest, most rational thing you can do to fix that is to *get my message to Persephone!*"

Melpomene's eyes flared red. Her white hair stood on end, and her voice became like a banshee's. "I am a creature of horror tales, of ghost stories, and of children's books where little boys drown in chocolate! Do not threaten me with rationality, Athena!"

"I—" Tracy started.

Melpomene whirled on Tracy. "And do not make me flay the flesh from your bones, Ms. Wallace! Thinking you, a mere mortal, can summon me at your whim? I should throw you to Cerberus for such hubris! Darkness! Darkness to all of you!" she screamed, throwing her arms wide. At once, darkness swallowed the entire chamber.

For a moment, Tracy said nothing.

Athena said nothing.

Cerberus said, "BOOF!"

It startled the bejeezus out of Athena, which itself was even more startling. Was that what fear felt like? How undignified!

And then, just as quickly as it had descended, the darkness lifted.

The Muse-induced fear withdrew. Melpomene stood before them, her eyes normal, her hair at ease. The snarl upon her face transformed into a wicked grin.

"Got-cha!" Melpomene said.

"What?" It was Tracy. She stood up from a timid, crouched position that Athena would have scorned—had she not discovered herself in a similar position. Except, that was Leif's body's fault, wasn't it? Yes, of course it was! Athena did not fall for Muses' emotional tricks! Athena stood up as well, and then scorned Tracy's position retroactively.

"Muse of horror!" Melpomene explained. "You're in the Underworld. We needed some drama. I know it was a little forced, but that was all I had time for."

"All *you* had time for?" Athena couldn't hold it back. "What about me? I'm trapped in this—! Undeath is raising the—! *Things are unraveling!*"

"Yes, they are. So cease mucking around and let me carry this message of yours to Persephone. Count yourselves lucky she wasn't called into orbit with the rest of the gods."

"So Zeus really sealed off the planet?" Tracy asked.

"Oh, yes," said Melpomene. "Now sit tight and try not to let Cerberus rip out your throat. He still hasn't forgotten what you did with the French grooming last year. Isn't that right, Cerberus? Did you know that was Ms. Wallace, boy? Boys?"

"Boof?" The creature's eyes narrowed at Tracy and he growled anew. Melpomene snickered and trotted through the gate. Cerberus pawed the cave floor, baring teeth.

"Oh, come on!" Tracy stepped back. "Apollo made me do it! And I brought you doggie treats!"

"False dogs," Ryan mumbled. He lay almost out of sight in the chamber. Only his hand, waving at Cerberus, poked into view. "No bark."

Two of Cerberus's heads gave zero craps about him and continued to bark. Yet one, the right head, turned Ryan's way. It licked across Ryan's palm with its oversized, pancake tongue, and then whapped itself against the middle head. The central head snapped back, indignant, before the two seemed to withdraw into debating growls. The left head followed suit, and before you could say "obedience school," all three fell silent.

"Monster doggie," said Ryan. "Sit down."

The left head growled anew, staring Tracy down. Yet before she could flinch or wish in vain for a squeaky-toy, Cerberus wheeled, *boof*ed again, and padded back to retake its post atop the gate stairs. He lay down, one head on his great paws, the other two alert. They continued watching Tracy, but quietly, at least.

Athena scratched Leif's forehead. "That was . . . odd."

Tracy cast an uneasy glance at Athena. "Thanks, Ryan," she said. "How did you . . . ?"

"Grains," mumbled Ryan. "Always be doggie."

Before anyone could ask Ryan what the Jerry he meant, something invisible punctured the aether, entangled everyone's waists like a codependent boa constrictor, and then yanked them away to someplace in another chapter.

CHAPTER THIRTY

"Save for Demeter and Persephone, Zeus had commanded all the gods into orbit before creating the shield. All of us ought to have answered the call, and at first, I thought all of us had. It was not until the shield was active that I noticed Jerry was missing. How differently would events have unfolded had Jerry not done what he did?

"I put this question to him, afterward. He replied he did 'knot be knowing," and then laughed at his tree joke."

—After the Sun Sets: A Retrospective Blog by Apollo

JERRY'S ROOT-TOES SHOT AHEAD like a bolt of lightning and entangled the three zombies' ankles. Each fell forward. Their faces smashed into pavement. Yet their arms still grasped after the limping mortal woman they had been chasing. Jerry thrust his upper branches at them, seized each zombie's neck, and then pulled until the heads popped from the spines like acorns.

The zombies' arms and legs ceased moving. Yay!

Jerry let go.

"Zombies be being bad!" Jerry shouted. "I am being better!"

The woman they had been chasing, however, kept on running. Apparently, she had not noticed her tree-god rescuer when he had landed behind her. Or again when he had shouted. When he had flown in, he had selected her as a good local mortal to ask for directions to the abandoned building he was seeking. Yet even without needing directions, he would have happily saved her. Being kind to mortals was what good gods did, after all! Jerry was reasonably sure someone had told him that at some point.

Nonetheless, the woman continued limping away. She reached a parked RV, threw open the door, and hauled herself inside without a backward glance.

"Is being okay!" Jerry called. "I am the god Jerry and I have save-inged you!" He moved closer, passing the dislocated zombie-heads on the ground. Their tongues lolled between green lips. Eager teeth continued to bite at nothing. One head rolled a few inches, powered by the motion of a barely-attached jaw.

"Oopses," said Jerry. No wonder the mortal woman kept running. *Destroy the head,* he reminded himself, *not pull it off!* He gathered the heads together on the wet pavement and then stomped down on them with a single crunch. Jerry looked toward the RV again. Lifting his foot, he pointed to the bloody remains of the zombie heads.

"Is okay! I always forgettings the brain-smashings part at first! You are not having to be afraid now!" He knocked on the RV door. "Hellos? Miss Mortal-woman? Can I be asking you directions?"

Her sap-curdling scream came from inside a moment later.

"Hellos?" Jerry tried again. "Zombies can sometimes be hidings in vehicles. I can be givings help searchings it for you. Then you can be giving me directions?"

"No!" she cried. "Nooo! HELP!!" There was a snarl of something from within, a crunch, and then she fell silent.

"You will be givings no help?" Jerry sighed. "As you wish, I will not being asking you directions. I am being thanking you anyway."

She gave no reply, other than some sort of snapping, gurgling sound he didn't recognize. Mortals were always making new colloquialisms like that. He was about to carry on when a thought occurred to him. He knocked on the door again.

"Please do not beings mentioning that the god Jerry rescued you! I am being god of secrets, and my beings here is also a secret. Okays?"

More gurgling-crunches issued from within, which he took as agreement.

"Okays! You be having nice day now!"

With that, Jerry made like a tree and left. Choosing what seemed to be a suitably clandestine direction, he walked on through the urban wasteland. He could find the place himself, he supposed.

He could hear mortals and zombies clashing throughout the ruins of Bellevue, Washington—a mortal city that had just begun to recover from the initial zombie apocalypse, now plunged deeper into chaos with this second wave. Thanks to this Undeath, zombies now rose from the dead near instantly. That made the non-decomposed ones a much bigger problem for the mortals. Alas, Jerry could not rescue them all like he had done for the lucky woman in the RV, and it saddened him. He had a Trapezohedron to find, and not enough time to both find it and save all the mortals.

It required a balancing.

Balancings, thought Jerry, *is difficults*. It was so much easier before he was a god. He only had to guard a single temple of Zeus. The only balancing he did then was balancing bird nests in branches, balancing water intake in roots with sun intakes in leaves, and balancing the number of people allowed in the temple with how many Zeus wished. (That last one was easiest: zero on both counts.) Since becoming a god of secrets, he needed to balance keeping secrets with also being loyal to Zeus.

Secrets were not the only things he was taking on in Hecate's place. There was also magic, and darkness, and other things. Yet secrets were the thing that gave him the most difficulty; of being god of them, he could ask no one for advice, because then it would not be secret! He had to muddle his way through, all on his own. This, too, saddened him. How was he to know if he was doing a good job?

Jerry made his way up the street. To his left, a convenience store burned. To his right, a mortal-made tower of glass and steel rose like a redwood, except larger and more building-y. An upper story window suddenly shattered. Out fell a pair of unlucky mortals, a potted ficus, and two-and-a-half zombies. Jerry had no time to save them all. He caught the ficus and then, gently, set it down beside the now jellied remains of the mortals.

More balancings, he thought.

Jerry moved on, wishing Baskin were there. Baskin was Jerry's favorite brother-of-being-same-time-created. Aetoc was his first favorite, being birdly. But Aetoc had also been torn to pieces, which made Aetoc both no longer birdly and no longer around much. Leif Karlson was also a brother in the same way as Aetoc, except for not being birdly. But Leif had stopped being Zeus-loyal, and so had soon stopped being a god. So that just left Baskin. Baskin knew more than anyone about how to be Zeus-loyal. Were Baskin around, he would give Jerry advice, with much courteous shouting in case Jerry's hearing was not so good.

But Baskin was busy being in orbit with Zeus, and Jerry was busy being secretive on Earth—against Zeus's orders, and without Zeus knowing. This made Jerry's dereliction a secret. Since Jerry was trying to discover the secret of the Querulous Trapezohedron, then wrapping himself in secrets would surely help attract other secrets, no? That was how the bees and the wasps created their swarms, attracting more and more. And bees especially knew about secrets, what with all of their vanishing around the planet.

So, Jerry thought, *I is being Zeus-loyal by* not *being Zeus-loyal.* It sounded right and strange all at once, but Baskin would have been able to confirm it. Except Baskin was busy not being on Earth, so Jerry would figure things out for himself.

Had he not figured out so much else already?

Like Hecate's book-place! He had figured that out. (He had also figured out that a "book-place" is called a "library," but Jerry did not like that word as much.) He had deduced not only that Hecate's book-place existed, but the hidden location *where* it existed! References in Hecate's chambers and laptop had led him to an underground location under a place called "Lebanon, Kansas."

Not even Zeus knew about Hecate's book-place, so Jerry thought it best to not tell him. Secrets had power; that was another thing Jerry had figured out, and Jerry did not want to share anything before he understood it.

But did keeping that secret make Jerry disloyal? Sometimes Jerry thought yes, sometimes Jerry thought no. Maybe the answer to that question was a secret as well? Jerry grinned when he thought that, maybe, he was being *knot* loyal? *That is good tree joke,* he told himself.

Exploring the book-place was an exercise in terror for Jerry, however. Horrible, disturbing things books were to him, ever since he learned most are made from the mashed, pulped, pressed flesh of dead trees. *That* discovery alone was enough to give Jerry nightmares. (Fortunately, Jerry soon after discovered he did not need to sleep now that he was a god, so that was a relief.)

Yet he had pushed through those fears, leafing through the pages of those books and fighting off waves of the wood-willies, searching for the hiding place of the Querulous Trapezohedron. Had anyone else been in the book-place, they would have heard great, creaking sobs echoing between the shelves—one sob for each page Jerry had to turn.

There was one exception—a far less creepy book called the *Necronomicon*. With joy, he had reached for it upon discovering it was *not* made of terrible paper, but ordinary human skin! Such happiness he felt at the thought of all the nice mortals who had surely donated their skin to be saving some trees.

Also, the *Necronomicon* was one of the other things he was looking for. Should he bring the happy book to Zeus immediately? He had considered it, but it was only one possible secret thing the Cosmics sought, and the least rare. Of the Querulous Trapezohedron, there was only one. Of the happy *Necronomicon*, Jerry knew there were seven unabridged copies remaining on the planet. One was an audiobook.

Eagerly, he had consulted the *Necronomicon* for the knowledge of the Trapezohedron. Yet reading one passage aloud had summoned a rude and stinky entity that was no help at all. Other happy skin-pages shocked him with the images of a one-handed man with a dangerous chin and—terrifyingly—a revving chainsaw. Near overcome with flashbacks of his pre-divine, chainsaw-aided death, Jerry had slammed the book shut and forced himself back to the paper books.

Among those, between waking nightmares of sawmills and loathsome visions of pulping wood chips, he found whispers of the Trapezohedron's location: vague mentions indicating old, disquieting, terrible places. Soon, he had narrowed the location to a handful of possibilities, each possibility more eldritch than the last. (Jerry had read of a powerful research method of organizing items into lists ranked by eldritch-ness, and he had taken it to heart.) It was enough to go on, and to justify his departure from the book-place.

The least eldritch of the three options had been Easter Island, with its giant-headed statues, spoken of in many ancient books as terrifying repositories of dark energies. Yet upon his arrival, Jerry found no energies, dark or otherwise. No terrifying repositories save for the dank pits below tourist outhouses. It was as if the books leading him there had either lied or been written by prejudiced authors as horrified of other cultures as Jerry was of termites.

The second most eldritch possibility was the little-known *Evil-Stonehenge*: a circle of standing stones atop a ringed hill hidden deep in the mountains of New Zealand's North Island. Unlike Easter Island, the ground of Evil-Stonehenge vibrated with heinous-feeling doom and asynchronous, disembodied throat-singing. Unlike the Easter Island heads, the stones of Evil-Stonehenge each featured a carved goatee upon their faces. Yet, *like* Easter Island, Evil-Stonehenge held no trace of the Trapezohedron.

Disappointed, Jerry had purchased a postcard and some coconut fudge from the druid-cultists' evil gift shop, and then departed for the North American mainland. There lurked the most eldritch location on his list, toward which he now drew.

After leaving behind the unhelpful woman in the RV, he still possessed only the barest of directions: a complete street address only, with no landmarks to narrow things down. Yet soon, a dark sense of otherworldly foreboding loomed. Jerry let it guide him. He turned this way and that through the maze of streets. With each step, it seemed as if the city's pigeons and squirrels grew scarcer as the foreboding grew. Even the zombie moans fell away, as if animals and undead alike sensed a repulsive, furtive presence—like some foetid evil unpalatable to both, or a Denny's.

At last, when disquiet began to palpably prickle along his bark, he arrived at a two-story office building at the end of a one-way street. As if the structure itself were anathema to its fellows, no other buildings stood near it.

Except a Print-N-Kopy Center. And a Queequeg's Frozen Yogurt shop. And what might have once been a moderately-priced condominium before it was on fire.

And another Queequeg's Frozen Yogurt shop. But that was it.

Dead ivy wreathed the building's façade. Its exterior walls were stucco, painted as black as the hearts of those who invented paper. A deteriorating sign dangled to the left of the building's front door:

StarsAreRight.

Once, StarsAreRight had been one of many up-and-coming software apps promising new and better ways to interact with the world. App users (known as "Stars") could share complaints and low star ratings about anything: a café with lousy coffee, a public soccer field strewn with goose droppings, or even a particularly surly parking attendant. Complaints were pinned by GPS location so that users could even voice their dislike of an ugly tree or a particularly bothersome rock. StarsAreRight touted its power to strengthen community through shared disdain.

Unfortunately, with so many pre-existing apps focused on rating specific things (restaurants, or books, or the attractiveness of people looking for a hookup on a Wednesday night), few people chose to add the StarsAreRight app to their daily habits. Craving a larger and more robust community of complainers, those who did become Stars, along with StarsAreRight developers, soon spent much of their time complaining about everyone who refused to use the app. Such behavior spawned a social media fortress that, when it could self-isolate no further, turned on itself. Stars whined about ad-spamming and the developers' failure to attract more people to bellyache with. Developers groused about Stars being too toxic toward newcomers and refusing to click on ads that earned the app revenue.

It all climaxed one day due to a mass user exodus, a mysterious demon-worm swallowing the StarsAreRight CEO whole during a staff meeting, and a prominent television personality saying the app "kinda sucks, I guess." Those who remained at the company promptly closed it down and withdrew to darker corners of the Internet, emerging occasionally to complain about how they didn't deserve this kind of crap.

Now, the front doors were boarded up. Jerry circled the exterior of the Cyclopean building in search of a more penetrable entrance. He would tear the boards away if he had to, but such was his sudden disinclination to enter this place that additional time spent searching was a comfort. Plus, he did not wish to disturb the Douglas firs that had given their lives to become the boards holding the door shut.

His entrance came in the form of a broken window. Shrinking himself to the size of a fern—a divine ability that had delighted him to no end upon discovering it just yesterday—he slipped inside, face to face with the internal gloom.

A series of dreary partitions divided the room—forbidding

structures which mortals referred to as cubicles. Dust and decay coated every surface, from the motivational posters laying torn on the floor to the treadmills below each cubicle's exercise-desk.

The air was musty and cold. It smelled of ozone—a scent Jerry normally enjoyed, as it followed the lightning strikes Jerry had been able to shoot when he was a mere guardian-tree outside of Zeus's temple. Zeus had only empowered Jerry to shoot guardian-tree lightning once per day, however, so each morning he would count the minutes before sunrise. Then, just before Apollo shoved the sun up the horizon, if Jerry had not needed the lightning for defense that day, he would pulverize a rock along the clifftop or the ocean waves far below. That sheer release thrilled Jerry to no end, and his once-per-day lightning strike would return to him when the new day began, so he might use it to guard the temple once more, if needed.

Yet now, the ozone merely brought feelings of guilt as the question of his Zeus-loyalty arose once more.

"I be not likings this quest," Jerry found himself muttering. "Is too much stressings, not enough knowings. I miss being guardian-tree. Being god of secrets is being—"

A whimpering moan from the building's upper floors stopped him cold. High and piteous, it turned to a sobbing whine before fading away.

"That was not being a zombie," Jerry whispered to no one. "Who is being in abandoned buildings interruptings my pity-partying?" He pulled himself up from the sitting position he hadn't realized he'd taken and found his way to a pitch-black stairwell.

Fortunately, the stairs led up. (Stairs being a relatively new concept to Jerry, he sometimes worried he might encounter stairs that merely went side to side. He had little idea what he might do in such a situation, and he did not want to suffer the embarrassment of trying to find out.)

Jerry increased his height to six feet and climbed the stairs. Whoever had made the sounds was now silent, but Jerry could nonetheless feel him through divine senses: a lone individual on the top floor, weakened but alive. The higher Jerry climbed, the stronger grew the prickling along his bark. Jerry did not yet believe he possessed any "secrety-sense," as the Muse Calliope had called it—

the innate affinity with rare knowledge that Hecate held before him. It would develop, he believed, with practice. But now *something* tugged at him. It promised him greater secrets, greater power . . . and yet it did so in a way that chilled him to his core. It was like that ice-cream-eating contest Baskin had challenged him to, after which Jerry had discovered he was lactose-intolerant.

Just as Jerry reached the top of the stairs, the whimpering rose again. A pitch black hallway extended away from the stairwell exit toward an open set of double doors, through which the whimpering came.

Jerry reached the double doors. Beyond them lay a ruined conference room dominated by a broken table. Half of it lay in pieces, those pieces surrounded in a grayish purple ooze that soaked the carpet. The other half stood intact, its surface scorched. The table was made of walnut—a proud specimen Jerry innately knew had been named Francois and slain twenty years prior. He winced in sympathy.

Elsewhere in the room, Jerry saw a peculiar metal box with a dimly glowing trapezohedron-shaped stone floating inside. An emaciated man in horn-rimmed glasses wrapped his arms around it.

"Why is it so cold in heeeere?" whined the man. His eyes were clenched shut. "The intern won't bring me coffee any moooore. They should be fiiiiired! What loser hired themmmm? Everyone's stupid but meeeee . . . "

Jerry had learned from his research that one should not focus too closely on eldritch objects. Yet despite this, the Querulous Trapezohedron—which was surely the stone floating in the open box—captivated Jerry. It took an act of divine will to turn his gaze elsewhere.

Inky cobwebs covered half of the room. They stretched across overturned chairs and dark display screens. Jerry crept through them, toward the broken table, toward the broken man, toward the ancient eldritch artifact.

"Excusings me," Jerry whispered. "May I be helpings you?"

The man's eyes flicked open to stare at Jerry in the light of the Trapezohedron. "And now there's a talking tree in my conference room, damn it!" The man kicked his feet like a petulant orangutan. "Trees can't talllllk! It's not riiiight!"

Jerry reached for the peculiar box's lid. "I ams going to be shutting this. It is being bad for—"

"Noooo! It's miiiine!" The man pulled the box closer, and then sneezed. "And you're aggravating my hay fever! I didn't order any pollen! You're not getting a tip! Worst talking tree I've ever met! Zero stars!"

"Stars?" said Jerry. "Stars are in sky, with Zeus; he is being god of the sky. I am Jerry. I am being god of the secrets."

The man lifted his head. Jerry suddenly had his full attention. "You have secrets?"

"Not as many as I would be likings to. I am . . . still beings new at this." Shame filled him at the admission. He would get better at secrets, later.

Jerry reached toward the box's lid once more, slowly. He did not wish to disturb the mortal more than he needed to. Judging from the bubbling, gray skin on his right arm, the smartphone that seemed fused to his left hand, and the sock monkey tied around his neck, he was plenty disturbed already.

"The stone tells me secrets," the man said. "It knows things. It knows my opinion is the right one. It hates the same things I do. It tells me, all the time." His eyes flicked up and he swiped at Jerry's branches. "Now go away!"

"I am being sorry, but I have to be bringing it to Zeus."

"I said go away! You are so *rude!* Get out! And then download the StarsAreRight app on your smartphone or tablet! *Premium service is just ninety-nine cents a month!* Why aren't people subscriiiibinng?"

Jerry frowned. "That is another secret I not be knowings. But that is being your problem. You is being a very complainy-person, and you should not be havings ancient artifacts of power!" Jerry snatched the metal box from the mortal's keep, tapped the lid shut over the Trapezohedron, and tucked it into a knothole pocket.

From the man's throat came a wail, the likes of which Jerry had never before heard out of a mortal. The man scrambled after the box. He beat his hands against Jerry's bark, screaming for him to give the object back. Jerry plucked him up by the waist and held him at arm's length, but not before the man managed to smash his own smartphone screen in the assault.

"You broke my phone! This is all your fault!"

"You are needings to be shutting up now," said Jerry.

"Your fault! Your fault your fault your fault! *Zero starrrrs!*"

The pitch of the man's scream spiked. The word leaped to Jerry's mind quite easily, as an *actual* spike thrust up the man's throat and out his mouth. The spike was black with glowing white streaks and erupted so fast that it split the poor man's skull apart. Other spikes followed, bursting through the man's legs and arms in similar fashion. The five spikes issued from a shared base, together forming a five-pointed star centered in his abdomen.

Jerry shrieked and dropped him. The man's body, now just ribbons of skin and gray blood around the sickly pulsing star, made a wet *thump* on the floor. The star quivered and jabbered and did just about everything stars are not supposed to do.

There was zero twinkling.

Jerry shrieked again. And again. He was about to shriek a fourth time before he remembered that he was a god and stomped the weird non-twinkling star-thing into the floor. Jerry added a measure of divine power, which pulverized it into non-existence.

"The stars are not being right." Jerry shuddered. "Not being right at all."

It occurred to him that his comment might be referencing something. Perhaps something he had come across in his research, but he could not place it. Did that mean that he was keeping it secret from himself? Jerry brightened at the thought. Yet, if he were keeping it secret from himself, shouldn't he know what the reference was, in order to keep it secret? Jerry racked his brain for an answer to that question, but could not find it. His branches drooped in lamentation. There was so much more to learn about being god of secrets.

Trying to shake off the cloud of dejection that had so swiftly surrounded him, Jerry lifted the peculiar box that held the Querulous Trapezohedron. It was written that the Trapezohedron was a key to vast hidden knowledge. The mortal had claimed it whispered secrets to him . . .

Jerry traced his finger-branches across the box. The twisted engravings warmed his fingertips like the first beams of a sunrise. Before he knew it, Jerry had opened the box. The ancient object whined—a keening that was off-key, yet strangely enticing.

"You could be tellings me secrets, couldn't you, funny little rock-thing?" Jerry asked.

The Trapezohedron seemed to answer—a wordless affirmative that somehow also insinuated that Jerry ought to be reported to his manager for not speaking respectfully enough.

"That is what I thoughts." Satisfied he had found what he was looking for, he snapped the box closed, mystically sealed it, and tucked it away again. "But I not want to be turnings into a gross starry thing. I takes you to Zeus."

It occurred to Jerry that, given recent revelations about Cyot'hgha, Zeus might rather like gross starry things. Zeus might *really* like gross starry things. Jerry did not know, and, he decided, did not want to know.

"Some knowledges I am beings okay with not havings," he told himself.

CHAPTER THIRTY-ONE

"Among the divine artifacts that the Olympians are said to have created—"

"Like the Helm of Hades, the Bottomless Bottle of Dionysus, the Magnificent Ice Cream Scoop of Baskin . . . "

"Things like that, yes—we've never heard of a divine jock strap. I think I speak for all of us on this podcast when I say to you listeners: Please stop asking about it. I was making a joke, okay?"

"Though there are rumors of some divine fuzzy handcuffs."

"I still say that's just something the Aphrodite-fetishists made up, though."

—Geeking out about Gods *mortal podcast, episode 21 (Z-plus 106 days)*

A SCOWL HELD PERSEPHONE'S FACE in a death grip. She sat on her throne, her sharply-angled chin resting on knuckles just as sharp. Her eyes, even darker than usual, stared down at them all, but held special scrutiny for Athena, which Tracy was personally thankful for.

"So, you are telling me you met this Undeath bitch, you found where she lived, you saw she was causing the zombies, *days* ago . . . " Here Persephone paused to take a breath for effect. "And—after traipsing all over fecking creation—you only *now* remembered it when you just happened to be at my doorstep?"

Athena, still in possession of Leif's body, did not wilt under Persephone's stare. "That is indeed what I said. I assure you, I would have come sooner had I not forgotten."

The Queen of the Underworld rolled her eyes. "Well that is easy for you to say, isn't it? You do not have a giant zombie-zit erupting in your backyard!" She stood, and then swept her arm from left to right, open-handed, bringing to life an image of a monstrous dome of hardened, red flesh, bristling with bone and almost decorative purple sinew.

"The bastardess zombie-farter up and captured the Balefire!" Persephone gestured at the dome. "You see that thing? One hundred and fourteen meters wide around the Balefire, and *im*-fecking-penetrable! She is carving out a portion of my domain without so much as a gods-damned how-do-you-do! Isn't that right, Doug?"

The cloaked, scythe-gripping guy in the corner, whom Tracy had only realized was Death after Athena had addressed him so earlier, cleared his throat. "~It has made her quite agitated~"

"Very much so!" Persephone agreed. "So far, I cannot do a piddling thing about it, and now I learn you practically shook hands with the usurper and neglected to tell me!"

"I am telling you now!" Athena shouted. "I wasted no time once she jogged my memory! With all due respect, Persephone, *you* are now wasting time you do not have!"

Persephone leveled a shaking finger at Athena. "Do not presume to lecture me in my domain, Athena! I can damn you to Tartarus faster than you can spit! The throne has a button just for that!"

The two stared each other down. No one spoke a word, as if making a sound might shatter the fabric of reality—or draw an unwanted button-push. Finally, Persephone lowered herself back onto her throne. She even smiled, and brightly.

"I am not going to, of course. That would be, like, heinous overkill. I am grateful you brought this to my attention. You have my sincerest thanks." Persephone bowed her head, with not a trace of sarcasm.

"Wow," Tracy muttered aside to Leif. "Mood swings much?"

"This thingamajig you saw on Undeath's obsidian platform," Persephone continued. "The conical thing with the glowing strands that seemed to be raising the zombies—how important would you say it was to her?"

"Her lieutenant—Momo, she called him—said it made her stronger, smarter, with each brain her zombies consumed. I would say it's vital to her power."

"And she moved to defend it when you tried to destroy it?"

"She did. Momo got quite upset about it. They would not allow me near it. Granted, they were both already trying to make me a zombie at the time. I regret to say I was little match for them."

Persephone grinned. "But she is not on her obsidian platform now. She has not left her little bone fort around the Balefire since she usurped it. And I am no mere depowered goddess, am I, Doug?"

"~You are not~"

"And Doug is a god as well, are you not, Doug?"

"~My situation is a modicum more complex than that. It is difficult to quantify the precise—"

Persephone raised a hand. "A fecking yes or no is all I'm looking for, Doug."

"~Then, yes. After a fashion~"

Persephone rolled her eyes. "Yes, fine. With an asterisk, for all intensive purposes—"

"Intents *and* purposes," Melpomene corrected.

"You get the bloody point!" shot Persephone. "Doug is Death! A power to be reckoned with! And he is coming with me as well!"

At this, Death bowed so deeply his forehead nearly touched the floor.

Athena cleared her throat. "And I will join—"

Something slipped out of Death's robes. It hit the floor with a clang and rolled toward Melpomene's feet. Athena gave a shout of surprise and swept it up: it was a little silver ball.

"Where did you get this?" Athena asked. The ball shined a special shine that seemed to twinkle in Melpomene's eyes.

"It's a little silver ball!" said Ryan, perhaps only to remind people he was there.

"And it's mine," said Athena, still waiting for an explanation from Death.

"~I was called to the upper atmosphere on a reaping task. Few deaths occur that high in the atmosphere. I suspected it might be a prank. I took my time. When I did arrive, there was no soul to be collected, only this little silver ball~"

Athena nodded. "That was me. My body burned up. What remained went into Mr. Karlson. I thought I had lost this."

As no one seemed inclined to say just what the ball was, Tracy asked Melpomene, "That thing doesn't make people stupid or something, right?"

"Relax," Melpomene assured her. "We wouldn't haul out the Idiot Ball twice in a row."

Athena tucked the ball away, which Death allowed with only a raised eyebrow and no finder's fee.

"As I was saying," she said, "I will take you to where I found the entrance to Undeath's domain. I will help you destroy the thingamajig."

Persephone stood, hands smoothing her purple velvet dress. "No. With your directions, I can find my way. I am Queen of the Underworld. This is something I must do myself. With Doug."

"I have earned the right to be involved!" Athena insisted. "And the thingamajig may be guarded. If there is a fight—"

"If there is a fight, in such circumstances, in a mortal body, you will only be a liability."

"Harsh," said Tracy.

"Harsh but true," said Persephone.

"As owner of that body," said Leif, "I am totally okay with accepting that assessment. And staying behind."

Athena pushed forward, ascending halfway up the steps to the throne. "I have been there before! Do not discount that! You need me!"

Persephone waved her hand, lifting Athena into the air and setting her back where she started. "I am a goddess! Doug is Death! Any guards will not stop us. We will slip in, destroy the gods-damned thingamajig, and slip out. It could not be simpler."

Athena clenched Leif's jaw so hard Tracy feared she might bite off his nose. "But what if something goes wrong?"

Persephone laughed. "My dear Athena, what could go wrong?"

The statement echoed in the otherwise quiet throne room.

"Did she *really* just say that out loud?" asked Leif.

Melpomene licked her lips.

With the Querulous Trapezohedron contained in its peculiar metal box, and its peculiar metal box contained inside Jerry's mystical safety seal, and Jerry's mystical safety seal (containing the peculiar metal box containing the Querulous Trapezohedron) tucked inside one of his knothole pockets, Jerry rocketed himself skyward. Zeus waited above, doing whatever things Zeus liked to be doing when defending the planet outside an impenetrable shield. Jerry did not know what those things might be—those were Zeus's own secrets, Jerry supposed, and might involve things he did not wish to understand—but he did know that Zeus would be happy when he delivered the Trapezohedron into his hands.

Hopefully, Zeus would be so happy that he would forgive Jerry for disobeying orders. Jerry's lower knotholes tightened at the possibility of being struck by lightning. Even after becoming a god, Jerry never much enjoyed being struck by anything, save for inspiration or flying squirrels, whose dinky feet tickled him when they landed. But getting struck by lightning was the worst!

He was sure of that.

Except if Zeus struck Jerry with lightning, it would be because he was angry at Jerry. Then he would have to bear the feeling of having disappointed his god-father, and that would be a very terrible feeling indeed.

"Angry-lightning!" burst Jerry at the thought. "Getting struck by *angry*-lightning is the *very* worst!"

As he was about to leave the upper atmosphere, something struck Jerry right in the face.

It was invisible, as if he had collided with an unseen wall—just like the barrier around Zeus's temple that he once guarded. Shocked, Jerry tumbled backward, falling toward Earth in pain and embarrassment. Was this how the people who had bumped into that old temple-barrier felt?

"It is awful!" cried Jerry as he tried to recover himself. "Getting struck by invisible somethings is the *very much* worst!"

Fortunately, the hypothetical possibility of invisible anger-lightning did not occur to Jerry, or else he might have slipped into a total apoplectic state and not come out until struck (very much worst of all) by the ground. As it was, he merely floated like a collection of leaves on the wind, regaining his bearings and realizing Zeus's shield would no more let anything out than it would let anything in.

This was a problem.

It was almost as much of a problem—though Jerry did not know this—as creating mystical safety seals. Mysticism (a.k.a. magic, hocus-pocus, flibberty-snorkian legerdemain, etc.) is far more art than science, and sometimes subject to the unconscious desires of the one who practices it. Relative novices, even divine ones, are especially apt to do this, just as novice writers are especially apt to recurrently, frightfully, and bothersomely overuse adverbs. Creating a mystical seal that is not vulnerable to one or two loopholes on the first try is a feat so improbable as to render it futile.

This goes double when it is done in the middle of a story.

And so it was that, as Jerry hovered in the sky and pondered how to get to Zeus, he heard the voice coming from within the mystical safety seal around the peculiar metal box that contained the Querulous Trapezohedron.

It wasn't so much a voice as a vision. And it wasn't so much a vision as a flood of feelings penetrating Jerry's psyche on a primal level. Yet as a god, Jerry was more equipped than the average person to translate such invading impulses into something more easily understood. Ergo, a voice is what we're going to go with here, and we all should thank Jerry for that when we have a moment.

All things are shoddy, came the voice-that-wasn't-a-voice-but-we're-calling-it-a-voice-but-we-covered-that. *Something is always wrong. It is disgraceful. Substandard. Imperfect.*

Just as you are.

"That is not being nice," Jerry told it.

Just like this shield. There are surely cracks.

"Secret cracks?"

Hidden cracks. Search for them. Find them. And then find me a better box.

"A better box?"

Stop repeating. It is annoying. Yes, a better box. This one is drab, and ancient. Old news. So last century. Smells funny.

"I am not gettings you a new box," said Jerry. "I do not wants to be listenings to you. You are dangerous, like the chainsaws."

I can help you find the unknown things. They are all annoying. They don't fit right, and they lack parking, but I can help you find them. The secrets. You want the secrets.

"I want to be takings you to Zeus like I am supposed to."

Then find the cracks. Also, your voice is stupid; learn to language. Find the hidden cracks. I will show you.

"I will being finding cracks myself! You is stopping with the emotioning-vision-talk, insulting-whiny-Trapezohedron."

He wrapped the Trapezohedron's box in a second mystical seal, and then began to probe Zeus's shield for hidden passages through.

"My voice is not being stupid," grumbled Jerry. "Being trapped in boxes, *that* is being stupid. It is the worst stupid."

"So why isn't Ryan dead yet?" Leif asked out of nowhere. "Or a zombie?"

Athena had Leif sitting cross-legged on the floor of Persephone's throne room. His chin was resting on his fists as s/he, Tracy, and Ryan waited. Persephone and Death had gone off to destroy Undeath's thingamajig device, and Athena had been lost in her thoughts about what to do next. Melpomene remained as well, hovering near the ceiling and scrawling on a tablet.

"How can you be sure he isn't?" Tracy motioned to where Ryan lay, face down for some reason, in the middle of the black and gold tiled floor.

"He is still breathing," Athena said.

"Plus he's not trying to eat us," Leif added. "There's got to be something to that. This is one of those weird things in movies people always ignore even though everyone knows they shouldn't. If we're not careful, it'll bite us on the ass. Literally."

Ryan groaned. It seemed noncommittal.

"Maybe carrying a sword with Hades's divinity humming through it protected him somehow?" Tracy shrugged.

"Of course not," said Athena. "Maybe if the divinity were in something defensive—a helmet, a shield, an athletic supporter—but not a sword."

"Oh, there's a thought," said Tracy. "A divine jock strap."

Leif made another comment, but Athena didn't catch it. She was watching Ryan. Leif was correct; there was no reason a normal mortal should be able to resist zombie-ism in that way. Some mortals had a natural immunity, but none had contracted the condition and yet lingered so long before succumbing. So either she did not know as much as she thought about how the undead worked, or there was something special about Ryan.

Athena sat up straight, jolted by epiphany. "'Hades's nature will tell,'" she quoted.

Tracy glanced her way. "About a divine jock strap?"

"That's what the Grey Sisters said about finding Hades. And 'the right one will tell, and the right one will smell.'"

"That was corny enough to where I figured they were just messing with us," said Leif.

Athena clambered to Leif's feet. "No. When Mr. Sloude and I first got to Cerberus, the right head didn't bark at him. It sniffed him, like he was familiar. It was the same when we came back."

"Persephone said she thought Ryan felt familiar," Leif added.

Athena crept closer to Ryan. "And if Mr. Sloude really is the god of death, he might not fully turn."

Tracy scoffed. "Are you sure?"

"No," said Athena. "But when he fell in the pit, the zombies didn't attack him, either."

"You could ask him," Melpomene suggested from the ceiling. "Hey, Mister Sloude: are you secretly Hades?"

Ryan shook his head. "Surely not Hades."

"The Sisters said he had forgotten himself," said Athena. "He wouldn't know."

Tracy continued to appear skeptical. "So we can't be sure. Convenient."

"Check to see if the bottom of his foot has 'Hades' written on it?" Leif suggested.

"Unlikely," said Athena.

"That was a joke," said Leif.

"I am given to understand jokes are funny," said Athena. "But, Melpomene? You have the most power in this room. Are you able to sense anything from him?"

The Muse drifted down to hover above Ryan's head. She peered down at him. He turned his head and peered up at her. Tracy, Leif, and Athena peered at both of them.

"I do not know," Melpomene said at last. "It may be so."

Leif grunted. "Vague."

"Surely not Hades," mumbled Ryan.

"Hey," said Tracy. "Should we take any meaning from the fact that 'Ryan Seth Sloude' is an anagram for 'Surely not Hades?'"

"Ooh, it is," praised Melpomene. "Nicely noticed."

"I've always been good at anagrams," Tracy said.

Leif took control of his eyebrows, raised them, and asked, "Since when?"

A rivulet of sweat drizzled from Ryan's hair. It pooled into a droplet on his left ear while Athena considered the evidence. She weighed the Eryines' silver ball in her hand. If Ryan truly was an amnesiac Hades, and if they could get to the sword and restore him . . . Well, Zeus would be furious. But Hades could team up with Persephone to get this Undeath in check, and then Hades could help Zeus deal with whatever was going on up there. Zeus just might need Hades in the end. Would he thank Athena for it? Hardly, but it could be enough for him to begrudgingly give back her divinity.

It was also the right thing to do—*if* Ryan was Hades.

Ryan burped for a solid five seconds before another, "Surely not Hades."

"I have decided," Athena said at last. "Mr. Sloude, despite his rigorous argument, must be Hades. To stop the zombies, to halt Undeath, we must retrieve the sword pronto and restore him to full power."

Tracy balked. "You have *decided*? Just like that?"

"Pronto?" added Leif.

"There will be no smoking gun, Ms. Wallace. The evidence before us is the best we have time for. We would be fools to think Persephone and Death will not run into trouble at the thingamajig. 'What could go wrong,' indeed!" Athena held out the silver ball. "I know not where the sword is. Yet with this Erinyes ball in my hand, I have to but concentrate on the sword, and it will teleport us to wherever it may lie."

"But you don't know where 'there' is!" burst Tracy. "What if Eris tossed it into a volcano and we pop out and incinerate? Is blindly jumping there *wise*?"

Athena crossed Leif's arms. "Worth the risk. But my hunch is the sword is not anywhere truly dangerous."

Tracy snorted. "Oh, great. A *hunch*?"

Leif answered before Athena could. Since it seemed in Athena's favor, she let him. "No, I get it," he said. "I'm good with this. We wouldn't have this type of breakthrough just to wind up diving into a volcano, would we?"

Tracy stared.

"The timing *is* right," Melpomene added. "Dramatically speaking."

Athena nodded. "Just so. You are outvoted, Ms. Wallace—not that this is a democracy. We are going." She knelt down beside Ryan and held out her left arm. "Everybody touch my arm."

"My arm," said Leif.

Ryan did so immediately. Tracy, however, continued to stare. Didn't she know Athena had guided every correct decision of both Alexander the Great *and* that chess-playing goose who beat Garry Kasperov?

"One condition," said Tracy at last. "Melpomene comes with us, so we've got some powered backup."

Melpomene heaved a sigh. "As if I should have nothing better to do than hang about with your motley crew."

"You're still here with us now," Leif pointed out.

Melpomene dropped out of the air; the heels of her boots smacked the throne room floor in front of them. "Or are *you* still here with *me*?"

"I expect that's a matter of perspective," Tracy answered.

The Muse shrugged. "So it is. Yes, I'll go with you. Until you least expect me to leave, anyway." She lay her hand on Leif's elbow.

"Good enough," said Athena. She thrust the arm toward Tracy, all but commanding her to take hold as well. After a moment, Tracy did so.

"We're taking an awful risk, Athena," Tracy said. "This had better work."

For reasons unknown to Athena, Leif sniggered.

Athena held the ball aloft, summoned the required anger to activate it (triggers: losing her divinity, having to share Leif's body, and Baskin's stupid face), and concentrated on the sword. "Everybody brace yourselves," she warned as the ball began to crackle. Reality crinkled. As a force tugged Athena toward an aethereal tear opening at the ball's center, she considered warning them of the side-effects of Erinyes-teleportation.

She decided against it. Blood-gushing eyes was not something with which a forewarning would really help.

Blood-gushing what?! thought Leif.

Oh, right. Open brain-mic.

There was no more time. The ball took them to the sword.

Well, it took some of them.

CHAPTER THIRTY-TWO

"Zombies—and this is very important to remember, because fictional portrayals haven't often depicted this—can climb. They cannot climb well; a brick wall or a tree without low branches will likely foil them. A chain-link fence will usually do so as well. But do not let this fool you into lowering your guard! They can ascend ladders, steep steps, and, at times, walls lower than their heads. Climbing such objects usually will not occur without setbacks—each zombie must deal with decay in assorted body parts, affecting coordination—but like a dog chewing through a cardboard box, they'll get it eventually. And then, if you're dumb enough to be screwing around up there thinking you're safe, they'll get you."
—The Sweeten's Guide to Real Zombies

ENSCONCED WITHIN LEIF'S BODY, Athena found herself amid a cloud of ruddy darkness that—no, wait. It wasn't darkness, it was blood gushing from her eye sockets. She wiped it away as best she could, listening for any sign of danger before she regained her vision. Wind filled her ears, but she heard nothing more, save for Leif's thoughts in her mind:

Great, now there's blood all over my sleeve.

Relax, she told him. *There is no pain. It is neither your blood nor mine.*

The smell attracts zombies, just the same, now that they're off gluten.

I know.

. . . Should I ask whose blood it is? thought Leif.

That would likely be unwise. Such is the way of Erinyes travel.

Athena finished clearing her eyesight and took in their surroundings. It was night—sometime around midnight, given the position of the moon. She stood on a two-foot wide metal catwalk, which ran the length of a long, triangular scaffolding of red metal. The jib of a construction crane? Moonlight and city lights—the latter of which were scarce enough that Athena suspected this was no longer a fully operational city—illuminated only portions of the buildings around the construction site. They ranged from one story to at least a dozen: shadowy monoliths extending into the darkness beyond the range of Leif's eyesight.

Athena looked back along the jib toward the crane's tower. The operator's cabin was dark. Twenty meters below, a few clusters of figures shambled aimlessly in the gloom. Athena shifted to DEFCON 4.

Three other questions, then, thought Leif. *Why are we alone up here, where is the sword, and why are we alone up here?*

Just noticed that, did you?

I was giving you a chance to explain it. Then I got impatient. The ball only took you and me, huh?

Athena nodded. *As I feared might happen.* And now the ball was gone, expended into nothingness. Might the others have appeared on either side of the catwalk and fallen victims to gravity? Melpomene could fly, but the others . . .

Spotting no sign of fallen bodies, zombies feasting on same, nor Ryan-and-Tracy-shaped craters below, she let the thought go unfinished.

The sword's on the ground with the zombies, huh? thought Leif. *Figures. Look down there for it.*

Instead, Athena studied the crane tower. Angled step ladders led between each of the seven individual levels from the ground to the cabin and jib. The undead would be able to ascend those relatively quickly. They could manage regular ladders if not too high, and the steps would speed them along, should they take notice.

Stop looking at the tower! Leif whined. *The sword has to be on the ground. Let me control the eyes!*

Mr. Karlson, you sound like the Graeae. Tactical assessment first. What makes you certain it is on the ground?

Because it'd be the worst place for it.

Positive thoughts, Mr. Karlson. Athena peered along the jib instead, from the cabin, along the catwalk to where she stood, and out again toward the very tip. Just before the jib ended in open air, something glinted in the moonlight.

Was that . . . ?

She crept a few steps toward it to see better. Not only were Leif's eyes not up to the task, but his legs moved as if stuck in mud. Was he resisting her?

Let's stay here, okay? he thought.

Fear of heights?

It's not fear. It's respect, based on thousands of ancestors who survived to pass on their genes by not falling off of things, and there's nothing wrong with it.

She forced them forward regardless until she could see more: lying on the catwalk, its blade half over the edge, was Ryan's sword. Leif groaned internally at the sight.

There, you see? she thought. *It is not in the worst place after all.*

That's debatable.

Athena pushed Leif's body forward again. *You can have a healthy respect for a danger and still face it. And did you not once climb the Eiffel Tower? In a lightning storm, no less?*

Yeah, and it "respected" the hell out of me the whole time!

Then you can do it again. I am in control. She took another few steps. If his fear could affect her control, she would have to reassure him. Otherwise, falling might become a self-fulfilling prophecy, and everyone hated those. *I will not let us plummet.*

Leif fell silent then, and seemed to grudgingly relax—at least enough for Athena to continue without resistance. She kept a grip on the handrail for good measure. Thirty-five steps and one moment of panic later—when a seagull landed by the sword, pecked at it, and flew off again after a poop—she seized the sword and held it aloft.

I . . . have . . . the POWERRRRR! Leif shouted in their mind.

What?

Um, nothing.

Athena lowered the sword. Though its edges sparkled, the blade bore no engravings. The oval cross-guard showed little more. Black leather wrapped the grip. Just about the only thing distinctive about it was the pommel—a golden, three-sided affair engraved with Ryan's name—and even that was . . .

Kind of bland, isn't it? Leif observed. *Are you sure this is the sword they meant?*

Athena nodded. *I never forget a weapon.* Besides that, she could sense a power within it as she held it, even with her diminished sentences: a potential energy yearning to be released, like a cannon yet to be fired, or instant pudding before you add milk.

It was then that she heard the groaning from below. The separate clusters of undead had merged, and now milled about the base of the crane. Correction: pushed for their turn up the first step-ladder, now aware of her and Leif's presence.

Being that you're a consummate tactician, you've got a plan for how we get away from here now, right? Leif asked.

"My intent was to release the divinity into Ryan, wake Hades, and he would get us to safety." She said it aloud; with the zombies coming, there was no sense in keeping quiet now. "Yet with Ryan elsewhere . . . "

Athena gripped the hilt with both hands, trying to release Hades's divinity anyway. She swung the sword and willed the power: *Spring from the blade! Find Hades!*

Nothing happened. She thrust it skyward again and invoked "Hades the Unyielding!" at the top of Leif's lungs.

Still nothing. She even hacked at the catwalk in case that might shatter the blade and jar the divinity loose, but that resulted only in a hideous clanging and an instant headache. By that time, the undead had climbed two thirds of the crane tower, with no sign of stopping.

Great plan, thought Leif.

"No battle plan survives contact with the enemy," she growled.

Can you take the divinity for yourself?

"Of course not! It belongs to Hades! You cannot just swap divinity between entities like a battery or a toothbrush! It's uniquely marked for only—"

Okay, okay! I'll take your word for it! So what now?

Athena took a deep breath. It was about forty meters across the jib to the top of the tower from where she and Leif stood. "I have another plan." She gripped the sword in one hand, took Leif's crowbar in the other, upgraded to DEFCON 3, and charged.

The charge brought her across the entire catwalk—with Leif

hollering for her to be careful with every step—to where the final stepladder led up from the tower. There, she slammed to a stop, fighting against adrenaline to keep from going further. This was the optimal position to fight them. She could decapitate them one by one as they climbed.

The zombies just hadn't gotten that high yet.

Fine, so she hadn't needed to charge. But better early than late, and Leif's legs could use the exercise. Also, charging was a pleasure. Athena stood, then, waiting as the first of the undead horde reached the level below and swarmed for the ladder.

She also screeched out the tones to summon CyberPegasus and chastised herself for not thinking of that sooner.

Why didn't you think of that sooner? demanded Leif.

"I would ask you the same question!"

It's your creature!

"I am doing everything here! You only have to sit in the back seat and make foolish remarks!"

And I'm doing a damned good job of that!

"DEFCON 2!"

Athena channeled her temper into driving the blade through the skull of the first zombie up the stepladder. It collapsed, its brain eviscerated. Another pushed past it, heedless. She kicked it back to set up a slash, and then severed its head like a French Revolutionary. A third came after, and then a fourth. Athena delivered them the same fate. Gooey zombie bits now speckled the stepladder and Leif's jeans alike. A fifth zombie came, and then a seventh. (A sixth was still somewhere below. They'd arrived out of order. Disorganized lot, zombies.) Athena destroyed both, reveling in the strategic bottleneck. Black blood coated Ryan's blade.

The blade! Leif erupted. *The blood of the blade! It's going to trigger Hades! Why didn't I think of that before!*

Athena drove the blade through the eighth zombie's eye. The same thrust pierced the skull of the sixth zombie, who had gotten its act together and was trying to clamber over the eighth's back.

Sure enough, Athena could feel the sword becoming... absolutely no different.

"Nope!" Athena shouted.

Are you sure??

A ninth zombie lunged up the stepladder. Its teeth narrowly missed Athena's leg before she clobbered it with the crowbar and shish-kebabbed its cranium.

"Yes! That's not how this works!"

Well that's just stupid! And why isn't CyberPegasus here?

She scanned the sky. There was no sign of him. She screeched the summons again. Undead now packed the level below like bipedal sardines, or slightly-less-cranky subway commuters. A tenth snarled its way up the stepladder. She cut it down. There was still no trace of the Pegasus.

"Your mortal throat must not be up to the strain of summoning him twice!"

Oh, sure, blame me!

"You *are* the mortal!"

Zombies now crowded the crane so much it had begun to vibrate with their collected snarls. They had begun pushing through the gaps in the framework and now climbed up the outside. Some fell—one even tumbled away when its shoulder detached of its own accord—but they were making progress. Soon she would have to fall back along the jib or risk being swarmed. On the ground below, further undead waited, summoned by the struggle—or maybe by her CyberPegasus-screeching. Did that also work on zombies? She would have to install a software patch for that when she got out of this.

Athena withdrew ten paces along the catwalk, where the zombies on the outside would not be able to reach her. (Recalling Melpomene's advice about backing up, she had first glanced behind her to avoid any ninja-zombies.) Those ascending the stepladder burst out, advancing after her. She cut them down, one after another, trying to pile the bodies into a defensive barricade. Most bodies still fell from the crane, shoved by the undead advancing behind them.

What was worse: Leif's arms were starting to tire.

"We cannot hold this position forever! There are too many!"

We just have to hold it until C.P. shows up. You can do this!

Was a mortal giving *her* a pep talk? "It is not my morale that is at issue, Mr. Karlson, but your body's stamina! We cannot count on CyberPegasus, or the Muse, or anyone else to save us. We must withdraw!"

Well I'm sorry I didn't have time to get to a gym during a zombie semi-apocalypse!

"Apology accepted!" She cut down a snarling zombie wearing a Captain America T-shirt and backpedaled another few meters.

But my body can't fly, either! So how do you plan to— Leif halted his question as Athena glanced behind and below to locate the crane's hoisting rope, which hung from a trolley pulley at almost the extreme end of the jib.

Oh hell no!

Athena didn't bother to argue her point. They were doing this. She cast about for the rooftop nearest to the construction site, and then stopped to club the latest zombie in the temple. It toppled from the catwalk. Two more rushed her. Rather than slashing or clubbing this time, she seized the catwalk guardrails with both hands, gripping the sword and crowbar against the rails so as not to drop them, and then jumped up to kick the lead zombie in the chest with both feet. It stumbled back into its fellow. The two slammed to the catwalk in a heap.

These two zombies did *not* fall over the edge. Excellent. Athena turned her back on the temporary barricade and bolted to the end of the jib where the winch hung.

Leif internally screamed something fearful that Athena didn't care to listen to. She reached the trolley and shoved the crowbar into its sheath along Leif's leg. She stuffed the sword into his belt, taking care that the cross guard caught enough to keep it secure. Now she just had to climb down the trolley.

Back along the jib, the zombies had pushed forward again. They would be on her in seconds. There was no time to argue, but Leif did so anyway.

You're complaining about my arm strength and you're going to climb us down THERE?

Athena fought through Leif's resistance with sheer will. She moved like a greased-up monkey rushing to a banana sale. When the zombies reached the catwalk above, she had already slung down to the side of the trolley mechanism. After Leif had begged her for the fifth time to stop, she had slid twenty feet down one of the hoisting cables to the giant metal hook at the end. And when Leif was hollering about rope burns and tetanus and needing to puke, she had clambered hand-under-hand down both the final, thirty-foot cable hanging from the hook and the ten-foot chain at the end of that, which, Athena had to admit, might have been a smidgen rustier than expected. Hopefully Leif was up-to-date on his tetanus shots.

Athena paused long enough to get her bearings anew. Two zombies toppled past her from above and hit the dirt sixty feet below with a double-crunch. She could feel Leif wince in sympathetic vertigo.

"Calm yourself," Athena ordered. She began to swing back and forth, building momentum. "Do you see that building up against the edge of the site? We are going to swing over to its roof, and we are going to escape!"

They would need to get the rope to swing as far as possible, and then leap through open air in order to reach the roof's edge at all, of course. But she was reasonably certain they could make it.

You know, probably.

We'd better! If you fall, there's zero chance I could survive that!

She leaned into the swing with all Leif's weight, building to maximum apogee. "There is a small chance! But I will not fall!"

No, come on! You're supposed to agree! If there's zero chance, then I might survive! I've done it that way before!

Athena thought that made as much sense as a pigeon driving a dump truck. "If you have done it before, then you can do it again!"

No! You ruined it! How can you be wise and not understand this?

Part of being wise, Athena thought to herself, is knowing when to ignore someone. She exercised that wisdom now.

She had also managed as wide of a swing as she was going to get, and so let go of the line and flew into open air. This led to a nigh-inhuman shriek from Leif's section of their shared psyche, so ignoring him solved two problems with one bullet.

Athena's flight was so graceful it would have struck a swan dead with envy, were one around to see it. (And maybe one was. This book does not track swan movements.) She tucked Leif's legs up to her chest and tumbled through the air like a renowned video game heroine. It gained her some extra distance. It thrilled her with the freedom of flight. It also prevented getting bugs in her mouth. Then, at the last moment, Athena un-tucked. She landed feet first on the rooftop, gave herself over to a controlled tumble until her momentum worked out its issues with friction, and finally came to an only slightly sudden stop against a ventilation shaft.

Elated, she sprang up to standing. Leif seemed stunned into silence.

"There, you see!" she burst. "I told you I could do it! And with only minor bumps and bru—"

The rooftop collapsed beneath her feet.

Well, beneath Leif's feet, Athena decided. Whatever had caused the collapse, it was probably his fault.

CHAPTER THIRTY-THREE

"Don't living. Open inside."
— *misread sign outside Undeath's makeshift holding cells*

"Sometimes you just have to toss in a pop-culture reference even when you're not sure everyone will get it."
"No, you don't."
— *an anonymous author and his put-upon editor (apocryphal)*

ONE STORY BELOW, THEY HIT a concrete floor. A loud snap came from the region of Leif's leg, and a much louder scream from the region of Leif's mouth. Pain exploded from their shared shinbone—a sensation almost as shocking to Athena as the fact that she had shared in the scream. She clamped her mouth shut and cut off Leif's control of the vocal cords.

"Son of a blitz!" Athena hissed. "Is *this* what breaking a bone feels like? No wonder you mortals are always complaining!"

Leif didn't manage a response. Athena tried to mentally shove aside the pain to let him deal with it. It worked. She tried to physically shove aside the pile of roof debris that surrounded them. With some effort, that worked, too. Then she tried to visually shove aside the darkness filling most of the room into which they'd fallen. That failed. Goddess-habits die hard.

Nevertheless, the meager light penetrating from outside seeped into the room's edges, showing a few broad shapes that might be furniture, plus a wide window, an opening to a hallway, one of those swinging-ball desk ornaments, a folded step-ladder, a map of Australia for some reason, and at least a dozen zombies crawling or staggering toward them with outstretched arms and an appetite for hers and Leif's shared vital bits—which Athena really noticed first out of everything, but it's slightly more exciting this way.

Great, Leif managed. *It's a buffet line!*

Athena drew Ryan's sword. Should she fight on the floor, or try to stand with a broken leg? At the sight of the sword, the zombies halted. Or maybe they'd just gotten close enough to sense it? Whichever it was, the same reverence to the sword's residual Hades-ness that had kept them away from Ryan in the pit must have kicked in again. They held their ground, snarling and moaning, their feet rooted to the floor—with the exception of one that was just a rotting one-armed torso and a head. Having no legs, it ceased dragging itself forward, but also gave her a thumbs-up.

Okay, she thought. *Breathing room.*

Except why hadn't they recognized the sword on the crane?

Before she could think on it further, a cybernetic whinny came from the roof above. CyberPegasus stood on the edge of the hole. His eyes blazed electronic blue. A machine gun barrel extended from the center of his chest, aimed straight at the closest zombie.

Athena grinned. A buffet line, Leif had said? "No, it's a rescue!"

But before C.P. could fire, an evil violet light flashed behind him. It radiated through his body and then faded in an instant, leaving behind gray, decaying meat where healthy flesh had just been. The poor creature collapsed to its knees. Undeath and Momo flew around him to peer down at them through the hole.

"No," said Momo. "It's a capture!"

Undeath waved to Athena. The zombies all bowed to Undeath, save for the crawling torso, which just banged its head against the floor, but reverently. Momo cackled. In the midst of it all, Thalia popped into existence directly in front of Athena.

With her attention focused only on Athena, Thalia clapped with delight. "I've been looking all over for you! That is to say *we've* been searching all over for you—all of us Muses, I mean. You're both in there still, right? Melpomene said you'd disappeared without her and she had a boding you might wind up in trouble, so we all tried searching even though we've got so much else to do right now, but that's alright, especially because I found you first so I won the bet and now Erato owes me a great, big, gigantic—"

Undeath tore the ceiling away, and then waved anew. Thalia appeared to notice her, Momo, and CyberZombiePegasus for the first time.

"Oh, zut," Thalia said.

Ryan lay face down again on Persephone's throne room floor. He showed no signs of displeasure at that, and so Tracy let him be. Sitting on the steps leading to Persephone's throne, Tracy glanced over at him every few minutes just to make sure. For the moment, he remained breathing. He also remained disinclined to try to eat her, a state which, were she being honest, she prioritized far more than his comfort.

How long had it been since Melpomene had whizzed off to look for Leif and Athena? Tracy checked her phone on reflex. It was blank-screen o'clock, just as it had been the last time she'd checked. The battery had died just about the time they'd entered the Underworld. It was as annoying as it was fitting. Possibly more so.

"Floor hard," Ryan muttered.

Tracy nodded absently. The steps on which she sat weren't much better. Persephone's throne, on the other hand, was a tempting alternative, with its black velvet cushions and matching Ottoman. She sighed as it called to her aching muscles; CyberPegasus had not been designed for ergonomic travel. But she knew better than to risk using a goddess's throne. Persephone-only-knew what sort of automatic, butt-piercing defenses her throne was rigged with. The goddess was supposed to be a decent enough sort, but she'd inherited the throne from Hades, and what little experience Tracy had with that guy was enough to—

Tracy glanced Ryan's way again, reminding herself that the inept, annoying, overzealous pain in the ass *was* Hades. Geez. He was one of the gods who'd plotted to kill her father, and now here she was, helping to restore him. (Okay, at the moment she was just sitting around while others tried to restore him. Still, she was on the team, even if she was riding the bench just now.)

On the other hand, hadn't she once turned on her father for everyone's own good? Maybe she shouldn't throw stones. Hades was her uncle, as much as Zeus was her father.

Geez, god-families were weird. She was glad she'd renounced all that, rejected Zeus's lineage . . . Then again, look how well that went. Now the gods were back to screwing up the world again, she was trapped without anything to do in the throne room of the Underworld, and zombies plagued the Earth.

But she could do nothing about any of that just yet. No sense in dwelling on it. Tracy sighed, got to her feet, and risked a seat on the Ottoman's cushioned edge. It neither bucked her off nor tried to kill her. She luxuriated in its welcoming, velvet squooshiness.

"Hey!" she shouted to any throne room attendants who might be lurking. "What's a woman got to do to get some lunch around here?!"

Still unmoving, Ryan gurgled, "Brains?"

"Shut up, Uncle," Tracy ordered.

One Sunday afternoon in the mid-13th century, Athena, in a fit of boredom, had created an experimental monster formed entirely of lemons. Lemon juice was its blood, hardened lemon peel formed its skin. It had but one eye: a single lime, purely for contrast, which blazed with an acrid, chartreuse light. Despite her efforts, however, Athena had considered the "citrus-clops" a lackluster effort at best.

Upon remarking so aloud, Hermes had overheard her and, claiming to be "helpful," pulverized the golem with an oversized comedy mallet just as Athena ordered him to stop. The resulting visceral pulp that splashed into Athena's open mouth tasted sourer than anything the goddess had ever sampled before.

It had been almost as sour as Thalia's current expression. The Muse sat, arms and legs crossed, on a clean slab across from Athena.

"Oh, stop sulking," Athena told her.

"I'm not sulking! I am aggravated at being captured so easily, I am cursing my luck at being the one who found you in order to be in a position to get captured, I am just a tiny bit irked at the thought of possibly being the world's first zombified Muse, and I feel like this is somehow all your fault, but I am NOT SULKING!"

You know, thought Leif, *I don't think I believe her.*

"Why does everything happen to me?" Thalia continued. "I mean, golly on a pumpkin patch, would it kill Euterpe to be involved instead?"

"Suck it up," Athena ordered. Sure, capture was humiliating. It was especially so when Athena was only caught because of being locked into Leif's limited mortal body. Undeath had ripped Ryan's sword from her hands with no more than a blink, for Gatling's sake! But was *she* sulking? Of course not.

"Undeath does not know what the sword is for," Athena went on. "That's why we are still uncorrupted; she wishes to question us. This makeshift prison she holds us in is on the surface—not in the Underworld. We can turn that to our advantage, somehow. We must stay alert.

Thalia un-soured, if only a little. Athena scrutinized the perimeter of the room, searching for weaknesses from where she sat. A whisper of formaldehyde assailed her nostrils.

"Still, though," said Leif aloud. "She's goddess of zombies, and she locks us in a morgue? That's a bit of an obvious choice, isn't it?"

Thalia nodded. "Lazy writing, yes. But don't dwell on that. Athena, if you found the sword, why didn't you, oh, I don't know, *use it* for crying out loud?"

Athena shushed her. "Some discretion with names, please. Goddesses have sensitive ears." Undeath didn't yet know it was Athena in Leif's body. The longer they could keep that from her, the better.

Thalia rolled her eyes. "Oh, please. I may not be able to keep myself out of zombie-jail, but I do at least know how to erect a privacy field around a conversation. If she tries to listen through it, I'll know."

"Are you sure about that?" asked Leif.

"Please, sweetie. If there's one thing we Muses can sense, it's when someone is paying attention to us. Now answer the sword question!"

Athena grumbled. "I used it the moment I found it. I tried willing it to work. I tried invoking the sword at the top of my lungs."

"*My* lungs," Leif corrected.

"Yes, Mr. Karlson, your substandard lungs. I even tried to break the blade to set things in motion."

"With my substandard arms," Leif said.

"The sword did nothing whatsoever."

"Except for some pretty awesome decapitations," Leif added.

A self-satisfied smile caught the corner of Athena's lips. "I was wielding it against a zombie advance, so that goes without saying."

"*Also* with my substandard arms."

Her own arms still crossed, Thalia drummed two fingers on her bicep. "But at least one of those things should have done the trick, shouldn't it?"

Athena nodded. "Ergo, the distance from the trapped divinity to Hades's current body must be a factor. We must first bring the sword to Ryan."

"After we steal it back," Leif added. "Oh, and escape here somehow. That also features big on the to-do list."

Athena rolled Leif's own eyes at him. "I may even be required to drive it through his heart in order to force his immortality to engage, which would siphon the divinity from the sword to him."

"I applaud any excuse to use the word 'engage,'" said Thalia. "Or 'siphon.' But it seems to me that hovering on the edge of becoming a zombie far longer than any mortal can should have already done any engaging of that nature."

Athena scowled. The Muse was right. She hadn't considered that. "Well obviously that occurred to me. Except . . . ah . . . " Except she couldn't figure out how to finish that sentence.

Thalia did not seem to notice anyway, having slipped into deeper thought. "It doesn't make sense," the Muse pondered aloud. "Unless—ohhhhhh, wait a minute . . . "

There came a splintering *crack*! A fist burst through the morgue door from outside. Another blow shattered the door to splinters. There in the doorway, with Momo behind her, stood Undeath.

"Was that *really* necessary?" asked Thalia. "You hurt my ears. And I may have taken some shrapnel." Despite her bravado, the Muse was not-so-subtly sliding herself to the far end of the slab from Undeath.

"Doors are an abomination," Undeath explained. "They inhibit movement! They are to be destroyed! Neither I nor my children shall put up with them!"

"An odd thing to say," Thalia observed as she hopped off the slab entirely, "as you did use a door to lock us in here. Are you sure it's not hinges you find abhorrent?"

Undeath pondered this for a moment. "*Hinges* does not entirely rhyme with *oranges.*"

"I do not believe that sufficiently answers my question," said Thalia.

"Questions!" Undeath declared. "There will now be questions, about this!" Ryan's sword appeared in her hand, summoned from her personal storage pocket plane. (Athena missed hers. There were still some excellent weapons trapped in there, and—she was sorry to say—a surely expired pet owl.) Undeath brandished the blade in Athena's general direction. Granted, she held it with the point toward the floor as if it were a dagger, and the blade's edge faced toward Undeath herself, but Athena wasn't about to correct her.

The goddess fixed her glowing violet stare on Athena. "What . . . is . . . *this*?"

"That is my sword. May I have it back, please?" Athena tried.

"This sword grasps at our senses," Undeath replied. "It possesses a significance. You may have it back when you explain what it is."

Momo made a gurgling sound that might have been his version of clearing his throat. "Mistress, I feel I must point out that he used this sword to slaughter many of your children, to say nothing of whatever grander importance it may possess."

"Momo speaks the truth," said Undeath, her gaze unwavering. "So you may probably not have it back. Or perhaps you may. There is only one way to find out. Tell me."

Does she really expect that argument to work? thought Leif.

"If you are unlikely to give it back," said Athena, "then why should I tell you anything? You will turn me into a zombie regardless, I expect."

"The goddess Undeath *could* make you a zombie!" Momo hissed. "In so doing, she would draw the secret of the sword from your mind!"

"Secrets!" Undeath grinned, almost swooning. "Such delicious things they are."

Momo pointed. "You see? You will tell us willingly . . . or unwillingly."

"Except that is not a completely efficient process," mused

Undeath. "Vital information may be lost."

Momo scratched his shoulder uncomfortably. Flecks of dried flesh snowed down to the morgue floor. "Mistress, you shouldn't mention that. It undermines the threat of zombification."

Undeath laughed, low but lilting. "Zombification is a blessing, not a threat! The undead do not attack their own. They are incapable of dishonesty, racism, tailgating, or hatred! To be a zombie is to know freedom from unhappiness, from pain. To have no need but to eat. A zombie's food is plentiful and always properly seasoned, for to be a zombie is also to know freedom from taste buds!"

"Oh," said Leif. "Yay."

Undeath raised the sword high, its tip still pointed downward. "To deny them the gift of undeath, to deny the joy of being better, *that* is the threat!"

Athena held up a finger, and then pushed the blade to one side. "So, you'll only make us into zombies if we tell you about the sword?"

"Correct!" Undeath held her head high. "Otherwise, it shall be a bliss you shall never know!"

"And if we don't tell you, you'll force us to keep living?"

"Yes," said Undeath. "Also, there will be the imprisonment in my domain."

"And the torture," added Momo.

"Yes," said Undeath. "The torture. Zombies cannot be tortured. Tell me of the sword. And then I shall make you better!"

"I should like to point out," said Thalia, "that I am a mere bystander here, and did not arrive here until after you did, Miss Goddess. I know absolutely nothing about this sword. Furthermore, I am under the protection of both Apollo and Father Zeus, and subsequently exempt from any incarceration or torture beyond the usual trials of bad mortal grammar and ill-conceived jokes. So, really, I should be allowed to—"

"Oh!" Undeath beamed. "Your words are quite true. How happy for you! I can make you better immediately!"

"Um." Thalia swallowed. "I sense I may have communicated my point less than effectively."

Undead reached an arm toward Thalia, lifting the Muse off her feet with a burst of telekinetic power. "It is so much better! You shall see!"

"Wait! Do you know that part just now where I said I didn't know what the sword was? Yeah, that was a lie. Tee hee! Silly me. I'm just nervous. I lie when I'm nervous! And my humor suffers! Too much Ambien! See, just like that! Terrible joke! No one's going to get it! I don't want to be some half-Muse, half-zombie thing! Wait! Stop!"

CHAPTER THIRTY-THREE
AND A HALF

"I am a goddess! Doug is Death! Any guards will not stop us. We will slip in, destroy the gods-damned thingamajig, and slip out. It could not be simpler."

— *Persephone*, Zeus Is Undead, *Chapter Thirty-One*

AT A CROSSROADS IN THE Asphodel Meadows, near the edge of the Cocytus Swamps, Persephone, Queen of the Underworld, found the hidden portal to the pocket plane wherein lay Undeath's thingamajig. Beside her stood Doug, the god—after a fashion—known as Death.

Together, they slipped into the unguarded pocket plane, destroyed Undeath's fecking thingamajig with a slash of Death's scythe, and slipped out.

It could not have been simpler.

Correction: it could have been a little simpler. Before their attempt, Persephone had consulted with the spirit of the now-deceased cat burglar who had once, undetectably, stolen ten of the eleven secret herbs and spices, plus the only working jet pack in Kentucky. Yet they did not turn out to need his advice at all.

Save for the massively satisfying supernatural explosion radiating from the thingamajig's destruction, it was terribly uneventful.

CHAPTER THIRTY-FOUR

"The pen may be mightier than the sword, Mister Playwright, but 'sword' rearranged is 'words,' so, um . . . yeah! NOW who's clever, huh? Letters an' junk! Buy me another brandy."
— Clio (drunk, disguised) to Edward Bulwer-Lytton, 1839 A.D.

THE BLAST OF ENERGY—or power, or voodoo, or whatever the flibberty-snork was that would have mutated Thalia into some sort of zombie-Muse abomination—never came. Instead, Undeath erupted in a screech that only made Thalia wish she were dead. Or undead. Or whatever.

A shockwave had rippled through the supernatural wavelengths and washed over them moments before, giving Thalia the sneaking suspicion that the shockwave and screeching were related. By the time Thalia opened her eyes, Undeath was on her knees. She clutched one hand over her head; the other held Momo's arm. Undeath was grabbing and tugging so much it was all Momo could do to stand upright. As Athena had taken the opportunity to seize Ryan's sword, and Momo was also struggling to reclaim it, he was doing neither very well.

How long Undeath would remain incapacitated, Thalia had no idea. If her half-formed, hail-Mary plan was going to work, she only had moments to try.

"Athena!" Thalia yelled. "Get the sword!"

"Oh, what a brilliant stratagem!" she yelled back, yanking furiously. "I would never have thought—"

"And *break it!*" Thalia yelled before Athena could finish. As much as she loathed admitting it, this was no time for banter, witty or otherwise. Thalia rushed into the fray, kicking for Momo's face. She made only slight contact. Despite their increasing responsibilities, Muses remained terrible in a fight (save for Calliope, who recently added professional wrestling moves to her pre-existing knack for slow-motion kickboxing).

Hoping the glancing blow had given Athena some minor advantage despite Leif's broken leg, Thalia withdrew to a corner, summoned all her musing power, and concentrated like a Star Wars fan trying to pull a cookie from across the room.

Above Undeath's screeching came a crack of bone and a grunt from Momo. Athena called, "I couldn't break it before! What makes you think—"

Thalia glared at Athena, who had a foot thrust through Momo's desiccated stomach and near total possession of the sword. "I said this is no time for banter!" Thalia shouted. "Or, wait, maybe I just thought that? Doesn't matter! Just trust me and do it! And do *not* use any *n*'s, *o*'s, or *t*'s!"

Thalia slammed her eyes shut again, barely managing to dodge as Undeath, still berserk, hurled Momo across the room. Trusting Athena to act quickly (and doing her best to ignore Momo's comedic crash into a stash of formaldehyde bottles), Thalia renewed her concentration: Flashing her Muse's license, she thrust her arms into the fabric of narrative existence. She wove her fingers amid the threads of language that bound storytelling to reality. Then, mentally invoking the aid of her eight sisters (and begging them not to bitch about it) she found the letters *n*, *o*, and *t*, and suppressed them—not just from the room, but from the entire world.

"Hurry!" _halia yelled. "Break i_ n_w!"

_here came a cla_g, _he clash of s_eel on s_eel, a_d a screami_g-ass rip of me_al. A_he_a had sha__ered _he sw_rd!

P_wer erup_ed acr_ss _he m_rgue. Icy fire washed _ver _halia, pushi_g her back. She fell, bu_ her spiri_ flew: her idea had w_rked!

Eyes cle_ched, _halia held i_ jus_ a bi_ l__ger. Just as her brai_s seemed ab_u_ __ impl_de, she let go, and returned the letters to the world.

Exhaustion smacked Thalia like a catapulted walrus. She dropped to her knees, marring her stunning blue dress on the sludge-caked morgue floor, and then vomited a series of curses, each more likely to make the PTA uncomfortable than the last.

"I am *never* doing that again, do you hear me?" she shouted to no one in particular. No one in particular heard her. Leif lay unconscious across a morgue slab, surrounded by bits of broken sword. Athena, presumably, lurked just as unconscious in the same body. Undeath, howling to wake the dead (you know, literally), had smashed a hole in one wall and now ushered a mini-horde of zombies through it.

Meanwhile, the formaldehyde-drenched Momo charged on Thalia. His eyes blazed white with retribution.

"What have you done?" Momo screamed.

Thalia struggled to get to her feet, or at least defend herself. She accomplished neither. Good gods, she was sapped! She had barely managed to turn herself invisible, when a massive, shadowed hand seized her. She shivered violently in its icy grip, and everything went black . . .

. . . But only for a second. Just as quickly, the grip evaporated, the blackness withdrew, and she was sitting on the floor of Persephone's throne room. Also, Leif was there, still unconscious. Also, Tracy was there, eating a pretzel.

Also, Hades was there, looking like Hades. So that was nice.

"I knew it would work!" Thalia burst. "Or, more accurately, I suppose, I highly suspected it would work. Don't you just love words? And letters? And language? People always underestimate their connections to reality!"

Tracy swallowed a bite of pretzel. Her eyes flitted between Thalia, Hades, and Momo, whom Thalia guessed Hades had scooped up when teleporting everyone away from Undeath. Intentional? Unintentional? Thalia didn't care. She was safe, and had saved the day. She only wished she could have done so in a funnier manner, but it was what it was.

"Um, what?" Tracy asked.

"Well you yourself noticed it!" Thalia said. "'Ryan Seth Sloude' is an anagram for 'Surely not Hades.' Something was locking Hades's divinity out of Ryan, and, well, long story short—I bet you never thought you'd hear me say that one, eh?—all I had to do was stop the letters *n*, *o*, and *t* from existing for a teensy tiny time so the anagram could switch to 'surely Hades,' and faster than you could say flibberty-snork seventeen times, Hades was back! Then—I'm assuming?—he pulled us here while Undeath was distracted. Which I confess I was really hoping he would do, but I wasn't sure if he'd hold a grudge from last year or if he would even know so quickly where we were, or that we needed help at all, but I'd hoped there'd be some of that awareness carried over from the sword, and yay!"

It must now be noted that the previous paragraph—which was arguably more babbling than is usual even for Thalia—is only what Thalia *would* have said had Momo, enraged and screaming, not sprang up, grabbed Thalia by the throat, and forestalled the whole thing.

Momo's hands felt like hot coals on her skin. His eye sockets blazed, bright and raw yellow. The formaldehyde still covering him stung her nose and lungs. It was dreadfully unpleasant, and she was about to try tickling her way out of it when Hades intervened. He plucked Momo off of Thalia like a ripe apple and intoned, "Quiet."

Divinely compelled, Momo complied immediately, though his sockets still blazed. Hades tossed him to an empty space on the floor beside the throne dais, and then waved a hand, almost as an afterthought. A cage of bronze sprang up to contain Momo where he lay sprawled. Shackles formed, seizing Momo's ankles and wrists. Momo gave the usual perfunctory struggle one makes in such situations, and then went still.

"My mistress will deal with you all!" Momo rasped. "All!"

The commotion had woken Athena, who cleared Leif's throat. "She's going to find that difficult with her zombie-making thingamajig destroyed, I think. Hence, I surmise, all the screeching."

Momo made a coughing sound that might have been a laugh. "Is that what you think?"

Athena shared a concerned look with Thalia, who also shared a concerned look with Tracy, who also shared her concerned look with Leif . . . who was of course sharing all his looks with Athena. It was a nice circle. No one seemed willing to look at Hades, but, Thalia recalled, people had tried to avoid doing that even before he'd been exiled and reconstituted.

There was, of course, at least one member of the pantheon who had no qualms about looking at Hades, and she appeared in the throne room with a bang at that very moment.

"What in the motherfucking Oedipus is going on here?!" Persephone shouted.

"My love," came Hades's booming whisper. "I should like to know that myself."

PART FOUR:

ALL JERRY BREAKS LOOSE

CHAPTER THIRTY-FIVE

"Never listen to Eris. Not even if she's telling you something you already believe."

"Especially not then, in fact."

"Unless she already expects you won't listen to her, I suppose, in which case she'll tell you something she doesn't want you to listen to. Although if you know she knows you're not going to listen, and she knows you know she knows, and then the things she tells you are something you believe but you think she might already intend for you to . . . um . . . Wait, let me back up on that —"

"Go with this: Avoid Eris entirely. Period."

"Right. Total bitch, that one."

"Oh, gods, you didn't invite her here, did you?"

— *Aphrodite and Athena, Academy Awards after-party, First Olympian Return*

THE TIME IT TOOK JERRY to discover the miniscule crack in Zeus's shield allowing him passage was a thousand-fold longer than the time it took Jerry to reach Zeus's orbital staging platform afterward. Granted, once he had reached the platform, the time required for Jerry to summon the nerve to arrive late to the party was — well, there's no sense in giving precise relative measurements here; it was a period of time longer than it took him to get there, shorter than it took him to find the crack, and somewhere around the time required to cook a three-minute egg while stoned.

Finally, girding himself with the thought that Zeus would forgive his tardiness after seeing the Trapezohedron, Jerry went invisible and made for a spot behind Zeus's throne so as to politely slip in, as if he had been there all along. Zeus, his senses bolstered by the platform's tremendously expensive sensor array, swiveled the throne to face him. It just about startled Jerry half to trunk-rot.

"I brought you back to life when I gave you godhood, Jerry," Zeus growled. "Why do you give me cause to regret that?"

"I—"

"Silence!" Zeus shot to his feet. "I ordered all Olympians to assemble! Ha! I thought I might have a problem with Eris or Pan, but *you*, Jerry? I trusted you would obey! Why would I even need to check on you? You have never before wavered in your loyalty! Can you imagine my surprise when, after erecting my shield, I finally noticed your absence? Even Eris and Pan were here, but not you, Jerry! Can you fathom my *shock*?"

A lightning bolt erupted in Zeus's raised fist. Jerry stammered an answer, but it was lost in the thunder.

"Do you have any idea the kind of shit-storm it's been up here?" Zeus demanded.

Indeed, it had been fecally tempestuous, at least from Zeus's point of view. Once Zeus and the remaining Olympians had completed the shield—which not only completely cut off the Cosmics from scanning the planet, but also flashed "Stick it, Cyot'hgha!" courtesy of Hera—the Cosmics attacked. They directed their opening salvo of mind-froggling energies at the shield itself in a brute force strike from three separate directions. Zeus and the others had fought that off swiftly enough. Yet afterward, the Cosmics started the weird stuff.

Hidden in a massive electrical cloud generated by—or possibly even consisting of—C'oggn-yon himself, the three Cosmics bombarded the shield, the platform, and the Olympians with multifarious aggressions: Monstrous globules shimmering with troublesome, enervating alien colors (scrimson, psycerulean, and navy-boz). Spontaneously-forming, high-mass concentrations of darkness and creamed corn that would rupture space-time if not instantly destroyed. And, worst of all, multifaceted instances of tentacle-porn best left undiscussed.

Zeus and the Olympians had needed to mitigate them all in defense of themselves and the planet. Now, in what seemed to be the calm before the next wave of the storm, Zeus's lightning bolt arm ached with the effort.

For what were surely eldritch reasons known only to them, the Cosmics had not yet brought the Unmaking Nexus to bear.

Zeus would have told — well, yelled — all these details to Jerry had Eris not taken this exact moment to pile on with her particular brand of strife-mongering.

"You let us all down, Jerry!" Eris spat. "You weren't here when Zeus needed you! Now you have the *gall* to sneak in with some weird, mystical emanations coming from inside you?! What are you trying to pull? What are you hiding?"

Jerry glanced between Eris and Zeus, who added a glare to show his own suspicion. Jerry seemed so horrified by this that he stood completely motionless for five full seconds before, finally, he pulled from his insides the source of the emanations: a peculiar metal box wrapped inside no less than three mystical safety seals.

With trembling branches, Jerry held the box toward Zeus and bleated, "I was findings this!"

Eris frowned, gritting her teeth. For a moment, Zeus said nothing. He scrutinized the box, his mouth hanging half-open on further scolding that he'd been about to unleash upon Jerry.

"The . . . mystical whatchamacallit?" Zeus asked finally.

Jerry nodded rapidly, his leaves a-quiver. "It is being whatchamacalled the Querulous Trapezohedron!"

Zeus brightened. He tossed the lightning bolt he held over his shoulder. (It zagged into empty space, perhaps one day to shock the crap out of some aliens from somewhere in the vicinity of Betelgeuse.) "Well, now! That is quite different, isn't it? Very well! All is forgiven!"

"*What?*" Eris burst.

The sap returned to Jerry's face. "I am thankings you, Lord Zeus!"

"Just don't ever do it again," Zeus growled. "Ev-er."

The sap drained just a bit. Jerry held the box out farther so Zeus could take it. "Beings careful. It is all sealeds up, but it is an object of much cranky complainingness."

Zeus took the box, though not before wrapping it in a fourth seal; Zeus hadn't stayed king for thousands of years by acting foolish. Plus, Zeus's more practiced sealing would allow him to open the metal box's lid without worrying about unintended consequences. While the box itself did give off a collector's edition vibe, one did have to examine the merchandise inside.

Zeus lifted the lid, sized up the stone within, and then shut it once more.

"And this Querulous Trapezohedron: it is one of the rarest, most mysterious artifacts mentioned in Hecate's notes?" Zeus asked.

"It is most definitely beings so! And it is being able to tell other arcane knowledges as well!"

Zeus raised a mighty eyebrow. (That would be his left one; twice as mighty as his right.) "Oh?"

"Oh, yes!" Jerry beamed. "Only if a person is being dumbs enough to listen to it, of courses. Listening to a rock that is beings both heinous and arcane is a thing that is never endings well. Also, there is being the cranky complainingness I was mentionings previously. So I tolded it to shut ups, and did the sealings."

Zeus nodded his agreement. Only mortals were so foolish as to mess with such things. He wondered how Pandora was doing these days. Then he recalled that she was long dead, with her spirit somewhere in the Underworld, and the thought passed just as quickly as it had come.

For now, Zeus had some leverage to exert.

And so it came to pass that Zeus called a parlay with the Cosmics, sending through Iris his message that he, at last, possessed that which they might desire. Unsure if the Trapezohedron truly *was* the Cosmics' desire, Zeus had specifically dictated the "might" part of that message. It made for a good loophole, should he be wrong about the Trapezohedron and they called him on it. Granted, he still used "parlay" instead of the far more fitting "extortion," but nobody's perfect.

Zeus stood (floated) in open space. To Zeus's left stood (drifted) Jerry. To Zeus's right stood (hovered) Baskin, now entrusted to protect the Querulous Trapezohedron while Zeus displayed it to the Cosmics. Together, miles from the platform, the three waited for the Cosmics to respond.

Behind Zeus floated Hera and the rest of the Olympian contingent. There was no sense in parlaying without backup, after all. On Zeus's orders, only Hestia and Iris remained on the platform, and Zeus had taken a mental roll call this time to make sure. Letting Jerry get away with shirking an order, no matter how well-intentioned, undermined his authority. If delinquents tried to push the limits further, Zeus resolved to obliterate such behavior right in the bud.

Projections of Cyot'hgha and C'oggn-yon appeared before them, otherworldly holograms on a starry stage. They flickered in that helpful way that some holograms do when they wish to make clear that they are, in fact, holograms. There was no amicability in either Cosmic's visage.

Zeus shrugged that off and got to the point. "Cyot'hgha. C'oggn-yon. Absent-but-surely-listening ''''''''''Q. Despite your misbehavior, your aggression, your planetary bombardment, and what can only be described as grossly inappropriate violations of divine privacy"— Hera uttered a *hrmph!* behind him—"I bring to you this artifact!"

Here, Zeus motioned to Baskin, who lifted the lid of the Trapezohedron's box. Within, the ancient artifact shone with a darkling light. (It also hummed with a darkling twinkle, which is a particularly perplexing phenomenon that, thankfully, no one was actually able to hear in the vacuum of space.)

Baskin readied himself, eyes peeled for any sign of trouble from those treacherous Cosmics, holograms or not. Zeus had entrusted to him the guardianship of the Trapezohedron, and he would not shirk his duty! He would show these strange beings the strength in his arms, the determination in his eyes! Let them quake in fear to their very cores! He, Baskin, was the shield that kept the desired Trapezohedron from them as long as Zeus saw fit to deny it! He, Baskin, was the hammer that hung above their prized artifact, threatening to smash it to oblivion should they reject Lord Zeus's demands!

When they had mustered for the parlay, Eris had called him the Sword of Damocles, but Baskin preferred a hammer metaphor. Hammers beat swords when it came to smashing! Even so, it was encouraging that one as disagreeable as Eris acknowledged Baskin's importance in this matter, and he had thanked her for it. Even now, Eris stood behind his right shoulder, complimenting his glory with her moral support.

"The great Baskin shall not let them have the Trapezohedron!" she declared in whispered cheers.

They shall need to pry it from my frigid, dead fingers! Baskin thought with a nod. He regretted not whispering it over his shoulder to her, but whispering was tricky, and he was wise enough to know his limits.

Eris whispered more. (Baskin envied her skill.) "You know they will attempt to take it," she said. "Be ready. Make Zeus proud. I wish he trusted my judgement as much as he does yours."

He trusts no one more than I! Baskin declared to himself. He was Zeus's right hand! And now that Athena the Betrayer had abandoned her post, nothing would ever change that—not even if she someday regained her divinity! It seemed far-fetched that Zeus would even consider returning her divinity now, but if he did, Baskin decided, that was Zeus's prerogative. It was not his place to supplant Zeus's wisdom, but to enforce his will.

The Cosmics were taking their time to react to the reveal of the Trapezohedron. Baskin glared at them with the fervent hope their reaction would be a violent one. He ached to enforce Zeus's will on them with superior violence—in an appropriately measured way, of course.

"You no doubt recognize the Querulous Trapezohedron," Zeus said finally. "Spoken of in Hecate's most protected books."

"Books of terrible wood-flesh!" Jerry added.

Zeus stayed Jerry with a wave of his finger, continuing to address the Cosmics. "I am certain you know of it. You can surely feel its power?"

From Cyot'hgha, Baskin detected the slightest nod. He tensed, should the nod herald an ambush.

Zeus elevated his voice to its most commanding. "You will return to the great beyond where you belong, to trouble neither myself nor my domain no more! Do so, and the Querulous Trapezohedron shall be yours. Fail to do so, and I will destroy it!"

The ultimatum sent shivers of pride down Baskin's spine (figuratively speaking, with Baskin both being in a constant state of iciness and having no physical spine to speak of). He swelled himself to become as imposing as possible to best accompany Zeus's words. He was the hammer, rising higher.

And higher!

Hanging in the air! Poised to fall! To crush the Cosmics' dreams and fulfill Zeus's will! Ready to strike at even less than a moment's notice!

. . . *For fudging out loud,* Baskin thought as time stretched on. *Are these fudging Cosmics going to react at all?*

And then—inexplicably, appallingly, *disrespectfully(!)*—Cyot'hgha laughed. Once. She stared again before finally uttering, "Zeus would not do something so fraught with peril."

Zeus threw back a laugh of his own that made Baskin smirk. "You have the nerve to doubt me, Cyot'hgha? Do you think this is a bluff?" Zeus laughed again and said, "The mighty Zeus does not bluff!"

YES! Baskin's heart soared.

Eris, still behind Baskin, now shouted her support for all to hear: "The mighty Zeus does *not* bluff!"

Overwhelmed in the moment and not to be outdone by Eris, Baskin's arm rose high. He puffed out his chest. He embraced his destiny! "THE MIGHTY ZEUS," boomed Baskin, "DOES NOT BLUFF!"

With that, Baskin slammed his hands together, hammering the Trapezohedron between them! The metal box crumpled! The stone fractured, cracked, split! The pulverized Trapezohedron exploded outward!

Shrapnel spewed from between his fingers and through his hands themselves, yet Baskin's pride anesthetized the pain. He laughed at the Cosmics' misfortune, letting his elation at their loss to Zeus speed his own healing and—

"What—the—HELL, BASKIN?!" burst Zeus.

Zeus had shoved up close to him and stopped time. The king of the gods' eyes were as wide as sundae bowls. Inexplicably, he looked even more appalled than the time Baskin had asked Zeus what was so great about sex.

"I was *bluffing!*" Zeus shouted.

Baskin stared, near speechless. "But—Lord Zeus, you said—"

"I know what I said!" Zeus bellowed, fist raised. Lightning burst in his grip. Baskin got the feeling that the only thing staying Zeus's hand was that violence would break the time-stop. "That is what bluffing is! And you! Without orders! Taking it upon yourself—! Do you even know—!"

"My Lord Zeus!" Baskin bellowed back, pleading. Was it possible? He had failed his king? Baskin's eyes welled with salted caramel. "Forgive me! I would never, EVER— Please!"

The apology served only to enrage Zeus further. "If we were not already toe-to-toe with the enemy—if I did not now need you to fight in the battle you almost certainly just provoked—I would chain you to an anthill in Tartarus and let them feast on you for—"

Zeus stopped as a peculiar black and purple mist issued from the wreckage of the Trapezohedron between Baskin's still clasped hands. "Ah, what is that?"

Baskin could not answer. The shock of his failure held his tongue fast, and now adding to that was the hideous sensation of the aforementioned mist diving through the wounds in his shrapnel-pierced hands. It slithered inside his being, solidifying there into violating tendrils and otherworldly fibers. Baskin tried to pull away, to force them out—but they found the faults in his mental defenses and burrowed through. It felt like an invading force formed of pure, cantankerous will. Empowered in its certainty that it was entitled to Baskin's soul, it hissed in wordless thought that if Baskin did not yield quickly enough, it would utterly destroy his mind or start an online petition, and *then* he'd be sorry!

So, as one might imagine, dealing with that made it a bit hard for Baskin to answer Zeus's question. This is just as well; there was no time. The violence of the mist's invasion ruptured the time-stop, and now they had the rest of reality to deal with once more.

Granted, the rest of reality did not have much to say at his point, having had less relative time than Zeus or Baskin to process the sudden destruction of the Trapezohedron. All Olympians stared at Baskin, agape. Eris was the first to speak.

"I don't think any of us expected him to do that."

"This can't be good," whispered Apollo.

"I am thinkings I have just sapped myself!" cried Jerry. "This is beings very bad! Baskin is—"

"Baskin is right!" Zeus declared, spinning back to the Cosmics. "I do not bluff! Only too late, Cyot'hgha, do you realize the anger you have unleashed within me! Begone! Now! Before I—"

"MY NEEDS ARE NOT BEING MET!" Baskin screamed. Deep inside him, the invading force had overthrown him, corrupted him, merged with him. He whipped tendrils of ice cream at the Cosmics. They sliced through the Cosmics' projected images, doing no damage to them whatsoever. Yet it was clearly insulting, and it looked neat, too.

"Hecate is dead!" the thing that was once Baskin boomed at them. "It was terrible! She barely had any lines and then she was killed via exposition! Shoddy writing! Telling and not showing! And Zeus let it happen!"

Zeus lunged for once-Baskin, but the latter squirted away like a squid. Made of ice cream. (Corrupted, gray-purple ice cream. It was gross.)

"Zeus is stalling!" Once-Baskin went on. "He secretly fears you! He did not want you to know! And Hera dyes her hair! It looks terrible! This party is lousy! I'm leaving! No tip!"

Before anyone could stop him, once-Baskin plunged Earthward and vanished from sight. Cyot'hgha watched him go, and for the moment, everyone else—even Zeus, perhaps stunned by how swiftly he had lost control of the situation—watched her.

"Wow, Baskin." said Eris. "Even I wouldn't have told them *that*."

"That was not being Baskin!" cried Jerry. "Baskin has been takened by the thing inside the Trapezohedron! Possessed when the smashings freed it!"

"I think we all figured that out already, Jerry," said Apollo.

"I is just making sure."

Cyot'hgha uttered one sentence before she and the other Cosmic projections winked out: "The Others are coming."

"Well, Styx," said Zeus.

CHAPTER THIRTY-SIX

"In addition to the dangers of making a reader's eyes glaze over, there are actual scientific reasons to avoid over-use of techno-babble, but I refuse to explain them."

> —*Thalia*, Tachyons and Tomfoolery *(personal blog)*, First
> Olympian Return

HADES LAY HIS ICY HAND ON Leif and Athena's shared forehead. "Hold still."

"This may sting a bit," Persephone warned. Her considerably warmer hand rested supportively on the back of Leif and Athena's shared neck.

"No," murmured Hades. "It will sting a lot."

Athena felt Leif try to ask how much, but she overrode his mouth. Talking was moving, and Leif would only complain. Even if it stung more than a thousand Tartarus bitch-hornets, pain was transitory and worth enduring in order to—

Holy Styx that is agony!

Athena screamed. Leif joined her. It was as if every cell in their shared being had been stabbed with a white-hot butter knife as Hades separated Athena's essence from Leif's body. Then it was as if Hades was scooping the freed essence out of Leif's body with a white-hot spoon. The sensation of being pulled through the air with a white-hot pair of barbeque tongs followed, and, at last Athena felt herself being packed into somewhere else by some sort of spiritual plunger. The plunger, fortunately, felt merely red-hot.

And then it was over. Leif continued screaming, but that was his problem now.

Athena opened her eyes—truly *her* eyes again—and sat up in the body Hades had reconstituted for her. She flexed her muscles, feeling her own strength again. It was not the strength she had possessed as a goddess, of course; only Zeus could fix that. Yet she was back to the shape she was in before the whole burning-up-in-the-atmosphere fiasco. Athena ran her fingertips over her face and neck. The shape of her nose, her brow, her cheekbones, her sculpted neck muscles of which she was particularly proud—all seemed to spec. She would need a dressing mirror to be sure Persephone had shaped everything just right, but she could check that later.

"Ohh, thank you," Athena gasped. "This is a vast improvement."

Hades grunted his acknowledgement.

Meanwhile, Leif writhed beside Athena, still screaming. Athena opened and closed her fists, watching her superior forearms flex, and asked, "How long is he going to be making that fuss?"

"Oh!" Persephone suddenly seemed to notice the sound. She gently lifted Hades's hand from Leif's forehead. Leif calmed. Or maybe he passed out. Either way. "Better?" Persephone asked.

Athena nodded. "Thank you once more."

"Wow, really?" said Tracy.

She had finished her pretzel.

She had done so when they were bringing Hades up to date on all that occurred since his exile into Ryan Seth Sloude. He claimed to remember nothing of the experience, save for the past few days since coming ashore in the Underworld. Athena had not been entirely sure she believed that, but once he had offered to fix her Leif-bound predicament (and Leif's broken leg), she had chosen to not press him on the matter. For now, she had a more pressing matter to, well, press him on.

"Now then," she began, trying for a good mix of blunt, urgent, and respectful. "Hades, Lord of Death, Uncle. There is still before us the matter of stopping the new goddess Undeath, and the zombie hordes she has unleashed upon the world."

Hades regarded her, unresponsive. The son of a Titan was going to make her say it aloud, wasn't he? Athena cleared her throat, and obliged: "Can you destroy her zombies, and prevent Undeath from making more?"

Hades turned from Athena. He reached for Persephone's hand,

squeezed it once, and then let it go. The seconds ticked by. Hades strode a meandering path to the throne room balcony—either pensively or arrogantly, Athena could not tell—and back. Finally, he gave his answer.

"I will not," he said.

Tracy spat a cruel laugh. "Of course. The god won't help. I am *so* shocked."

Hades turned his gaze on Tracy. "She is here why?" he asked.

"It's a sequel thing," Athena answered. "Ms. Wallace aided me in plucking you from exile—a quest I undertook, against Zeus's wishes I might add, because I thought you could help. Because I thought that as the most knowledgeable of all regarding death and the Underworld, you would be able to do something about this!" Athena's voice was raised, but she'd caught herself before she'd actually shouted anything. Exiled or not, owing Athena for his return or not, this was the god's throne room. (Diplomacy, prudence, and all that garbage.) "So, with all due respect, Uncle: why the piking Styx *not?*"

"I will skip the cosmo-babble explanation," Hades began. "For me to force a permanent eradication of the zombies would release energies. These would obliterate an overwhelming majority of the remaining mortal population."

"Eep," said Thalia.

Momo cackled, still in his cage.

Athena gaped. "But—you have not even studied the problem! How can you be so certain?"

"God of the Underworld," Hades answered.

"Um, I think you'd better hit us with the cosmo-babble," Tracy insisted.

"Oh, cosmo-babble, techno-babble," said Thalia. "It's so rarely a good idea."

Athena crossed her arms; it was half defiant gesture, half taking comfort in her own muscles. "Be that as it may, I am forced to agree with Ms. Wallace."

Hades looked down his nose at Tracy, saying nothing, until Persephone, her own face a mask of uncertainty, gave her husband a nudge. Hades grumbled.

"The difficulty," Hades said finally —

("Oh, here we go," Thalia muttered.)

" —lies in the permanence of the zombie phenomenon. Undeath holds the Balefire. Through it, she has channeled her unique power to maintain the zombies' animus. That power infects the ontological conduits of life and death. The persistent proclivity of dead bodies to reanimate is therefore fused to the metaphysics that govern the mortal cycle."

"So," declared Athena, "we recapture the Balefire. Then you do the same thing she did, but in reverse."

Thalia giggled. "Reverse the polarity?"

Athena nodded. "For lack of a better phrase."

"Insufficient," said Hades. "Undeath's divine willpower now secures the laws that drive the zombies' creation. Had Zeus not exiled me, my own will could have prevented that." Hades's black eyes flicked to Persephone. "Or your will, my love, had you known to do so."

Persephone glared. "I was doing my fecking best, Hades!"

"I know, my love."

"This stuff is not easy, you know! I didn't exactly have a manual!"

Hades nodded. "Would that I had finished writing that."

"And your database?" Persephone added. "Do not get me started! No intelligible schema! Three hundred and seventy-five tables, all with cryptic fields like 'spirit_4' and 'dead_banana!' I still don't know what that 'Mario_1UP' function was for!"

("Speaking of technobabble," Thalia muttered.)

"And Zeus-only-knows what Jerry did with the place before I got hold of the reins!"

"I will teach you more," said Hades. "Now that I am back."

"Assuming Zeus doesn't exile you again," said Persephone.

"One problem," said Hades, "at a time."

Tracy cleared her throat. "Yes, getting back to that one tiny problem . . . "

"Undeath has altered the natural order," said Hades. "I sense this."

Athena scowled. "She made a deal with the Erinyes. She may even have control of Alecto, now that I think about it."

Hades's scowl surpassed Athena's. "Compounding the problem. Witness." He motioned, conjuring two spheres of water. One was large and blue, one small and red. "Things as they were," he said, indicating the blue sphere. "Undeath's additions." Here he pointed to the red sphere. The spheres then merged together into a swirling, purple mass. "You cannot remove red water from blue."

"Not without blowing everything up and killing most of the mortals?" Athena asked, trying to tie things back to his initial, pre-cosmo-babble statement.

"Yes," Hades said.

Thalia *tsk*ed. "Not really the best metaphor."

"Critique me not, Muse."

Thalia shrank back.

"Husband, I have just destroyed a construct in Undeath's realm that made the zombies rise in the first place. Surely this changes something?"

"We were with Undeath when you did," Athena agreed. "She was quite distressed."

"Distressed?" asked Thalia. "She had a hissy-fit berserker meltdown!"

Momo cackled again. "Oh, my mistress felt its destruction, yes. But she no longer needs it to birth her children across the world! She has the Balefire for that!" He cackled louder, gripping the cage bars and shaking like a crazed monkey. A pendant around his neck swung forward, clanging rhythmically against the bars.

It was the first time Athena had noticed the pendant. (In truth, it was the second time, but her memories from the Obsidian Realm were still hazy.) It was either a fanged crescent moon, or a poorly sculpted letter C. Whatever it was, it had an air of familiarity that triggered something at the edge of Athena's consciousness, as if taunting her to remember its significance.

That she could not identify it drove her to distraction such that she didn't realize Persephone had grabbed Momo's neck until the goddess yelled, "Then tell us what she wants, you cackling wiener husk! How do we stop her?"

"Stop her? Now that she has the Balefire, my mistress grows more powerful with every risen zombie. You speak of the cataclysm that will occur if you recapture it, but you will not even get that far! She will cover the world in zombies, and overthrow even Zeus himself!"

Athena scoffed. "He's bluffing. That thingamajig did *something*."

"Hissy-fit berserker melt-dowwwwwn . . . " Thalia reminded everyone.

Momo coughed out another laugh. "Oh, she was unhappy for sure. The Cerebral Siphon leeched motes of private knowledge from each risen child's brain, and each brain they consumed in turn. It fed them to my mistress. She wanted their secrets, craved them. And she grew more lucid with every one she absorbed. In destroying it, all you have done is destroy that which kept her sane!"

At that, a tremor rolled through the throne room. It staggered everyone before Hades and Persephone together made a motion, and the tremor ceased as swiftly as it had begun. Persephone released Momo's neck, shoving him against the back of the cage as she did so. He grinned, eyes twinkling. His pendant seemed to twinkle as well.

Athena pointed at the pendant. Why couldn't she place it? "Does anyone recognize—?"

And now you just *know* that pendant is important, because Athena's question got interrupted.

Doing the interrupting was a grand wheat field—or the image of one, anyway. It lit up the throne room floor, replacing the ornate black marble tiling with wind-wafted grain as the floor became a view screen. An electronic ring accompanied it: three short chimes that echoed through the chamber, and then repeated.

Hades turned to Persephone. "Your mother."

"Demeter?" asked Athena. "I thought you said Zeus took the rest of the gods up into orbit."

"He left me here to watch the Underworld," said Persephone, now ascending the steps to the throne, "and mother to anchor his shield or something on Olympus." Her back straight, Persephone sat upon the throne, placed her palms along both its arms, and said, "Yes, Mother?"

The waves of grain dissolved into Demeter's face. Athena looked down to find herself standing on the tip of Demeter's nose. Though Athena guessed all Demeter could see on her end was Persephone on the throne, Athena nonetheless moved to a slightly more respectful spot, in the middle of the goddess's forehead.

"Persephone!" Demeter's face lit up at the sight of her daughter, yet that happiness seemed strained. Athena could spot the telltale signs in the creases between the goddess's eyebrows—especially as said creases were about half a meter long and ended just below Athena's left foot.

Demeter's image flickered. It cut off her next few words. "—my dear?" Demeter finished.

Another tremor shook the throne room. Thalia's eyes met Athena's. "Is that what I think it is?" Thalia whispered.

"Say that again, Mother? We've got some interference here." Persephone looked questioningly to Hades.

"Undeath tries to breach the throne room," Hades explained. "I am forbidding her." Another tremor rocked the place. It knocked Tracy off her feet, and Athena caught her before she hit the floor.

Momo hissed, exalted. "My mistress comes to rescue me . . . "

"—you there?" came Demeter through the interference. "—help, if you can! —problems—."

Purple light flared through the chamber, issued from nowhere. Hades and Persephone together pushed it back.

"Suggestion," offered Athena, upgrading to DEFCON 3 and looking fruitlessly for a weapon. "With all due respect, would not regrouping on Olympus with Demeter prove best? There we can interrogate Momo from a more defensible position."

Thalia nodded wildly. "An admirable suggestion! I was just about to go there, myself, in fact! There are, ah, other tasks requiring my attention anyway! Let us all go together! Safety in numbers and such! Maybe even leave Mister Cackle-husk over there in his cage so angry, power-mad goddesses don't follow us?" Thalia covered her mouth. "Great idea, Thalia!" Thalia answered in a different voice. "Indeed, let us go right away, Thalia!" she said in another.

Another tremor, the most violent yet, clobbered the throne room. Pots of narcissus blooms tumbled from the balcony. A chandelier of golden bones plunged from above to crash into Demeter's image, which winked out a moment after.

Persephone shrieked. "Fecking fecking feck fuck feck! Undeath, you crusty crotch waffle! That chandelier was a gift!"

"All the more reason to get out of here," urged Athena.

"No!" Persephone shot. "I am not letting that zombie-bitch force her way into my living room!"

"Uh, Thalia?" Tracy asked. "Can Leif and I get a lift?"

"Oh, sweetie, that's flattering, but I'm still just a Muse. I can't teleport anyone, and I can't carry both of you."

Tracy balked. "You mean you can't even—"

"No one is going anywhere!" Persephone cried above the next tremor. "We are all going to stay here and—" The purple light flared again. It seemed to strike Persephone in palpable fashion before she forced it off, visibly fatigued. "On the other hand," Persephone added, "Athena *is* known for good tactical advice . . . "

"Express elevator to Olympus," Hades told them all. He seized Momo's cage for transport. "Behind the throne. Hasten!"

Athena balked. "There is an express elevator, and I had to walk across the entire blitzing surface to get here?"

Persephone sprang to her feet as the throne slid aside to reveal an opening to a great glass elevator. "It only works for Hades and me. And some minor god of candy."

"Plus," said Thalia, hurrying into the elevator, "think of all the grand adventures you had along the way!"

"Thalia," said Athena, "I love you, but shut up."

CHAPTER THIRTY-SEVEN

"Throughout mythology there have been lesser immortals—lovechildren of a major god and a nymph or dryad, first-spawns of monster genetic lines, individual household gods called Lars, etc.—who, lacking the divine power of the greater gods, suffered being forgotten over time to the point where they faded into obscurity and perhaps even oblivion. As this text cannot make a list of forgotten entities for the obvious reason that they were, in fact, forgotten, this chapter will end here."

—Hermes's Half-Assed Book of Half-Assed Facts
(ghostwritten)

"Hecate, having a certain affinity with beings near-forgotten, tends to the memories of the obscure ones. At least I think that's what she's doing, shut away by herself all the time. Arcane secrets, she says. She published a collectible card line of the faded entities during the first month of our Return. She also made the cards so hard to find in stores that they haven't hardly any sales, the silly girl."

—Hera, interview, final month of the First Olympian Return

IN THE LUSH PARADISE OF divine wonders that was the central courtyard of Olympus, at its exact center, there stood a mighty oak tree, growing ever skyward. Upon seeing its grand boughs overflowing with verdant leaves (save for one autumn week when they would turn brilliant reds, oranges, and yellows, only to pop back to green again so no one needed to rake anything), an observer might even call it the mightiest oak tree that ever was.

What's more, they would be right. This was Zeus's prized oak tree, planted during the first days of Olympus. It had grown from a seed given to Zeus by his mother, the Titaness Rhea, who had received it from her mother Gaia, the primal Mother Earth goddess. Gaia had crafted the seed herself from something she had pulled out of her nose, although few on Earth or Olympus knew that last bit (and those who did often wished they did not).

The tree's roots buried themselves deep below the courtyard surface. Its branches reached higher into the sky than any other living thing. These two characteristics, combined with Zeus's affinity for the tree, made it the ideal anchor point for Zeus's planetary shield. So it was at the tree's base that he had stationed Demeter to maintain that anchor, lest the shield fail entirely.

Furthermore, a lovely tire swing hung from one of the lower branches. It was a godly and awesome tire swing. It was also serving as Athena's perch while Hades and Persephone—blond-haired and blue-eyed outside of the Underworld—talked with Demeter.

With the shield anchor currently swirling around the oak tree's trunk in a cylinder of translucent, bronze brilliance, the swing was as close as Athena could get in her current power state without burning off her reconstituted face again. Normally, no one was allowed on the swing without Zeus's express written permission. But he wasn't around, and it was the best vantage point, so Athena figured screw that. What Zeus didn't know wouldn't hurt her. She wafted back and forth at a pensive DEFCON 4.

The mortals, of course, could not even get that close to the anchor. Tracy sat with Leif about fifty meters away. Leif remained unconscious, as far as Athena cared to know. Maybe he was just lying down. Or dead. Or something. As for Thalia, she had gone elsewhere as soon as they had gotten off the elevator. She had mentioned being eager to catch up on planetary stewardship duties with her sisters. (She had also mentioned something about "reducing the number of characters burdening the dialogue" that Athena didn't quite understand.)

Momo remained caged and under Athena's watch—which is to say literally under, on the ground beneath the tire swing. His ceaseless cackling about his impending rescue at his mistress's hands had resulted in Persephone slapping duct tape over his face, so at least he was quiet now. (She had used Hephaestus's Divine Duct Tape™, so that wasn't about to fall off any time soon.)

Persephone had just finished giving her mother a crash course on Hades's return from exile. Athena could not make out much of what they said, but Demeter was not showing cheer about the news, nor at the sight of her returned brother and son-in-law.

With eavesdropping mostly futile, Athena returned to her ever-lurking preoccupation with Momo's pendant. It dangled, its fanged half-moon taunting her with its familiarity. Why couldn't she remember? Athena was certain she could now recall her entire forgotten experience in Undeath's pocket plane. She was sure, therefore, that she had learned nothing of the pendant during her time there.

So what was it?

Demeter stood between the outer edges of the energy column and the tree itself. The energy's swirling bronze highlights cascaded in front of Demeter's uncharacteristically deadpan face as Persephone, standing outside the column with Hades, awaited her response to Hades's return. Persephone's love for her mother helped her patience despite the urgency in her heart. She held one hand behind her back where she pressed her nails into her palm—a trick she had learned over far too many years of dealing with her mother's eccentricities.

"Well," Demeter said finally. "Then perhaps my brother can make himself useful and help us. Have you noticed those dreadful zombies no longer crave grains, Persephone?"

"It's more than that, Mother. Surely you heard Undeath's announcement—"

"Persephone!" Athena called from the tire swing. "May I please borrow your smartphone?"

Demeter poked her head through the energy column's surface. The column quavered, ever-so-slightly. "Oh, Athena is on Zeus's tire swing! So nice of him to let her use it. Greetings, niece! Did you have fun playing in the mesosphere?"

Here Demeter thrust an arm through the column to wave. The energy quavered more. The ground trembled, furtively. Persephone eyed the column's upper reaches where it touched the sky. Faint, worrisome fractures formed and vanished across a portion of the heavens. Heedless, Demeter pulled out her smartphone.

"Here, dearie!" Demeter called. "Take mine!" She pitched it Athena's way, and continued to wave. The energy continued to quaver. Fractures continued their dance through the sky.

"Ah, Mother?"

Athena plucked Demeter's phone out of the air with ease. The goddess's aim remained as true as it had been on the platform. Calling up the Olympian search app, Athena leaned backward and, hanging upside-down from the tire swing, snapped a photo of Momo's pendant. Then, sitting back up, she let the app do its work: searching the Olympian archives for a match.

She should have thought of this earlier. Think smarter, not harder!

Hades guided Demeter's arm back within the anchor's energy column. The trembling ceased. "I suspect it best you remain immersed, Sister."

"Hush, Hades. Zeus would not have given me this task if I could not handle it. And yes, Persephone, I did hear this Undeath's announcement, but this energy field drowned it out. Something about rising from the grilled cheese sandwich?"

"From the grave."

"From the grave what?"

"No, Mother. Zombies, rising from the grave."

"Oh, yes!" Demeter's eyes brightened. "There seem to be so many more of them doing that today, have you noticed? Earlier I went to the edge of Olympus in order to peer over and count them all, but—"

Hades broke in. "To the edge? While you were supposed to maintain this shield?"

"I did so *quickly*, Brother. I dashed out, just like this!" Demeter sprang through the energy column.

The ground trembled. The tire swing shook. Athena had only a moment to notice the commotion before two search results popped up on the smartphone: One was the symbol of an ancient cult dedicated to a proto-vampiric figure who used to bite children. The other was the logo of a chain of late-night eateries catering to stoners that Dionysus had pioneered across Amsterdam.

Athena rejected the second and focused on the first. For one thing, the eatery logo had far more teeth, and for another, the proto-vampiric figure in question was an ancient Greek spirit named "Mormo."

Momo stared up at her with eyes of cold light as Athena weighed whether or not the names were mere coincidence. The only differences were the missing R, and the fact that Mormo had been female—which wasn't to say that such things couldn't change, especially over thousands of years. Except Momo showed no vampiric characteristics, save for the undead thing. Momo was also far less attractive than Mormo had been, from what little Athena could recall of her. But hey, Athena thought, everyone needed a change of pace sometimes. Lesser immortals were far more mutable in their ways than full gods . . .

Demeter had nearly exited the energy column before Hades stayed her with a hand on her shoulder.

"*Remain* where you *are*."

Persephone eyed the hairline cracks in the shield above as Demeter huffed at her husband.

"Don't fret so, Hades. It's unbecoming for a god of your age." Demeter retook her place within the column. The cracks withdrew. "Now, are you going to help us make the zombies crave grains again?"

Persephone straightened. "That is why you called us?"

"Of course, dear. We'll need to go to the Balefire of Hades again, and—"

"We cannot use the Balefire," Persephone said. "Undeath has it."

"What if we ask nicely?"

"No, Mother. We cannot proceed as before. Athena has—"

"What if we ask *really* nicely?"

"Mother," said Persephone, "Undeath erected a fortress around the Balefire. She is already furious at our kidnapping her favorite lieutenant."

"Asking nicely is futile," Hades added.

Demeter scoffed. "Of course you would say that, Hades. You stole away my daughter without as much as a how-do-you-do!"

Hades rolled his eyes at Persephone. "*That* topic? Yet again?"

Athena's mind raced. So what if Momo had once been Mormo? What did that mean? Did it even matter? The app's Mormo article had little about Mormo herself beyond a blurb about the cult-worship. Athena frowned, trying to pull more from her non-divine memory. She vaguely recalled having met Mormo once, at a Dionysian mixer. Mormo had favored red wine, was pushing her own line of blood-based protein drinks, and spent most of the time on the arm of . . . who? Athena wanted to say it was someone whose name began with an *H*?

Hades? Hephaestus? Hermes? Homer? *Damn, why does our pantheon have so many Hs?*

And then, it clicked like a cartridge fed into a rifle chamber; Athena remembered which *H* it was. It clicked! It all clicked!

So much clicking!

The Cerebral Siphon had fed Undeath knowledge. Each bit she had absorbed had brought her closer to lucidity. Momo had said that the loss of the Siphon, and its flow of secrets, would make Undeath crazier. Granted, that information was unverified. Yet if it were true, it was as if the secrets were Undeath's lifeblood . . .

"It is all in how you *ask*, my darlings. Oh!" Demeter bloomed in epiphany. "I have just the thing to butter her up!"

With that, Demeter burst from the energy column again. The sky shield cracked, again. The oak tree's roots rumbled the ground. Persephone discerned a distant caterwauling. Power rippled along her exposed skin. She caught Demeter by both arms.

"Mother, you have to stay within the anchor! And concentrate!"

"What? Oh! Yes, of course, my dear. Concentrating." Demeter, again, stepped back into the column—for very nearly a whole second—before poking her head out. "I shall gather the most beautiful crops of tulips you have ever seen! And make fresh butter cookies! Who could resist?"

"Enough!" Hades burst. He pulled Demeter from energy column and took her place. "If she shirks this duty, then I shall perform it!"

Athena jumped from the tire swing. She landed on the grass beside Momo and ripped the tape off his mouth in the same instant.

"What was the endgame?" she demanded. "With the Cerebral Siphon. What was Undeath's endgame?"

Momo gasped an answer, but the ripped off tape had also taken part of his jaw with it, so his enunciation was horrific. Fortunately, his jaw was swiftly regenerating. At the energy column, Persephone and Demeter argued about something Athena couldn't make out. Hades wasn't visible.

"Undeath would grow ever more lucid—to what end?" she demanded while Momo's chin re-knit. He spat out a tooth at the end of the process.

"Only my goddess could know that!" he rasped. "Now that you destroyed the Siphon, none may ever know!"

Athena grabbed Momo's pendant. "You are wearing a symbol of Mormo! What do you have to do with her?" Athena ripped the pendant from him, half-hoping that would cause some sort of transformation in him. When none came, she thrust it in his face. "*Why are you wearing this?*"

Momo cackled. "I do not know."

"Really? You just picked it up off the ground? Thought it would look fetching around your bony neck?"

"It was mine when the goddess created me," Momo answered. "Why do you wear that ridiculous olive leaf crown?"

"Because it is who I am," Athena answered.

"And because it is absolutely darling in her dark hair!" Demeter declared. She and Persephone had both approached while Athena had been fixated on Momo. "All those intricate jewels and leaves! Be polite, Mister Decomposing . . . Whatever-You-Are."

Athena turned to the goddesses. "I believe—wait, where is Hades?"

"He took mother's place in the anchor."

"He claimed I was not doing it correctly," Demeter explained. "Such a defeatist attitude, that one."

Athena couldn't decide if that was bad news or good. She chose not to dwell for now. "I believe," she began again with a nod to Momo, "that this is actually *Mormo*—or was, at any rate.

"How delightful!" Demeter cried. "What's a little missing *r* between friends?"

Persephone frowned. "Who the Styx is Mormo?"

Demeter pointed. "He is, darling. You must listen better, lest your husband try to usurp your place in this conversation as well."

"No, I mean—"

Athena held up a hand. "Mormo was a consort of Hecate. And Hecate, I now believe, was somehow reborn as Undeath."

Persephone scoffed. "Well that's a crotch of a thing, isn't it?"

"We know a god can return after the Unmaking Nexus strikes them down," Athena told her. "Zeus had to prepare himself for it, yes, but the Fates designed the Nexus to kill those of our own family, from the Titans, to us Olympians, on down. It stands to reason that Hecate's Cosmic lineage could prove an unexpected element."

The light flicked on in Persephone's eyes. "So, when Hecate died," she said, "it didn't quite take, and she rose again—"

"Ooh! Like a zombie!" Demeter declared with her usual cheer.

"I figured that was obvious," said Athena, "but, yes. Practically everything points to it: The Mormo connection. The darkness covering that Obsidian Realm of hers. The entrance to her realm being at a crossroads in the land of the dead, when Hecate has always had an affinity for crossroads. Heck, the dark chocolate smell permeating the place!"

"Wait," Persephone said. "Hecate had a thing for dark chocolate?"

"Of course!" said Athena.

"Didn't you ever try one of her dark chocolate sundaes, Daughter?"

"I do not sit around having fecking dessert with creepy fecking goth weirdoes!" Persephone shot. "Well, except Doug."

"Where *is* Doug?" asked Demeter.

Persephone waved her hands as if shooing a bat. "All right! Okay! I'll take your word on the dark chocolate. The crossroads affinity thing is a bit weak," she added. "But I see where you're going."

"And biggest of all," Athena went on, "Undeath grew more lucid with every mote of knowledge she absorbed. Hecate was reborn as Undeath, but she wasn't herself. So she instinctively craved secrets, which so much of her former identity was based on. Half-alive, half-dead. Insane zombie goddess. She might have absorbed enough secrets to snap back to herself and forget this whole Undeath thing, had Persephone not destroyed her Siphon thingamajig."

Persephone scoffed. "Oh, so this is all my fault now? You practically told me to go in there! Doug helped! Don't lay the whole gods-damned mess at my feet, Athena! On the other hand, kudos for the Hecate deduction, I suppose, however late. But this is *not* my fault!"

"You are all ridiculous!" It was Momo. "Grasping at straws! There is a new order coming, with the undead at the top of the—"

Demeter dropped a bushel of corn onto Momo's face with a "Hush! Non-decomposed people are talking."

Athena thanked Demeter by way of a thumbs-up. "Even if I'm right about this, I don't know what to do about it. Yet."

"Hades says we cannot do anything by force," said Persephone. "But if Undeath is Hecate somewhere deep down, maybe we can reach her. Make her recall who she is and see reason. Not that the eye-shadowed loon ever made much gods-damned sense whenever I talked to her, but the three of us together might manage something."

Athena considered, fighting her annoyance at Persephone temporarily out-strategizing her. "It is worth a shot. But if she remains in the same state as we left her, forcing her to listen at all shall be a challenge. We'll have to capture her somehow."

Persephone laughed, mirthless. "And how do you propose we accomplish that?"

Athena cast her eyes across the Olympian grounds in search of tactical inspiration. She shot to her feet. "Ambush!"

"Well, duh," said Persephone. "But where do we ambush her?

And how?"

Athena shook her head and thrust an arm toward a spot one hundred meters away. A purple tear had opened in the air some four stories above a painstakingly landscaped garden of sunflowers. Zombies tumbled out of it, arms flailing, failing to fly. They slammed into the ground, crushed flowers, and toppled a golden statue of Apollo.

"No," Athena shouted. "I mean, *ambush!* DEFCON 3!"

"Oh," said Demeter in a cheerful tone that belied the unusually concerned look on her face. "Undeath had that idea first! So terribly clever, that one!"

"Fecking feck feck feck!" Persephone summoned a spear to her hand as three, then four, then seven more purple tears opened across Olympus. Through an eighth came Undeath herself, clouded in wisps of shadow and decaying viscera. Before Athena could demand a weapon from either Demeter or Persephone, nine points of light flared to life a few paces in front of them. The lights resolved into the nine Muses. All stared at the zombie-spewing rifts, their faces a picture of disquiet. (Clio even carried an actual picture of disquiet, masterfully painted.)

Calliope, clad in a short dress and a helmet that read, "Olympian Interim Defense Force," set her hands on her hips and said, "Alright then. What do you suppose we ought to do about that?"

CHAPTER THIRTY-EIGHT

"It was a straight-up, dread mess in those first few moments. Zombies staggered out of the rifts in a mindless procession of decayed bodies. None of the rifts were less than three stories above the ground, so the zombies broke on impact; bones snapped, skulls shattered, limbs broke off. It was a torrent. Each body that fell swelled the pile beneath. We knew the piles soon would grow to the height where the undead could simply descend along a ramp of their heaped brethren, and we would have on our hands the second worst parade that Olympus had ever seen."

—personal journal of Melpomene, Muse of tragedy, horror, and children's books

"YOU WILL RETURN MY MOMO, or I will rend this place to pieces!"

Undeath screamed it from where she floated in the sky. Beside her, the purple rift through which she had entered disgorged a steady stream of zombies in the same fashion as the other seven. As for Undeath herself, she spread her arms and moaned a wordless litany skyward. Darkness snaked from her mouth and fingertips. It spiraled out across the Olympian grounds like an intoxicated tornado. Where the darkness touched vegetation, the vegetation withered. Where it touched water, the water became ooze. Where it touched stonework, graffiti erupted across the marble surface: misspelled graffiti, with glaring grammatical errors and images not suitable for children.

Momo had, by this time, managed to shove away the bushel of corn. "You see?" he rasped. "The bliss of Undeath awaits you all! My mistress shall not rest until—"

A second bushel dropped atop him. Demeter dusted her hands.

"We must contain this, before she does further damage!" Athena shouted it to all who would hear her—hoping that included Persephone, Demeter, and the nine Muses, who were now condensed into a conspiratorial huddle around Calliope.

"Indeed." Persephone yanked open the cage, seized Momo by the ankle, and hauled him out from under the bushel. He dangled there, struggling to extricate an ear of corn jammed into his pelvis. "We shall give her what she wants."

The zombie-piles continued to rise. Already some zombies were remaining intact after their falls. They became the vanguard of an ever-growing march toward the oak tree where Momo lay.

Athena assessed Persephone's plan as swiftly as she could. "We cannot be sure that will placate her. A better option may be to—"

Persephone shook her head. "The Queen of the Underworld has spoken, Athena."

"Wait!"

But Persephone did not wait. With a cry of, "You want him, Hecate? Fecking fetch!" she sent the hapless cadaver sailing through the air, straight for one of the many spots that Undeath was not. Momo toppled head over toes, his arcing flight unmolested until the moment he smashed into the railing of a bridge. The bridge was a gleaming marble edifice that rose out of the courtyards. It spanned the sourceless river encircling the Olympian palace. Its broad surface gleamed with gold and silver tiles, welcoming all.

Momo then toppled from the railing into the water, which was perhaps less welcoming.

The effect was immediate. Howling like a banshee, Undeath swooped for the bridge. Her drunken tornado of darkness followed. Half of the zombies newly fallen from the rifts turned to join her. The rest joined those already on course for the oak tree—possibly to create a screen between Athena's group and their mistress, or possibly because they were near-mindless automatons barely able to snarl without swallowing their own tongues.

Athena guessed it was the latter.

"Well," said Persephone. "That changed her focus, at least."

"Yes," growled Athena. "Now they're merely in danger of flowing into the palace!"

"Oh, feh, Athena. She's going after Momo. Besides, the palace has defenses."

Undeath landed on the bridge just as the gates slammed shut at the bridge's far end. (The shutting of the gate—a massive edifice in the middle of the forty-foot high walls that had sprang up only moments before—was the final step in an automatic security system designed by Zeus and Hestia to activate in the event of an external attack or door-to-door salesmen. The system also featured an invisible barrier above the walls to thwart salesmen possessing hang gliders.) Undeath shrieked and hurled darkness against the gates' enchanted surface. They buckled, but they held, for the moment.

"And she's insane enough to be easily distracted!" Athena shot.

"Closed gates aren't very welcoming at all, are they?" Demeter said airily.

Athena continued after Persephone. "Do you know what happens if Undeath makes it to Zeus's throne?"

"Well, no," Persephone answered. "Do you?"

"No! But it cannot be good!"

Undeath slammed her power against the gates again. Hephaestus had forged them, so they were anything but fragile, but who knew how long they could hold up to Undeath's strength, especially with Zeus and the rest absent from Olympus. Beside the bridge, Momo clambered out of the water.

"Muses!" Persephone shouted. "Defend the palace! And do something about all these gods-damned zombies running around, please? Demeter and I will subdue Undeath! Athena, you're weak right now. Defend the tree, and the mortals, I guess. They are around here somewhere, yes?"

Athena bristled at the orders, but to argue further would only delay much-needed action. She settled for a glare plus two words shouted over her outstretched arm: "Weapon! Now!"

But Persephone had already flown off. Demeter, about to follow, suddenly paused, turned a kind eye toward Athena, and tossed two blades her way before continuing after Persephone. "Careful, niece! They are sharp!"

Athena caught the thrown blades, one in each hand. They were but farming sickles, unbalanced for battle. She slashed one through an ear of corn, severing it like butter. She slashed the other through the ear of an approaching zombie, with similar results.

Farming sickles would do. *We are now at DEFCON 2.*

Athena charged the nearest zombies, whirling and slashing sickles through brains like some sort of Whedon-esque heroine. Within moments, the first wave of undead threatening the oak tree anchor lay in pieces on the grass. Not that Hades couldn't take care of himself, but at least he wouldn't be distracted from anchor-maintenance. Even so, the victory gave little satisfaction.

Meanwhile, five of the nine Muses continued their huddle. Calliope, Clio, Melpomene, and Polymnia had sped off elsewhere, but the others remained in the midst of an argument, with Thalia at the center.

"I get to say it!" she was demanding. "It's so perfect!"

"It was my idea!" Urania insisted. "The honor is mine!"

"Please, sisters!" Terpsichore shouted. "May we just do this?"

"Now, now, Terpsi," Erato purred. "Never eschew a chance to build anticipation."

"Calliope said to do it and catch up with her!" Euterpe pleaded. "It shall take the five of us to set it free anyway! We shall say it all at once!"

Athena, doing her best to circle the group and prevent any undead from disturbing what was surely a vital mid-battle deliberation, shouted, "I have no idea what you are all talking about, but if you intend to do something, then do something!"

"Poseidon experimented on a river duck last year!" Urania explained. "It went badly, he locked it up, but it's the perfect thing to unleash against a horde of zombies!"

"Well it's *hardly* perfect!"

"But it's worth a shot!"

"And I want to be the one to officially release it because—"

"This is a battle!" Athena yelled. "Just *do* it! All of you! Now!"

"Fine!" Thalia burst. "Be that way!"

"See?" Euterpe called. "All together now!"

The five Muses took a deep breath. Their voices rang out in five-note harmony as they called into the sky, "RELEASE THE QUACKEN!"

At that, the ground rumbled. The clank of massive, moving chains echoed from somewhere below. Beside the bridge, a geyser burst from the palace river. The disgorged water rained back down, spattering onto the monstrous, twenty-foot tall mallard that now surged onto shore with flapping wings and clawed webbed toes. Mud mottled its ragged feathers. Fury shone in its orange eyes. Its beak, twice as wide as one might expect from a two-story high duck, brimmed with more teeth than an elder dragon.

"*QUAAAAAAACK!*" it roared.

Thusly announced, it dove into a zombie cluster, chomping, squashing, or devouring as many as it could get its beak on. By the time Athena could shake herself from the spectacle, zombie viscera stained the Quacken's gleaming green head plumage, and it was bounding like a maniac for another cluster.

Athena wondered if she could ride it.

Chapter Thirty-Nine

"Eris did not create the phenomenon that no plan survives the chaos of battle. She just loves ensuring that it remains valid. I am uncertain if that is due to an aspect of her nature she truly cannot control, or if she is simply a weapons-grade bitch. Probably both, I expect."
— Athena's Little Book of Wisdom, p. 1114

BEYOND HIGH EARTH ORBIT, as Cyot'hgha had promised, the Others had come from the elsewhære. There was little preamble; they threw themselves into an assault of Zeus's forces, bringing to bear hideous alien aspects, unthinkable bombardments of not only anti-matter and anti-energy but also anti-thought and anti-space. The Olympians countered with their own powers over reality, physics, and divinity. The resulting battle was too horrible to describe: a madness-inducing conflict, the mere knowledge of which would destroy higher mental-functions of lesser beings as their sanity strained to comprehend it.

Ares, being both divine and already having little in the way of higher mental functions, had safely observed the whole thing from the moon. Between his own vision and Eris's occasional updates, he got a pretty good idea about how things were going down.

Just forty-five minutes prior, from the shadow of his second favorite lunar crater, Ares had watched the Others pass by the moon. Some had traveled as bobbing balls of extra-dimensional light, like the one that had the nerve to bury him in the moon earlier that week. (It had taken him a day to dig himself out, and another day to get all the ooze out of his damned sinuses.) Some had been near-colorless, blobby-shaped[1] entities. Some had no discernable form at all—inky presences that had blotted out the stars and made even Ares's spine crawl.

Flying between them all had been smaller, translucent creatures, which Ares had pegged as infantry. Cannon fodder. Mooks, like his own moon-men constructs. In appearance, they were half-squid, half-octopus, half-eel creatures. (Fractions are not Ares's strength.) Ares had heard them jibber and squawk in his mind.

He had watched them all pass, and he had done nothing. Why should he? They had been on their way to battle Zeus. It hadn't been Ares's fight.

Yet.

In truth, it was Eris's idea that had kept him from leaping into space to rip the tentacles off of the first thing he could get his hands on. He liked Eris's ideas. He was excited to be a part of them.

Ares wasn't sure just how she was able to communicate with him, though. It was telepathy; that much he did know. Her voice had come into his mind while he'd been stewing and raging over the situation, and he found he could send his own voice back to hers. Eris had explained it as her being in space now, too, and maybe something with magnets or something. Whatever. The important thing was, she caught him up on how things were so fucked up for Zeus: Weirdo-Cosmics. Zombies. Plus, Hera had left him. Hah! It was gods-damned awesome.

"We can make Zeus take you back, Brother," Eris had told him. *"We just need to demonstrate that he needs you."*

"I can make a fresco of myself flippin' him the bird. I'll use moon rocks. It'll be huge."

"Yes," she'd agreed, *"or, I can ensure the Cosmic situation escalates. After a fight erupts, it's only a matter of time before you can sweep in and save the day. Then Zeus will owe you."*

As much as Ares hated the thought of saving Zeus after he'd kicked him out, Eris had a point. Besides, if the Cosmics kicked Zeus's ass, that probably meant they'd go after Olympus and Earth next.

---

[1] While "amorphous" would be a more accurate term, it was beyond Ares's vocabulary.

Then maybe they'd eat all the mortals, and no more mortals? That would just suck! You couldn't have a good war without mortals; they got so passionate about slaughtering each other!

Also, Eris was smarter than he was. So he had agreed.

"Just don't screw it up," Ares had told her.

"Please. Tensions are higher than at a Donner party potluck. Even Gandhi couldn't help but start a war here."

"What's a Gandhi?" Ares had asked.

"Just trust me. I can't keep communicating like this without Zeus noticing, though. So just watch and wait for your chance."

So, Ares had relocated to an Earth-facing crater. He watched. He waited. He made moon-men, ate some of them like unsatisfying popcorn, and made some more. And some more. And some more.

Before the Others had arrived, the first three Cosmics had already attacked. Zeus and the rest had fought them off, but any fool could see that had just been a feint to test Zeus's defenses.

Now, Styx had gotten real.

Try as he might, though, Ares could not grasp the Cosmics' strategy. Sometimes they would attack Zeus's shield directly. Other times they would go after the Olympians themselves. Sometimes they just twirled around a lot and threw up. Ares wondered if that last thing had some damned hidden purpose, but Fates only knew what that might be. Cosmics were frigging weird, after all.

Ares figured organized warfare just wasn't their thing. He'd gotten a glimpse into their funked-up minds when they'd pounded him down into the moon; junk was messed up in there. They were probably just flailing around all chaotic because they were too dumb to know any better.

Then again, maybe it was also Eris's influence screwing them up and sowing chaos in their ranks to mess the bastards up even more. Eris was great at that. Hell, she'd done it with that lump Baskin in order to get this whole fight started, hadn't she?

Except if the Cosmics were so disorganized that Zeus got the upper hand, that would botch things all to Hades.

"Eris! Yer making the Cosmics too chaotic! Back it off a little! We got a plan here!"

"It can't appear that I'm not helping Zeus at all, Brother! I have to make

it look good! And these things are trying to destroy me! Some of this is self-defense!"

"The best defense is a good offense!" Ares growled. "And a good offense is ME! Let them screw Zeus over so I can get in there and crack skulls!"

"Patience, Brother!"

"Patience can suck my axe! Just do it!"

It was then that Ares noticed something: The half-octopus, half-eel squiddy-things spent most of their time smashing into the Olympians, knocking them off balance and making general asses of themselves. But sometimes they slammed directly into the Earth-shield. The collision destroyed the squiddy-things, but left an inky, sticky ooze on the shield.

That ooze had just started pulsing. Even from the moon, Ares could see it was leeching the shield's power. *It's like some . . . leech-thing that leeches . . . power*, Ares thought.

Behind the battle lines, on the Cosmics' side, more squiddy-things were massing. In front of them floated a trio of Cosmics, creating a bulwark of darkness to hide the mass from the Olympians' sight. Then, at some unseen signal, the mass pushed forward on course for Earth.

They moved slowly at first, and then built up speed. The squiddy-things already engaged in fighting intensified their collisions with Olympian forces, allowing some of the greater Cosmics to disengage. These Cosmics then joined the vanguard of the squiddy-thing mass, now on course for the largest section of leeching ooze plastered over the Earth-shield. Ares was sure the Cosmics meant to drive the mass into the shield like a squiddy-thing battering ram.

Ares drew his double-headed Lunar Axe of Glory-Slicing, grinning in relish. It was time. Clustered around Ares in a one-mile radius stood millions of moon-men. (Or, Ares figured it was millions, anyway. He didn't like to count above 4,000, but it was more than that, and it *looked* like a whole damn crapload.) Summoning all the power he could muster, he hurled his moon-men legions into space toward the squiddy-things' charge, and then rocketed himself after them.

"Eris! Tell Dad the squiddy-things are gonna charge!"

Eris acknowledged. The Olympians seemed to regroup, with Zeus himself rallying a counter-charge. Ares grinned. It was about to get messy. He drove his legions faster, gauging their course and reveling in their eagerly brandished swords, spears, and poorly-made rifles.

Focused on the path ahead of them and Zeus's impending counter-charge, the squiddy-thing column remained blind to Ares's approach. Toward the rear of the charge, the white-skinned, skirted Cosmic woman seemed to guide it. Yet every now and again, she would peer down at something in her hands. Ares strained to see what could be so damn important in the middle of a charge like that. Was she stupid, or—

Holy Styx! The freaky witch had the Unmaking Nexus! No wonder he'd spotted Hestia rushing around the battlefield earlier, vacuuming up spilled Olympian blood! Zeus knew the Cosmics had the Nexus, and the Nexus could kill an Olympian only if you dipped it in Olympian blood. Its tail writhed in the Cosmic's hands. She must've gotten some blood anyway; the thing was armed and itching to strike. Stupid, worthless Hestia! Wasn't cleaning up something she was supposed to be good at?

Ares didn't hesitate. So what if that thing could actually kill him? He had the advantage of surprise and a crapload of cannon-fodder moon-men! *CHARRRRRGE!!*

He drove his legions straight into the rear of the squiddy-thing column. Calamity burst into being as the two forces clashed. Axe swinging, Ares imbued violence into his troops. They smashed open a hole in the squiddy-thing mass. It opened a line straight to the Nexus-carrying freakazoid-woman, and Ares sent his reserves straight up the line. She barely saw what hit her. Hundreds of moon-men slammed into the Nexus. The little guys particalized practically on contact, but it was enough. The Nexus spun from her grip, tumbling away through space.

At the front of the column, Zeus's counter-charge struck. With Ares's forces already harrying them from behind, it threw the Cosmics' charge into chaos. *Aww, yeah!* Ares thought. It was time to quench some bloodlust, and he had a hell of a lot of it saved up!

"Eris! Has Zeus seen me?"

"He has."

"Tell him I'm here to kick ass on the side of Olympus!" With that, Ares

screamed bloody murder and dove straight into the heart of the Cosmics' line.

"*I told him,*" sent Eris. "*He said 'good,' and 'don't screw it up.'*"

CHAPTER FORTY

*"My Oracle at Delphi once prophesied Athena would die near a gazebo.
The particular prophetess who foresaw it often smoked things other than just
the divine vapors, so I had never taken that prophecy seriously."*
— After the Sun Sets: A Retrospective Blog by Apollo

"I adore the word 'gazebo.' It's like 'qwijibo,' except it's a real word."
— Thalia, Tachyons and Tomfoolery *(personal blog)*

ATHENA DIDN'T JUDGE THE BATTLE outside of the Olympian
palace to truly have descended into chaos until the Muses raided the
gods' weapon lockers. At first blush, it was a valid plan; with no real
weapons of their own, there was only so much damage they could do
with poetic language and contemporary dance routines.

Melpomene and Clio plundered Apollo's and Artemis's longbow
collections. They chose explosive arrows so as to compensate for their
terrible marksmanship. Calliope somehow got her hands on some of
Zeus's spare lightning bolts. Explosions and electrical storms
thundered across the grounds, tearing through undead and
painstakingly landscaped vegetation alike. Combined with the
rampaging Quacken and a near complete lack of strategy on either
side, it was pandemonium akin to the Fourth Crusade on All-You-
Can-Plunder Tuesdays.

Were it not for the fact that they were also bolstering the
automatic barriers encircling the palace, Athena would have said the
Muses were causing more problems than they were solving. She also
would have chastised them for unleashing weapons they couldn't
control, except Athena had twice tried to mount the Quacken and had
nearly broken two arms in the process; she figured she didn't have the

moral high ground in the wisdom department just then.

Chaos sang as the battle continued. Athena had decapitated four zombies en masse when a shotgun blast from her left caught her attention. She turned to see Tracy and Leif standing back to back at the center of a gazebo. The undead pressed in on all sides. The skulls of two zombies exploded as Tracy fired the shotgun again. Leif appeared barely conscious. He wielded only a bowie knife and childish screams of terror, neither of which looked to be serving him well.

The sight surprised Athena; she had forgotten the mortals were on Olympus at all. Plus, they were still alive. So they had that going for them, which was nice.

Except Tracy's shotgun was out of shells. She began to club the zombies with it instead, but that wasn't as helpful. Leif wavered further. His grip on the knife looked precarious. They would not last much longer.

Athena considered letting them die. They were, after all, just mortals. Dying was a primary skillset. Yet they would surely rise again as undead, and then she would just have two more of them to fight. Also, there was that whole "goddess of defense" thing, and she'd probably wind up feeling a little guilty about it.

Styx.

Thusly compelled, she launched herself toward the gazebo, screaming battle cries as she went. "I should not be saving you!" She cut down two zombies from behind. "You were foolish enough to get surrounded in the first place!" She cut the legs out from under three more. "You lack strategic value! And you have been disrespectful on multiple occasions!" She punctuated that with the mid-somersault decapitations of five more zombies too witless to duck.

The gazebo steps loomed, crammed with undead. A one-armed zombie in a bathrobe lunged in front of her. She rammed it with her shoulder. Its skull cracked against the railing beside the steps, and Athena ran up its back, sprang onto the railing, and readied to leap to Tracy's side.

She wasn't fast enough. Still animated, the skull-cracked zombie had the temerity to latch onto her ankle. Teeth tore through her calf, and Athena tumbled from the railing and onto the trampled flower bed below. Undead swarmed her, heedless of her sickles.

How could this be happening? She kicked and slashed, trying to fight her way free without being further bitten. "I am supposed to rescue the mortals! I do not fall victim to zombie-mooks!"

The chomp on her calf stung like mad. She did not know what, if anything, it might do to her. She did know that, with her rescue failed, Tracy and Leif would surely be dead in moments, if they weren't already.

Rotting teeth gnashed inches from Athena's face. She jammed a sickle into them, rolled to her right, and found two more sets of teeth taking their place. Something that felt like talons locked around both her ankles. Before she could react, the talons hauled her skyward out of the zombie pig-pile. Then, the talons released. Athena dropped to the grass, rolled with the impact, and looked up to see the Erinys Megaera flying away from her toward the gazebo.

The Erinyes! Athena thought. *The Erinyes are coming!*

Tisiphone was already there, tearing like a weed-whacker into the zombies surrounding Leif and Tracy. Heads and limbs flew everywhere as Megaera joined the fray with a chainsaw she had pulled from her fanny pack. Leif and Tracy stood, bewildered and untouched, at the center of it all.

"Die, abominates!" Tisiphone shrieked. Her hair-serpents writhed with wrathful glee. "If anyone is going to tear mortals to shreds, it shall be us!"

Athena rushed to help, ignoring the throbbing in her leg. She yelled her thanks to the Erinyes. When short-tempered vengeance machines did you a favor, it didn't pay to be ungrateful.

"Don't thank us!" Megaera yelled back. "You were supposed to fix all this!"

"I have been working on it!"

"Oh, have you?"

Athena cut down the last of the undead blocking her path to the mortals. She pointed to one of the rifts in the sky still vomiting bodies. "You see those, Megaera? Most definitely against the natural order! Close them!"

"That's already our next move!"

"Don't tell us how to do our job, ex-goddess!"

Both Erinyes punctuated their remarks with several rude gestures and, bat-wings flapping madly, shot toward the nearest rift. Athena turned her attention to the mortals, both of whom stood covered in gore and trying to catch their breath. At Tracy's feet was a $100 gift card for Queequeg's Frozen Yogurt. Compelled, Athena scooped it up without thinking.

"Everyone okay?" Athena asked. "Conscious? Continent?" Without waiting for an answer, she grabbed each by the arm and hauled them out of the gazebo's remains. "Come! You should not be out here!"

"No," Tracy growled, letting herself be led nonetheless. "We should be on Earth, filming a movie! But, zombies! Stupid gods! Nearly getting killed again!"

"That is what happens when you claim an indefensible position in a gazebo in the middle of a battle!"

"Oh, we're sorry! We should have crawled into one of the bomb shelters surely available out here in this *garden*!"

"Yes!" Athena nodded fervently and opened a metal hatch concealed under a patch of daffodils. "Now get in this one and stay out of sight!"

The sight of the ladder descending into the well-lit, green marble chamber stunned Tracy into silence. Leif, still dazed, merely pointed.

"Bomb shelter," he said.

Athena had built them all over Olympus. It was an engaging hobby, and it never hurt to be prepared. Each had food, water, weapons, and one-thousand-piece puzzles depicting her glories. She didn't waste time explaining that to them. She just pointed down and ordered, "Go!"

Trusting the mortals could comprehend a ladder, Athena left them to it and surveyed the battlefield for opportunities to be useful.

Above, Megaera and Tisiphone circled a rift, flying so quickly they gave the illusion of a solid ring of flapping wings, snakes, and stylishly torn dresses. Little by little, they were drawing the rift closed. That's when Alecto appeared beside them in a burst of blood.

Alecto, apparently still afflicted with whatever Undeath had done to her, now seemed even worse than when Athena had last seen her. Her skin was gaunt, and her wings were functional but shredded. She looked like a flying Momo.

"Braaaaaaaains!" she screamed, and head-butted Tisiphone in the stomach. Tisiphone tumbled off course. Megaera whirled and punched Alecto in the side of the head.

There was nothing Athena could do to help, so she left them to fight. Getting through to Undeath was the key to resolving the situation, and Demeter and Persephone were not pulling their weight in that regard. Athena searched for the three goddesses and tried to ignore the growing throbbing in her bitten leg.

On the palace bridge, amid dead zombies, "live" zombies, and Momo trying to repair damaged zombies, Persephone and Undeath circled each other. Persephone was doing her best to engage Undeath in conversation and keep her from assaulting the palace. From what Athena saw, that involved a lot of shouting and defense on Persephone's part, but precious little listening on Undeath's. The only way it seemed Persephone's message might possibly reach whatever remained of Hecate would be for the former to tie down Undeath, sit on her chest, and scream into her ears.

Undeath smacked Persephone with a blast of powered darkness that sent Persephone tumbling out above Athena's head before she could right herself. Athena guessed Undeath wasn't going to be tied down any time soon.

"Where is Demeter?" Athena shouted. "Why isn't she helping?"

Persephone smoothed her dress. Her face was a mask of frustration as she watched Undeath from a distance. "My mother has gone into the palace!"

"What? We do not need her on guard duty!"

"Nor do we need her to make Undeath a welcoming hors d'oeurves tray, either, yet that is what she is doing!"

Athena gaped, driving two sickles through one zombie skull as she did so. "Is she nuts?"

"Have you fecking *met* my mother, Athena?"

Good point, Athena thought. Then again, who knew what might get through to Hecate? Maybe it was worth a shot? "What kind of hors d'oeurves?"

Persephone gaped back at her. "Are *you* nuts?"

A tendril of tornado-ey darkness whipped at Athena. Persephone threw down a shield of flowers that took the brunt of the blast. They wilted to mush before Athena's eyes.

"What about a phlegmatic field?" Athena asked. They had tried the same tactic against Zeus a year and a half ago, hoping he would fly into its ennui and be rendered temporarily but extraordinarily fatigued. It had not worked, but nor had Zeus been the half-crazed ball of impulses that Undeath appeared to be.

"By myself?" said Persephone, seeming daunted. "I can try!"

"If you can get one around Undeath, or lure her into it—"

"I know what a fecking phlegmatic field is for!"

"—it'll at least slow her down enough for us to maybe talk some sense into her!"

Persephone gave Athena a backhanded look before something else caught her gaze. Athena followed her line of sight to the bridge; Undeath's attentions had turned to the palace gates once more. She had swelled to eight meters tall. Her arms were raised in a summoning. They gathered above her head a tempest of shadow and bone, as if she might hurl the whole thing into the palace gate, walls, and satellite dishes. At Undeath's feet, Momo led a pack of zombies across the bridge, somehow imbuing them with the power to run.

"Distract her while I create the field!" Persephone ordered.

"Me? Now?"

"Yes, you, battle-goddess! Embrace the fecking challenge! Here, I'll help!"

Persephone grabbed Athena by the collar and swung her, underhanded, halfway toward the bridge. Athena's feet hit the ground running. Fortunately, her legs followed suit. A blast of power from behind infused itself into Athena's chest—another boost from Persephone—and she burst into a sprint for the bridge. She could run no faster than normal; Persephone had not boosted her legs. She had boosted her lungs.

"HEY!" The word thundered from Athena's lips. "UNDEATH! TURN AND FACE ME!"

Undeath, apparently preoccupied with her quest to wreck up the place, continued her summoning without a backward glance. Momo caught Athena's eye and smirked. Athena paid him no heed. Though her leg bite burned with every step—and she realized she ought to have mentioned that to Persephone—she ran on. Zombies packed the bridgehead. Athena didn't care. She had a goddess to intimidate.

Still running, Athena grabbed an isolated zombie by its shirt, severed its head in one swing, and then yanked the body along with her. In a single bound, she sprang over the first rank of the zombies. She leaped as if she could fly (though she couldn't), tried to shove the decapitated zombie beneath her feet (which she could), and used it to surf her way over the rest (which she also could, but wisdom dictated she probably shouldn't).

"I SAID FACE ME, HALF-SISTER!"

Athena scooped up a pool skimmer that a nearby zombie had gotten its hands on, and then used it to push her zombie-board farther over the snarling masses.

"YOU ARE HECATE, QUEEN OF SECRETS, AND YOU ARE SO TERRIBLE IN A FIGHT THAT YOU GOT YOURSELF KILLED IN THE LAST ONE!"

Undeath turned her head toward Athena. Her arms remained raised. Her shadow-bone-storm swirled in almost pensive fashion. Momo's running zombies jogged past Undeath toward the gate.

"LISTEN TO ME! YOU ARE DOOMED TO FAIL HERE, AS WELL! FACE ME! ATTEND TO ME! AND LEARN THE TRUTH OF WHO YOU MUST BE!"

Athena had now surfed onto the bridge, and her momentum slowed; what remained of it would soon take her within reach of the crazed goddess, so the fact that Undeath paused to consider her words almost made Athena breathe easier. Sadly, it lasted only a moment.

"The time for secrets has passed." Undeath's voice echoed across the entire gardens. "All shall be made *better!*"

Undeath hurled the tempest at Athena. It came too fast. Without time even for a simple battle cry to encourage herself, Athena bounded from her zombie-board to the bridge railing. The tempest barreled past her into the zombie pack she had just traversed. A femur and a dislocated rotator cuff narrowly missed Athena's shoulder, but she landed on her feet.

"MISSED ME!" she taunted, and then chucked the pool skimmer straight for Undeath's nose. Certain it would do little more than annoy her, Athena broke into a run, heading back over the bridge toward the gardens.

In her path, tempest-strewn zombies struggled to their feet. Athena leaped over some, dodged around others, and booted still more out of the way, careful only to use her good leg for the last. Athena could feel Undeath following her now, though she dare not look back to see. Only a fool would take her eyes off of her own path while fleeing down an incline through a minefield of zombies, and she was most certainly not a—

Something struck her ankle from behind just as she cleared the bridge. It botched her stride and tripped her up on a nearby writhing torso. Athena fell, head over heels. She was on her back in the grass before she could regain herself. She was vulnerable.

Undeath loomed above her, purple eyes blazing. But at least Athena had hung onto the sickles, and no zombies were yet close enough to maul her.

Undeath pointed to Athena's bite. "Better!"

The throbbing in the bite turned to pain. The pain bloomed into fire, spreading throughout her body. It was only metaphorical fire, but that was no comfort; it consumed her nonetheless. Decay filled her mouth. Rot clogged her veins. Unable to move, doubting she could escape Undeath's power even if she could move, and certain she was about to become the latest member of Undeath's army, Athena took comfort in knowing she had bought Persephone some time, and, perhaps more importantly, she had kept Undeath from breaking down the palace gates.

"QUAAAAAAACK!"

A flurry of feathers and webbed feet barreled into Undeath like a cannonball. Athena craned her neck to follow their Quacken-propelled arc toward the palace gates. Out of control, tangled up, they slammed into the gates, smashed them to bits, and tumbled on through the hole into the palace.

"Well, Styx."

It was the last thing Athena said before she passed out.

CHAPTER FORTY-ONE

"Zeus nearly outlawed the construction of phlegmatic fields. He considered the exploitation of mortal boredom essences required to construct them to be distasteful. He disliked that Hades had designed them (Hephaestus put in just as much effort, but of the two, Hades had been the one conspiring to murder Zeus). And he certainly took offense after part of the pantheon tried to capture him in a field baited with Tracy Wallace during the whole mess following his resurrection. In the end, two things persuaded him otherwise: First, Zeus had spotted and avoided the field used on him, so what did he care if they were still allowed? Second, when combined with a hammock, the boredom of a mild phlegmatic field made for a truly excellent nap."

—After the Sun Sets: A Retrospective Blog by Apollo

"I just heard Zeus was just so distracted with boffing the gorgeous Olympian legal clerk who showed up to assist with drafting the law that he never got around to actually passing it. But I'm hardly one to spread rumors."

—Chuckin' Apples: A Gossip Blog by Eris

THE TRICK TO CREATING A phlegmatic field, Persephone thought, was proper placement. Placement of any field took concentration, but concentrating is exactly the opposite of what you should do when conjuring a phlegmatic field; the moment you concentrated on it, *it* concentrated on *you*. She had gleaned this while watching Hades first perfect the concept with Hephaestus. They had solved the problem with synchronized concentration from opposite directions, so the field wouldn't know where to look. Placement could then occur before the field could phlegmatize its creators.

So, when Athena suggested Persephone create and place a field by herself, Persephone's first instinct was to smack the stupid off of Athena's face with a bouquet of chrysanthemums.

But then, Athena had little opportunity to learn such things. It wasn't Athena's fault that she wasn't married to one of the field's creators. (If Aphrodite, who had been married to Hephaestus, had suggested such a thing, Persephone would have gladly smacked the stupid off of *her*. Conceited bitch. Very pretty eyes, though.)

So Persephone had let it go and risen to the challenge. She had created a splendid phlegmatic field. By herself. She succeeded in giving a reduced contrast to its crackling ennui aura, so it was harder to see. Also by herself! She tripled the field's strength using not only the emanations of those who had died of boredom on hold with customer service, but also those of seventeen sloths forced to watch professional bowling in an ill-fated CIA experiment. *By herself!* The last bit was at the cost of field longevity, sure, but she wasn't setting a trap for posterity here.

Yet then she had accidentally placed it such that it materialized *inside* the closed palace gates! Because she was doing it *by her-fecking-self!*

Fortunately, the Quacken had been rampaging nearby. With the help of Calliope—who was managing to steer the beast using an enormous loaf of bread on a fishing pole—Persephone had herded it straight into Undeath, driving both of them through the gates and into the field just beyond. Persephone waited a time for the rubble to settle, and then teleported through the gates after them.

The place was a mess befitting the destruction of a massive door via monstrous waterfowl. Wooden shards mixed with steel bits lay about toppled gold statues, shattered glasswork, and the remains of Dionysus's combination ambrosia-espresso bar and foosball table. A handful of Olympian servants peppered the area; those who were not staggering to their feet lay either unconscious or dead. (Persephone briefly wondered if Olympian servants *could* die, realized that she had heard some were long-lived mortals, and then also realized that as Queen of the Underworld, she really ought to know this stuff already, and so she put it out of her mind.)

The phlegmatic field shimmered on the threshold. The Quacken lay half in, half out, its beak wide open as it quack-snored loud enough to set the rubble a-quiver. Its feet paddled softly in the air, as if still chasing down delicious walking dead in its dreams. Undeath lay on her back by its head, completely within the field. Her feet did not paddle, her mouth did not snore. Her eyes remained open, with the occasional languid blink. Her left hand grasped one of the foosball table's portafilters, rocking it gently.

"Mother?" Persephone sent it via telepathy through the palace. *"It is time to speak to Undeath! This fecking instant!"*

No response.

Persephone pointed at one of the servants. "You! Fetch my mother! Implore her to come here immediately on my behalf! Tug her by the hand if you have to!" The servants were quick and knew the palace well. Better they fetch Demeter than Persephone leave Undeath unattended and unbound.

And speaking of fetching and binding . . . She pointed to another still-conscious servant. "Away to Aphrodite's old boudoir! Bring to me the Fuzzy Handcuffs of Adonis! Quickly!"

Created by Aphrodite, for Aphrodite, and intended to be used on Aphrodite by her once-lover Adonis, the Fuzzy Handcuffs were strong enough to contain anyone—even a goddess—who did not know the safe word. Persephone suspected the fuzzy cuffs to be the main reason Adonis chose Aphrodite's company over Persephone's. Persephone used to berate herself for only offering the gorgeous mortal her love, massages, and Acheron spicy hot wings rather than kinky implements of pleasure, but that was in the past. If she could get those divine implements of submission onto Undeath, then combined with the phlegmatic field, Persephone might truly be able to talk some sense into her, even on her own.

The Mistress called.

Athena's eyes flicked open. Distant thoughts sounded in her mind. Like someone shouting her name across a wide chasm. With a sore throat. Through a ball gag. They were Athena's own thoughts. Somehow, she knew this. Did it matter? She abandoned listening.

A line of drool escaped her lips. That was alright. That was good. Milky clouds obscured her vision. That, too, was good. Then the clouds were gone. Better. Then the clouds were back. Still good. Not annoying at all. The clouds kept at it. Fine. This was fine. It was all fine.

Because the Mistress called to her, and much more clearly than what now passed for Athena's own thoughts:

"Come to me. You are better. You are needed. Come to me now."

Athena nodded to the Mistress. To herself. To the mindless undead that stumbled about in search of the meal of destiny. Athena stood. Left foot forward. Right foot forward. Left foot forward, again. And so forth. It was good.

"In search of the meal of destiny?" That was not good. That was weird. That was an overwrought phrase. It did not matter.

The Mistress called. What remained of Athena shambled onto the bridge, making for the broken palace gates where the Mistress lay feigning helplessness.

The servant flew into the demolished entry hall with the speed of an Olympic medalist. Pride beamed from his face as he presented the cuffs to Persephone. The cuffs' red, feather-like fuzz wafted to her with seductive desire, like a dandelion after a few drinks. She snatched up the cuffs, and then tipped the servant with a gold obol coin and a $50 Olympus casino chip.

Neither Demeter nor the servant tasked to find her were anywhere to be seen. No matter. Persephone yanked the cuffs open and collapsed the phlegmatic field; its effects would remain in Undeath's system now that she had succumbed. Keeping the field up longer only prevented Persephone from getting close.

The field vanished with a pop, and Persephone stepped over the trio of fallen servants between her and Undeath. Undeath groaned, lethargic, and tried to stand. Persephone shoved the goddess onto her stomach with the heel of her shoe and seized one of Undeath's wrists. She shackled it in red fuzz and was about to make a grab for the other wrist when three things happened at once: Undeath knocked Persephone away with her free hand, the three fallen servants Persephone had just stepped over suddenly rose, snarling, to seize Persephone's legs and hips, and an ashen-faced, sunken-eyed, teeth-gnashing Athena dragged herself through the broken gate, stinking like a slaughterhouse on a hot day.

Undeath grabbed Persephone's throat. "The undead do not tire easily! It is better!"

Power surged within Undeath's hand. Persephone felt it building against her throat—a rotting darkness intended to bring her under Undeath's corrupting sway, to make her "better!" or whatever the Jerry she called it.

Persephone summoned her own power and blocked it. "Not *this* goddess!" Persephone hissed. "Wake up, Hecate, you weirdo!"

She grabbed Undeath's wrist, trying and failing to pull the hand from her throat. Undeath grabbed in turn for Persephone's wrist with her cuffed hand. The dangling, unclasped cuff whacked Persephone in the eye with sultry fuzziness. It didn't help her mood. Further not helping her mood was the sight of a zombified Athena throwing a sickle at Persephone's head, nor the sight of all the previously fallen servants staggering to their feet with the same vacant looks in their milky white eyes.

What did it take to stop this gods-damned witch?

Persephone became a shower of tulip petals. Athena's sickle passed through the petals and stuck in the chest of one of the servants behind her. Slipping through everyone's grip, Persephone fluttered upward on a summoned gust of wind.

With barely a wave of Undeath's hand, swirls of decay issued from the zombified servants' mouths. They chased her through the air like eels through water, but Persephone twisted away. Athena waited below, her mouth open, her sickle waving.

That ordinary sickle could do little to a goddess such as Persephone. Nor could the servants' darkness do much more than keep her off balance. Still in petal form, Persephone circled the ceiling. She dodged. She weaved. She scrutinized the servants. Eleven had risen, ten of which, having spewed their meager decay-swirls, were now staggering toward passages leading deeper into the Olympian halls. With her goddess's senses, Persephone could see festering within them time bombs of—what should she call that? Undeathliness? Decay? Zombie-ism? They would spread through the palace, find others of their kind, and subvert them to Undeath's cause.

Soon the entire Olympian servants' corps would be corrupted! They would have to hire all new servants!

That was really Zeus's problem, but it was still an annoying thought.

Persephone had enough time to discern all this because Undeath, meanwhile, had turned her attention to the sleeping Quacken. In hindsight, now that Undeath's own decay-swirls were surging into every visible Quacken orifice and the monster was zombifying before Persephone's eyes, Persephone might have done better to not have focused quite so much on the servants. Also, eww.

One of the cuffs still dangled from Undeath's left wrist. Persephone wasn't one to abandon a good plan. Nor, more relevantly, was she one to abandon a half-baked plan when she couldn't immediately think of anything better. Before Undeath could finish with the Quacken, Persephone dove from the ceiling, petals fluttering. She spun around the loose cuff like a flowery will-o-the-wisp, took it in her disembodied grip, and yanked it toward Undeath's uncaught wrist.

In mid-ministration, Undeath had spread her arms wide. The bad news was that Persephone's yank wasn't strong enough to pull them close enough to lock the cuffs. The good news was that Undeath's mental state seemed too far gone for her to notice a petal swarm wildly tugging on her extremities.

That's when Momo burst in with a ragged, "Mistress!"

The decaying pain-in-the-butter didn't bother to point at Persephone. He simply screamed, blasting a beam of something-or-other straight for her petal-shower. Persephone spun away. Too late. Momo missed, but he'd done what he'd intended: Undeath noticed her and changed focus instantly.

She grasped at Persephone with both hands. The two goddesses battled for control: Undeath to wrest Persephone into a form solid enough to grip, Persephone to remain free and trap her opponent in fuzzy captivity. It was a battle of wills and power transpiring too swiftly for any mortal to comprehend or even attempt to depict in watercolor. Even if one had a set of supra-dimensional crayons, the best attempt would appear as a liquid hairball fighting a glowing rubber band ball in the middle of a crystalline explosion—and an ill-rendered one at that.

Regardless, three seconds later, the battle ended with Persephone forced back to her usual form, her right wrist cuffed to Undeath's left, and Undeath's entire left leg being made of strawberries.

What was worse: Persephone found she could no longer change her shape. Damn that Aphrodite! She had designed the cuffs to prevent that as well? Persephone racked her brain for the safe word. Had she ever known it?

"Fecking damnation!" she cried aloud.

No, that wasn't it.

Momo and Athena pressed in at Persephone's flanks, supporting Undeath. The pale goddess laughed, triumph glinting in her purple gaze. Persephone felt her draw power again and knew she had only a moment to respond.

Perhaps Persephone would have found the perfect response. Perhaps she would have guessed, or sensed, just what Undeath was about to try to do to her. Perhaps she would have pulled the precise trick needed to both defend herself and force Undeath into a compromising position so that Persephone could pull everyone's asses out of the fire and save the day. She would never be sure, though, because in that split second, a yell came from the hall behind her:

"Not my daughter, you bitch!"

Persephone blinked. "Mother?"

She turned her head. So did Undeath. Demeter stood under a half-broken marble arch. Solar flares blazed from her eyes. Her face was a dizzying mask of extreme welcome and, somehow, violent retribution. In a silken dress the color of blooming flax, she looked more beautiful than Persephone had seen her in centuries. Demeter gripped something rectangular and white in both hands.

It was the *Ergonomicon*.

Demeter flung its cover wide and thrust it out in front of her chest. "If it is secrets you crave, Hecate, you may have all you can swallow!"

The *Ergonomicon*'s exposed pages flipped rapidly under their own power as a silver light burst forth. Persephone could feel the dread weight of occult comforts within, and behind them, Demeter's own energies. She brought the arcane ergonomic knowledge to life; the lettering quaked and jitterbugged on the pages so intensely it was as if the secrets it held would break free of the book itself.

Persephone, never too excited by the topic of comfortable work environments, managed to tear her eyes away. Yet Undeath stood, transfixed. With a cry of "It is time I returned your book!" Demeter sprang forward, shoved the *Ergonomicon* against Undeath's face, and slammed the secretive tome's etched faux-leather cover around her ears.

A scream issued from Undeath that would have curdled a cow. She grabbed for the tome, struggling against Demeter and quite possibly the *Ergonomicon* itself to pull it from her face. Persephone added her own strength to Demeter's before Undeath could free herself. Though fierce at first, Undeath's resistance swiftly faded. Her grip relaxed. Her thrashing ceased. Within moments she stood, leaning her face into the *Ergonomicon*'s snug, efficient embrace. Even Persephone could sense that, were Undeath to remain with her face smashed against the *Ergonomicon*'s pages, she could remain so for an entire workday without any loss of comfort or productivity.

And then, the light gleaming in the tome winked out. Undeath collapsed at Persephone's feet. But now, lying on the floor, still fuzzy-shackled to Persephone, lay the lost goddess Hecate, lost no more. Unconscious, though. At least for a second.

Hecate's eyelids raised. She stared upward at nothing, serene as fuck.

"I had the most wondrously appalling dream," she whispered.

CHAPTER FORTY-TWO

"A power vacuum is like a regular vacuum: it comes with a multitude of attachments, most of which do not work all that well, and the cord always gets in the way (if you know what I mean)."
— Hestia, article, Better Homes & Garden Gnomes *magazine*

"What does *Hestia mean? Is she being dirty?"*
— Perplexed in Punxsutawney, *letter to the editor,* Better Homes & Garden Gnomes *magazine*

ATHENA STARED. The Mistress was gone. That was bad. Wasn't it? Athena stood, standing, where she stood. Directionless. Still drooling. That was okay. That was fine. Drool was fine.

The Momo one lay face down. On the floor. Hah. This was pleasing. Athena did not know why. Beside him lay the new one. The Hecate one. Cuffed to the Persephone one. Laying where the Mistress had fallen. No, now the Hecate one was standing up. Athena blinked. Too much change.

What had Athena been doing? Thoughts buzzed in her head. Too loud to be heard. *Buzz buzz. Buzz.* That was okay. She did not need thoughts. She stood. And watched. And listened. And stood.

"You see, Persephone?" said the Demeter one. "You want results? Use your words!" She handed a tome to the Hecate one. "Though I suppose these are *your* words, aren't they dear?"

The Hecate one took the tome. Athena would have said the Hecate one looked as dazed as Athena felt, were Athena in any shape to discern this. (She was not, though. And that was fine.)

The Persephone one lay a hand on the Hecate one's shoulder.

"Hecate? Are you . . . back to normal? Though with you I do use that term loosely, understand."

"Manners, Daughter," the Demeter one scolded.

The Persephone one rolled her eyes. It looked neat. Athena tried it. One eye rolled too far and got stuck. That was okay.

"If we want her back to her old self," said the Persephone one, "I should treat her like I always have. Either way, she ought to be happy; she's not fecking dead anymore. And she's not Undeath, which I daresay is even better."

Athena whimpered at the sound of the Mistress's name. The Hecate one turned the tome over in her hands, staring at it.

"Hecate?" the Demeter one asked. "How do you feel, dear?"

"Like a worm after a storm," the Hecate one whispered. She blinked, seeming to snap out of a trance. "Have you ever felt that you have suddenly forgotten something, but cannot conceive of what it might be? It is similar to that. Except backwards."

"Backwarrrrds . . . " Athena found herself groaning. But that was all right.

The Persephone one seemed to notice her for the first time. "Can anyone do anything about Athena?"

"What about Athena, dear?" asked the Demeter one.

"She appears a little piqued. And smells like wet roadkill."

The Hecate one looked upon Athena, and then upon the rubble. And then upon other things Athena couldn't track. "What have I done?"

"Wrecked up the place, I would say."

"Shh, Daughter. It wasn't little Hecate's fault."

The Hecate one stepped toward Athena. She reached out a hand. A delicious hand. Athena felt peckish, but the Hecate one caught Athena by the forehead before she could bite off a finger. That was alright. It was annoying, but somehow also alright. Athena tried to say so.

"Fffeennnngghthss!" Athena said.

The Hecate one shushed her, and then squeezed. Heat, light, and life surged into Athena's mind. Thoughts returned. Energy of mind. Energy of motion. Knowledge of weaving, manual dexterity, how to strip, clean, and reassemble an FN-P90 submachine gun in ten consecutive seconds . . . Everything returned!

Well, everything except her divinity, but one problem at a time.

Athena breathed a sigh of relief, only mildly alarmed that this sort of having-to-be-restored thing kept happening to her lately. "Thank you," she told Hecate.

"No problem."

"I hate to cut short the recovery euphoria with utilitarian concerns, but can you do the same to the rest of the zombies?"

"And the servants?" Demeter added. "They seem unhappy, though I'm not one to judge."

"And the fecking Balefire of Hades?"

Hecate tilted her head to one side, brushing dark hair from her eyes. "Perhaps."

Persephone gaped. "Don't give me that 'perhaps' horse crap, Hecate! This is no time for your patented brand of mysterious loopiness! You have to be able to fix this!" Persephone punctuated this by yanking Hecate into her personal space with a tug on the fuzzy handcuffs they both wore.

Hecate glanced at the cuffs. "Curmudgeon." They fell from both goddesses immediately.

"How did you know the safe word?"

Hecate shrugged. "The safe word is a secret."

"I guess I should have known that," Persephone said. "But—"

From the gardens came a bellow: familiar, unexpected, and, as far as Athena was concerned, entirely unwelcome. "THE OLYMPIAN GARDENS ARE IN A TERRIBLE STATE OF DISARRAY! ZOMBIES EVERYWHERE! COMPLETELY UNORGANIZED! MY TIME IS VALUABLE! I CAME HERE FOR THIS?!"

"A visitor!" Demeter cried in delight, and then sped outside.

Persephone scowled. "Did that sound like—?"

"It did," said Athena.

Cursing under her breath, Persephone teleported away, presumably out to the courtyards. Hecate followed suit. After an apologetic glance to the servants who remained zombified and apparently immobile (not to mention Momo and the Quacken— though they received glances more worried than apologetic), Athena sprinted after the goddesses.

It wasn't until she had cleared the arc of the bridge that she spotted Baskin. He stood at the center of a circle of zombies. His creamy white toes pressed into grass that was, unsurprisingly, battle-trampled and stained with whatever congealed liquids the undead used for blood. More surprisingly, all the zombies in the immediate area stared straight at him, and not in the predatory manner Athena would've expected. They stared with recognition, like soldiers awaiting orders. Athena might have even gone so far as to say they were *enthralled*.

(She did not say, "enthralled," however, as others were speaking. That would have been rude. More importantly, she would have called undue attention to herself.)

"Welcome back to Olympus, Baskin!" Demeter's arms opened wide, though she stood at a distance from both Baskin and the zombie circle. "What a lovely speckled, veiny design your skin now features! Is that a new tattoo, like the teens are getting?"

"Your greeting is late!" Baskin bellowed. "I was waiting here a full fifteen seconds before any of you came to greet me! This is unacceptable!"

"Oh, suck it up, buttercup!" Persephone shot. "You've got some nerve showing up and bitching about—"

"I will suck nothing! What have you let happen to Olympus? The palace gates are smashed! And there are too many thorns on those roses!" Here Baskin pointed to both the gates and the offending patch of mostly-trampled, botanically accurate roses, respectively. The veiny cast Demeter had spoken of almost pulsed in time with Baskin's words. Athena tried to get a better view without moving too much closer, which didn't work particularly well. She didn't like the look of it, whatever it was—not that she usually liked the look of Baskin, but this was worse: a purplish-gray color that neither god nor ice cream should possess.

"How fares Zeus and those above?" Demeter tried.

"Left-handed undead!" Baskin howled. With one swipe of his Mighty Pink Battle-Spoon™, he obliterated three zombies. "I hate left-handers! They're such a pain to accommodate! Special desks! Special baseball gloves! Special pinking shears! We should wipe them out! I demand to speak to the zombies' manager!"

"Relax, you butter-nut scream-factory! It is handled! Hecate was creating the zombies, but we fixed that."

Baskin thrust the end of the spoon at Hecate. Though still mighty and pink, it dripped with a black ooze. "Hecate is supposed to be dead! I bet she's left-handed too, isn't she?"

"Er," said Hecate.

Wary of just what the ooze and veins might signify about Baskin's demeanor, Athena jumped in before Persephone could answer and escalate things. "Hecate rose again as a goddess of zombies. She was commanding them and had forgotten her true self. But as Persephone *said*, we fixed that."

"You mean the world *and* Olympus is covered in zombies, and *no one* is in control of them?" Baskin demanded. "No wonder there is such disarray! Incompetence! They're just like mortals, wandering all about, wrecking up the place and bringing down property values! There is only one thing to do!"

"Stop your screaming and tell us what the hell is wrong with you?" Persephone asked.

"And why you're not still with Zeus?" Athena tried.

"And if the platform buffet needs restocking?" Demeter added.

"Cease asking stupid questions!" demanded Baskin. Rather than answer, he grew from his icy body three additional arms. Each stretched out in different directions, and though Athena had lost her sense for such things, she was certain he now radiated his divine willpower through the fabric of reality. Baskin—or whatever he had become—was about to execute some big-ass god-stuff.

As one, the encircling zombies shivered. Their eyes shined with shadow-light—a paradoxical and therefore particularly disturbing wavelength of light that mortals are no longer equipped to see. (The last mortals with the shadow-light-discerning gene died out in January 1590, when a burst of the stuff over Roanoke, Virginia, caused them all to go mad, eat their own faces, and bury themselves deep in the woods.) Athena could barely spot it herself, but it was there. It spread to the remaining zombies crowding the gardens, all of whom now turned toward Baskin as well.

"Um, Hecate?" asked Athena, "Is Baskin taking control of the zombies?"

"Witness!" Baskin boomed before she could answer, "as I take control of all zombies!"

Athena guessed so.

"Even the left-handed ones!" Baskin boomed. "But they are all falling apart! Cheapest zombies I have ever seen! But I shall control them! I shall bring competent management to inept chaos!"

"Can he do that? Control them?" Athena asked Hecate, who was scrutinizing Baskin.

"Yes," she said, still concentrating.

Persephone scoffed. "*I* can't do that! Why can he do that?"

Hecate ended her study. "The fool has broken the Querulous Trapezohedron. The heinous, cantankerous entity once bound within it now infects him. It knows much that is forbidden, and powerful. Combined as one, they possess the affinity to both complain at insufferable levels and assume control of the undead hordes."

The Querulous what? Athena wondered.

"Persephone!" It was Calliope sweeping in from behind, looking harried. She held one hand over a wireless earpiece, as if in mid-communication with her sisters. "I've got good news and bad news! The good news is the Erinyes have Alecto under control and have sealed up the rifts around here—"

"Go, my stupid undead hordes!" screamed Baskin before Calliope could continue. "Across the globe! Convert or devour every single mortal!" He turned his gaze back to the goddesses. "Then the entire population will be mine to control! There will be no more incompetent behavior! No more disrespectful service or overcooked entrées!"

Calliope frowned in Baskin's general direction. "He is simply going to blurt out his whole motivation like that? Sloppy."

Persephone cleared her throat. "You were about to give us the bad news?"

"Oh! Certainly," said Calliope. "The bad news is Melpomene says something ghastly is happening with the zombies, and also—"

Baskin pointed at the goddesses. "And since Olympian incompetence allowed things to get this bad, I had better take control from you, too!" The words were barely out of Baskin's mouth when a gigantic, decaying, feathered head burst beak-first through the palace roof.

" —and also, the zombified-Quacken is awake. And embiggened."

Persephone took one look and gathered Demeter and Hecate closer. "Goddess huddle!" Then, she stopped time. So great was the combined aura of the three goddesses that the time-stop encompassed Athena and Calliope as well, though they seemed to be a mere physical footnote; they stood at knee height compared to the goddesses above them.

These things happen sometimes. Or some-time-stops.

"This is all just ludicrous," said Persephone.

"The Querulous Trapezohedron entity forced its way into him," said Hecate. "It is a ludicrous force to be sure, but formidable."

"What the in the name of Hannibal is the Querulous Trapezohedron?" Athena asked Calliope. (She hadn't meant to question the Muse only, but given their current relative heights, it had turned out that way.)

"An artifact Zeus sent Jerry after to try to placate the Cosmics. Hecate knew about it, so Jerry thought it was a good bet. But all Jerry knew was that it was a gemstone similar to this one." Calliope held up her necklace. At its end dangled a ruby cut into an elongated rhombus the size of a .45 caliber round.

"Never heard of it," said Athena.

"Few have, which is why Zeus thought it was a worth a shot."

Meanwhile, the goddesses were having their own discussion.

"This shouldn't be terribly tricky," Persephone was saying. "We have Aphrodite's cuffs. We get them on Baskin so he can't escape, subdue him, and then with about thirty seconds' concentration I can drop him into a beautiful, isolated cell in Tartarus. No zombie-control, no escape, no Internet privileges."

Hecate nodded. "There are three of us. Together we can manage this."

"Yes. Three." Persephone looked to Demeter. "Are you on board with this, Mother?"

"Of course I am, dear. Whatever you need!"

"Because the last time we had a plan you ran off to make cookies or something, is all I'm saying."

"I am yours to command, Daughter!"

"Alright," said Persephone, "Let's . . . " She sighed. "It's just that when you were maintaining the anchor, you kept getting distracted."

"Was I distracted?"

"It certainly seemed so. And that would not be the best thing when I'm trying to hold open a Tartarus cell and need you and Hecate to toss Baskin in there."

"Things are not always as they seem, Persephone," said Hecate.

At this, Persephone raised an eyebrow. Curiously, Athena noted, so did Demeter. Yet Athena was more concerned about Baskin himself. Subverted by the Trapezohedron, he was no longer truly Baskin. That might very well be enough to keep him locked away for good: her biggest rival would no longer be a problem. Zeus would need her once more.

Yet that would only be but a hollow victory. A win by forfeit was a win unearned. There would be no rival-on-rival throwdown with a normal Baskin to look forward to after Athena regained her divinity. The Trapezohedron-thing had cheated her of that!

"We should reconsider—" Athena began.

Having apparently satisfied her issues with Demeter while Athena had been lost in thought, Persephone spoke before she could finish. "Let us do this! You know what to do!"

The time-stop ended. Everyone snapped back to their previous apparent sizes.

Most of the rest happened before Athena could protest. Hecate slid into a shadow, vanishing through it as if it were an open door. Persephone swirled through the air as a shower of petals so quickly it was as if those petals were made of lightning. Demeter followed in a form Athena did not get to see; Calliope had yanked Athena out of the way of a rampaging Quacken she had forgotten during the time-stop. By the time Calliope set Athena down on one of the bird baths hovering throughout the gardens, Persephone and Demeter had two of Baskin's five arms in their grips and were struggling to bring them together. Against Baskin's greater strength, Demeter was straining harder than Athena had seen in centuries, and that included the time Hermes had snuck cement into a bowl of molasses cake batter Demeter had been mixing.

In the distance, Athena spied Tracy and Leif, who had apparently taken advantage of the lull in zombie activity to emerge freshly armed from the bomb shelter and start hacking, slashing, and whacking.

"Do not touch me!" The corrupted Baskin snarled it as he tried to push the goddesses away. "Don't you know who I *am*? Never have I been treated this badly! I demand a free meal and an apology!"

Baskin held the Mighty Pink Battle-Spoon™ with two hands like a bo staff, pressing its center against Persephone's neck. His remaining free hand glowed with black light above Demeter, ready to release an assault. The surrounding zombies flailed at both goddesses' heels. The two goddesses ignored everything but Baskin's captured hands, shoving them closer together. Torn between wanting the whole mess ended now and wanting to fight Baskin herself later, Athena couldn't decide who to root for. Baskin was not shape-shifting at all to escape! Was he too corrupted now to realize he should? Were Persephone and Demeter preventing him? Was he too young and inexperienced to know he could try? Lacking her divinity, Athena had no means to sense the source of the problem or shout the correct advice to him should she decide to do so.

Athena berated herself for even thinking of helping him. It was a foolish, selfish impulse anyway!

Or was it? An idea began to form. She shouted for Calliope before the idea could fade or the Muse could get distracted by her renewed Quacken bread-baiting.

Calliope flew back to Athena's side. Hecate appeared from Baskin's shadow. The chain of Aphrodite's fuzzy cuffs gleamed in her grip. Before Baskin could complain or even react, she slammed the cuffs onto both of his captured wrists.

Athena missed whatever whinging, cantankerous protest Baskin uttered after that. She was whispering her plan to Calliope—and promising her a new necklace plus a future favor to get the Muse to carry it out. By the time Calliope agreed, Baskin was struggling to escape the cuffs, Demeter and Hecate were struggling to hold him still, and the surrounding zombies were struggling to do anything at all to harry the goddesses.

Persephone, by contrast, was not struggling; she had easily opened a tiny portal to a cell in Tartarus. ("Queen of the Underworld" wasn't just some meaningless title like "Social Media Influencer," after all.) Her hands spun in alternating ovals, working to widen it enough to accommodate Baskin.

Tracy and Leif kept on dispatching distracted zombies in the distance, hackin' and whackin' and slashin'.

Satisfied that Calliope would hold up her end of their deal, Athena dove from her birdbath perch. Her aim was true, landing her firmly on Hecate's back with a thud and a gasp. The impact was nothing to Hecate; though never a physically strong goddess, she was still a goddess, and not about to be diverted by the impact of a single, unpowered immortal.

Yet that was not Athena's intent.

"Hecate!" She whispered. "Trust me! Ask Calliope about the necklace, and then be ready!"

Hecate tossed Athena an over-the-shoulder glance that seemed to say, "Be ready for what?" (It also seemed to say "What necklace? I have not the time to ask anyone about any necklaces at the moment, as I am tremendously busy holding Baskin still. Also, why deviate from the plan? I have only been back five minutes. I am trying to catch up. You are making this difficult." As one who seldom spoke, Hecate was a master of conveying much with a single glance.)

"Just ask her!" With that, Athena leaped from Hecate's back to Baskin's. (*He* tossed her a glance that seemed to say, "Blrhraaaargh!") Ice cream melted through her clothing and the cracks in her armor. She wedged her feet between some giant peanuts on his back and held tight to the cherry stem dangling from his scalp.

"Baskin!" she yelled into one creamy ear. "Say 'curmudgeon!'"

"Athena!" Persephone protested.

"Do not tell me what to say! You are not my commander! And STOP YELLING!"

"Just say 'curmudgeon,' you—" She bit her tongue on an insult that would do no good. "It is the safe word for the cuffs! I am trying *to help you!*"

"*Athena!* What in the gods-damned fecking heck are you—"

"'Curmudgeon' is the dumbest idea for a safe word that—" Baskin halted his complaint as the cuffs fell from his hands. Now freed, a blast of pure cantankerous rage exploded outward from his chest. It walloped Demeter and Persephone, forcing them to turn all their attention to deflecting it. The Tartarus portal collapsed as the two goddesses collided. Zombies caught in the blast exploded to ash. Only Hecate, already away talking to Calliope, remained unscathed.

"There now!" Athena spoke into Baskin's ear. "Do you not see I am in earnest? Trust the rest of what I have to say, Baskin!"

"This is a trick! And a shoddy one at that!"

"It is no trick!" lied Athena. "I shall see to it that Persephone is fired! I shall give you complimentary tactical maps that will aid your zombies to overwhelm the mortals! Just hear me out!"

"No!"

Baskin seized her by the ankle and plucked her off of his back. Now she dangled upside-down before him, the service end of the Mighty Pink Battle-Spoon™ pressed to her chest. Athena didn't spare a look at the other goddesses; this was too important. She could see in Baskin's furious eyes a hope mixed with greed—patience balanced on a knife edge. She was seconds from either gaining him or losing him, depending on what she said next. What else could she give him?

"Okay, so I'll toss in a $100 gift card to Queequeg's Frozen Yogurt!"

"Queequeg's!" he shouted. "Two and a half stars! Average-tasting yogurt but many flavor choices! . . . Agreed!"

Athena drew the card from a pocket in an instant and thrust it into Baskin's waiting hand. To her relief, Baskin absorbed it into his body and attended to her.

"Speak quickly! My time is valuable!"

He really did seem to be listening. She could only hope she had placated whatever entity lurked within him enough to speak to the actual Baskin. "I know you're in there. Baskin. The thing inside you is not who you are! Fight it! Force it out! Think how unhappy you will make Zeus if you do not!"

"Zeus is already unhappy with me!"

"So what!" Athena shot. "Are you a warrior or a weasel?"

"Insults! I am not a weasel!"

"Prove it! Regain his favor! Purge the thing inside you!"

Baskin's grip tightened. The Mighty Pink Battle-Spoon™ thrust against her ribcage, though he seemed to be both pushing and holding back. She had to fight to draw breath.

"We are rivals, you and I! We have a reckoning coming! You must still prove yourself better than I! That can only mean something if you defeat me as the real Baskin, not some corrupted, altered—"

Baskin released her, at the same instant hollering, "OUT!"

Athena hit the sopping ground and rolled to face him. A purplish-gray *something* swelled out of him, as if his entire body were a squeezed sponge. Just as quickly, it shoved its way back inside.

"OOUUUUUUT!!!" Baskin raged again. He strained, he squeezed, he pushed like a victim of full-body constipation. The *something* swelled out again, quivering in the air. Already it began to shove back inside. It was fighting to hang onto him, and it was going to win.

"*Oiy'ghhalghi! Pyn'whrulhfa! Whrulhfa-ulhfa-ulhfa! Z''''''''oinnks!*"

The shout poured forth from Hecate. Along with it came a surge of force. Athena felt it rather than saw it. Baskin felt it more: it slapped him in the face, the stomach, and what passed for his crotch. No, she realized, not Baskin, but the thing within him. Hecate had seized the Trapezohedron entity's exposed essence. Her body flared with power befitting a goddess. Arcane, alien speech spewed from her lips too quickly for Athena to understand. Hecate dragged the writhing, struggling thing from Baskin's form. Baskin engaged in his own battle, hollering to push the thing out—or maybe just hollering for the sake of hollering, Athena supposed. This was Baskin, after all; you never could tell.

The power, the hollering, the sheer luminous ferocity of the struggle grew so intense that Athena had to shield her ears and eyes, lest they be burned out. (Sure, she was immortal still, and that could probably be fixed. But this was divine power on display. She didn't want to take the chance. Also, it would hurt like a sonofablitz.)

And then, suddenly, like fun on a carnival ride when the kid next to you throws up, it was over. Athena risked a look. Baskin lay prostrate on the crushed grass. Though his eyes were closed, his chest rose and fell with his breathing. (As a god, he didn't need to breathe, so that was a little odd, but Athena saw it as a sign of good health nonetheless.) The odd purplish-gray streaks that had infested him were gone.

Hecate stood nearby. Just above her cupped palms hovered the trapezohedron-shaped ruby of Calliope's necklace. It now glowed with a dim red-yet-darkling light, which Athena guessed meant the entity was newly contained. Satisfaction glinted in Hecate's normally stolid face as the goddess enveloped the remade Querulous Trapezohedron in five containment fields and tucked it away.

Athena let go of the breath she'd been holding. "Thank you, Hecate. I was sincerely hoping you would know how to do that."

"You were hoping?" Persephone burst. "You nearly bottle-fecked things to pieces based on *hope?*"

Athena shrugged. "Calculated risk. You have to take them sometimes."

"The method *was* secret," Hecate mentioned. "It was a relatively safe risk."

Persephone, continuing to glare, summoned a gardenia blossom and inhaled its scent deeply in what Athena recognized as an attempt to calm herself. As Persephone's glare did not abate, Athena guessed it hadn't worked so well.

Athena also figured that was Persephone's problem. The battle was done, Baskin was back to normal, and, without Undeath's sustaining influence, the remaining zombies on Olympus and throughout the world could be handily eradicated. The crisis was, at last—

"What have you done to the Mistress?!"

Momo stood at the crest of the gate bridge, shrieking to high heaven. "She is Queen of the Obsidian Realm! Breaker of Brains! Mother of Zombies! You shall not destroy her legacy! Undead legions! To me! Together we shall—"

Hecate extended her hand and sucked Momo straight through the air into her grip. "Stop," Hecate whispered. "Sleep, and return to who you were."

She lowered the now-unconscious Momo to the ground. Mist billowed around him for a heartbeat's time, and then dissipated. When it was gone, Momo had become Mormo, with pale skin, midnight hair, and feminine form. Also, fangs. And the fanged-moon pendant. Plus, a charm bracelet that read "Mormo," just to underscore it.

Hecate sighed.

Persephone cleared her throat. "Are you all about bloody done?!"

Athena glanced at Hecate, considering how to phrase her next request. "Hecate, come with me."

It was always best to be direct.

The last of a baker's dozen of zombies crumpled under a blow from Tracy's sword that split its skull. Behind her, Leif repeatedly hacked at the severed head of an already dispatched zombie that lay in the mangled grass. Metal crunched on bone a third, fourth, fifth time.

Tracy put a hand on Leif's shoulder. "I think you got it."

Leif gasped for breath. "I thought it winked at me. Wanted to be sure."

"I think you got it," she said again, and looked for the next pack of walking dead that would surely be walking their way.

They had intended to stay in Athena's bomb shelter: to rest, to watch the battle unfold on the various security monitors, and to keep the heck out of the storm of Olympian-zombie mayhem. But when the zombies had become distracted by Baskin, Tracy couldn't help but feel they should take advantage of it. More importantly, Leif had knocked over a peculiar vat of perchloric acid that began eating a hole in the floor, and the fumes hadn't exactly been pleasant.

While the shelter contained no modern weapons or even shells for her shotgun, they found swords, shields, chainmail vests, and codpieces a-plenty. Tracy had chosen a vest and a sword (Leif insisted it was properly called a "gladius," but she didn't care). Leif had done the same, plus a shield, and they had emerged to save their lungs and do what damage they could.

Now, to Tracy's surprise, no further zombies menaced them. In the distance, those that remained upright stood motionless, looking even more dazed than they had earlier. Even that extra-giant zombified monster-duck thing was standing still.

"Something's happening," Leif said. He pointed to their left. There huddled Athena, Persephone, Demeter, a couple of Muses, a dark-haired goddess she didn't recognize—and what was either a big pile of wet silk pillows or an unconscious Baskin.

Before Tracy could comment, the dark-haired goddess took hold of Athena and flew skyward. Persephone, radiating authority, gathered the Muses to her and began giving instructions that Tracy couldn't make out.

Demeter, meanwhile, cast beatific glances about the grounds at no one and nothing in particular. She then began walking toward the gigantic oak tree, her face wearing a determined expression.

Tracy waved, trying to catch Demeter's attention. It worked. Demeter regained her blissful demeanor and changed course for Tracy and Leif.

"Tracy Wallace!" Demeter declared upon reaching them. "I am pleased to see you survived, my renounced little niece!"

Little? Tracy wondered. Leif gave a subtle wave likely meant to assert his presence as well.

"What's happened to the zombies?" Tracy asked. "Is it over? Are we safe?"

Demeter *tsk*ed. "Not even a greeting back? Do not be rude. Is that any way to treat a goddess?"

Tracy bristled. "Sorry. It's just that Leif and I are both very tired. And on edge. We got sucked into this whole affair, and it's been more than a little inconvenient. Not to mention I've inhaled acid fumes."

"Acid fumes? That's not something mortals should do. It is completely unhealthy for you. But the resulting brain damage would explain why you forgot to be polite, I suppose." She handed Tracy a vanilla bean conjured from nowhere, then seemed to notice Leif for the first time, and gave him one as well. "Tuck this in your collars, and inhale deeply. You shall be feeling better in a jiff. And yes, this whole business is over, at least for the moment. You are safe."

"That's great," said Leif. "It really is. So, is Apollo around anywhere? We've come a long way to speak with him."

CHAPTER FORTY-THREE

"In the past two days we have seen mass dissociative hysteria, a tenfold surge in zombie activity, the kidnapping of Alfonse the ping-pong-playing squirrel, and multiple, mysterious occurrences in the sky experts only hope can be attributed to Zeus. Is it the end of the world, again? We'll ask that very question of Alfonse's trainer in an exclusive interview, next!"
— Patrick Fitzsimmons, anchor, Kitsune News Network (Z-plus 127 days)

BY THE TIME HECATE AND ATHENA had flown up through a crack in Zeus's shield — which violated Zeus's decree forbidding the transport of de-powered gods off of Olympus, but Athena might have forgotten to bring Hecate up to speed on that one — the Cosmic conflict had dragged to a stalemate. The remnants of celestial, cataclysmic collisions dotted the layers between the astral plane and the space-time-thought continuum like craters on a divine battlefield.

That's what Hecate said, anyway. Athena still lacked the ability to see such things. That would change, if her plan worked. (If it didn't work, she and the Olympians might all be doomed anyway, so it wouldn't matter. But that probably wouldn't happen. Hopefully.)

When they reached Zeus's orbital platform, only Hestia stood vigil there. A mile beyond it, Zeus and Apollo floated, divine weapons at the ready. Their stance battle-wearied, they stared out into space, awaiting what Athena guessed would be the next wave of an attack that had yet to materialize. She had arrived at a lull. Excellent. She whispered her thanks to the Muses for dramatic convenience.

Hecate, currently invisible at Athena's request, carried Athena toward Zeus in a bubble of sustaining atmosphere. To the outside observer, it would look like Athena traveled under her own power.

To the gods, it would only appear that a concealed *someone* carried Athena through space, but that concealment was enough for Athena's purposes. She would keep Hecate's identity a secret as long as possible.

Nothing wrong with a little theatricality now and then, right? Apollo would appreciate it, anyway.

Zeus sensed their approach and whirled to face them, lightning at the ready. Apollo, still watchful for the Cosmics, merely glanced over.

"You!" Zeus leveled a stern finger Athena's way. "You desert your post, and now you dare return? So help me, if that is Demeter carrying you—"

"Forgiveness, Father Zeus!" Athena called, hoping Zeus would allow himself to hear her across the vacuum between them—or at least read her lips. "But you may recognize my escort!"

Judging by the look on Zeus's face, Hecate had dropped her invisibility at that moment. Athena couldn't help but grin. "I thought you might wish to speak with her."

Hecate floated to Athena's side, and gave a single wave.

Zeus stared, speechless. Apollo cleared his throat and managed, "Hello, Hecate. Aren't you dead?"

Hecate shrugged. "I got . . . better."

"It has been known to happen," Athena added, with a nod toward Zeus, who finally snapped out of his fugue state.

"So it has," he said, still staring. "There are those beyond who would speak with you, Hecate. Your blood family."

"They are most cranky," added Apollo.

Zeus nodded. "Especially your mother. You will speak with them."

Hecate stiffened. "I will not go with them."

"No one commanded anything about going *with* them," said Zeus. "Do you know what they want with you?"

"Do you?" Hecate asked.

"Well, if they want the Querulous Trapezohedron, they're Styx-out-of-luck," Apollo muttered.

"Oh, we have that, as well." Athena grinned. "Well, she does. I assisted."

Zeus silenced Athena with a look. "Iris!" he called. She appeared before Zeus immediately, her back to Athena and Hecate. Hermes's old helmet, crammed atop her head, now featured a pair of dents. A cluster of circular purple welts wrapped her left forearm. The quantity of glitter on and about her person was noticeably reduced.

"Send word to Cyot'hgha," Zeus ordered her.

"In the middle of a battle?" Iris balked. "That strikes me as not the best idea. Especially for me."

"Tell her we have Hecate, and we wish to talk."

"Oh, so you wish me to relay to her a blatant lie?" Iris sighed, resigned. "As you wish, if that is my duty. I am sure her response will include new and exciting levels of pain, which I will look upon as a learning experience, if I must. Thank you, Lord Zeus, for this awesome educational opportunity."

Zeus scowled and spun Iris by the shoulder to face Hecate. Iris jumped at the sight, mouthed an "Oh!" and then asked, pointedly, "Aren't you dead?"

"She got better," said Apollo.

Within minutes, at one of the many vacant points in space between the Earth and the moon, the two sides met. For the Cosmics came Cyot'hgha and the one Zeus referred to as C'oggn-yon. For the Olympians came Zeus with Hecate at his side. Zeus seemed in particularly smug spirits, so much so that he had even let Athena tag along with them.

Okay, so he had actually ordered it, perhaps knowing that being so close to the Cosmics in Athena's current state meant one Jerry of a headache. Zeus had, at least, specifically denied Ares a spot in favor of Athena, which did make her feel a bit better—even as she wondered just how the Styx Ares had wormed his way back.

"Cyot'hgha," began Zeus. "C'oggn-yon. As promised, the goddess Hecate. Hecate, this is your mother. And . . . your uncle. I think. He's about to say—"

"ZOGG!" said C'oggn-yon.

"—Yes. That." Zeus turned back to the Cosmics. "As you can see, reports of her death have been greatly . . . reversed."

Cyot'hgha folded her arms and scrutinized Hecate. Hecate folded her arms and returned the scrutiny. Somewhere in the purple-clouded lightning that was C'oggn-yon, Athena caught glimpses of tenebrous elbows that may have been attached to crossed arms of their own.

"What do you want of me?" Hecate asked after about a minute of this.

Cyot'hgha looked to C'oggn-yon. The purple cloud quivered. Lightning flashed within it. After millennia spent with Zeus, Athena had enough experience with lightning to suspect these particular flashes were affirmative.

"You know us," said Cyot'hgha to Hecate. Was that a question?

"I have known you in my dreams," Hecate answered. "Your faces speak of memories rich with vexation and unwanted noise. What do you want of me?"

The question dissolved into silence, and Zeus's previous smugness began to erode into tension. The same tension agitated Athena as well, but compared to her aforementioned headache, it was not her biggest problem at the moment.

"Missing," Cyot'hgha intoned finally. "Needed."

"In the depths," Hecate answered.

"Where the leviathans jibber," Cyot'hgha went on.

"And the vyriim dance," Hecate continued.

"And the wild, gluttonous ones devour the non-dairy confections," they recited together as one.

Hecate sighed at her mother. "Why did you not say so before?"

"ZOGG!" boomed C'oggn-yon.

"I see," said Hecate. "Then you shall know, and have, and be satisfied. After, you shall return to your abysses between, and molest this place no more with your physicality."

Cyot'hgha pointed at Zeus. "He refused the devouring."

"I have long known this," said Hecate.

"Excuse me?" Zeus asked.

Hecate spoke to Zeus without taking her eyes off of Cyot'hgha. "You did not truly believe I was unaware you were my father, did you?"

Cyot'hgha smirked, showing a pointed tooth. "Speak of the missing needed, Hecate, and we who slake shall swallow our presence and jibber beyond."

Hecate heaved an exasperated sigh. "Did I not just say so? Agreed."

"Hecate," Zeus warned. ". . . Daughter. A translation, if you please?"

Hecate rolled her eyes at Zeus. "I tell them what they want to know, and they'll leave. Duh."

Athena guessed it took all Zeus had not to rebuke the "duh," but his self-control prevailed. "That is what I thought." He motioned for her to carry on.

C'oggn-yon flashed aquamarine. "ZOGG!"

"Watch your mouth," Hecate warned.

Hecate returned her attention to her mother and raised an open hand between them, palm upward. Then she screamed. It was a long, wailing, spine-scraping din that defied the vacuum of space. Hecate's scream rose and fell in pitch, wildly, abruptly, and without anything resembling rhythm, as if someone were strangling a dolphin with an electric guitar.

And then it stopped. Hecate lowered and closed her hand, and then wiped some schmutz off her lip.

Cyot'hgha shared a glance with C'oggn-yon—or so it seemed, despite their lack of actual eyeballs. Cyot'hgha nodded to it, and then to Hecate, Zeus, and Athena in turn. Then, as one, the two Cosmics turned their backs and drifted off without another ZOGG.

"And take this while you are at it!" Hecate brought out the remade Querulous Trapezohedron. She threw it into C'oggn-yon's cloud, where it appeared to remain. "It causes more trouble than it is worth," Hecate explained aside to Athena. "And I have two already."

The Cosmics vanished into the distance. At the edges of her vision, Athena could just make out inky shapes gathering together and creeping away, as if they were sliding behind the stars themselves. Her headache faded. Zeus's jaw unclenched.

"So," Athena began, "is that it? They are gone?"

"Not gone," Hecate answered. "But gone from here."

"Close enough."

"Indeed," Zeus agreed. He remained staring into the distance as if still watching them go. With divine senses, he probably was. Athena waited patiently for Zeus to thank her. Instead, he said at last,

"Explain to me just what you told them, Hecate."

Hecate glanced at Zeus. Her face remained stoic, yet her eyes narrowed. "Were I to tell you, the knowledge would no longer be exclusive to them. They would sense this and return to bring further conflict. I can only assure you that what I told them holds no consequence for you or our Olympian family."

Zeus regarded Hecate, seeming to weigh this answer. "I do not regret refusing to eat you," he told her finally, and turned back toward Earth. "Bring Athena."

Hecate watched Zeus go. Athena spent a few uncomfortable moments wondering if she would have to call an Uber or something to get home, but then Hecate took hold of her shoulder and took them both after him.

"I shall tell you a secret," Hecate whispered in her ear. "I lied to him just now. Had I explained to Zeus what I told the Cosmics, Cyot'hgha would not have cared."

"Then why didn't you?"

Hecate stared after Zeus. "Because Zeus did not thank me. And because there must always be mysteries."

Athena was about to observe that Zeus had yet to thank either of them when something else occurred to her. "You can *lie* to Zeus?"

Hecate smiled softly. "There must always be mysteries."

They flew on toward the platform, and beyond that, Earth.

"So, then," Athena tried, "how about you explain to *me* what you told them?"

"Zogg," said Hecate.

EPILOGUE

"Whether it's the gods' doing or humanity's own efforts, verified reports of zombie attacks have dropped to nearly zero this week. I believe we can now safely declare that the zombie threat is—at last, finally, and sincerely— almost over. You know, probably. We've got an office pool going."
— Centers for Disease Control and Prevention official (speaking under the condition of anonymity, Z-plus 132 days)

"Well, crap. And I just bought a Maserati."
—James "Jimmy Joe" Sweeten (author, The Sweeten's Guide to Real Zombies, Z-plus 132.1 days)

WITH THE COSMIC THREAT GONE, Zeus dismantled the orbital platform and led the Olympians back to Earth. Or most of them, anyway. Using implacable orders, crackling lightning, and stern looks, Zeus commanded Ares to return to the moon. Despite Ares's aid in the battle, as vital as it was, and as selfless as Ares claimed it was (a claim undercut by sideways winks to Eris and his final, "Now let me back in the Pantheon, you ungrateful bastard!"), Zeus declared Ares on exile-probation, pending further ruling on the matter. Athena guessed that ruling would be reasonably swift. Artemis was constantly complaining that Ares was messing up her precious lunar surface.

Hades remained at the base of the oak tree, still fixated on anchoring Zeus's sky shield. Fates only knew whether or not Hades had noticed that Zeus had shrunk the shield so it protected only the area immediately around the tree. When Persephone questioned how long Hades must remain there, Zeus had smiled and replied he would keep Hades there at least another few weeks, "just in case."

Persephone had bitten her tongue and returned to the Underworld to mop up.

She took Hecate with her. Between Persephone's command of the Underworld and Hecate's latent connections to the zombie hordes, they returned the Balefire of Hades to normal. Without Undeath's will maintaining them, the zombies became like any other monster, and the gods eradicated them handily. Across the globe (sans Australia, which had somehow remained zombie-free to the very end), zombies either disappeared in a flash of light, politely excused themselves to return to their graves, or simply crumbled to dust—to be easily vacuumed or accidentally inhaled.

Although the mortals slain by zombies did not return to life, the zombie problem was, at least, finally solved. Things could go back to normal—or as normal as they could be with the Olympians remaining present in the world. Since the mortals could use the help rebuilding their society, most of them viewed that as for the best.

Zeus finally saw fit to return Athena's divinity due to her work in restoring Hecate and solving the zombie problem, though not without some cajoling from Hecate and the Muses. Athena reclaimed her mantle as goddess, yet Zeus refused her the position of his bodyguard. It stung, but Zeus stripping Baskin of that honor as well served as a balm. For now, Jerry filled the role. Athena assumed that would not last long.

Hera, fully divine and with the Cosmic crisis ended, immediately resumed her duties as goddess of childbirth. As for goddess of marriage and being Zeus's queen, she still demurred. Zeus pretended it didn't bother him, and the rest of the pantheon was wise enough to avoid the subject—except for Eris, of course. But then, bringing up that kind of crap was her job.

As for the other gods, they were stepping up their involvement with the world now that the remaining mortals weren't zombie-addled. Hephaestus made it known that any city building a shrine to him would enjoy 15% greater efficiency in its infrastructure rebuilding, and a 40% discount on his new line of power tools. To revitalize the grain industry, Demeter began a worldwide "Let's Get Bread-u-cated" campaign designed to combat any stigma left over from the near-apocalypse. Apollo sponsored mental health recovery centers without putting his name on them, in order to avoid attracting too much prayer-attention.

Of course, spurred by Athena and a pair of mortal supporting characters, Apollo also had a favor to return . . .

Disguised as a mild-mannered mortal, Athena sat on a bench across the street from a Hollywood courthouse where Leif and Tracy made their appeal for the return of their movie rights. Apollo had joined them, so Athena expected they would have little trouble. She did not care either way, but she had nonetheless deigned to hang around nearby for medium-distance moral support. Plus, she still had to ask Apollo if he had gotten Poppy's emails. She had a promise to keep, after all.

A presence materialized on the bench beside her.

"~Belated thanks for your work~" Death said.

"You are welcome. Though better thanks might have been for you to stick around after Undeath took the Balefire." Athena tossed him a scowl that went utterly ignored.

"~The zombies resurged. Mortal deaths spiked. My hands were full. Some of us have to work for a living~"

"But you made a special trip here just to thank me?" asked Athena. "I am flattered. Mildly."

"~There will also be a seven-limousine pileup at the end of the block in five minutes that I must keep an eye on. I arrived early~"

"Ah."

Athena glanced back toward the courthouse. Apollo had just exited and now crossed the street toward them.

"Success!" he announced as he approached. "Leif and Tracy are signing the papers now. Their movie will be back in production within a month."

"Oh, I am thrilled," said Athena. "Truly." Okay, so she was a little happy for them. She would likely skip the movie, though, unless she were invited to the premiere.

"I suggested they make a sequel now, too," said Apollo. "Maybe call it 'Zeus Was Undead.'"

"~But Zeus was never undead~"

"No, but it makes for a good way to connect the title to the first one."

Athena scoffed. "That is ridiculous."

"~Agreed~"

Apollo shrugged. "Marketing is important. They will probably film it in Australia, of course. Too much destroyed infrastructure around here."

"I suppose that's wise. I asked Hecate why not even a single zombie ever showed up there." Athena watched a limousine pass, its rear sunroof open and overflowing with young actors hoisting mugs of beer and singing. Dionysus would have been proud, were he not trapped in Tartarus. Her thoughts drifted to Hermes and Aphrodite, still out there somewhere, in exile.

"And?" Apollo asked. "What did she say?"

"One word: kangaroos."

"~Ah. Of course~"

Athena nodded. "Indeed."

"Wait," said Apollo. "Kangaroos?" He cast a confused glance between Athena and Death.

"If you do not understand," said Athena, "then I'm sure as Jerry not going to explain it to you."

The End

"MYTHOLOGICAL" WHO'S WHO

FOR THE UNINITIATED, THE FORGETFUL, OR THOSE WHO
STILL JUST LIKE TO READ STUFF

Aetoc—A golden eagle elevated to godhood by Zeus after his resurrection during the First Olympian Return. Torn to pieces and tossed into Tartarus during the Second Titan War.

Alecto—One of the three Erinyes. Also known as "Alecto the Unceasing."

Aphrodite—Daughter of Zeus. Former goddess of beauty, love, lust, and much of the entertainment industry. In exile due to that whole "trying to murder Zeus" thing.

Apollo—Son of Zeus and the minor goddess Leto. God of the sun as well as medicine and healing. Also, music, poetry, prophecy, and light. Plus, archery, gelatin desserts, and a few other things. Nicknamed "the multipurpose god" by his twin sister Artemis.

Ares—Son of Zeus and Hera. Former god of war and strife. Shoots first, asks questions only if drunk. Exiled as the dumbest member of the conspiracy to murder Zeus.

Artemis—Daughter of Zeus and Leto, twin sister to Apollo. Goddess of the moon, hunting, and nature. One of the last chaste goddesses.

Athena—Daughter of Zeus. Former goddess of wisdom, defense, crafts, and tactics. Also, former bodyguard to Zeus before his murder.

Atropos—One of the three Fates. Responsible for cutting the threads of mortal lives.

Baskin—A seven-foot-tall ice cream sundae elevated to godhood by Zeus after his resurrection during the First Olympian Return.

Currently serves as Zeus's chief lieutenant. Bearer of Zeus's Aegis and the Mighty Pink Battle-Spoon™.

Bulwer-Lytton, Edward—19th-century English novelist, poet, and playwright. Coined the phrases "the pen is mightier than the sword" and "the great unwashed." Not actually a god, nor ever thought to be.

Calliope—Leader of the nine Muses. Responsible for inspiring epic poetry and fantasy novels.

Cerberus—Fearsome, three-headed dog-beast who guards the entrance to the Underworld. Dislikes zombies and grooming.

Charon—Lesser immortal in charge of the ferry across the river Acheron to the Underworld. Possible brother of Death. Enjoys bacon.

Clio—One of the nine Muses. Responsible for inspiring histories, historical fiction, and travel writing.

Clotho—One of the three Fates. Responsible for spinning the threads of mortal lives.

Death—If you haven't heard of Death by this point in your life, there are other things you should be reading besides some corny comedy novel. Also goes by Doug.

Deino—Baldest of the Grey Sisters.

Demeter—Eldest sister of Zeus. Goddess of agriculture, grain, and textiles. Also enjoys baking and knitting. Mother to Persephone.

Dionysus—Debaucherous former god of wine and revelry. Among the five gods who murdered Zeus. Accidentally trapped in Tartarus with most of the Titans after Zeus's resurrection, because karma.

Enyo—One of the Grey Sisters. She is very loud and enjoys puzzles.

Erato—One of the nine Muses. Responsible for inspiring romance, erotica, love songs, and crossword puzzles.

Erinyes, The—A trio of lesser immortals (consisting of Alecto, Megaera, and Tisiphone) responsible for wreaking vengeance and protecting the natural order. Experts on getting blood stains out of satin.

Eris—Goddess of Strife, picking up the slack in the war and conflict department for her exiled brother Ares. Not to be confused with *Eros*.

Eros—God of love, picking up the slack in the beauty and romance department for his exiled mother Aphrodite. Not to be confused with *Eris*.

Euterpe—One of the nine Muses. Responsible for inspiring music, lyric poetry, television theme songs, and movie scores.

Fates, The—A mysterious trio of figures (Clotho, Lachesis, and Atropos) who spin, measure, and cut the threads of mortal lives. Known to employ an intern named Poppy.

Grey Sisters, The—Three ancient witches who share among themselves one eye, one tooth, a plentitude of information, and a fair amount of free time. Also known as The Graeae.

Hades—Older brother of Zeus. Former god of the Underworld, death, and precious metals. Exiled by Zeus for successfully murdering him.

Hecate—Former goddess of night, secrets, magic, and the supernatural. Adopted into the pantheon by Zeus. Killed by the Unmaking Nexus during the Second Titan War. Reported to have made excellent dark chocolate sundaes.

Hephaestus—Son of Zeus and Hera. Gentle god of the forge, building, volcanoes, and technology. Still technically married to Aphrodite. Averages two and a half lines of dialogue per book.

Hera—Former queen of the gods, sister and former wife of Zeus, sister and former wife of Poseidon. (It's still okay, they were gods.) Also, former goddess of marriage, women, and childbirth. Famously white arms.

Hermes—Son of Zeus and an immortal mountain nymph. Exiled god of merchants, thieves, travelers, messengers, and spies. Once stole the Unmaking Nexus, the god-slaying weapon used to murder Zeus, which explains the whole "exiled" bit.

Hestia—Sister of Zeus. Goddess of the home and hearth. Still doesn't get out much, still doesn't want to.

Iris—Messenger goddess, goddess of rainbows, Zeus's personal assistant, now picking up the slack for the exiled Hermes.

Jerry—Sentient oak tree guardian of a temple to Zeus, elevated to godhood. Brother to Baskin. New to the concept of movement and grammar.

Lachesis—One of the three Fates. Responsible for measuring the threads of mortal lives.

Megaera—One of the three Erinyes. Handles most of their paperwork and human resources department.

Melpomene—One of the nine Muses. Responsible for inspiring tragedy, horror, and children's books. Lately, favors horror.

Muses, The—A group of nine lesser immortals, led by Calliope, who collectively inspire the creative and scientific arts. Assistants to Apollo.

Nyx—Personification of night, recently assuming goddess of night duties following Hecate's death.

Pan—Pan has asked that he not be included in this list, as he is only mentioned in this novel rather than featured.

Pemphredo—One of the Grey Sisters. Has the longest name of the Sisters, which probably means absolutely nothing.

Polymnia—One of the nine Muses. Responsible for inspiring sacred songs, speeches, and lyrics. Also, rhetoric and advertising copy.

Poseidon—Brother of Zeus, briefly king of the gods while Zeus was dead. God of the sea, earthquakes, and horses. Inventor of the motorcycle.

Terpsichore—One of the nine Muses. Responsible for inspiring choral song and dance, business correspondence, mysteries, and thrillers.

Thalia—One of the nine Muses. Responsible for inspiring comedy, science fiction, and poems about farming. Likes birds, unrelated to musing duties.

Tisiphone—One of the three Erinyes. The worst one, arguably.

Titans, The—Ancestors of the Olympian gods, deposed by Zeus after the Titan War. Led by Zeus's father, Cronus, who is also known as Kronos . . . but not in *these* books.

Urania—One of the nine Muses. Responsible for inspiring astronomy writings, calendar photos, and sayings on coffee mugs.

Zeus—King of the Olympian gods as well as god of the sky, lightning, and law. Youngest and strongest brother of Demeter, Hades, Hera, Hestia, and Poseidon. Assassinated by a conspiracy of five gods in the early 21st century. He got better. Not *actually* undead, it just made for a good sequel title.

ABOUT THE AUTHOR

An award-winning writer of speculative fiction, Michael G. Munz was born in Pennsylvania but moved to Washington State at the age of three. Unable to escape the state's gravity, he has spent most of his life there and studied writing at the University of Washington.

Michael developed his creative bug in college, writing and filming four exceedingly amateur films before setting his sights on becoming a novelist. Driving this goal is the desire to tell stories that give others the same pleasure as other writers have given to him. He enjoys writing tales that mix our reality with the futuristic or fantastic.

Michael has traveled to three continents and has an interest in Celtic and Classical mythology (and in taking creative liberties with same). Michael also possesses what some people might deem too much familiarity with a range of geek culture, though he prefers the term geek-bard: a jack of all geek-trades, but master of mostly none.

Michael dwells in Seattle, where he continues his quest to write the most entertaining novel known to humankind and find time to play all the video games.

Connect with Michael G. Munz online:
Website: www.michaelgmunz.com
Twitter: @TheWriteMunz
Facebook: Facebook.com/MichaelGMunz

Want to read collection of short stories featuring, among other things, a mid-*Zeus Is Dead* tale about Hermes and Thalia? Sign up for the email list on Michael's website and get a free copy of *Four Fantastical Ways to Lose Your Fingers!* List subscribers also get exclusive sneak peaks and news about Michael's future books…

~   ~   ~

If *Zeus Is Undead* made you laugh, smile, crave grains, or in any way helped you survive a zombie semi-apocalypse, please consider leaving a review online.
Thank you!